ORIGIN STORY

ORIGIN STORY

JENDI REITER

SADDLE ROAD PRESS

Saddle Road Press
Ithaca, NY
saddleroadpress.com

ISBN 9798987954157
Library of Congress Control Number 2024932659

Cover art © Jim Shaw
Author photograph by Ezra Autumn Wilde

Other works by Jendi Reiter
Swallow
Barbie at 50
Bullies in Love
Two Natures
Made Man
An Incomplete List of My Wishes

Contents

This is my earliest memory of comics:

The first panel is a mystery. Too young to read the set-up in the daily news lying on Bubbe's plastic-slipcovered couch.

Nothing before this, then: white curls and black rosebud lips of a blonde beauty in see-through pajamas. Her hand slides under her pillow as she lies down.

Black and white stripes uncoil and strike. Sunburst lines of pain behind her silent scream.

Dick Tracy stands behind her bed, saying words to other stone-faced men in suits. Her dead arm dangles over the edge, the white hair a waterfall hiding her face. Did any of them see the snake? Where is it now?

I'm a grown man and I still don't sleep with my hand under my pillow.

PART I

VAYEIRA

SEPTEMBER 1996 — JANUARY 1997

Be secret and exult,
Because of all things known
That is most difficult.

—W.B. Yeats, "To a Friend
Whose Work Has Come
to Nothing"

My hands were tied to the bed when the timer went off.

His body sprawled upside-down across me, crushing my face into its sticky warmth. My pulse throbbed around a core of pain, from my bruised throat to the buzzing length jammed up inside me. I couldn't squirm away, I had to take it. Muscles seized in panic, clung to a last refusal, released into hot oblivion.

"Uh-oh, Peter, was that the oven or the smoke alarm?" Julian lifted his head from between my legs and sniffed the air.

"You don't cook much, do you."

"Skipped a generation." Rolling gracefully off me, he slid the vibrator out of my hole and lightly stroked and kissed my spent cock. I shivered, this time not from pleasure. The same gentle touch migrated up to my face, which he wiped with a scented tissue. I licked my lips, causing him to smile. After untying the cords, he rubbed my unbound wrists, as if to soothe bruises that weren't there. His dark brown eyes held a flicker of concern, when I'd hoped to see only the stoned bliss of a good fuck. But why should this morning be different from all other mornings? I guess because it was the new year, by my people's calendar, and because hoping for the best while enjoying the worst is a Jewish tradition as old as chopping off the tip of your dick for the Almighty.

"You okay, darling? Did I hurt you?"

"Not enough," I teased. I smoothed his wavy auburn hair and kissed him deeply, inhaling his honeyed scent. He let out a contented sigh and wrapped the blanket tightly around us. Though he'd lived in Manhattan for six years, my Georgia-born boyfriend claimed the late-September cold snap took him by surprise every time.

I twisted away from his embrace. "Promise I'll be right back. I just have to check the oven. Unlike my ass, pie crust is a delicate creature."

"I'm glad someone is using it. Phil used to dry his socks in that oven."

I made a face. "You don't do that, I hope."

"Certainly not—they're cashmere." He patted my rear. "Go, my appliances are lonely without you."

Another hint—in true oblique Southern style—about wanting me to move in. My best friend Phil, Julian's last boyfriend, had died a year ago (*pneumonia*, his parents called it), and a wave of anxious monogamy had swept away the mutual friends left behind.

The apple cranberry pie was kind of crisp around the edges from baking ten minutes extra, but otherwise a good copy of the recipe photograph in Bitsy Selkirk's *A Table to Celebrate: The Best of Southern Living.* I never follow directions to the letter anyway—except in bed. I penciled in a note about the cooking time, then closed the book so Jule wouldn't catch me in the heresy of disagreeing with his Mama's published words. There, I had something presentable to contribute to Rosh Hashanah dinner at my father's house tonight.

"Preheat oven to 350 degrees, tie up the chef and bake until you come on his face? I hope you wrote that all down."

Julian, nude, came up behind me and leaned over my shoulder, smiling. He knew me too well. Lovers for five months, we'd been friends for three years before that, wanting each other so much that we let everything imaginable get in the way to save us from each other. His humor was sharp sometimes but never sarcastic at my expense, unless you count the way he despaired of my taste in clothes. Bringing his work home, you might say. Not that this was my home.

I gave him an affectionate squeeze. "Quick, take a picture of this beauty before my family sticks their forks in it."

Once Julian got behind his camera, nothing else existed for him. Being naked together in the kitchen was no distraction. He shot the pie as carefully as the high-fashion models for his magazine advertisements. He also understood not to ask me to pose with it. Julian didn't take offense easily, except at truly important (to him) misdeeds like women wearing tennis sneakers with a business suit. That made him a good guy, in my book. And an unusual addition to the Edelman family. But that was moving way too fast, even in my own head.

Jule would meet me at Dad's brownstone that evening with the dessert because although it was Sunday, I had to work. I taught yoga and strength-training classes at the Ironman Gym in Chelsea on weekends, and trained with private clients part-time during the week. In between, I picked up whatever odd jobs would prolong the losing battle to keep up the rent on my Upper West Side hole in the wall. I actually liked being a dog-walker, but Dad would never find out. Just once, I'd called in my alumni connections to get a position in Columbia's student tutoring office, but those freshman poli-sci nerds, just bristling with utopian self-esteem, were as depressed to see me as vice versa. Welcome to the future, dudes: 26 years old, Ivy League graduate with honors, able to lift 200 pounds in a single bound, now working minimum wage to explain the difference between "oligarchy" and "oligopoly". Oh, and with a brief detour through some scandalous photos in *Gay Downtown*. Don't say everyone doesn't get their fifteen minutes.

It wasn't that I had no ambition. The many things I dreamed of doing—bodywork therapy for people with AIDS, rescuing homeless cats, writing a superhero comic book—didn't pay a living wage. So there you go. All I had to do was smash global capitalism, and I'd be fine.

*D*ON'T JUST DO SOMETHING—SIT THERE, read the poster on the wall of my yoga studio, words over a stock photo of a skinny blonde white woman in lotus position on a mat. Every gym offering attracts a certain body type, as people are hoping for enough look-alikes that they won't feel ugly or weird when they're all suffering on the floor together. Yoga people are usually stringy and wrap themselves in layers of clothes in all seasons. I'd been practicing long enough that I'd stopped noticing my differences in the mirror: over six feet tall, heavy-muscled arms and shoulders, sweaty black chest fuzz that I refused to wax into alpha-gay conformity. Kids in school used to call me Frankenstein till yoga taught me how to move. Now, I soon found my familiar zone and relaxed into positions that an untrained mind teaches the body to fear as uncomfortable. That was the real help I tried to give in my classes, not how to lift your leg an inch higher behind your back, but how to ask yourself with an open mind, *What's the worst that could happen if I did this?*

Resting in corpse pose at the end, I could faintly smell myself, Julian's body odor mingled with mine, in the pores of my face. I smiled. A little arousal goes fine with enlightenment, you ask me.

Thoughts are supposed to flow without clinging or aversion. In that flow, I couldn't hang on to his sweet parting kiss without also recalling the way he couldn't meet my eyes when I joked about our bondage games. Though kink had been my idea from the start, he worried about me—or himself, for liking the power I gave him. So far I put up with the mistrust because neither of us was ready for another argument about the last time I'd taken too big a risk. Let's just say my ass was literally in a sling, and then out of a job, since I'd blown up my State Assemblyman boss's pretensions to heterosexuality. Julian had given up his biggest celebrity PR client rather than keep working for the campaign that had thrown me under the bus.

He never showed any hint of resenting it, but just in case, I made sure he had all the cream pies he could eat.

After class, I would have barely enough time to hop the train uptown, change into my good outfit (navy blazer, gray slacks, gray button-down), garnish the whitefish salad I'd made the night before, and look for a cab to Greenwich Village. Neither Dad nor my stepmother Ada could cook, so the rest of the meal would probably be roast chicken and sides from Zabar's, and my half-sister Prue's vegan nut loaf, a staple cuisine of the Michigan Womyn's Music Festival she'd attended last month. Prue was starting her sophomore year at Hampshire College, studying folk music and computer programming.

Jule would tell me to appreciate the positives. In the Selkirk family, a five-course gourmet meal was typically paired with a black eye or a belt to the backside.

I listened to the radio in my apartment while I went over my shirt with the iron one last time. Too late for "Prairie Home Companion", but I also liked the political programs. Skipping around some boring financial gab, I came in partway through an episode (pre-recorded, but new to me) of Dad's syndicated weekly talk show about his professional specialty, civil liberties and the law.

"—This is Nathan Edelman at 'Rights on the Left'. We're talking with Dr. Christine Kline, author of the new book *The False Memory Epidemic*. Dr. Kline, it's your contention that the sexual abuse cases that are all over the news lately—celebrities coming out with recovered memories of incest, allegations of Satanic cults in your local preschool—that these so-called memories are a kind of mass hysteria? How could that happen?"

"What you have here is a dangerous alliance developing between the Christian Right and the pro-censorship radical feminists. They have a common interest in spreading lurid stories to prove that the sexual revolution has failed women and children. Then you have the therapists, possibly well-meaning, who want to find a magic bullet to fix all their patients' problems—even if it means digging for memories that aren't there."

"But why would patients want to believe that? Wouldn't anyone rather remember a happy childhood?"

I recognized Dad's "friendly witness" questioning voice, higher-pitched and more inquisitive than the relaxed baritone he used to lay a trap on cross-examination. The radio shrink must have won him over with her swipe at the anti-porn panic. While some kids might have been embarrassed that their father defended the First Amendment rights of peep shows, I was relieved he wouldn't toss my room to find my shoplifted *Playgirl*s. Damn, there I'd gone and scorched my best shirt. Sex daydreams and ironing don't mix. Just ask Betty Friedan.

Dr. Kline picked up Dad's question and ran with it. "Everyone's childhood is unhappy in some way. Mature people get over it and don't look for someone to blame for the setbacks we all experience in life. But there are a lot of immature people who still feel entitled to that fantasy of unconditional love and perfect need-satisfaction from infancy. Seeing themselves as victims is a way to demand care from an uncaring world. It's no coincidence that the ritual-abuse paranoia has been stoked by the same fundamentalists who believe angels and demons are battling over whether you masturbate."

My father chuckled. The sound grated on my nerves. How did he sleep at night? Dreamlessly, I'd bet, with no undigested ghosts from his sober media diet of *New Yorker* features and political biographies. I supposed I should be grateful to him for switching on the light and returning the monster tentacles and disembodied hands to their true form as blankets humped on a bed.

"But how could a person have vivid physical impressions of something that *didn't happen?* What's actually going on there?" he asked Dr. Kline.

"Children's fantasy lives are often more real to them than the boring grownups' world. Add the Oedipus complex, throw in some shame around their sexual awakening in this puritanical culture, and it's easy to see how their minds connect two completely unrelated experiences. Something they saw in a movie that made a strong impression, a vivid dream—even, unfortunately, schizophrenia. My point is, there are a lot of explanations more plausible than an epidemic of predatory uncles."

"Well, that's good news."

I didn't see how he could say that. It would make *me* break out in a cold sweat to believe that the majority of people around me should be wearing tinfoil hats.

I shut the radio and finished getting ready, but I felt kind of distracted all the way to Dad's place. Angels and demons. Heroes and villains. In some sense I believed in all of those, an invisible Gotham City underlying my ordinary New York of pigeon shit and rent strikes. The Joker, the Penguin, Two-Face, they became villains because they rebuilt their lives aroud the One Terrible Thing somebody did to them. What if Batman had gotten over his parents' murder in therapy instead of fighting crime? I pictured the Dark Knight showing up at his stepfamily's house with a bowl of whitefish salad, and realized once again how ridiculous my inner life was.

J ULIAN WAS WAITING on the steps of Dad's brownstone, looking fantastic (naturally) in a soft olive-green blazer and brown shirt that hugged his slim but well-defined body. A suit vest without a tie, I'd never have thought to do that. Clothes weren't my thing but I was starting to enjoy having a trophy boyfriend. He made Bedford Street look like a movie set. Jule was nervous, though; I could tell from how his eyes darted round when I kissed him hello, like he was expecting someone inside the house to chase him off with a shotgun.

I rubbed between his shoulderblades. Yeah, I still had the touch. His posture relaxed. "Hey, don't stress," I said. "You know all the major players. Dad thinks you're great, and I heard Ada's having a good day. And there's pie!"

"Wonder if it tastes as good as the chef." He flashed that bright-white smile. "Sorry to be high maintenance, sweetcakes. It's just different, being introduced as your boyfriend. No one's ever... well, you know."

"Too much too fast?" My turn to worry.

"No!" Julian boldly took my arm to lead us upstairs. "You're lucky, that's all. You can always be yourself here."

"About *this*... yeah. Just remember something, okay? You know how they say it's not polite to discuss religion, politics, or sex at the dinner table? Well, that's *all* we talk about."

"Oh-*kay*. But use your safeword if you need me to switch to 'How about those Mets?'"

"Avocado." I winked.

Homes have their signature smells, like bodies: a mix of old standby recipes, cleansers or perfumes, used books or tobacco smoke, that the painted walls and upholstery breathe out as they age. The familiar atmosphere and noisy conversations of my childhood home engulfed me as soon as we walked inside. And as usual, a part of me strained for that missing note, the voice or the scent of someone who hadn't lived there since I was a bar mitzvah boy.

Julian needn't have worried, because we were instantly swept into the festive chatter. Dad wore one of his many novelty neckties, this one with bees for the "apples and honey" symbolizing a sweet new year. As straight guys go, he was easy to shop for. My petite stepmother, her energy burning bright as the cigarette between her racecar-red lips, drew Julian into a debate about movies while they laid out the food. Their conversation partner was a man I didn't recognize, maybe one of Ada's poetry professor colleagues. He had that melancholy, refined quality, though his suit was too expensive for a writer.

I chose to catch up with my sister about her summer adventures. She and three other Hampshire girls had chipped in to rent an RV for the music festival. Their destination: a huge Midwestern field where thousands of women discovered the joys of life without electricity, running water, or the need to wear shirts.

"Okay, so we did *not* smell good by the end of the week, but it was amazing," Prue gushed. "For the first time, I could just *have a body*, not worry about how anyone labeled me or who's going to try to touch me."

"That's awesome...but honestly, not the outcome I would've predicted from a crowd of music fans getting naked in the mud," I joked.

"Well, that's the difference between men and women. Trust me, you see one naked grandma washing dishes in a kiddie pool, you've seen 'em all."

"So, no girlfriend for you yet, Prue?" my eavesdropping father teased. My sister seamlessly transferred her scornful glance from me to Nathan. The running joke in our family was that Prue was in the closet because it was the only place she could get any work done.

My cousin Ben, a cantor at the Park Avenue Synagogue, and his wife Amy completed the group squeezed together around our dining room table. Ben and I had been best buddies back when the only "dungeon masters" in my life wielded 20-sided dice. He was a Lawful Good if there ever was one. They were here, instead of with Aunt Nora and the rest of Dad's family in Brooklyn, because it was too hard for Amy to be around all those grandchildren after her last miscarriage. Sometimes Dad could be really thoughtful like that.

I loved having Julian with me at parties. He could work a room without calling attention to himself. Mostly he did it by listening to other people's shtick, like Dad and Ben sparring good-naturedly about how to be a Jew without believing in God. As for me, after an hour of the Phil Spector Wall of Sound, I was itching to step outside, smoke a joint, and try to remember my own name.

Dad had seated me next to the mysterious silver fox, who introduced himself as Dennis Campbell. Gay for sure, but not sending vibes my way. Quiet, watery blue eyes, firm Yankee jaw. I had a flash-forward of how Jule might age, gentle and elegant, if he reached fifty—damn it, *when*. Think negative; think negative. We were tested all the time, and so far our number hadn't come up.

"You probably don't remember me, Peter—I was Lew Aronson's partner." Dennis smiled sadly. "Not in the legal sense."

"Oh gosh, I'm so sorry." It seemed right for me to take his hand again, and his brief answering pressure confirmed it. "He and Dad were friends since...*forever.*" My father's Brooklyn Law School classmate had died of cancer in January.

"Well, I guess the Sixties do feel like an eternity away, now. Or maybe not so much. Back then, we were all afraid of dying in the jungle, shot by some other scared kid defending his shitty country—not an enemy you can't see, that didn't even have a name when Lew and I were discovering the bathhouses." A big sip of Manischewitz did not give him the hit he was expecting. "Ugh, this stuff. I'm glad I'm Episcopalian. We know how to drink. Anyway, sorry to be a death's head. I should save it for Yom Kippur, except...I'm not a *bit* repentant."

Baruch ata, Adonai Eloheinu, melech haolam, shehecheyanu v'kiy'manu v'higianu lazman hazeh. Ben chanted the blessing and the rest of us echoed with the translation: "Praise to you, Adonai our God, King of the Universe, for giving us life, for sustaining us, and for allowing us to reach this season."

The ritual satisfied, we returned to our conversations and feasting. The Zabar's holiday platter was not as good as my mother's cooking in the old days, but better than what I could afford to buy on my salary. Sometimes family gatherings felt like my personal soup kitchen. Perhaps that embarrassment made me paranoid that Ben was dodging me when I tried to join his conversation with Julian across the table. Everyone brought their losses to the party, weighing them down, walling them in. Like Dennis, who would sometimes start his anecdotes with "Lew thought—" or "Lew used to say—", skip a breath and carry on. I found out he was a partner in a small firm specializing in family law. They'd litigated some high-profile cases defending gay parents' adoption and custody rights.

Dad and I cleared the main course dishes and plated the desserts. The kitchen was the part of our house that had changed the least since I was young. The gold-speckled white formica counters, brown brickwork linoleum, and faded baby-blue wallpaper patterned with lemon trees were a 1970s time capsule. The floral cushions and heavy wooden furniture were long gone from the living and dining rooms, replaced by smooth off-white couches and geometric rugs the year after Dad and Ada married. An improvement, but a culture shock when I crossed through the kitchen doorway.

As I set my pie on the table, Dennis stood to take the brandy and the cheese platter from Dad. Though shorter than both of us, Nathan grasped

Dennis's and my shoulders in a big welcoming gesture that stopped us from sitting down right away.

"So glad you two are hitting it off. Peter, this job is going to be great for you. You'll be great."

Job? I looked blankly at Dennis, away from my beaming father. The whole group seemed to be watching us, their talk stilled by the arrival of sweets and liquor. Dennis gave a magnanimous shrug. "We were having too good a time to talk business, but yes, from what Nathan has told me, you'd be a natural for the paralegal position in my office. Your government experience would be an asset in researching our politically sensitive cases. And you seem like you'd enjoy the fight for justice!"

Sitting down was not enough to drop me out of target position. The rest of the party broke out with congratulations and encouragement, as if I'd already won the trial of the century. A cold dead weight settled in my stomach, followed by the acid of shame at my ingratitude.

What about Julian? Did he also want this for me, or was he worrying that six months from now, the *New York Law Journal* would report on finding me, Dennis, and the guardian *ad litem* having a three-way in the courthouse men's room? No, I was being totally unfair. Jule had been my number-one defender even when he thought I'd never be with him. His warm, hopeful brown eyes met mine, giving me courage to take a deep breath and force my voice down to a steady, manly pitch.

"Thanks, Dennis, it's really nice of you to give me a chance—" Shit, that sounded defensive. "But I don't feel like I belong in an office job, right now. Something more hands-on, with people..."

The genteel older man seemed disappointed but not offended. "I won't lie, there's a fair amount of paperwork, even for us partners, but I think you'll find the human interest factor satisfying enough. Come visit us tomorrow before you make up your mind."

They wouldn't leave it alone. I had to come out with it. "Actually, I... I'm going to take a job with my mother."

Nathan's cheeks flushed redder than his neatly clipped goatee. He didn't quite succeed at masking his anger as laughter. "What, you'd rather be picking peanuts on a kibbutz, the rest of your life?"

No mistaking Jule's feelings now. Fear of loss, naked on his face, too soon and all-consuming for him to get mad that I could move to Israel without telling him. Which I would never do.

"No, she's moved back to New York, for awhile." Dad was startled but I gave him no time to quiz me. "She came home in June because Grandpa Saul was dying, and she realized she didn't want to be so far away from her family anymore, so she's going back to social work here. She just found an opening for me in her new program."

"Doing what? You don't have a master's degree," Dad pointed out the obvious. The problem was, Mom hadn't given me any details yet. I just knew in my gut that I'd be happier there than fighting paper battles.

"It's a program for at-risk kids. They're still putting it together, but it sounds exciting. Innovative," I enthused. I hadn't been a politician's aide for nothing.

Dad sniffed. "Well, that's what your twenties are for, nowadays. Experimenting." At my age, he'd had a federal court clerkship and a baby son on the way. Contrast that to yours truly and Prue, whose latest contribution to the store of human knowledge was the song "Cow Mother Is Bleeding".

"Y'know, when I got accepted to the Fashion Institute, my Daddy said no way in hell was he paying for me to, quote, 'take pictures of ladies' panties,' but he sure wanted a lot of copies of my Juliette Binoche profile in *Vogue*!" Julian said with a little laugh. As intended, everyone forgot about me and peppered him with questions about what the Oscar-nominated actress was like in real life, and whether Ralph Fiennes's character in "The English Patient" had done the right thing collaborating with the Nazis to save his married mistress's life. As if my boyfriend was a moral philosopher as well as a style guru.

He tried, anyway. "Maybe it depends what kind of person she was? If she wanted to die for the Allied cause, then no, but if she would have put herself first, then yes?"

Ben fired back, "No, a person that selfish doesn't deserve to live."

I avoided Julian's gaze and admired my slice of pie. My opinion on adultery and karma would not be popular at this table. When I raised my head again, Jule was still looking at me. Widening his eyes like a scared cartoon character, he silently mouthed the safeword, "Avocado!"

I mimed a kiss, so small a gesture that only he would notice it, I hoped. No, I didn't care. For those few seconds, we two were the only people in the room.

[EXCERPT OF SCRIPT FOR *THE POISON CURE*, VOL. 1, ISSUE 1]

Pharmakon does not sleep. But when the moon is full,
he goes to his bath.

A round white moon over a black city skyline fills
his apartment window. Close-up on same view as he
pulls the curtain. Room goes dark.

Scene shifts to small windowless bathroom. Candles
flicker against tiled walls, one at each corner of
a foaming bathtub. Water moves as if boiling, or
alive.

Pharmakon faces himself in the cabinet mirror. His
tall muscular body is dressed in well-fitting but
nondescript business clothes: white dress shirt,
gray trousers. Staring straight ahead with no
expression, he wipes his face with a washcloth till
greenish streaks appear on his brow and cheeks.
What looked like skin is a foundation of makeup.
Cleaned, his face is the pale green shade of
radioactive material, and seems longer and thinner,
like a skull or insect.

He strips in the next panel. His chiseled nude form
is the same shade of green. He pours a vial of red
liquid into the bath. The waters heave.

Pharmakon lies in the bath. The candles flare and
dim back down. Sparks of energy pop overhead like
soap bubbles.

*He has no dreams of his own. So he walks in the
dreams of others. The ones who need him. They tell
him what he must do.*

Close-up on candles. They change hue from green to
cheerier shades of pink and white. Pulling back, the
scene is now a birthday party. A girl blows out nine
candles. Two girls her age sit at the table, a woman
and a man stand behind her. Top half of man's face
in shadow. Next panel, close-up again on the girl
and the man, detail of previous image, showing their
resemblance.

Return to the green bathtub. Pharmakon's head and
body are entirely underwater but visible below the
surface, framed in remnants of foam. His eyes are
open. He is thinking—seeing? listening?

She wishes... She wishes he would stop...

When he rises from the tub, Pharmakon is a handsome
man with normal skin tone, looking mostly the same
as in the first panel, but fresher and healthier. He
blows out the candles and puts on his bathrobe. The
tub empties in the foreground, while Pharmakon is
visible in rear view through the open door in the
background. Final panel close-up on a ruby-red drop
of blood circling the drain.

[INTAKE REPORT ON TYLER WICK]

Barbara Hauser, Home Manager, Gateway House
New York City
September 5, 1996

Tyler is a 15-year-old African-American/Dominican
male. He was assigned to Gateway House by the
juvenile court after he pled no-contest to a
charge of shoplifting [see enclosed file]. Tyler
has been intermittently homeless since his mother,
Sami Benitez, passed away from cancer in 1993. His
father, Marcus Wick, was fatally shot in 1990 during
an altercation with police. A grandmother and an
aunt are still living, but are not appropriate
caregivers at this time because of conflicts over his
sexuality. His last foster care placement with the
Andersons also failed for reasons that are disputed:
he claims bias, while the they allege that he was
hostile to their daughter and stole her clothing.

Tyler's mental health needs have not been properly
addressed because of his disrupted living situation.
He believes he has an alternate female personality
which he calls "Tai", and periodically demands to
be addressed by this name and female pronouns. From
his past evaluations [see enclosed file], this seems
to be a dissociative trauma response. One of our
main goals at Gateway House will be to assist him
in integrating his feelings and sense of self.

Tyler has many strengths to build on. He is an
intelligent young man who can be persuasive and
charming, though he needs work on managing his
aggression. He applies himself best to projects

that he chooses on his own. A talented artist,
he wants to become a professional cartoonist and
commercial illustrator. A successful outcome for his
case would be a permanent foster-to-adopt family
with the resources to send him to art school after
he completes his GED. As placements for homosexual
youth can be a greater challenge, Tyler's initial
stay at Gateway House is planned for 90 days,
renewable depending on need and availability.

I WAS A GROWN MAN with a collection of mint-condition "Tales from the Crypt" comics, but the picture over Rabbi Saul Hauser's cluttered writing desk made me flinch away as if I was still eight years old. My late grandfather's West End Avenue apartment was a mile north and several zeroes on the bank acount away from my closet-sized HQ. The central living-dining room was a temple constructed of wood and paper, with floor-to-ceiling bookcases of carved walnut lining the walls between tall skinny windows. For a few spots of color, niches too oddly shaped for books held pottery collected by Grandma Reyna from vacations in Florida and the Holy Land. She was gone too, nearly ten years now. Just Mom and me left, taking our first shot at deciding what to do with all this stuff.

"You're going to take this one, right?" I gestured toward the picture, rather than touching it. People get zapped for things like that in the Bible. It's like the world's first Hazmat manual.

"Please, if we start redecorating now, this place'll be even more of a mess. First things first." Mom gently restrained my arm. "Besides, it'll scare the kids at Gateway House."

"It scared *me*." Past tense. I didn't want to be a downer. I dug in my memory for happier images from this place: chopping nuts for Grandma's honey cake, story time with the Rabbi's illustrated book of folk tales. The scent of old paper made that one easier to retrieve.

Mom chuckled. "Not for long, I don't think. You did your bar mitzvah *Dvar Torah* on the *Akedah*, don't you remember?"

The *Akedah*, the Binding of Isaac, otherwise known as that awkward father-son road trip in Genesis where Abraham thinks God has commanded him to sacrifice the clueless boy. Caravaggio's painting, reproduced on the framed poster over Grandpa's desk, dramatized the moment when Isaac comprehends his fate and squirms in terror under his father's grip, while an angel rushes down to stay the old man's knife.

I shrugged. "Probably only because I could copy from Grandpa's book. I had more important things to worry about, back then."

"I'm sorry." She put her arm around me and rubbed circles on my back, the way she did when I was a kid and couldn't sleep. Not for the first time, she said, "You understand why I had to leave."

"The divorce wasn't *your* fault."

"You were so brave. I could always count on you." Brightening up, she turned toward the kitchen. "Let me make us some coffee and a snack. I have some business I want to talk about before we get lost in the clutter."

We sat at the oilcloth-covered table with Folger's Instant and a tin of butter cookies. The thin china cups with flaking gold trim reminded me of Grandma Reyna, translucent and fragile like her aged hands. My mother presented a different picture, though. Her hands were strong and square like mine, with blunt fingers and callouses from gardening on the kibbutz that had been her home for the past decade. We'd both inherited the rabbi's height and sturdy physique, an ongoing source of insecurity for my mother, who was concerned about looking feminine. Though her clothes were modest and practical, she never left home without makeup and at least one item of simple gold jewelry. Since returning from Israel, she'd taken up wearing skirts again and had her light brown hair professionally styled with blonde highlights. At 51, Barbara Hauser (formerly Edelman) was the perfect image of a reliable, sympathetic social worker. I wondered if she'd miss working with her hands in the dirt. I was glad she'd come home, but it also meant I could no longer escape to our bunkhouse in the olive grove when New York made me crazy.

Mom broke her cookie in half, an old habit, pretending to herself that she wasn't going to finish it. "So here's my idea," she said. "Two of them, actually. Remember I said I had a spot for you at Gateway."

I nodded. She'd filled me in on the basics of the program earlier. One of her former colleages at the state Office of Children and Family Services had started this nonprofit to run a therapeutic group home for kids aged 11-17. With some government grants and a lot of volunteer labor, they'd bought and renovated a decrepit townhouse in the West 100's that now had room for eight youth and two live-in staff, including Barbara. They took in kids who were homeless because of family trauma or addiction, and prepared them for permanent foster families or independent living.

"I want to hire you as a mentor for the kids. It's a lot like what you were doing as a Housing Works case manager, back in the day, but more fun, because you know, they're mostly healthy, they've got their lives ahead of them. They didn't choose to be in this crisis."

I let that pass. Barbara's take on my old HIV+ clients was nothing you wouldn't read in the news weeklies. Coming from a more conservative religious background than Nathan, she'd needed a little time to adjust to my coming-out, but ultimately nothing shook her faith that her only child was a Good Boy.

My duties would include leading support groups, one-on-one guidance, homework coaching, and of course, filling out a lot of forms. It did sound more creative and independent than Dennis's paralegal job. The catch was, it was part-time and paid less. I could probably juggle the schedule with most of my yoga and bodywork clients, but my paycheck-to-paycheck life wasn't changing anytime soon. Yet another unresolved issue between me and Julian, who thought that moving in with him would solve all my problems. I would tell him that was a decision I would make because I *wanted* to, not because I *had* to, but then the air would be full of his unspoken insecurity about why I didn't want to, and I really couldn't come up with a reason.

"I hear you about the money problem," Mom assured me. "That's the second half of my offer. This apartment is mine now. The co-op maintenance comes out of the estate, at least for the next few months, while we get Papa's antiques and papers sorted. But I can't use it because I'm living at Gateway."

"And then you'll sell it?" I cut in. I guessed where she was going with this, but it exhausted me to think of moving again in such a short time.

"Not right away. It needs fixing up. The lawyer said the market isn't strong right now. Besides, I have a plan, if you'd just listen." She smiled to take the edge off her words.

"Sorry, Mom. I'm still getting used to all the changes. I always thought you'd put down roots in Israel for good." I recalled the sunset-colored stone buildings, loud meals at communal tables, the shimmer of hot air over ploughed fields. "What about that guy you introduced me to last time— Dov?"

"That's over." Her mouth made a disapproving click. I waited for more information. She sighed impatiently. "You really want to know, Dovid wanted to move faster...physically...than I was ready for, and he got very pushy when I put him off. You know how men are." She refocused on me with a kinder look. "Oh, not *you*, boychick, I mean typical men."

"Sorry I asked."

"I'm fine. Permanence is over-rated, isn't that what you yoga people say? 'Be Here Now.' When I think how many unstable living situations my Gateway kids have been through, I shouldn't complain."

"So you want me to give up my studio and move in here?"

"Please think about it. Not only rent-free but I could maybe find you a little stipend from the estate to help organize Papa's things. His publisher's antsy for that second book he never did finish. The papers are all here somewhere, you'd just have to put them in order for the editor. I don't have a head for that stuff. So you stay here a year, maybe more, that's plenty of time to save money and get on your feet again."

I looked around at the whitewashed cabinets with their foggy crystal knobs, the once cheery buttercup-yellow walls baked by time to a parchment color. Could I charge for doing renovations too? I felt like a convict on work-release. "I'm not ungrateful, Mom. It makes sense. I hate needing help, that's all."

"It's not charity. You deserve this. All I want is for my son to be free to do good work and not worry. We're never going to become rich from a life in social service, so why not take a little reward from heaven when it falls in your lap?"

"Okay. Let me sleep on it." But I knew she knew I was sold.

While Mom pulled up the crackling window blinds, I gave myself a quick tour of Grandpa's file cabinets to assess the size and awfulness of the job ahead. The man had a memory like a labyrinth that only he could navigate. Grandma Reyna had frequently found his scribbled Talmudic notes turning up in her recipe box or among her sewing patterns, as he would write on the nearest piece of paper whenever an insight came to him.

I wasn't surprised to find a folder of old birthday cards, and a bundle of yellowing letters postmarked 1968, wedged in the drawer that seemed to contain most of his research for the unfinished book. The return address on the old mail rang an off-key bell. *Rabbi Norman Ahrens...Fort Lauderdale.* I shook my head, like a shoe full of sand. Nothing came back to me but the smell of seaweed and some girl with grape-flavored lip gloss who had forced me to kiss her. The top letter, full of news about people I didn't recognize, included a long discussion of some unorthodox notions Grandpa apparently had about Adam and Eve, hence its inclusion in this drawer. I sighed and put it back. This book was going to be a real Frankenstein's monster.

"I'm going to need a better desk lamp, and a new computer to transfer files off this ancient one before it self-destructs..."

"Sure, sure," Mom clucked. "Fix it up however you want. Bring your boyfriend over to redecorate."

"Um, I don't think repainting the bedroom will be the first thing on Julian's mind," I needled her. "You know how men are."

Her blank look wavered on the edge of taking offense. My mother was never good at understanding other people's jokes.

[Intake Report on Prudence Porter]

Celia Moreno, LICSW, Mass. Dept. of Children & Families
  Somerville, MA
  April 12, 1982

Prudence Porter (Prue) is an eight-year-old
Caucasian girl in the custody of her mother,
Ada Porter, an adjunct instructor in the English
Department at Boston College. Ms. Porter was put on
administrative leave following a manic episode and
is currently being treated for depression and self-
harming tendencies as an in-patient at Metropolitan
State Hospital in Waltham. As the father lives in
another state and is not available to participate
in Prue's care (no further information was
provided) and there are no relatives in the area,
DCF recommends a 30-day foster placement while the
mother's condition stabilizes...

[Excerpt from *The Akedah, Sacrifice and Sanity* by Rabbi Saul Hauser (Hebrew Studies Press, 1981)]

...Modern scholarship on Genesis 22 has of course been
dominated, some might say overshadowed, by Kierkegaard's
infamous "teleological suspension of the ethical": the question
of whether G-d's command may override the fundamentals of
commonly understood morality, using the limit case of a father
killing his own child. Familiarity does not make this scene
less terrible to contemplate, hence the anxious proliferation of
arguments and counter-arguments to create a screen of words to
shield our eyes.

Sidestepping rather than disputing the rights to this well-
trodden path, I propose instead to consider the *Akedah* as a stark
depiction of the *psychology* of an encounter with G-d. Abraham is
no philosopher, rationally weighing the pros and cons of obedience
versus human rights, as if these were equivalent data points.
Knowledge of G-d's will is not information but an *experience* that
calls all other knowledge into question: even the most inviolable
taboos, the most primal bonds of affection, those that the human
animal knows as essential for continued existence, long before any
conscious "morality" is overlaid on them.

To recognize the voice of the living G-d is, sublimely, to die—for
Abraham most of all, for G-d demands not his mere physical life,
but the tearing of the web of beliefs that constructed his virtue, his
identity, and his relations to others—what we moderns might call
his sanity. And yet—once having heard the command of the One

who is Truth, he counts that world of illusion well-lost, and realizes that only now has he begun to live...

[Extract from a letter to Rabbi Saul Hauser from Rabbi Norman Ahrens, postmarked Fort Lauderdale, FL, Dec. 5, 1968]

...Can I still wish you *mazel tov* on Barbara's getting married? Atheist or not, he did the right thing with the baby on the way, and

that's what matters. Talking about G-d is our job, but what a surprise (and relief!) to find out how little difference our opinions make, compared to just putting up with people.

Annette and the baby are well, sleepless of course, but blissful in that Eden from which we clumsy papas and grandpapas are exiled.

Speaking of which, thank you for the draft of your article on *Parsha Bereishis*. I'll admit, it disturbed me. Specifically the idea that Adam and Eve would *need* to protect their sexual privacy from the Father— well, I don't see where else you can go from there except a Freudian debunking of the whole creation story.

Now I'm the one worried about atheism—some contradiction, old friend?...

[Extract from a letter to Rabbi Saul Hauser from Rabbi Norman Ahrens, postmarked Fort Lauderdale, FL, Feb. 13, 1969]

...Poor Barbara, please give her my condolences about the miscarriage! At least she was at your place when she started to bleed, not home alone as usual. G-d was looking after you all, though I'm sure it doesn't feel that way at the moment.

It's brave of you to keep writing meanwhile. You can't let go of the Garden of Eden, I see. Good that you toned down your speculation about the fig leaves. Not to rain on your parade, but I still wonder if you're ready for where this road leads. You see a parallel between Freud's backtracking on incest with his seduction theory, and the doctrine that Adam and Eve caused their own loss of innocence. But isn't G-d by definition good? It seems to me we can't project human family dynamics, with all their pathologies, onto the Creator without missing the essence of G-d's holiness, His difference from us.

That's just my two cents—our old teachers would be disappointed to see how I've given up writing altogether, since taking over this congregation! Believe it or not, I enjoy the grunt work more—what kind of windows to install in the new building, visiting little old ladies and their cats, etc. They say an administrator rises to the level of his incompetence—well, here I am!...

[EXTRACT FROM A LETTER TO RABBI SAUL HAUSER FROM RABBI NORMAN AHRENS, POSTMARKED FORT LAUDERDALE, FL, MARCH 1, 1970]

...At last, a grandson—may he be the first of many! What a smart boy your Peter looks already, with those bright eyes. An old soul. Now I hope your worries about Barbara will be over. It's strange how some new mothers are more depressed, the longer they've been waiting for that miracle baby. Afraid to get their hopes up? Just a personal observation—these days a rabbi has to be a shrink, as well!

Barbara is made of stronger stuff, I think. Full of faith, always looking to take care of others. You say she and little Peter are inseparable—just as they should be! Tell Nathan to get used to warming up his own soup for a few months. We modern men must share the load. But Annette insists I tell Barbara not to feel guilty about stealing some sleep, even if she has to take a pill now and then...

I PICKED AN OAK LEAF out of Julian's hair, a papery brown curl stuck in his sun-tinted auburn ones. Star-shaped maple leaves pasted a red and yellow collage over the slow-moving stream on the grounds of Spiral Gardens, a wellness institute in the Hudson River Valley. We'd scored a day at the spa because Julian was photographing a celebrity profile piece for *InStyle* about a former supermodel friend of his who'd reinvented herself as a spiritual fitness life coach or something like that.

"Just call her whatever she says she is. It doesn't have to be logical," was my boyfriend's experienced advice, as we sat on the hillside and watched the leaf patterns ripple and shift. "The buzzwords change, but people always want the same things: to stop worrying, feel prettier, and believe they get a second chance." He snapped more photos of the peaceful bronzed landscape, though he'd told me the magazine would try to get by with stock images of October foliage so they could pay him less.

"Well, we got one." I lightly nuzzled the hair above his ear. He picked up my hand and kissed it. It sort of made my chest hurt. Having something makes you remember not having it.

"I'm so glad you let yourself take this weekend off, finally," he sighed. "Have you talked to Barbara? Is everything under control with Tyler and Quito?"

I was grateful he understood that I couldn't go AWOL from my teen clients, even for a day. Simmering feuds and sudden blow-ups between the seven current residents of Gateway House were a regular consequence of love-starved kids claiming their territory and our attention. Q was a runty, doe-eyed Puerto Rican who'd been pimped to men and so was freaked out by the gay guys in the house, which would be me and I guess Tyler (Mom and I disagreed how to label him). But the little dude felt compelled to pick fights with us instead of leaving his bogeymen alone.

"Yeah, thank God, Mom's a miracle worker. Q's only been there a week and she just found a single lesbian foster mom to offer him a shot at penis-free living. Wish I could break through to Ty, though. I think his art is the key, but he won't let us see it yet."

A sweet-toned gong echoed through the crisp air, calling us to the big house for the guided meditation ceremony. The presentations and trade show would be in there, a low-slung, streamlined white modern building with spa and gym facilities, and no doubt a cafeteria that smelled like freshly pulped vegetables. I gave Julian a last kiss. "Ready for your green juice cleanse and astral body projection?" I teased.

He wrinkled his perfectly straight nose. "Don't get your hopes up—or any other body part. Cheryl's publicist said this expo was Christian-flavored."

"You okay with that?"

"Sure." He didn't look at me. "If it keeps Cheryl Kingston's nose clean, who am I to judge?"

We sat on soft foam-plastic chairs and breathed in the sounds of pre-recorded monks chanting. We pushed our seats back and stretched to the unseen sun. We felt our Higher Power inside our chests like a tiny golden flame. Silence and clean air felt good. Not being the one to hold the space felt even better. No teaching for me today. If anyone got shanked with a sharpened eyebrow pencil, I could look the other way.

Julian had quickly introduced me to Cheryl before this medicine show got started. The tall, slim blonde with the gentle smile was not pretentious in the way I expected professional Christians and good-looking people to be. She reminded me of Farrah Fawcett, if more "Burning Bed" than "Charlie's Angels".

The book and course series she was launching today was called *Fit for a King* and it was about leading a clean and healthy life through meditation on Bible verses, a simple Mediterranean diet, repetitive exercises, and "mindfully decorating the temple of your body". Her presentation was relaxed and sincere, a plain voice for a colorful personal testimony: from *Mademoiselle* cover model to coke-sniffing centerfold, to a six-month stint in minimum-security for possession, where she found Jesus in a 12-Step group run by a priest doing time for a DUI homicide. It didn't make me want to accept the gospel or get my eyebrows plucked, but I respected her optimism, as one idealist to another. The exact method wasn't as important as passing on the hope that people in the shit could crawl to higher ground.

After her spiel, people dispersed to their small-group workshops or the juice bar. I eavesdropped on Cheryl's interview with the *InStyle* reporter. Julian was happily absorbed with his camera, his worries for his old friend set aside. The girl from the magazine was playing devil's advocate, pointing out that it was unusual to include make-up and skin-care tips in a religious self-improvement plan.

"God is simple, because He wants even people like me to understand him," Cheryl countered. "He came so that we would have life abundantly, and our life is in our bodies. We're a part of His beautiful creation."

I was curious how Julian took that, as he was more conflicted about the God stuff than he cared to admit. Underneath his flippant one-liners was a buried insecurity that he wasn't living up to the example of his pruny missionary sister in Uganda. But I didn't want to distract him at work, so I snuck in late to the "Mission X-Force" weight-lifting class. Pumping away my troubles was another treat I didn't have enough time for since the Gateway House job started.

The bulging and grunting in that class would have put the muscle queens at my Ironman Gym to shame. Here, though, I didn't feel caught in the crossfire of cruising glances. The trainer was a bull-necked young guy with earnest blue eyes and shaggy blond hair like He-Man from the Saturday morning cartoons. Because it was safe (and totally inappropriate), I found myself getting turned on by the fog of man-sweat that thickened in the room. Julian was the one who excelled at hookups. When I tried, I felt like those guys were fucking their way right through me, passing like solid flesh through a ghost.

My focus shot, I ducked out when the trainer began his sales pitch. In the back garden, I wandered toward the outdoor tai chi group to establish cover for status, as they say in the spy novels, then staked out the far side of the building to light up the joint I'd smuggled in my coat pocket.

I breathed out sweet clouds. The leaves lost their edges and became a dancing veil, a gypsy's fringe of coins. I would miss Quito; he had a line on some strong shit.

Too soon, Julian came looking for me. He didn't smoke so I didn't offer. "You stressed?" he asked, sniffing the air.

"Give me a break," I groused, though his tone was mild. "I can't do this around the kids."

"You don't light up every night in that mausoleum you live in? A bag of Doritos, the Dead Sea Scrolls, and thou..."

"If *thou* came over more often, *thou* would find out." I poked his rear for emphasis. I had no problem sleeping at Julian's place sometimes, but I wished he was doing more to help me bring Grandpa Saul's apartment back into the land of the living. Did he resent me for taking Mom's offer of shelter instead of his?

"Seriously, that place makes me feel like I've wandered into a Scooby-Doo cartoon."

"Isn't the whole point of Scooby-Doo that ghosts aren't real?"

Julian suddenly pulled me around the corner. "Quick, let's get out of here."

"You want to skip dinner and find a place to fuck?" My mind, or something, was still in the weight room with the Masters of the Universe.

"No. Shut up." Julian shook his head, embarrassed by his rudeness. "Sorry, it's just—"

Another voice broke in. "Hey...it *is* you. I was hoping...Julian Selkirk? Do you, uh, remember me?" We were face to face with the big blond from Mission X-Force.

Jule did his best to give the guy a cold stare. I saw his body tense. It made me edgy too, not knowing how to protect him without making a scene. And from what?

"It's Brent. Brent Harrison, from Marietta High," the guy pushed on.

"Yeah. I know."

Brent rocked on his feet, wanting to move closer but stopped by the force field of Julian's unfriendliness. "Look, I've always wanted to say—" He flicked a glance at me, wondering if I belonged in the audience for his true confession.

"This is my boyfriend Peter."

"Oh, okay. Cool," Brent said quickly, his enthusiasm pitched too high. "You're still like that. I mean—" His face colored.

"That you're nothing like me? I think you and your friends made that clear a long time ago. Now leave us alone, we're working."

"No! That's not true. I've wanted to tell you I was sorry, for so long. I chickened out that night because I was ashamed. Of—of what we used to do together. That I wanted it too. I struggle with the same things you do."

"Darling, I don't *struggle*. I've completely surrendered to this one," Julian parried, giving me a wolfish look. I tried to reciprocate, though I hated parading our private feelings to score a point.

Brent forced a smile. "I bet. He was killing it in my Mission X-Force class just now. Any chance you want to go on tour as a bodybuilder, Peter?"

Jule didn't let me respond. "*That's* what you're doing now? Tossing pianos in the air for Jesus? I thought you'd be a lawyer in your daddy's firm."

The big guy bowed his head. "Wasn't for me. I kind of hit a rough patch, couple of years ago. Went into the hospital. Anyhow, working out always helped me channel my feelings, you know, and when the Mission X-Force guys came back to do a show at Roswell Baptist, I felt inspired to join up. You remember how awesome those stunts were, when they came to our school?"

"Yeah, I do. It was a big homo circus." Jule turned to me. "These ex-football stars and wrestling champs would do a strongman act in our gym, then when we were all excited, they'd invite us to a show at my church where we got free hot dogs and the hard sell to come to Jesus. Welcome to separation of church and state, Georgia style."

Brent's sad expression deepened. "You really don't have any good memories from back then, do you."

"I remember your dick tasted pretty good on prom night. Did you enjoy that? Or was it more fun watching your wrestling buddies break my ribs in the parking lot afterward?"

"Please forgive me. I hated myself so much," Brent said.

"And you don't now?" Some compassion crept into my boyfriend's voice. I relaxed a little. Jule's rare flashes of anger could be intense but never lasted long. He liked to say he was content with his low expectations of humanity.

Brent's eyes shifted. "I've found a way to make peace with my temptations without hurting other people."

The warmth vanished from Julian's face. "Same shit, different day. Tell it to the next kid who thinks he deserves to bleed out for being a faggot. I'm not a Christian anymore, I don't have to turn my cheeks for you."

He yanked me away. I followed Jule to our rental car in the lot. "Drive," he said, tossing me the keys.

"What about Cheryl?" We'd planned to hang around through dinner so he could schmooze with her and maybe line up more jobs.

"Fuck it, I'll call her tomorrow."

Stomach growling and bladder bursting, I took us down the highway, while Jule pressed his face to the window, streaking it with mostly silent tears.

I let cruise control help me out so I could lay one hand on his arm. He locked his fingers through mine, digging into my palm. He was fit but no bruiser, with an artist's graceful hands, not a boxer's. Had he flung them up that night, to protect those dark eyes, that face that was pure gold for the treasure-hunters in Chelsea's back rooms? Or had he cradled them beneath him, to preserve his fingers' agility with a camera, his ticket out? I gripped harder, aching to transfer pain from him to me, to feel it flow through and out like a lightning rod, into the wet empty night.

"Babe, you want to talk about...?"

"What's there to say?" He didn't even try to turn the hitch in his voice into a laugh, but he thumped my hand gently on his leg, to assure me I wasn't the target of his anger. This almost made me join him in breaking out the Kleenex. He was so damn polite. Not just in the Southern way of fuckbuddy Brent, consigning you to hell with a handshake, but truly kind.

"I wish I'd cruised that Mission-X fucker in his weightlifting class. You know he wanted it. I wish I'd taken him out back and bit his nuts off," I said.

Now Julian did laugh. He scooted over to lean his head against my shoulder. "And I wish you could build a time machine and go back to 1989 and be my prom date."

"Would they have actually let us do that?" My Brooklyn private high school had been too counter-cultural to hold a prom, but they minded their own business about who paired off with whom.

"Are you shitting me? After we got expelled, Daddy would've shot you and packed me off to one of those therapy camps where they give you electroshock while running a slideshow of the Calvin Klein catalog."

I shuddered. "Ugh, sounds like *A Clockwork Orange*."

He made a sour face. "That's what you *would* think, that the worst part is that horror-movie bullshit that makes the news up north when you need Christians to laugh at. But it's not. The worst is when you think you've found a little corner of your life where you can be real with somebody...and, BAM!" He smacked the dashboard. "You're just roadkill on the highway to heaven."

Spotting the Golden Arches, I steered toward the off-ramp. "Let's stop for a bit."

"No, I'm okay. I don't want to talk about it anymore."

"Yeah, but I smoked a blunt and I need some carbs, stat." I pulled a grin. "I'm everything they warned you about in 'Okie From Muskogee'."

True to his word, Jule kept us on lighter topics, like his profile of Cheryl, while we refueled and finished our drive home. I kissed him on the head before I went up to the counter for our shakes and fries, and held his hand as we ate under the grease-hazed fluorescent glare. They didn't pay well enough at Mickey D's to fight the culture wars. Long as you didn't deal drugs or take a dump on the floor, the staff left you alone.

J ULE SURPRISED ME by offering to spend that night at my place. It was a nice gesture because I had an early morning group session at Gateway next day. Half a dozen jittery or sullen teens learning to listen to each other's feelings, rehearsing for peaceful coexistence with the families we hoped to place them in. Despite wanting only to hate him, I remembered Brent dropping a mention of his hospital stay. What if he'd found a place like Gateway instead of the closet-case Bible counseling he probably got? Well, maybe then he'd be Julian's boyfriend instead of me. My concern for gay liberation didn't extend that far.

My room had once been Grandma Reyna's, where she knitted and watched TV on the day-bed, and after her passing, a guest room gradually taken over by boxes of yellowing paperbacks, seldom-used clothes, and tchotchkes whose sentimental value was lost to memory. My first project on move-in had been to turn my new den into a replica of the one I'd left. Goodbye fluffy area rugs and pressed-tin pictures of Florida sailboats, hello "Batman and Robin" poster (Chris O'Donnell's nipples!), laptop, and queen-size bed with navy blue sheets. I could promise Julian that nothing and no one would intrude between us in that bed tonight.

I was lost in the relief of a hot shower when he knocked on the bathroom door. So, not even waiting for bed, fine with me. I called him in, and in a few moments his smooth, sculpted body was pressed up behind me under the spray, cocooned in a curtain of steam. He wasn't hard yet, but I stiffened as soon as his soft, hot bulge rubbed against my ass cleft. I turned around to kiss his mouth. Water streamed down over his closed eyes. His hands glided down my back, and lower. But all he wanted to do was hold me. I tucked my face into his neck. Words came without thought, from my heart into my throat, into the air, the space between us that for once I wanted to close completely. "This won't end," I breathed in his ear. "I won't go."

"Peter, I love you, so much." Because he knew it was easier for me to swallow a dozen loads than to shape my mouth around those words, he put his fingers to my lips and let me kiss them instead. We soaped and rinsed each other until his long, beautiful cock was pulsing in my hand, as eager as mine.

"Hang on, condoms are by the bed," I remembered.

"Can't wait," he gasped.

"You want to…" I took a deep breath and slowly turned my rear toward him. I was clean, and though I'd never dared ask if Julian was as exclusive with me as he seemed to be, I trusted he wouldn't do anything stupid that could hurt me. Realizing how much trust that really was, I shivered as if the shower temperature had plummeted.

"No, never!" Poor Jule was freaked out now. Neither of us could shake the memory of how his first love, my best friend Phil, had died last year.

I stroked his softening erection. "Don't worry, I know just what you need."

As we towelled off quickly, I knelt on the bath mat (a grubby, embarrassing pink floral *schmatta* I hadn't had time to replace) and sucked him back to stiffness, pumping my dick with my hand till I felt arousal spread over my whole body like a suit of electricity. He was soon confident enough to pull me away to the bedroom, where rubbers and lube could make the rest easier.

Julian laid me back on the bed. I pulled my legs up and drew him in.

Breathing low and fast, he took me with strong, steady thrusts. Mostly I close my eyes when I come because I love the vanishing, the sinking into the darkness of my mindless senses, but I couldn't stop gazing at his joyful face and masculine body rising above me.

We rolled ourselves up in the sheets, naked chest to chest, cozy as a sleeping bag. I was dozing off when Julian's loud, uneven breathing in my ear alerted me that today's bad memories had hit him all over again. I saw tears in his eyes, but he smiled through them, determined, and put his hand over my heart.

"*This* is what I have faith in now," he whispered. "Nothing's more sacred than this."

I was his world. He was at peace because of me. Didn't I love him? What could be wrong with this? I touched his hopeful face. He was generous, caring, a star in every way—okay, so he was too squeamish to handcuff me and raise welts on my ass, but maybe he was right to steer me away from the dark side for awhile. It wasn't like he fell short of my dreams of the perfect boyfriend, but like I couldn't picture those dreams at all, couldn't remember imagining a future where I'd have all of someone's life and he'd have all of mine.

Did I love him? I closed my eyes and listened to my body. Echoes in an empty well. How could I not *know*? I'd taken it for granted that I loved people in the normal, average way: Mom, Dad, Prue, my friends. But Julian's love went too deep, hitting the blank spot in my programming, the part where, if this was the last two minutes of a "Twilight Zone" episode, I'd look in the mirror and discover I was really a cyborg or a dead man.

I wished this wasn't my apartment so I could leave. Julian was right, and wrong. This *was* sacred but he deserved to have it with someone better than me. Then finally something ripped open in my heart. A gasping loneliness, a drowning animal furiously clawing upward for air. "I'm gonna love you the way you want," I forced out, a vow with the voice of a threat, a fuck-you to myself or the robot overlords who had mis-wired me.

Julian's face lit up. He drew me into his arms and I clutched him tight. I felt small, wet, soft like a fish who was born to breathe in the waters that had choked me a moment ago. I slipped into sleep.

And dreamed of sitting on a hard seat in the dark. The curved rim chafed the backs of my legs. My feet dangled in space. It felt like the first time I sat on the grown-up toilet but I couldn't see what size I was in the pitch blackness. Soon as I had this thought, the tickling, pulling sensation down below told me I had to pee like crazy, but I wasn't allowed. This wasn't a bathroom, it didn't smell like it. Rubber, gasoline, thickness of air closed in by concrete. Bucket seats of an antique car, no softness over the springs. But a huge someone pushing me into smallness, the driver's hot weight like a bolster bulging against my hip.

The door flapped open to my right and another body squeezed in on my opposite side, where there hadn't been a seat before. When I looked ahead or at myself I was still blind, the motionless air a sack over my face. I didn't dare turn to either side, nor look behind, as the rear doors flapped and slammed, flapped and clicked shut. With each new passenger the Model T sagged back on its rear wheels, till I could swear our front end was lifting off the ground. A question rasped indistinctly from the back seat, and the driver spoke. "We can't leave till they're all here."

But how many could there be? Vertigo, the car angling upward. We were going to suffocate in here, too many mouths breathing the garage's trapped oxygen. Another murmur from behind my head. The driver replied: "I don't know this one." They meant me, the stranger—they were going to throw me out like the stowaway girl on the spaceship in "The Cold Equations". But instead the garage door flew open at our rear and the light flooded in, the magnified sun off the sea, blue-gold, rippling and rushing. And we rolled backward into it, speeding back and down, plunging vertically like a snapped roller-coaster car, screaming toward the bottomless ocean...

[Drafts of moral inventory for week of 4/16/92, journal of Brent H., Love in Action residential program, Lawrenceville, GA]

I had a song stuck in my head today because I was on kitchen duty and I listened to the trucker's radio through the back door when he delivered our bread. I should have turned the water up louder because I have to avoid False Images. I didn't go out to see him and I didn't think about whether he looked like

~~Come and go with me /Please say you'll never~~

I overheard a worldly song by accident today and allowed it to mislead me into thinking about someone I sinned with in school. Julian and I were in Glee Club senior year. I did it for my college resumé so they wouldn't think I was a dumb wrestler. Now I see I put the False Image of success ahead of avoiding temptation because he had big brown eyes and sang tenor to my bass and would take the music seriously when I wanted to, instead of messing up like the other guys to get a laugh. His hands were really strong for a skinny guy. One time when our group was on an overnight bus trip for Battle of the Bands we shared a bathroom and

Come, come, come, come... come into my heart

I was struggling with temptation today because something reminded me of a guy in high school who sinned with me on an overnight trip. J.'s father had problems with alcohol and hit him sometimes. I am lucky that my father isn't like that, but he was busy with money problems at the firm and I didn't feel close to him. I see now that J. and I were confused about our identity as men so we tried to give it to each other but that was a false image. That's why I let him

Way beyond the sea

[JULIAN: FIVE PHOTOGRAPHS]

Peter, shirtless, buying onions at the summer market. Mulch steams in the sun, around small tight mounds of clipped bushes that relieve Union Square Park's honeycombed cobblestones. He's unafraid of smells, his sweat and the green stewing herbs he rubs between his wide fingertips. His shoulders roast red-brown in the glare. Later, after this picture, they'll peel. He thinks I'm looking at other people. That I'm working, even on an unchurched Sunday morning, to make a stranger's captured style pay off for me. A toddler in sagging shorts undoes my shot of her caregiver's layered chocolate braids. It's hard to tell who belongs to whom. Peter's afraid of children. He pivots away to the tomatoes, weighing one in his hand like a swollen organ, smoothly removed, ready to be healed by the knife.

Peter lighting the Havdalah candle. This was a hard one to take. The flash would have disturbed him. The braided taper stands out, its light ringing the rim of my empty wineglass. He's left his over. I don't know what he believes, but we do this every Saturday night, if we can. For his God, that's enough. The dim kitchen fuzzes his face into shadow. He never minds it when the picture comes out that way.

Peter, dressed in red. He's the Flash, he's a tinfoil thunderbolt slapped onto Spandex pecs, second-prize cosplay winner in a midtown Sheraton where I join the crowd of robots and werewolves winking our cameras' soul-stealing eyes at him. He's proudest when he's someone fictional they adore. Tonight, out of character, I'll pretend the new scars on his back have something to do with justice, a fight he didn't choose but had to win.

Peter looks like his sister. They both have one foot out the door of their bodies. Ready to light out. She's tuning her guitar. They're laughing because he can't sing. *D-I-V-O-R-C-E.* I swear, neither of them know how a shirt should fit. I may be just a coal miner's daughter, but I can carry that tune, for them.

Peter, bleeding. This time it's an accident. Other people think he's brave. The way he stands at the sink, not cursing or crying out, as the half-sliced bagel grows spongy and pink. Looking into his own hand like it's going to tell him something, like he's found the motherboard behind the panel. It's on me to wash him, teasing his fingers open. This time he asks for the picture. He says he's not high. I only smell copper and cooling toast. We look through the lens together, at the water where spirals of blood and soap dissolve and combine.

“SHIT, I GOT BLOOD ON MY BLOUSE,” Tyler complained.

I wrapped the gauze tighter around the teen’s hand. “Would this be a bad time to say, you should’ve thought of that before you smashed a glass door in?” We Gateway staffers were also supposed to correct him for using female words for his clothes, but as anyone will tell you, I’m not the fashion police.

“Bitch confiscated my sketchpad.” In a lower voice he muttered, “Sorry, I know that’s your mama I’m talking about.”

“Well, what did you do?”

“What’d I *do*? It’s just wrong. What the fuck else is there *for* me to do? I don’t watch that old-lady daytime TV, I can’t have my music...”

I waited for the outburst to finish. It wouldn’t help to point out why the kid’s Sony Discman and headphones were also in the time-out cabinet in Barbara’s office. At first, I’d (secretly) doubted her strictness in discouraging “Tai”, his female alter ego, from manifesting. But he was twice the troublemaker on the days he whipped out the shoplifted press-on nails and refused to answer to “Tyler”. As a boy, he was clever and quiet, didn’t start fights but could finish them. Tai, on the other hand, was the kind of girl who’d cut you for borrowing her hair gel without permission.

Barbara and Dr. Marla Fuller, our psychologist in residence, theorized that if we could teach Tyler to integrate those feelings into his normal persona, he could take responsibility for his aggression and channel it in more acceptable ways. Which was maybe their way of saying that a ripped black Dominican dude in scarlet lipstick freaked them the fuck out. I’d expected better from a group home that billed itself as gay-friendly, but what did I know—nobody wants to adopt Dr. Frank-N-Furter. I had to keep my priorities, as they say, *straight*.

“Would you cover for me? Just this once?” Tyler—or should I say, *Tai*—wheedled.

“Man, you know I can’t do that. This is my job. And how would I even pretend this didn’t happen? Am I supposed to say, ‘Sorry, Mom, I was playing baseball in the hallway?’” The glass window panel in Barbara’s office door hung in vicious-looking shards from the frame. He’d been planning to reach through and unlock it from the other side. Instead, I’d have the fun task of picking up the sharpest bits with heavy-duty rubber gloves and taping cardboard over it till the volunteer handyman came next week.

"I didn't mean that," Tai said, though I was sure he'd been testing my loyalties. "Just sneak in real quick and grab my sketchpad, lock up again, and hide it someplace safe till I've done my time for this shit."

"Something in there that you don't think they can handle?" I tried once again to help him open up. "I know you've been through some rough stuff, but it's nothing to be ashamed of."

Tai pouted, angry at his own embarrassment. "It's none of their business, is all. They look at my drawings so they can ask me bullshit questions like, is the dead guy in the alley my father, or do I fantasize about being a superhero because I'm afraid to trust people. They don't think I've got a brain, I can make up *new* stuff? Nobody asks fucking Stephen King if his mom was a demon-possessed sportscar."

He'd touched a nerve. I had to give him credit. "Superheroes, huh? You know my weakness."

Was that the hint of a smile? "Well...there's this one character I draw a lot, who's got super powers, but I don't know if he's a hero yet. I can't get the story straight in my head, it always goes too many places at once." He scuffed the toe of his sneaker back and forth on the linoleum. "Anyway, maybe it's dumb to write it down. Don't want people to see what crazy shit I think about."

"Do you want me to look at the sketchpad or just hold it for you?"

Perhaps surprised that I would bother to ask permission, Tai gave me a real, warm smile this time. I wished the last visiting foster parents could have seen him that way. "You can read it, Pedro..." he added in a stagey whisper, "if you dare!"

Right then, Barbara rounded the corner with Micah, a very well-behaved fat 13-year-old who'd come to us after an attempt at hanging himself from a light fixture. He joked about the failure in group in an apologetic way that made me sad. The staff loved him. His brown baby-face paled when he saw Tai's bloody bandage. I moved to reassure him but he shrunk away toward my mother instead. She stroked the back of his neck like an owner soothing a nervous dog, a gesture that I'd outgrown at his age (or felt I should have, anyway) but that he seemed to revel in.

"It's okay," I said to no one in particular, putting my hands up. "He didn't take anything. Just some anger management problems."

Barbara succeeded in keeping a poker face about the violation of her inner sanctum. "Tyler, you're missing your GED prep class. Go take off that outfit and put on normal clothes, then come back and clean this up.

I'll give you a remedial lesson when the others go out for movie night. Peter, can you stay and make sure he does it?"

Here was my chance to get out of this mess and leave the kid to snatch his own contraband. I felt for him, but my job and my free apartment were at stake if I got caught siding with a client who broke the rules (not to mention her door). Could I stop sabotaging myself for once?

"I can't, I was just on my way to rehearse the mock interview with Cara," I lied. "She blew off our last session, and the foster parents are coming to meet her at the end of the week." Cara was a 13-year-old whose intelligence and sweet nature were hidden by her extreme social anxiety. We were helping her with social scripts so she wouldn't clam up and fail to bond with the prospective family. Since she also had no sense of time management, it was all too easy for me to invent an appointment that she would simply "forget" to attend. I'd catch up with her for real tomorrow.

Barbara frowned. "All right, I'll do it. You walk Micah down to his appointment with Dr. Marla."

The boy shook me off. "I can go myself." I shrugged and left them all to their problems, ignoring Tyler's desperate eye-rolls.

CATCHING UP ON PAPERWORK for the rest of the afternoon mellowed me out. I wanted to give Cara her best shot at this placement, and not just because I owed her my alibi. She was one of the few whose troubles were only a matter of perception, an un-damaged soul obscured by the stupid labels that society puts on a bashful black girl. And what really was the untold story in these folders full of smiles, these applications from would-be moms and dads proving they had a clean bill of health, a spare bedroom and a BBQ grill?

I grabbed a slice of pepperoni pizza with the kids before they went out to the movies, then announced I was going to send a few faxes and head home for the night. Barbara herded Tyler off to the computer lab for the lesson he'd missed when he was playing burglar.

They'd swept up the glass but the cardboard patching the broken window was slipshod. A perfect excuse for me and my roll of duct tape to be in the office, to which I had a key, of course. I convinced myself that's all I was doing here, up till the moment I took the sketchbook down from my mother's closet shelf.

An image flashed in my mind's eye: Dad's home office, a poetry book tucked between two volumes of First Amendment case law, Polaroids of an unknown little girl spilling from the opened pages... My pulse pounded in my throat and my head felt heavy as a bowling ball, as if anything in Tyler's drawings could match the shock of that day in 1983 when I'd discovered the existence of my half-sister Prue inside the silver-and-white cover of Ada Porter's *Moonflower.*

No one saw me leave with the pad under my bulky parka. So much for Julian's advice to wear more form-fitting clothes. Julian...if only he was around tonight, but I couldn't even call him because he was on an overnight flight to Hawaii for a photo shoot at dawn. He believed in bending the rules to help people. Would he tell me I'd done the right thing? Maybe by the time he checked in with me, I'd have lost the nerve to ask. I let myself fantasize about bathing in the surf with him, and wondered why I had picked such an uncool career.

Rain speckled the windows of my apartment. I sat at Grandpa Saul's writing desk with a banana soymilk smoothie and Tyler's drawings, beneath the poster I'd bought to replace the Biblical filicide—Bette Davis as Margo Channing. Flipping through the boldly colored pages took me back in time: showing off my reading skills at this very desk, my grandfather's thick finger like a Torah-scroll pointer guiding me through Superman's speech bubbles. If I didn't make any mistakes, he'd give me 35 cents to buy the next issue at the newsstand where he purchased his cigars. I would pretend we were old men together, sitting on a park bench with the new comic book that I was too excited to open, while he read the *Jewish Daily Forward* and smoked the stinky tobacco that Grandma Reyna wouldn't allow in the house.

I inhaled, half expecting the store's atmosphere of newsprint and bubblegum to waft up from Ty's striking images. He didn't yet have a professional's grasp of anatomy and perspective, but in some ways the art was stronger for it, confident in its passionate distortions. The absence of a storyline made me stare harder at the inked faces, searching out their secret lives.

A green-skinned Titan immersed himself in a bath that boiled over with reddish bubbles. A bald, skeletal, nude woman curled on a bed, holding a plump baby to her hollow chest. In a disturbing sequence of optical illusions—had someone given the kid a book on Escher?—the baby's body morphed into part of his mother, so that in the final drawing, the circles of her new full breasts only vaguely suggested the small head and body they had once been. Feeling oddly nauseous, I flipped that page over quickly, but saw the same woman attached to a tangle of tubes pumping rainbow-colored fluid from a tank with a skull-and-crossbones label. I felt my own skin twitch as if punctured. Of course—I shivered with relief as the metaphor made sense—Ty's mom, undergoing chemo.

Ashamed at having understood too much, I skimmed the remaining pages, which held somewhat sinister erotic drawings of the emerald giant with various men. The last spread showed a beautiful young man, pale and thin in a hospital bed, being brought back from death by a kiss from a hulking male nurse. I gasped at this last scene, its tenderness a surprise in this dystopian portfolio. Tears sprang to my eyes, with a memory of Phil dying in Julian's arms, his ugly, pointless end. As their loyal friend on the sidelines, their silent rock, I'd ached for a share in that devotion—even, one night, dreaming a shameful dream that it was me in that sickbed, with no duty to speak or move, only to soak up love. The ultimate submissive. Now all that adoration was mine and sometimes it made me feel I was being burnt alive. I missed Jule so much, because when he was here, I still couldn't have him.

Sleep wouldn't come. Porn? Weed? *Mystery Science Theatre 3000?* I twitched beneath my blanket, knowing what I needed, my resistance breaking down. Before I could think twice, I was out in the chilly dark, another hunched raincoat shuffling down the stairwell to the downtown #1 train. Waiting, riding, walking, all the distance between me and my old neighborhood was for nothing. It was just as easy to find that unnumbered basement-level door, give the password to the man who answered the flat-sounding buzzer, and hand over the folded cash.

"Long time no see. What're you up for?" Bernie asked, picking out a room key with a delicate pinch of his thick fingers. He was bald and paunchy but strong, built like the executioner in a Bugs Bunny cartoon.

"Keep it safe. Nothing that'll leave a mark. My boyfriend doesn't like it." I'd semi-consciously rehearsed this on the train, the words of a subbie, not a cheater.

A stereo played Metallica at low volume in the shadowy foyer, but this apartment wasn't a nightclub. No one danced here. The narrow room housed the sheeted slab of a bed and a rack of clamps and cuffs. I'd been here before. First the blindfold, then the backwards shove, the wrenching of arms, shoulders, thighs, into spread-eagle lockdown. The burn of muscles holding position, the dizziness of air crushed out of lungs by a burly master straddling me to tighten the cold metal. Then he left. The waiting, part of the terrible thrill. Hard to explain to someone who hasn't done it, which fortunately no one could ask me to do, since I had a gag in my mouth. It could be like strapping into the cockpit of a racecar, or suiting up to dive into the black depths of the sea. This image recalled my now-recurring nightmare of the car crash in the ocean, so I shoved it aside with my mind, the only part I was free to move.

The gag was ripped off. A rubber-sheathed dick pressed my mouth open instead. I liked blowing without condoms better but I had said safety first. I loosened up, tilted back. My throat would be raw. Ah, nice warm lube. These guys were pros. A bigger one rammed me. On my next gasp I smelled leather like a new car, the gloved hands that steadied my head. I was in a trance, breathing barely enough to stay aware of the shockwaves below as pain split in half and birthed pleasure.

Alone, unlocked. Wet. I sobbed when the room's timer light switched on. Forced again into the life others knew, homesick already for the safest place inside me.

[EXCERPTED EMAIL EXCHANGES]

Sent: October 16, 1996, 11:45 PM
From: missionxbrent@aol.com
To: jselkirkphoto@aol.com

Hi Julian—

I got your address from Cheryl. Sorry to freak you out. I didn't mean to give you the big sales pitch for my life, like I'm all fixed now, right? :) My head was still in doing my show. That's mostly my social life now, so I forget how to ask "where's the bathroom" without turning it into a darned altar call. Well, God works in mysterious ways.

You probably don't want to hear from me, but I'm trying one more time to say I'm sorry about prom night. I was trying so hard not to have those wrong feelings for you anymore, I just froze up.

Anyway, next time you're down visiting the family, let me buy you a coffee and catch up? We're not touring on Thanksgiving or Christmas. Sorry to hear about Carter's accident. We prayed for them in church. Glad the twins weren't hurt.

Peace out— Brent

Sent: October 18, 1996, 7:06 AM
From: jselkirkphoto@aol.com
To: missionxbrent@aol.com

Don't ask me why I'm writing back to you. Hawaii is boring. Tropical storm hit the beach before I could, so I'm in the hotel business center waiting for my model to finish throwing up. Oysters, not dieting. I hope.

So you heard about my dumb-ass brother. Mama just told me Stef
kicked him out—DUI with two kids in the car, no shit—but Daddy
wouldn't let him stay in the spare room, even though they've got
enough space in that house for Sherman's troops. Keep an eye on him
for me, okay? Sign him up for your church softball league or something.
I hear sobriety can be lonely. No experience with it myself.

Forgive you? What do you think you did? I wasn't expecting you to
declare "I am cocksucking Spartacus" but friends don't let friends get
blood on their tuxedo. You're lucky it wasn't a rental. I have standards.

As for "wrong feelings"—are you still gay and taking cold showers, or
did Jesus electroshock you into kissing girls the way you used to kiss
me?

—Julian

Sent: October 18, 1996, 12:20 PM
From: missionxbrent@aol.com
To: jselkirkphoto@aol.com

Hi again Julian—

Thanks for writing back! I get why you're bitter. Lots of hypocrites in
the church, and outside too.

Wow, you asked a tough question. I wish we could talk face to face
because anything I write is going to sound like Christian-ese to you.
I'm not "gay" because I don't want to label myself based on something
that isn't the most important part of my life. It's too much pressure to
throw away everything for some guy when you're both imperfect, and
then there's no God and what have you got? Hope it's different for you
and your lucky boyfriend. I see you still go for the same type ;)

Have fun in Hawaii. Have you read Cheryl's book yet? What do you
think?

Peace— Brent

Sent: October 20, 1996, 4:53 PM
From: jselkirkphoto@aol.com
To: missionxbrent@aol.com

I hope you and Peter aren't the same type. He gave his blood and
guts to this church anti-poverty program that hung him out to dry
rather than expose that the boss was on the down-low. Peter's dead
in politics now. Be careful Mission X doesn't leave you out in the cold
once you can't break bricks with your forehead anymore.

In other news of lost causes, I talked to Carter yesterday. Thanks for giving him the number of that support group. You probably know Stef took him back, minus car keys, and they're trying another marriage counselor. Poor guy, if I had to work for Daddy every day, I'd drink too—cyanide, not whiskey. But he *doesn't* have to. He's just afraid to face that none of us will ever be good enough for the old man.

Cheryl means well. I don't know about the woo-woo stuff. If we attract from the universe whatever we think about, why isn't Tom Cruise sitting on my face?

—Julian

[EXCERPT FROM ELAINE RAINDAUGHTER, "SUPERMODEL TO SAGE: AN INTERVIEW WITH CHERYL KINGSTON," WOMYNWISE MAGAZINE, JUNE 1997]

Discovered at fourteen in a junior swimsuit pageant in Miami, Cheryl Kingston became an iconic face of the late 80s in Vogue, Mademoiselle, and Femme NY, before a detour into drug addiction and jail time taught her to look inward for true empowerment. I spoke with her in April about reclaiming beauty and spirituality from a patriarchal society.

ER: In your recovery memoir, *Fit for a King*, you opened up for the first time about surviving male sexual violence. I think when someone's so successful at looking perfect, people forget there's a real woman under the surface. How did keeping that secret affect your life?

CK: When I was a *Mademoiselle* cover model, I made my body beautiful for everyone else, but I didn't treat it like the temple of the Spirit inside. No matter how much money I made or how many people desired me without knowing me at all, inside was an angry, empty little girl who was punishing me for not keeping her safe from those boys. I used to think I was tired from long workdays and travel as an internationally known fashion model, but now I know it was chronic fatigue syndrome from not listening to my emotional pain. I got addicted to diet pills, and when those weren't enough to make me feel peppy, cocaine.

Hitting bottom was the best thing that ever happened to me because I learned that all problems are soul problems. I could have stayed angry that I was in jail while the man who'd pimped me out to feed my habit went free. I could be angry all the way back to that terrible day that changed one little girl's life forever. But then I'd only have kept making myself sick and needing more drugs to numb the hurt. Medical drugs are as bad as street drugs. They can addict us to avoiding the source of sickness, which is unforgiveness.

ER: Sounds like you've worked hard to find peace. But I'm going to challenge you: How can personal forgiveness be enough to fight rape culture?

CK: I don't know about that. All I can do is work on myself. Forgive myself for attracting these painful lessons into my life. Then I can believe I deserve beauty, health, and pleasure. And so do you. So does everyone.

THE LANTERN OVER the Gateway House porch was cracked again, a moment of bored vandalism giving the lie to our name. The afternoon was darkening with the onset of winter, speedy winds swirling the brown leaves and splayed newspapers.

Going inside for a stepladder and a replacement bulb, I stopped to greet Mom and Dr. Marla in the common room. They were stuffing fundraising envelopes while watching CNN. Our newly re-elected President Bill Clinton was charming his way through a speech about cracking down on the culture of poverty. My mother got a paper cut, licked her finger and shook it off impatiently in the direction of the screen.

"He wants to be so tough on crime, he should spend a few days around here first."

"What's so wrong about what he's doing? Our kids shouldn't have to be afraid that their classmates are carrying guns," Dr. Marla objected. Our resident psychologist was a stocky black-haired woman in her fifties, with a penchant for zip-up jumpsuits, like she was planning to parachute out of a plane.

"When you expel that kid with the gun, where's he going to go? Out on the streets, selling drugs, because he can't get a job without a diploma. If he's lucky and he doesn't die, he might end up here. If not, his kids will."

"Maybe that's the best we can do. Save a few in each generation, put them in families where they'll have a better chance."

Barbara shook her head. "You'd think I'd stop wanting to save everybody. I've been doing this long enough. Tell me what good it does, Mr. President, to kick a family out of public housing because their father has a drug conviction."

"You're an idealist. That's why the kids love you." Dr. Marla swiped another envelope closed.

"Me? *I'm* the realistic one. Everybody does drugs, everybody has a weapon. Or something. Tax fraud, hit and run, shoplifting. Some people just keep secrets better than others, so they still have a roof over their heads."

One little repair job led to another. Solving simple problems calmed me and saved money for the group home, which, like most small nonprofits, measured its margin of survival in pennies. I was tacking down the curling doormat in the entryway when Ty and his new prospective foster parents,

Horace and Aletha Becker, returned from their first unsupervised outing. A black professional couple—he was a radiologist, his wife an amateur painter—the Beckers were looking to help out another teenager now that their adopted daughter had left for college. I waved back at their friendly greeting instead of shaking hands, as I was grimy from the soot and slush on the floor mat. A warm but authoritative figure, Dr. Becker was apparently the type to wear a suit on the weekend, while his wife's smart black-and-white dress seemed straight out of the abstract wing of MoMA, where the threesome had spent the afternoon. Ty, stiff in a checkered button-down shirt and navy blazer from our clothing drive, clutched a museum tote bag printed with that Lichtenstein painting of the drowning girl: *I don't care! I'd rather sink—than call Brad for help!*

I signed Ty into our log book, while Barbara, overhearing us, bustled out to greet the couple and discuss scheduling another outing after Thanksgiving. All the adults agreed that the visit had gone well. Ty's smile looked wavery to me, his eyes suspiciously bright with tears he'd taught himself not to shed. The moment they were gone, he pounded up the stairs to his room. Barbara shook her head. "He won't do better than those two. It's hard to find an ethnic match with resources for a special-needs adolescent. And isn't Aletha just lovely? She's very interested in helping Tyler get a real education in art, but he won't show her any of his drawings yet."

"Give him time, Mom. Teenagers are secretive."

"Don't I know it. You were such a quiet boy, I never expected you to have so many struggles later."

"I'm doing great. My life is great," I said curtly. "Are you really sure the Beckers are the best fit for Ty? They seem nice enough, but he looked pretty depressed wearing that preppy straitjacket."

"Oh, well, as for *that*..." She sighed. "You weren't here earlier but we had a little argument. He wanted to wear lipstick and these ugly cheap pearls that he picked up somewhere, and I told him no."

"They do know he's gay, right?"

"Of course. That's not the issue. He can do whatever he wants with his boyfriend when he's old enough to have one—"

"He's *fifteen*."

"But I'm not sending him down Fifth Avenue dressed like a transsexual prostitute. He's just re-enacting when he should be trying to heal."

"We don't know what he's trying to do."

"Trust me, I know self-sabotage when I see it." She patted my arm. "Try to get through to him, Peter. He looks up to you."

As soon as I had a free moment, I went upstairs to check on Ty. My first knock on his door was met with silence. "It's just me—Peter," I said on the second attempt.

"Yeah."

I took this as all the encouragement I would get, and cautiously opened the door. Ty was cross-legged on his bed, sketching furiously. He'd shed his preppy clothes and wore boxers and a too-small red camisole with lace straps. "Better put some pants on, my man, or I'm going to get in trouble."

"I'm not your *man*." But he got up, with resentful slowness, and scrounged up a pair of sweatpants.

I left the door open a crack, as per regulations, but closed enough for a mostly private conversation. "What are you working on?"

"Same as usual." He remained bent over his drawing pad. I could tell that he wasn't really drafting anymore, though, just digging in lines and scrubbing them out with a crumbly eraser.

Without really planning it, Ty and I had begun weaving a storyline around some recurring characters he drew, as a skill-building exercise that was more engaging than Regents Exam practice essays on plastics recycling and the three branches of government. He'd seen too much of life, or wanted to pretend that he had, to play along with the hokey conversation-starters of group therapy: rose, bud, thorn. But I could almost always draw him out by rejoining our shared fantasy world.

"I had an idea for that character we made up last time, with the super poison powers. You did a great spooky drawing of him in a bathtub— maybe that's where he transforms, like, with a potion or something."

"Lucky motherfucker." Ty flung down his pad. I finally saw the image: our green-skinned antihero gazing solemnly at his reflection while brushing on, or perhaps wiping off, the cosmetics that gave his skin a human tone.

"How do *you* want to transform?" I ventured.

Ty rolled his eyes at my Social Work 101 question. I let the silence fill up between us. No doubt he'd spent an exhausting afternoon being tactfully interrogated by the Beckers about his goals and hobbies. Noticing me glancing at his drawing, he took up the pad and flipped some pages over. He paused on an image I couldn't see, tenderly retracing some lines with his fingertip. Then, his face contorting from wistfulness to frustrated rage, he tore it out, crumpled it and flung it in the general direction of the wastebasket.

"Hey, wait, don't do that." I smoothed out the abused piece of paper on my lap. Two intertwined nude men came to life in the strokes of ink, the slight distortions of their angled limbs giving their coupling the edginess of truth, the strain and violence of two individuals starting to fuse into one desire. A closer look showed that one was the pale beauty from the hospital bed, and the other our toxic protagonist.

"Whoa, great plot twist! Is he the one who made the guy sick or...or can his powers *heal*, as well as kill?" My head tingled with excitement, the thrill of the breakthrough more compelling than the erotic embrace.

My enthusiasm was infectious, but only briefly. The light in Ty's eyes was again snuffed by shame. "Nah, fuck it, I don't want to work on this anymore."

"Okay." I tried to mask my disappointment in a neutral therapeutic tone. "Can we talk about that?"

"They keep pushing me to show off to my 'new parents' what a 'great artist' I am. What do you think Mrs. Becker's going to say about this shit? They'll send me back to Dr. Marla so she can tell me everything that's wrong with my head."

"Do *you* think something's wrong?" These mirroring questions felt fake to me, but that's how we were trained to talk to the kids. To be an echo chamber where their own words bounced back in the emptiness till they couldn't avoid what they were really saying.

"I think I'm real—*Tai's* real—but nobody else does. That's the definition of crazy, right?"

"Are you Tai—are you her right now?"

Ty cocked his head, calculating whether I was sincere or laying a trap. I wasn't sure myself. What I wanted to do, and what I was supposed to do, were—as usual—two different things.

"I'm her when I draw what I'm really into. Stuff that comes from someplace, I don't know, I don't think about it, it's just there. But Dr. Marla says I'm 'noncompliant' when I won't pick it apart in group, talk about how *sad* I am from working the street. It was just a job! Most jobs suck—if you know what I mean." Ty winked and made a wet popping sound with his lips. His eyes still held the pain I'd seen before. Or so I thought. Was I patronizing him, too?

"Please don't give up on your art. Try to cut Barbara and Dr. Marla some slack. They might not be able to handle *this*—" I indicated the erotic drawing— "but they can help you grieve for your mom and dad, and stuff like that."

Ty bristled at the mention of his parents. "How? By pushing me off on strangers? I told them, I want to go live with Aunt Carmen."

"We'll see how your Thanksgiving visit goes." The sister of Ty's late mother had so far not shown interest in giving the kid a home, but the holidays were a good time for familial guilt feelings. "But she's going to want the same thing the Beckers do."

"For me to keep all this shit inside, no matter what." Ty picked despondently at the lace neckline of his camisole.

"No, we just have to find the right outlet for it."

"Could *you* write it down for me, Pedro? I'll give you the drawings, you put it together like a real comic book. Then nobody has to see, unless we want them to."

"Thank you for trusting me." That was my mission, right? To win him over, steer him toward a future that was better than what he could envision. "But..."

"But what? It's your *job* to report on me?" Ty sneered.

"My job..." I took a breath to calm my heartbeat. How could he know that I ached as if it were me in those miserable borrowed clothes, propped up like a mannequin in my family's display of success? "My first responsibility is to take care of you. To make a space where you can find yourself, without being ashamed."

Homosexuality, my father said more than once, wasn't declassified as a mental illness till yours truly was three years old. He meant this as a supportive comment, a promise that he would remain in the enlightened vanguard. But I was more frightened by the idea that it had ever been in question—that from the ages of zero to three, as the much-speculated-upon gay gene replicated in my cells, I'd been legally insane, until some generous doctors gave me the chance to prove otherwise. Wasn't Ty—or "Tai"—like any other kid who eased his terror with a secret self, creating a diva or superhero to hold the part of him that was too large and precious for this world?

"Then we're on?" Ty pressed.

I gave him what I hoped was a confident smile, as I picked up an empty soda can from his floor and raised it in a toast. "Here's to the first issue of... *The Poison Cure*!"

[EXCERPT OF SCRIPT FOR *THE POISON CURE*, VOL. 1, ISSUE 1]

```
Hospital corridor. Rear view of tall man in
orderly's scrubs pushing a cart of file charts past
a painting of St. Vincent. Three panels follow him
walking past doorways with glimpses of different
families at bedsides: A father holds his newborn and
```

kisses his wife. Adult children comfort each other
as their elderly mother flatlines.

At the final door, the orderly pauses to watch from
a distance. This ward is set apart from the others
and has no visitors. The doctor pulls on rubber
gloves and a germ mask before entering.

Close-up through window slit. On the bed, a
beautiful young man with flowing black hair, aquiline
nose and high cheekbones. He lies unconscious
while doctor checks vitals. Next panel, the orderly
peeks at a file from his cart, finding the matching
room number. The name *Ryder Challis*. A list of
medications: AZT, 3TC.

As the doctor hurries out, flinging the hazmat gear
into the trash behind him, the orderly darts into
the room. His face is shown for the first time. It
is Pharmakon, with his normal human appearance.
Name tag on scrubs reads *Tod Gift*.

Bending over the bed, he plants a deep, tender
kiss on the patient's mouth. The kiss lasts into a
close-up in the next panel that shows healthy color
returning to Challis's pale face, while a faint
tinge of green spreads outward from the kiss onto
Pharmakon's features.

Challis opens his eyes. Faces inches apart, the men
look at each other with wonder and surprise. An
instant later, Pharmakon covers his now unnatural-
looking face with his sleeve and rushes out before
the patient fully wakes up to what has happened.

One duty ends... Another begins.

Scene shift. Dim locker room. Pharmakon changes his
scrubs for a green satin shirt, tight black pants.
He walks out into the city night.

A crowded upscale restaurant. Men and women in
business attire drink to unwind before the evening
commute. Focus in on a man in early middle age with
a square jaw and receding blond hairline. It is
the man Pharmakon saw in his dream of the girl's
birthday party.

Suave, Pharmakon leans against the wall by the men's
room, looking intently at the blond man, whose back
is to him. The businessman starts to sweat and
shift uncomfortably, like a junkie trying to hide
his need for a fix. Making an excuse about catching
his train, he says a rushed goodbye to his co-
workers. As he turns and spots Pharmakon, anxiety
gives way to an entranced expression.

*He'd always wondered what it would be like... Could
he take the chance... Where would they...?*

Breaking eye contact, Pharmakon slips down the
corridor past the restrooms to an alley out back.
The businessman follows at a careful distance. Next
panel, in the dark alley, hidden in the shadow of
dumpsters, Pharmakon has the man up against a wall,
deep-kissing him and reaching into his pants. The
older man clutches him in ecstasy.

Pharmakon is on his knees, going down on him.
The man's eyes widen and his face lights up with
overpowering pleasure—changing the next instant to
the contortions of shock as he claws at his chest
and collapses.

Pausing only a moment to zip up the corpse's fly,
Pharmakon disappears into the dark street.

The body lies alone in the alley with its eyes open.
Rain begins to fall. The first drops trickling off
him make the tiniest green flash as they strike the
puddles on the ground. Then all is gray.

"I'm sorry to make us miss our flight," I told Julian again, as I squinted through the drizzle on the windshield to see how traffic was moving up ahead.

Julian's leather-gloved hand fiddled with the edges of his Burberry scarf. "Enough. It's okay, truly."

"You could really have gone ahead without me. I don't want you to miss Laura Sue before she returns to Uganda." I'd said this before, too, but I still felt bad.

"Personally I'd rather visit her in that fucking war zone than the one in Marietta." He turned aside to the view of the East River, dark beneath our span of the congested Brooklyn Bridge. "Anyway, I'm sure we'll squeeze onto some flight tomorrow, if we're willing to layover in Cleveland in the wee hours. Just enough time to show the flag and get out."

"You're a good brother."

"And you're a good social worker. That and a buck-fifty will get you..." he rubbed my thigh— "a trip to the Mile High Club."

Dream on. It was the Wednesday before Thanksgiving, but instead of being on a plane headed for Mama Selkirk's turkey and trimmings, I was crawling toward the outer boroughs to hunt down Tyler, who'd gone AWOL from his Aunt Carmen's place. She'd called Dr. Marla to say he'd run off, and that good lady had decided I was the one to go investigate since "I had such great rapport with him." Not great enough, I guess, or he'd have called me to stop him from making such a stupid move.

On the other hand, maybe this was my fault. Julian and I had been all set to spend the holiday with Mom at Gateway till he heard that his sister's furlough from her missionary endeavors had been moved up from Christmas to this weekend. Was Ty testing me, or spiting me?

Some of the kids with family in the city were being allowed day or overnight visits in the week leading up to Thanksgiving, once we determined that the home environment was stable enough. Everyone had to be back at Gateway for the holiday itself, so the kids with nowhere to go wouldn't feel left behind. Meanwhile, Julian had gone all "not without my boyfriend" on his Mama when she entreated him to fly down for the family celebration—a point that he was forcing, not me. He'd sacrificed enough for our relationship. But Jule insisted: "Phil must've told you about that awful dinner party where I faked having a girlfriend, right in front of him? It didn't fool my family, only made him feel like shit. I want to behave better with you."

I don't know why they call them holidays when they're so much work. The only properly named one is Armed Forces Day.

Nearly an hour later, we were interrupting dinner at Carmen Benitez's apartment in Red Hook. I smelled spicy beef stew and fried dough. Social work is a lot of looking through doorways at tables where you won't be invited to sit down, and other places where you wouldn't dare. Either way, always carry granola bars in your coat pocket.

Carmen looked surprised, but not unpleasantly, to see Julian beside me in his slim-fitting trench coat like a detective in a French film. He has that effect on people. Ty's aunt was a sterner, dressier version of his late mother in the photo on his night table. Her red and purple dress was tight around the curve of her belly. Sounding worried beneath her short-tempered manner, Carmen said Ty had gotten into a shouting match with her fiancé while she was cooking and stormed out several hours ago. Something about refusing to do chores and make himself presentable for prayer meeting.

"Was he, uh, dressed normally?" I asked, not wanting to bring up the topic of feminine clothing if Ty hadn't forced the issue.

Her expression implied that "normal" for teen boys was still a step below acceptable. "Isaac told him to put on a tie for church. He believes in respect." The dark-browed face gentled with the shy pride of a woman in love with a strong man.

Hearing his name, a tall guy in a crisp white shirt and skinny tie came up and put his hands on her shoulders to steer her back to her duties. "Carmen, it's time," he said in a deep Jamaican-inflected voice.

Her body turned to him, but her eyes reluctantly lingered on us. "He's always had this problem, blowing up at nothing, but I thought he'd cool off and come back, like usual. I cooked his favorite *sancocho*."

"Can you think of anyone else he could have run to?" I asked as the door began to close.

"No, sorry, there's no one."

And doesn't he know it, I thought. Julian and I descended the building's dim, rain-slick front steps to my car, where he switched on the heater full blast. "Should we try the police station?" he ventured.

"And tell them what—to be on the lookout for an angry young Negro in women's underwear?"

"He's a runaway. He won't get arrested just for standing on a street corner."

"Seriously? Have you ever talked to any black people who weren't Naomi Campbell or your housekeeper?"

"Oh, suck my balls. On second thought, drive us out of here first."

I wouldn't give him the satisfaction of saying so, but I was actually heading for the precinct, if only because I was out of ideas and had to try something to justify this expedition. Perhaps realizing that future ball-sucking depended on his being less moronic about race relations, Jule reached out a supportive hand to me. "You're afraid he's gone back to hustling, huh?"

I considered the worst scenario. "You know what—no. He's pissed but not self-destructive. He has goals now, and he gets that he has to find a foster family he can play nice with, even if he's hurt that this wasn't the one. Ever since we've been writing the comic book—" An idea struck me, and a taxicab nearly did too, but settled for honking at my abrupt left turn. "Humor me—I have a hunch where he could be."

"I hope it's somewhere with a phone so I can call American Airlines."

"I promise."

Traffic was lighter as I detoured to Brooklyn Heights. There was a good chance Rogues' Galaxy would be open, holiday eve or not. Jonas and his core customers weren't the type to knock off early to cook stuffing. We wedged into a parking spot by the Promenade and walked head-down against the wet wind.

Yes, the little green spaceship on the Open sign was neon bright. I smiled at the familiar sound as I pushed the door open: instead of chimes, a motion-activated recording of a theremin's alien *wee-ooo*. Cheap ink, expensive plastic, glass cases displaying models of grimacing monsters and buxom babes with blasters. Luke Skywalker movie posters had yielded center stage to Will Smith from *Independence Day*, but the comic-book shop was still my time machine, the sanctuary I remembered from when I was Ty's age. Through Jonas' acquaintance with Dad, I'd scored a part-time job stocking shelves, during that blurry, terrible year when my parents' marriage imploded.

Gary Jonas had grayed early; fifty looked the same as forty on him. Rangy, lean-muscled, with a sort of slow swing to his walk, like a gunslinger. A quick grip of a handshake, then I introduced him to Julian, who made no move to reciprocate. My boyfriend's face was tight—impatient for me to stop reliving my childhood so he could start on his? I asked Jonas for the phone. "It can wait," Jule said, not budging.

"Looking for your stowaway?" Jonas asked me, with an amused twitch at the corner of his mouth. "I bought him a Quarter Pounder when you didn't come by suppertime. He's in the back."

I exhaled with relief. "Thank God I was right."

Jonas squinted. "You mean he didn't call you? He told me..."

"Nope. Spidey sense."

The older man laughed dryly. "Takes one to know one, is what it is. You and your sidekick think alike. Remember the time you used your key to sneak in here overnight, right after your mother tried to take you kids away to live in Florida?"

"Not really." Not at all, actually. What kids? I was Barbara's only one.

"Watch out for that short-term memory loss, my man." Jonas mimed a toke. "Nearly pissed myself when I saw you sleeping on the floor that time, thought some bum had broken in and OD'd."

"Well, Julian always says I dress like one." I glanced his way, but my joke failed to draw him in.

Jonas squeezed my shoulder hard. "I'll go retrieve your precious cargo." But Ty had already eased silently into the doorway dividing store from stockroom, watching us with longing eyes that spoke louder than the ready-to-argue set of his jaw. One hand dragged his overnight backpack on the floor.

Jonas helped him save face. "Ty, thanks for showing me more of your drawings. These characters have potential. Cult favorite, underground stuff, for adults, you know..." He skimmed the shelf of coffee-table-sized art books. "What I'm saying is bad for business, but don't read too many comics, not yet. Don't be derivative. You need anatomy, perspective—here." He handed the boy a hardcover book on classical figure drawing that must have cost upwards of fifty dollars.

Ty had the courtesy to look my way for permission, but Jonas didn't wait. "Happy Thanksgiving. Now do what Peter wants. Go home, apologize, do your work. We're all on your side here."

The kid mumbled his thanks, stuffed his prize in his backpack, and finally got a move on. I planned to drop him at Gateway and then speed over to the airport to find another flight to the sunny South. Julian, walking at a fast clip ahead of us, was taut with anger that I didn't understand. He didn't typically stress about lateness or changes of plans. At my car, he motioned us into the backseat and stuck out his hand for the keys. I tried to ask what was up but he cut me off. "I'm sure Tyler has a lot to tell you. Pretend I'm not even here." To underscore his words, he cranked the car radio to country-western. A dude with an exaggerated twang offered us a quarter to call someone who cared.

"What's buggin' *him*?" Ty stage-whispered over the whining fiddles.

"Don't change the subject. What the hell got into *you*, running away like that? Are you trying to get kicked out of Gateway?"

"No, man, I dunno, I'm sorry, but you know what it's like, when you're just gonna bust out of your skin if you don't go someplace to cool down?"

I don't believe in being honest with everybody, but I am with the kids, so I nodded just once. Ty went on: "But then I felt like an asshole, 'cause I'd taken my bag and walked out, and if I went back, it'd be like saying I was wrong and that fool Isaac could boss me around."

"Sometimes they can. That's how the game is played."

"I'm not stupid." Ty pouted. Even without cosmetics, I saw the teenage girl inhabit that face: vulnerable, defiant, straining to blossom. The pain in those eyes was liquid, bright. "She's having his baby."

"Yeah, looks like it."

"I thought that extra room they were fixing up was gonna be for me... Never mind, fuck 'em."

"They never said they wouldn't take you too. Right? You didn't give them the chance."

"I *said* fuck 'em. You never been in foster care. I know how this shit plays out. Their real kid always comes first. They want me to be a free babysitter and handyman. They catch me in high heels someday, decide I belong in a Hannibal Lecter movie and every weird thing the kid does from then on must be because there's a perv in the house. Am I wrong, Pedro?"

"I don't know. But for once you could wait and tell your concerns to the home-study social workers instead of running off like you know everything and don't need anyone."

Time to play the grown-up again. I hoped I'd always know to check myself when I started identifying too much with Tyler. I remembered how it felt at his age to be the family mop-up man, the afterthought, the obstacle to someone's fresh start. Too young to move out, too old to have his feelings coddled.

What feelings, Peter? I'd had a middle-class home, a supportive coming-out, a new half-sister who turned out to share my interests in Donkey Kong and socialist revolution. But Barbara loved me, and Ada didn't. My real mother left, and the woman Dad had been secretly fucking since I was in preschool—a bipolar, chain-smoking poetry professor—moved herself and her love-child in. Not that Prue and I were the type to throw chairs at each other on the Geraldo Rivera show. She lurked upstairs with her guitar, and I in the basement with my comics and weed, for about three months before we realized we had to join forces or eat TV dinners forever. Dad thought Ada was going to be the mom, and Ada thought I was. As they say, she knew a hawk from a handsaw.

Lucky Tyler, now, not appreciating his luck yet, coming home to Barbara's Thanksgiving table. I wished I could stay too, instead of spending the night in the airport with my angry boyfriend, en route to Cracker-ville. But I had a little shiver of anxiety that if I did this, or even spoke the wish aloud, Jule would give up on us.

The prodigal apologized to Dr. Marla and Barbara. He said he hadn't wanted to go to Isaac's anti-gay church so he went to show my friend Mr. Jonas his artwork and lost track of the time. I confirmed that this was more or less true and that he hadn't stolen the book, whose sticker price, I saw, was $79.95. While this performance was going on, Julian disappeared to phone the airline.

When he came back, he addressed Barbara, not me. "We're on the 11:45 tonight out of LaGuardia. I tried the airport motel in Atlanta but it was full, so I can make more calls or we can sleep on the plane."

"Stay for dinner first," Mom urged us. Julian hesitated, torn between wanting to send me to bed without my supper, and his Southern training to be polite to mothers and hostesses.

"Thanks, Mom, we'll take something to go," I said.

"I made stuffed derma."

"What's that?" my boyfriend asked.

"Mashed carrots inside of cow intestines," I said.

Julian shrugged. "Okay, not a car food, then." He pulled up a chair and sat. So that was settled. He was going to eat the worms and win the dare. The joke was on him because Barbara's cooking had to be superior to the marshmallows-and-lard cuisine of his native land.

He managed to ignore me throughout our quick meal via his usual trick of asking other people to talk about themselves. Mom was even a bit fluttery around him, modest about her achievements at Gateway, allowing herself to get misty over *kibbutznik* memories of oneness with land and people. Dr. Marla, that stolid butch, told us about taking a continuing-education class in art therapy.

"Did Tyler pick that book himself?" she probed.

"No, Jonas gave it to him."

"In any event, I'm glad to see him studying the classics for a change. He has too much talent to use it just for shock value."

"What could possibly shock a social worker?" Julian teased.

"Hardly anything," Barbara jumped in, with a giggle, "but we worry sometimes that the kids get stuck reliving the most disturbed parts of their experience, instead of expanding their imaginations to healthier futures. Stories about love and families, not always sex and violence. So they can learn to hope for that for themselves."

I thought about Ty's hopes and rude awakening at Carmen's. But that was his argument to make, and he wouldn't ever speak of it to these two, I knew. He'd have to bury it under pages of super-villain perversion and just let them try to crack Pharmakon's code.

"I understand what you mean," I said, "but that dark and heavy stuff is part of real life, especially for gay teens. Sex is scary and raw and could kill you, and is also what tells you you're alive. It's kind of—a guy thing? Everything's like a death-match—but it doesn't mean anyone's really going to die."

"I'm sick of that part of life," Julian shot back.

My mother favored him with an affectionate look. When he didn't elaborate, she said, "I agree. Times are changing, thank God. All I want is to show the kids that they can be gay or lesbian and still have a normal, safe life." A sidelong glance at me, her sterling example. I'd have paid someone a hundred dollars to pee on me right then and there.

BACK ON THE ROAD, with Tupperwares of pumpkin bread for a midnight snack. Julian had left the honky-tonk on full blast when I turned the key in the ignition. I punched the off button at the first red light, brushing his hand away from the volume dial. I didn't need Reba to teach me about the fear of being alone.

"Okay, enough," I said. "Why have you been so pissy since we found Ty? We'll only be a few hours late. I'll find some chore he can do to make it up to you for dragging us out of our way."

"*Chore?* What's he going to do, suck my cock? *I'm* not a chickenhawk."

"If my mother could hear you talk like that…"

Jule gritted his teeth. All right, bad time for a joke. I went on about my idea: "He's probably not reliable enough to assist at a shoot, but he could help you scout for props, set up the studio—"

"Really," he said, sharp as icicles. "You're that stupid. You don't see it. Or you don't *want* to see."

"Hey, that's not cool. Or comprehensible. Talk to me like a normal person or you're getting 45 minutes of polka music from here to LaGuardia."

He glared at me. "You have no boundaries. You have no idea what's appropriate. You and this kid, and he *is* just a kid—what is he, thirteen?"

"Fifteen."

"You're caught up in this fantasy together of being the next Batman and Robin or some shit, that he's going to pimp himself out for—"

"Wait, wait. Shut that shit down." I twisted around toward him, missing my merge onto the highway, which set off a cacophony of honks. "Don't make me have an accident."

"Can't handle the truth," he muttered.

"Not till the next exit."

Crisis averted, a few minutes later, I broke the truce. I'd been stewing over what he was implying. "Are you—*jealous* of Ty?"

Jule looked as offended as I felt. "Hell, no. I'm trying to protect him. Which should have been your job."

"From what?" A terrible thought surfaced. "Not...from me? Eew. You can't believe I'd ever—with one of my kids—eew!"

But the harder I pushed the horror away, the more it stuck to me, like a tar baby. I felt close to Ty, but not in that way. With *The Poison Cure*, I was giving him a space to be honest, in all his lipstick-loving manliness, his innocent lust and rage, which everyone else would trim away to adapt him to a world where gay black boys didn't find a forever family. But had I violated his private mind, taken advantage of his trust to see what I shouldn't see, even though he had offered it? A lump rose in my throat, a choking grief, followed by a cold wave of dread that I really was the subtle predator Julian saw.

"Not you, dummy." Jule laid his warm hand over my clammy one on the steering wheel. "God, don't you think I know you better than that? It's just, you couldn't protect yourself, when you were his age, and now you're letting Ty walk into the same trap."

"Now I really don't know what we're talking about." Julian was obsessed with rescuing me from my kinks—not that he'd hesitated to nail me to the wall last night—but I hadn't started those explorations in real life until college.

He breathed out slowly, steadying himself for something he'd rather not say. "Remember the camping trip we took with Phil, before he...got too sick? That night we all did true confessions about our first times?"

My friend's loving ghost calmed us as soon as we invoked his name, sending a piney breeze from that night two years ago to cool our anger and remind us to survive together. Yes, of course I could recall the firsts he and Julian had shared. Why hurt me now, with the unchangeable past?

Julian went on: "You told me that guy Jonas fucked you when you were thirteen. Right back there in his fucking stockroom. The one Tyler was in when we showed up. Did you mean that or were you bullshitting to impress us? Tell me and I'll back off," he pleaded.

"No!" My voice sounded loud in the confined space of the car. "Look, Ty is safe. The rest—this is not a good time, okay? I'm supposed to meet your homo-hating, gun-toting parents in less than 24 hours and I'm already exhausted."

"If Mama had owned a gun, my life would've turned out a lot better. And you still haven't given me a straight answer."

"There's nothing wrong with your life. You're gorgeous, you can charm a dyke out of her cargo pants, you make hundreds of dollars an hour to take pictures of handbags, and you own my ass. And I bet, when *you* were a miserable teenager stuck with all the family secrets, if a cool older guy had volunteered to teach you about becoming a gay man, you'd have dropped your pants too."

"Yeah, we all know I was born slutty, but *he* shouldn't have asked. That's the issue. You're not bad. You're the victim here. And Tyler's even more vulnerable."

"There *is* no victim!" I was nearly shouting. "Don't lay your Christian guilt trip about lost purity on me. I like Jonas—I owe him a lot. You want to talk 'firsts'? Mom and Dad weren't always accepting. Sure, in theory, but they didn't want to see it in their own son. They'd just look sideways at me like something was wrong that couldn't even be named. Jonas took me to my first Pride march. He showed me what I was, why I'd always felt different, and that it could be beautiful, like...superheroes."

"He should've done that without being a chickenhawk, is all."

"Shut up, Julian. Shut up or I'm gonna drive this car—"

—somewhere they can't reach us, a voice echoed in my head. I heard it alongside the traffic of here and now, like two radio stations playing at once. The strange one louder, no, we were there, I was *—coming with us. You'll like it there. She should have been mine—* Oh God, the airport sign up ahead, we were really going, all my fault because I *—always tell me the truth, because you're a good boy, but not everyone—* honking horns all at once the rushing darkness behind us the crying *I want to go home Peter I want Peter—*

"Peter? Peter! What's the matter? Pull over, right now." Hands gripping me, shaking, pulling the wheel my fingers were clenched around. A lurch to the side. Jolting to stillness. Something hard digging into my forehead. "Go home, go home..." a gasping monotone repeated. When I sucked in a deep breath, the voice stopped. It had been mine.

"Darling, what is it? Look at me." Julian cupped my cheek gently. I lifted my head from the steering wheel. He'd managed to stop the car on the highway shoulder. No sirens approaching, so far.

"How'd you do that?" I asked stupidly, gesturing at the road. "We're safe, right?"

"Drunk-dad driver's ed," Jule quipped, but then his tone became serious. "I do talk a lot of shit about my family, don't I? No wonder you had a panic attack. We really don't have to go, I promise. We'll go home, I'll stuff your turkey, and on Friday I'll find a one-day round trip to see my sister before she leaves this corrupt world behind." The pressure of him kneading my upper arm gradually brought me back to my body in the here and now. A body with a lingering sense of being too big, too developed, for the shrinking fear that had flooded every cell. "Poor sweetheart. I'm sorry."

"Me too. I don't know what the hell happened." I embraced him as well as I could with the seatbelts binding us.

"Meeting the parents is a big step. I understand if you're not ready for it. Especially these parents. Now move over and let me drive us back to my place."

I checked in with my gut. A surprising calm. The worst had already happened, though I didn't know what I meant by that, and had no desire to find out this minute. "No thanks, babe—I mean, you should drive, but I want to stick to our plans." I found the ability to smile. "I've been meaning to ask your Mama how to keep my soufflés from falling."

Julian kissed my cheek, mercifully playing along. "Thank you, darling. You are showing the reckless disregard for human life—usually your own—that marks you as a true member of the Selkirk family."

Nothing more was said about Tyler. I welcomed the upcoming distraction of somebody else's dysfunction. Departing planes zoomed overhead, their engines screaming of power, not distress. I dozed in the passenger seat, with my head against Julian's steady arm. Behind my flickering eyelids, the jet sounds conjured the green image of Jonas' neon spaceship, a tiny beacon of safety despite everything. A promise of escape bought with the ticket of homelessness—to return, if at all, changed by light-years, speaking a language unintelligible to the ones who had said they loved you best.

[EXCERPT OF SCRIPT FOR *THE POISON CURE*, VOL. 1, ISSUE 2]

The park at night. Backdrop of black skyscrapers dotted with gold windows behind a ring of trees. Foliage rustles. Scuffling, gasping sounds.

Close-up, inside view of the cluster of bushes in purplish shadow. Profile of Challis, face strained, eyes squeezed shut, a hand over his mouth. Next panel, pull back from same view to show both men's bodies: Challis kneeling on grass with pants down, bottoming for older man in a smart suit. Streak of greenish light at the background edge could be a passing car or a person approaching unseen.

Next panel, both men standing and dressed. Balding pinstriped gent seems embarrassed as he hands a wad of folded bills to the slightly smiling Challis. Green streak takes on more resemblance to human silhouette.

Challis, alone, turns to see a figure emerge from the trees: Pharmakon, dressed in trench raincoat and dark trousers. There is no green color on or around him. Now Challis is the one to look a little embarrassed, but by the next panel, his startled expression has relaxed into the seductive smile he puts on for clients.

C: *I don't know how you saved my life...but I know how I'd like to repay you.*

Pharmakon: *I don't know either. It's never happened before.*

C: (misunderstanding, draws nearer, smile widens): *That's what they all say, honey.*

P: (despite his next words, moving nearer, so their faces are almost close enough to kiss again): *You don't understand. Usually my touch... hurts people.*

C: (frowning a little but not budging): *Maybe I'm immune.* (Laughs suddenly.) *Get this—a month ago I could've died from somebody sneezing on me, and now—*

Challis leans in for a kiss but Pharmakon tilts his head back. Close-up of Challis' hand touching the bare skin of Pharmakon's neck. Energy radiates around the contact point. Both men close their eyes in ecstasy or pain.

Pharmakon looks exhausted, about to yield to a kiss, when Challis breaks contact: *Whoa. We'd better not fuck here or we'll cause a forest fire. Where're you headed tonight?*

Pharmakon sees a chance to change the subject: *Why do you still have to hustle? Now you're healthy, can't you—*

Challis curls his lip: *Look, all I want is to suck dick and write songs. One pays for the other. Good deal.*

P: *I'm sorry.*

C: (turning around, walking off into the bushes): *I don't need a hero, okay? Change your mind, I'll be around—same time same station.*

Moonlight and shadows. Pharmakon stands alone in the clearing. He thinks: *A hero?* Next panel, we see the moon is full, and his skin has turned green. Walking away, frowning, head down, he thinks: *That's the last thing I could be.*

[EXCERPTED EMAIL EXCHANGES]

Sent: November 19, 1996, 12:13 AM
From: missionxbrent@aol.com
To: jselkirkphoto@aol.com

Hi Julian—

How's life in the fast lane? Tonight was our last show till after Thanksgiving weekend. I'm always too pumped to sleep after these things. Pulled a great crowd of high school kids in the parking lot of Cornerstone Bible Fellowship, with a really cute chick fronting the praise band, and then our act. This whale of a girl was having some kind of seizure in the driveway, and we were scared it was allergies, but turned out it was like the born-again version of Beatlemania.

I'm being really bad here, but it reminded me of the time in Glee Club when you sprinkled your mama's ground-up diet pills on Ray-Ray Jones' powdered sugar donuts and convinced him it was the Holy Spirit giving him the shakes.

See, we had some good times. Anyway, that's what made me think of you. What's your holiday plan? Flying somewhere warm and glamorous? I'll be here—got a job as a campaign worker for the American Values Network.

Have a blessed day— Brent

Sent: November 21, 1996, 10:39 AM
From: jselkirkphoto@aol.com
To: missionxbrent@aol.com

American Values Network? What branch of the Illuminati is that?

Ray-Ray Jones was a moronic weasel. He couldn't even give a proper swirlie. Dropped his own retainer in the toilet when he was laughing it up about conditioning my hair with Ty-D-Bol. So don't flagellate yourself over him, unless that turns you on.

I'm exhausted today. 24 hours in Miami, not the fun part. I can't wait for the gritty realism trend to be passé. This round of pictures looked like a still from a docu-drama about crack whores. Do people need to feel guilty and serious before they can blow $500 on a pair of shoes? How sweet the sound, that saved a wretch like me—*ka-ching*.

Bitch all I may, I should probably drag myself back on a plane to see the family for Thanksgiving. Peter and I hardly have enough time alone, we're both working so hard. He teaches two yoga classes a week, as well as his job at the group home. The other night we finally went out dancing with his old pal Kevin from Housing Works and his boyfriend, but Peter was almost asleep on his feet after two beers. He just can't say no—anytime one of the Gateway kids gets a boo-boo, they send up that big Bat-signal in the sky, and he jumps off the roof. It's like I'm dating a single mother...with a dick.

Give my best to the Robot Sea Monsters— Julian

Sent: November 21, 1996, 6:41 PM
From: missionxbrent@aol.com
To: jselkirkphoto@aol.com

Hi Julian—

The American Values Network is a new political action group that supports candidates with traditional values in state and local elections. Kind of like a nicer, more grassroots Contract With America. The usual platform—fewer regulations on small businesses, schools that respect parents' beliefs, a flat tax, protection of the unborn, etc. They have some creative ideas for government cooperation with faith-based social service providers.

Peter sounds like a nice guy. Maybe he wants a family? Everybody does, I think, even though we complain about them. Gives us something to look forward to when we get older—can't live off the rush from those wrestling trophies forever. (One of the high schoolers at the Mission X-Force show called me "sir"!)

Sea monsters forever— xo Brent

Sent: November 21, 1996, 10:24 PM
From: jselkirkphoto@aol.com
To: missionxbrent@aol.com

Ah, my sweet Young Republican. I promise to take a flattering photo of you 10 years from now when you're caught in an airport men's room with a rent boy.

The thing is, it's not whether you want a family, but whether they want you. That must be why I keep coming back, like an idiot. I tell myself I'm checking on Mama's safety, or making sure my nephews learn there's culture beyond NASCAR, but what would make me truly happy is to figure out where I belong in this picture. Can't fit in, can't let go. I sound like a Pam Tillis breakup song. Creepy.

I just remember those moments when it all came together—singing in church, fixing Sunday brunch, Daddy throwing a ball in the backyard— did that actually happen or have I seen too many home-insurance commercials? Mama and Daddy still in love somehow, sometimes—well, there must be some hot stuff keeping them together, gross as that sounds. And I say to myself, that's what I don't have. The patience to slog through 10, 20 years of shit waiting for the next flash of magic.

If you're that lonely, what are you going to do? Can you find a girl who only wants to have sex once in her life, and pray for triplets? Touch my sister and you die, by the way. (Peter can totally take you down.)

  Yours in family values— JS

Sent: November 21, 1996, 10:45 PM
From: missionxbrent@aol.com
To: jselkirkphoto@aol.com

Hey Julian—

I'm nowhere near ready to get married. You're right, faith is hard, and love takes a lot of it. Only God can give us the strength to stick it out, when it's the kind of relationship He designed us for.

Do you want me to send you a videotape that helped me? (No, it's not a home movie of my butt. I know how your mind works.)

Praying for you— xo Brent

Sent: November 21, 1996, 11:38 PM
From: jselkirkphoto@aol.com
To: missionxbrent@aol.com

I don't need to see any more videos of some closet-case pastor and his Stepford wife. I've heard all the same sermons as you. When Daddy ran for city council, in '87, everyone was on their best behavior. Mama didn't walk into as many doors that year, if you catch my meaning. And I got packed off to a very special summer camp. Dickheads claimed they could straighten us out with cold baths and team sports, like I hadn't done that to myself and much worse. But the Holy Spirit blows where it will, and so does Julian Selkirk.

Enough of this—Peter just stepped out of the shower and I've lost the ability to use words properly. Wish you were here (not really)— JS

Sent: November 21, 1996, 12:41 AM
From: missionxbrent@aol.com
To: jselkirkphoto@aol.com

Hey Julian—

I'm sorry your family didn't realize they all needed healing, not only you. Thanks for trusting me again. I'm going to mail you a book called *The Darkened Mirror* that helped me through some hard times. See what Peter thinks of it, too.

Love, Brent

My boyfriend grew up in a magazine feature. Better homes and gardens, better people. Better not touch anything till you ask. The Selkirks' eggshell-colored house with a wraparound porch was tucked into a cul-de-sac of similarly substantial neighbors off the main artery through Marietta. The commercial strip, on our approach, boasted a modern red-brick church complex that Julian sped past with a tight expression, and a KFC with a 50-foot-tall mechanical chicken that rolled its googly eyes at us. These attractions gave way to small, closely spaced ranch houses where I assumed the service-sector townies lived, and then to discreetly marked turnoffs where clusters of fine homes hid among the trees.

"This must be where they filmed *All That Heaven Allows*," I quipped. Unlike Rock Hudson's smooth pompadour, my dark Ashkenazi curls, mashed sideways by sleeping on the plane, refused to be assimilated by the comb that Julian (of course) supplied from his carry-on bag. Certainly *he* did not look like he'd changed into his lightweight brown suit and Hugo Boss necktie in a gas station bathroom.

The Selkirks were strangers to me except for Julian's sister, Laura Sue, who'd lived in New York for college until her departure for the mission fields of Uganda. Her return for Thanksgiving was the reason Julian and I were enduring this performance of family togetherness. Besides her, the gathering comprised their parents, Bitsy and Bradford; Julian's big brother Carter, and his wife and twin three-year-old boys; and—

"What the fu— what's *he* doing here?" I hissed at Jule, barely checking my bad language within the sacred precincts of Mrs. Selkirk's rose-wallpapered vestibule.

Jule frowned, whether at me or at the surprise guest, I wasn't sure. "Something for Daddy's campaign, I guess. I told you, he's running for state Senate?"

"Oh man, tell me we're not going to be on TV?"

"I'm sure you're off the hook there." He squeezed my hand for just a second, to show he meant no criticism by it. Then he moved away from me to exchange cheek-kisses with his mother. She even smelled like roses from several feet away. Her hair, a brightened version of Julian's auburn, was rounded into stiff short curls. I followed them into a warm, noisy parlor filled with guys watching TV: two heavy-set, fair-haired men I assumed were Selkirk father and son, the kids wrestling on the carpet, and that fucker Brent. He had the nerve to grin and wave at me like we were at some kind of pep rally.

As the guys back-slapped Julian, Bitsy got around to shaking my hand, smiling with pursed lips. She was wearing pearls and a drapey powder-blue dress. I wondered how she could cook a turkey and trimmings for ten people without getting a spot on it. The fashion superpowers must run in the family.

"And you must be Peter. How nice of you to join us. Everyone, this is Peter, one of Julie's friends from New York."

Julian raised his voice above the din. "Actually, he's—"

"—very happy to be here," I spoke over him. "You guys have us beat for winter weather. I'm glad to catch a break from work." Keep talking, say anything until the moment is past.

"Peter works with disadvantaged children," Bitsy informed the room.

"Great, we'll call on you when the twins get cranky." Bradford peeled a grandson off his leg and came over to grip my hand like he was squeezing a lemon. Right back at you, old man; I bench-press 200 pounds. Surprised by my handshake, he chuckled and punched me on the arm. "No limp wrist on this one! You like football?"

I took the seat he offered me on the leather sofa, gratified to see Brent search for another spot. I decided to keep his expectations modest in case the next hurdle was a sports trivia quiz. "New York's more of a baseball town, but I usually watch the Super Bowl."

"That's because your teams are losers."

"Yeah, the Jets'll break your heart."

Carter's wife Stef, a tall thin blonde in a teal suit-dress and high heels, brought a round of beers for all of us except her husband, who was nursing a ginger ale. Each sip from the can seemed to remind him all over again that it wasn't alcohol, and he looked at it with a kind of disappointed surprise. Julian asked her for a rum and Coke, which he inhaled like a lost nomad at an oasis. He had the grace to act embarrassed when his sister caught him mid-chug. They retreated to a corner of the den to catch up on the progress of the gospel in Africa, or the ten reasons why she shouldn't be wearing clogs with that skirt.

An honest-to-goodness black maid, with a white frilly apron tied around her stout old body, was setting out steaming dishes on the long mahogany dining table. I could smell those sinfully good marshmallow-topped sweet potatoes that goyim count as a vegetable. I took it easy on the beer so I wouldn't fill up.

Carter's twins, with no such foresight, were stuffing their little mouths with Chex mix from the cut-glass bowl on the coffee table. Their dad protested weakly as Bradford swooped them up and bounced them on his knees, using their tiny bodies to mimic the arc of the football thrown for a long pass. "Come on, they love it," their grandfather proclaimed over the red-faced kids' hysterical squeals.

Brent added to the scrum by getting in their face with a camera to capture the heartwarming family moment for his next fundraising postcard. So of course Julian had to break off his conversation with Laura Sue to show Brent why he was using the wrong lens for this lighting—putting his hands all over Brent's tree-trunk-sized biceps to reposition him, as if Julian really cared about taking a flattering picture of his dad's big shiny forehead.

What they got instead was a nice action shot of little Brian or Kyle (nobody had told me which was which) being tickled till he burped up half-digested orange cracker mush onto the candidate's lap. Bradford's 100-watt grin transformed to an equally electrifying glower. Giving the kid a sharp smack on the rear, he handed him off to Carter, who shepherded his boys into the kitchen to be cleaned up by the women. I stood up to help them but Julian made a fierce "No" face at me that was, for one uncanny instant, a copy of his father's outraged expression.

While Bradford went upstairs to change clothes, we waited quietly around the laden table, the burnished roast turkey in the center sending out tantalizing odors, the pair of candles flickering on either side of the centerpiece (multicolored dried corn and cranberries in a ceramic holder shaped like an Indian head). Bitsy compulsively straightened the serving dishes, patting the sides to check that they were still warm. By unspoken agreement, no one as much as sipped from a water glass until the patriarch reappeared, in a tan suit and checked shirt that were nearly identical to his previous outfit.

"What a spread, right? Better than any of your fancy New York restaurants," he boasted in Julian's direction. Bitsy had seated us far away from each other. I was between her and Laura Sue at the foot of the table, while Carter and Brent sat on Bradford's left and right, with Julian between Brent and Stef.

"How about you, Pete—what do your people do for Thanksgiving?" Bradford bellowed genially at me, as if I was the first member of the Hebrew tribe to wander south of the Mason-Dixon line. Stef raised one sculpted eyebrow in a sarcastic expression that she erased before her father-in-law could see. I began to feel more optimistic that Carter would earn his 30-day AA chip.

"My mom's probably serving roast chicken to a roomful of hungry teenagers right now," I said. With a pang, I pictured Tyler burying his loneliness in tough talk and adolescent gluttony, pretending he didn't mind spending a family holiday with strangers. My father and Ada would be enjoying the hotel sauna near Grandpa Abe's retirement home in Florida, preparing to listen to his annual spiel about why we shouldn't celebrate stealing this country from the Indians. I wouldn't say Grandpa was a card-carrying member of the Communist Party, but that's only because he was too paranoid to keep the card.

To show what a good sport I was, I reached for the green bean and bacon casserole, but this was a faux pas. Bradford first had to lead us in prayer. We all bowed our heads. The flash of Brent's camera made one of the twins cry. Stef put a hand over his mouth, while deftly extracting the butter knife from his brother's nostril. I could see how she stayed so thin, never having a free hand to eat with. Laura Sue kept her head down and eyes closed even after the others had moved on to the amen's, like she was listening to a different prayer than the rest of them.

With some good food in me, I started to relax. I let the maid bring me another beer, for appearances' sake, though I wouldn't drink it. Julian was on his second or possibly his third rum and Coke. The laughter at their end of the table got louder. Bradford took a bite of stuffing and his face darkened with displeasure. "Too cold," he proclaimed, dropping the spoon on the starched white tablecloth. A temporary hush fell. Bitsy hurried to dab a napkin on the spot and carried the dish into the kitchen for reheating. Julian made some joke that I didn't catch, but it mollified his father enough for the conversation to resume. From what I could hear from my end, they were talking about his poll numbers. Brad was trailing his Republican primary opponent among women voters. "Any tips, Julie? *You* know all about what the ladies like," he baited his son.

My boyfriend's eyes blazed, but he set his lips into a charming smile. "Actually, Peter's the one you should ask."

"Switching teams, eh? Did you go to that camp to straighten you out, like this big fella?" Bradford thwacked Brent's meaty shoulder with enthusiasm, like an auctioneer with a prize bull. Brent beamed.

"What Julian means," I said, with considerably less warmth, "is that I was an aide to a state assemblyman for two years."

"Oh, how nice. Do you have any advice for Brad?" Mrs. Selkirk chirped, at the same time as Brent asked, "Why'd you quit?"

The real answer to both questions was the same: don't get photographed being pissed on by your boss in a sex dungeon. I regretted putting myself in a position to help someone like Mr. Selkirk get elected, though any politician who could win Newt Gingrich's home county would likely be just as bad.

"Not to be too stereotypical, but you appeal to women by taking care of children," I said. "Investing in education, welfare. Crime—but you've got to be careful, because moms think about what could happen if their sons got arrested, or shot by police. Everyone in jail has a mom too, you know."

"Oh, the blacks don't vote," Bitsy assured me.

"Not for you, anyway, Daddy," Laura Sue spoke up for the first time. Her soft voice was steady but I saw her hands trembling in her lap.

"Because it's the Republican primary, she means, and they're Democrats," Carter hastened to cover for his younger sister.

"No, no, what Pete's saying is real interesting," Bradford cut in. "D'you think I could peel some of 'em off? I don't care whether you're white, black, or purple, everyone wants the same thing, a safe neighborhood and more money in your pocket."

"We've been emphasizing family values," Brent declared. "Good churchgoing black families also want to end the culture of welfare dependency. Strengthening marriage *protects* women and children."

Laura Sue cleared her throat loudly and pushed away her nearly untouched plate of turkey and stuffing. I imagined she was counting down the seconds till she could return to war-torn Kampala.

"When are *you* planning on starting a family, Brent?" Julian said. "You don't want to wait till your eggs are dried up."

Bitsy stood. "Who's ready for pie?"

Even an ascetic missionary couldn't resist Mrs. Selkirk's pecan pie with caramel ice cream, not to mention the blueberry-lemon trifle and the peach coffee cake. Carter spoon-fed the twins whipped cream, looking happy at last. Mr. Selkirk had me caught up in what he considered a friendly debate about Clinton's welfare-to-work agenda, which I interrupted to compliment the chef.

"Mrs. Selkirk, how did you get the cake's texture so perfect? Every time I make it, I'm following what it says in your cookbook, but the peaches make the bottom soggy."

Bradford guffawed, turned his back on me, and struck up a conversation with Carter about the real estate market. Laura Sue murmured to me, "Male privilege—easy come, easy go."

"No worries—I'd rather have good pie."

She favored me with her first real smile. She looked young and sweet then, like Julian in a good mood.

Jule came round to our corner of the table, resting a hand on each of our chairs. "How's that culture shock treating you, Lulu?"

She leaned her head against his arm. "About as well as that bottle of rum is treating you."

He sighed, looking at me this time. "This place doesn't bring out the best in any of us."

Speak for yourself, I thought. Not only did real men not bake, it seemed they also didn't apologize. Though, to be fair, he had tried to acknowledge our relationship and I'd been the one to shut him down.

"Are you surprised by how awful we all are?" Laura Sue asked me sympathetically.

"Come on, there's no good answer to that," Jule teased.

"Are you happier in Uganda? Do you enjoy your work?" I questioned her instead. We'd barely spoken during the meal, but I was coming to think that her withdrawal was due to shyness rather than disapproval of my existence.

"You know, hardly anyone asks me that. They only say how brave and generous I must be, to bring Jesus and penicillin to the natives. Yes, I'm happy—*I'm* grateful for *them*, for being around people who know what really matters."

"And what's that?" Jule asked, a hint of a challenge in his voice.

Laura Sue seemed accustomed to ignoring her brother's irreverence. "Kindness. Taking care of each other. Depending on God to keep you alive each day, knowing everything you have is a gift."

"Isn't there, like, a civil war going on? Children chopping off people's hands with machetes?"

"Ah, Julie—you always think you're going to shock me when you point out that people are sinners." Laura Sue licked the last puddle of ice cream from her spoon, an adorable portrait of gluttony.

The elderly maid, whose name no one had bothered to tell me, bustled round the table, stacking dirty dishes on a platter that she hoisted with effort. Laura Sue and Stef joined in the task, and I followed suit, disregarding Julian's miming for me to sit with the other men and accept the round of whiskey that his father was pouring.

"They already know we're homosexuals, we might as well be polite ones," I told him. Laura Sue giggled.

Yet another football game was roaring away on the TV in the den. In the kitchen, the women were packaging leftovers while half-watching a black-and-white portable TV on the countertop. They were up to the scene in *It's a Wonderful Life* where Clarence the unlikely angel stops George Bailey from throwing himself off a bridge. I'd always appreciated the honesty of

Jimmy Stewart's wild-eyed despair, intruding into this feel-good holiday schmaltz.

"This is my mom's favorite film," I told Julian, who was tailing me with a glass of whiskey in each hand. We watched the alternate history of a George-less world unfold, a decadent town of broken people, up to the scene where Bailey pursues his amnesiac Mary, a spinster librarian who's understandably twitchy about being stalked with declarations of love. Her body language reminded me of Laura Sue, but I suppose it would have clouded the moral of the story if Mary had realized she could make a difference in the world on her own.

I took both glasses away from Julian and put them in the sink. He didn't protest. In the hallway, I slipped my hand into his. He stood very close to me as I perused the wall of family photos. The three children declared their genetic loyalties from the start. Carter had his Daddy's stocky fair-haired good looks, while Julian and Laura Sue took after Bitsy's fox-like delicacy and wariness. They seemed equally represented in the childhood pictures, then Carter's family dominated in adulthood, with his glamorous wife and chubby babies. There was one professional shot of an adult Laura Sue in her NYU graduation cap and gown. The latest image of Julian must have been taken the night of that infamous high school prom where Brent's buddies gay-bashed him. Posed at the foot of the curving staircase in this house's front hall, he gazed over the head of a cute freckled girl who resembled Doris Day. He had too much Brylcreem glistening in the auburn curls that flopped over one eye, and a wide forest-green bowtie (still his favorite color) sticking out from the slim-fitting tux. I touched the unsmiling face with my fingertip.

"I'm sorry I've been a bitch to you tonight." Jule's fingers caressed mine.

"Well...I'm sorry I didn't let you introduce us as boyfriends. I had some naïve idea that I could make them treat you better."

"Really? That's what you were thinking?"

"Of course—what else would it be?"

Julian didn't look wholly convinced, but he shrugged. "It doesn't matter. Nothing I do here matters. I don't think it would make a damn bit of difference to *my* family if I'd never been born!"

"But...you know...it means everything to me." I stumbled over the words, because they were so true, but there was no hesitation in our kiss. His lips were soft and eager, his breath fiery-sweet with rum. The tension in his body collapsed all at once into our embrace. I crushed him close to me. The din of sports fandom in the other room had faded away; all too soon I heard the floorboards creak behind me, and dropped my arms to my sides. Julian, however, stole a glance over my shoulder and pulled me back toward him, pressing our pelvises together till I thought Mrs. Selkirk's wall-mounted porcelain cherubs would blush in embarrassment.

"If you make me walk back into that den with a boner, I will seriously kill you," I whispered.

"Oh, *fine.*" He had to give my ass a hard squeeze before he let me go. But his eyes were fixed on the person behind me, who retreated with quick but heavy footfalls when I turned around. Brent's linebacker silhouette wasn't made for stealth.

I was way beyond too exhausted for this N-dimensional chess game. I wanted to ask Jule a lot of things, but mainly, how soon could I crash in the solitary guest bedroom where Bitsy had lodged me so we wouldn't commit sodomy under her roof. The bluegrass piano music tinkling in the distance affected me like a lullaby.

"Oh, it's Daddy's favorite song. Come on, we mustn't miss this."

"What exactly is happening?"

"Family tradition. A nice one this time, I promise."

He led me into a different parlor with doily-draped tapestry armchairs and an upright piano with Carter improbably seated at the keyboard.

"*How* many rooms does this house have?"

"Enough for every member of the family to nurse their own private hangover—that's the Selkirk Builders guarantee."

Everyone but Brent (to my relief) was gathered together. Bitsy made a little space for me on the hard-cushioned sofa. Carter played a tune that reminded me of "Prairie Home Companion" while Stef quietly tried to persuade her father-in-law that the twins should go to bed. "Let 'em live a little!" he boomed, bouncing them on his shoulders. Bitsy gazed at them with tenderness. At last Bradford deposited the over-excited boys on the rug. He strode a bit unsteadily over to the piano, tossed back a drink that he'd set on the lid (on a coaster, at least—Bitsy still had some authority), and sang in a rich, sweet baritone: *Never grow old, ah, never grow old, there's a land where we'll never grow old.*

A softer mood descended on the room. Even Julian, cross-legged on the floor at my knee, smiled a little. Bradford had a faraway look in his eyes when he crooned the last line. A strange expression flickered across his broad, ruddy face in the silence that followed—grief, anger, a prayer? It reminded me of George Bailey when the Building & Loan eats up his honeymoon money, tethering him yet again to the small world that revolves around him.

Shaking off his funk, Bradford cued Carter to pound out a jauntier tune. *I'm working on a building, I'm working on a building,* he caroled, grinning.

Laura Sue's reedy soprano chimed in. "C'mon Julie, we need you on tenor," Carter called out. My boyfriend joined the group at the piano, his clear, mellow voice soaring: *I'm working on a building, for my Lord, for my Lord.*

Brent reappeared in the doorway with a camcorder, as if he couldn't get any more annoying. The family continued singing: *If I was a drunkard, I tell you what I'd do. I'd quit my drinking and work on the building too.*

"Isn't that sweet? I made them all take lessons when they were young," Bitsy said to me.

Julian's mood was as volatile as his father's tonight. When the song ended, he plopped down on the bench next to Carter. "Still on the clock, Brent? Come on out, show 'em what you can do. Remember when we sang this in glee club?" He picked out a few notes on the keyboard.

Carter shook his head at his younger brother, either not knowing the tune, or sober enough to realize that Julian was about to do something ill-advised. Undeterred, Jule launched into a plaintive *a capella* melody: *As the deer pants for the water, so my soul longs after thee...* His hard stare at Brent clashed with the gentleness of the song.

Brent swallowed hard. I fidgeted on the sofa, thought about interrupting to ask for more pie that I didn't want, willed the twins to start bawling. Julian's bell-like tenor rang unbroken in the air for an entire verse, till Brent, lower lip trembling, harmonized with him: *You alone are my heart's desire, and I long to worship you.*

"Yeah, get on your knees," I muttered. Jule swayed at the piano, as if the liquor was catching up with him, and broke off mid-song, wiping his eyes. "Forgot what comes next," he slurred.

Brent tried to keep going, but Laura Sue interrupted loudly with a different melody: "In Christ *alone*, my hope is *found*—" She sang with more determination than skill. You could raise an army to that beat. Her father, reasserting control of the situation, thumped along on the piano lid with his big hand. Brent went back to documenting electable moments. When Laura Sue noticed the lens pointed at her face, she shut her mouth and stalked out of the parlor. Stef took that as her cue to haul her fussing children away, and the party was finally allowed to break up.

Though my bed was calling, I lurked in the front hall to make sure Brent and his highlights reel had hit the road. I wasn't letting Jule spend the night under the same roof as that guy. Mrs. Selkirk thought I was lost: "You're up these stairs, second door to the left, dear. And...try making the cake with peaches that aren't so ripe, and slice them thinner." She smiled like a mom this time, not a future senator's wife.

IT WAS HARD TO FALL ASLEEP without Julian. Not for the first time today, I craved the weed I hadn't dared smuggle onto the plane. My guest room was inhabited by an antique walnut vanity with lots of protruding knobs and spires, a bed of the same species, and thick reddish-brown paisley drapes that matched the bedspread. The heating puffed vigorously behind its ornate white metal grille. I tied back the curtains and cracked the window open, spilling the light of an almost-full moon across the floor. Far from keeping me up, the white glow was soothing. Daylight of a dream, a desert breeze's warm exhale, eucalyptus and olive leaves...

She was against my back, strong and ancient, gnarled holder of centuries of secrets. My secrets, though she stood on this rock-faced hill for all to see; no one knew her like me. They saw a boy in an old olive tree, a boy with fragrant leaves tickling his face, branches between his legs. In the lap of the tree, dozing like a baby, soft on softness, herself come alive. Leaves of hair curtaining down around my face, their green perfume for air, fullness pressed to my mouth with juice that trickled, tickled down to hands wiping, stroking, tingling below—

"Ow!" Jule exclaimed. I jumped awake. He was lying beside me, rubbing his bare chest, where I guess my elbow had jabbed him as a reflex. "Sorry, babe, you have a bad dream?" he asked softly.

My head felt fuzzy and my dick was throbbing hard. "No, I—a good one, I think. Can't remember. What were you doing?"

"This." He rolled over on me and tongued my lips while bringing his hand back to the straining bulge in my shorts. I opened my mouth and hugged him close. We ground against each other till we could hardly stand it. He bit my neck, I moaned, and he had the nerve to whisper, "Better be quiet."

"*You* be quiet," I muttered, running my fingernails over his balls, which predictably made him squeak.

"I have a plan." He got up, his cock now waving straight out of the slit in his briefs, and unhooked one of the curtain ties. Kneeling on top of me, he pulled my head back (not very hard) by the hair and wrapped the brocade strip around my mouth. "Don't worry, Mama has the maid wash these every two months."

I choked on laughter through my gag. Other muffled sounds came out as he pinned down my legs and teased my ass open with his lubed-up fingers. He buried his mouth in my hair to stifle his panting. He had condoms for both of us, to prevent any stains, I assumed. The mattress springs squealed when I thrust into his pumping hand. "Mmph," I pointed down at the tell-tale bed, shaking my head.

"I know what you like." He slapped my butt cheek, enough for a little pleasurable sting, and gestured toward the floor. Next thing you know I was face down on the carpet with his big hard shaft filling me up, reaching deep inside, taking me all the way. I bit down on the folded fabric. We cried out, one after the other, tumbled over, tangled and laughing.

Jule cleaned us up with some scented wet things that itched my skin. "Makeup remover wipes. Best I could do on short notice."

"Thanks, now my ass feels like a supermodel."

We climbed into bed together, but put our underwear back on, in case there was a house fire. The moon floated between the clouds. Wind-tossed branches rippled the trail of light on the floor, reminding me of something in my hazy dream. A home, safety, but far away.

Unusually for him, Julian didn't immediately fall asleep. He was content to lie with me and watch the sky.

"I missed you," I said.

He kissed my collarbone. "I'll always be there when you want me."

"Which I do. Whether or not I have the guts to say so."

"You're very brave, sweet thing. Believe me. I couldn't have faced this weekend without you."

"I wish you didn't have to hide, to put on a fake suit of armor, just to have a family. We need to be—I don't know—our *own thing*, stop trying to fit into our parents' idea of how we should've turned out."

"I've tried. That's what I want most, for us to be something real. But I've always been told that...*this*...doesn't last." He gestured at our half-naked bodies entwined. "Never mind, sorry to sound clingy."

"Go ahead and cling." I held him tighter.

"Really?" He pressed his face into my chest.

"Yeah, I'm not afraid of you."

"Should've spanked you harder."

"You noticed, huh?" We both laughed. I thought Jule was ready to doze off, but after a couple minutes he spoke quietly again.

"I keep coming back because they're always here. My family, the church—I mean, I don't *go* to church, but I don't have to, it's all around us in this town. And sure, sometimes it's shitty, but I know the possibility is there—that they'd always be waiting for me, if I changed."

"Don't say that, Jule, please. You're not going to change, because that's bullshit. Our love is as good as anybody's. Even Brent hasn't changed, he just wants to get as close to you as he can without fucking."

"Poor guy." Julian rolled over onto his back, staring upward. "I know I'm who I am and that's it. But it means something, anyhow, that constant devotion, like they taught us God has. Behold, I stand at the door and knock, et cetera. Like your family has for real, giving you a fresh start every time you need it."

"There's a lot about me they don't want to see, though."

"What do you mean?"

"I don't exactly know. That's just how it feels." I searched my memories for a reason. "They don't think of me as a grownup. Maybe they're right...I live in my grandpa's apartment, I work for Mom, I write comic books..."

"At last, I've corrupted you with my frivolous lifestyle."

I toyed with his wavy hair. My scalp massages could make him purr. He was just a guy, a good guy I wanted to have around, every day and every night, if it could be like this. This peace, the absence of fear, felt unfamiliar, and that was a strange thought in itself—had I, king of the yoga mat, been anxious so long it was second nature? "Hey, you still want to move in together?"

Jule lit up. "You mean it? Yes, of course!"

"Good, we'll start planning when we get home, okay? I have some work to finish in the apartment, then I'll be ready to go."

We kissed some more, wrapped arms and legs together, too lazy and content to follow through on the stirrings below, and out of condoms anyhow. As we came to rest, Jule murmured, "By the way...you said *love*."

"I did."

"Did you mean, like, gay men in general, or—"

"I meant love." My heartbeats almost choked me.

"Me too."

Thanks a lot, Julian. Of course he was snoring within minutes after that, and I was like a hospital patient with espresso in his IV drip. I had my fail-safe yoga mantras to bring me down, but before my first *Om*, I told Julian's God to do several anatomically impossible things. Maybe Grandpa Saul's papers could teach me how to swear in ancient Aramaic.

[EXCERPT FROM *THE DARKENED MIRROR* BY DR. DOREEN FLETCHER (BETHEL HOUSE PRESS, 1988).]

...In my practice I have known many patients who were wounded in their masculinity because of childhood traumas. Through therapy and prayer they were able to reach the shame, fear, and loneliness of the child inside. When they learned how to comfort and integrate this buried part of themselves, they found freedom from sexual compulsion. They no longer had to compensate for their broken sense of self by fixating on other men's bodies.

A distant or difficult father, or a mother who suffocates her children with her feelings, can interfere with the natural development of a boy's sexual identity. Studies also show that childhood abuse is common among men who later struggle with same-sex attraction. The reasons are complex. Predators may target boys who lack strong male role models. Boys molested by a same-sex adult can become confused by arousal. A mother who crosses boundaries with her son can poison him with disgust at natural sexual relations between men and women.

If you think this happened to you, *you are not alone*. No shame is too great to be healed by God's love.

Be cautious of counselors who say "forgive and forget". Forgiveness is our ultimate duty, but when you rush to forget, what you know in your "innermost parts" (Psalm 139:13) comes out in other ways: as sexual brokenness, addiction, promiscuity, and depression. Our Savior promised: "The truth will set you free." (John 8:32)

Patrick (not his real name) was a 25-year-old white-collar professional who came to me for help with a pornography addiction. Before meeting his girlfriend, whom he wanted to marry, he had compulsively engaged in sadomasochistic activities with older men. Now he was in love for the first time, but tormented by fantasies of his old behavior. He was ashamed of cheating on her and scared of contracting AIDS. In therapy we uncovered that he had longed for love and approval from his father, a career army man who believed in old-fashioned physical discipline. He sent Patrick to a boarding school where he was drawn into an inappropriate relationship with a football coach. Once Patrick could grieve his losses and give his inner child the safe masculine love he had missed, his unwanted attractions faded away. As of this writing he is happily married and expecting his second child.

[EXCERPT OF SCRIPT FOR *THE POISON CURE*, VOL. 1, ISSUE 3]

Early evening, summer, clear blue sky shading
into pink-tinged clouds on horizon. Wide view

of downtown city street with brownstones, cafes,
a couple of skinny trees in fenced squares on the
sidewalk. Group of women singing, led by man in
black with a book. Teen boy, baseball cap pulled low,
pauses to look in window of cafe behind the singers.

Next panel, closer view, shows that man leading
group is wearing a priest collar and the book cover
has a cross. Some women sing with clasped hands,
eyes closed. Other frown, hold signs: GOD'S PLAN =
1 WOMAN + 1 MAN. Cafe window has tiny rainbow decal
in corner, below weathered gold lettering: *Dorothy's*.
Teen boy slouches further into himself, walks away
quickly, nearly collides with tall man in green
shirt, whom we see in rear view entering the cafe.

Inside, next panel, warm golden tones contrast to
blue-grays of previous panels. Challis sits on a
stool on cafe's small open-mike stage surrounded by
tables, singing and playing guitar. He is relaxed,
gentle, handsome in loose open-necked blouse and
tight jeans. Warm smile when he sees Pharmakon, the
man in green, sit down at a rear table. Next panel,
end of set, stage bare, Challis moves a chair up
close to him.

Challis (leaning in, so his chin is brushing
Pharmakon's arm): *I'm glad you came.*

Pharmakon: *Yeah, I rearranged my shift at the
hospital.*

C: *No more miracle cures today?*

P: *I told you...that's not really in my line.* (Half-
smile softens his stiff face.)

C: *Lightning only has to strike once, right?* (Touches
hands seductively.)

P: (quick smile, then serious): *Speaking of
thunderbolts, what's with the Hellfire Choir out there?*

C: *Dorothy's is owned by the Gay & Lesbian Center.
The church down the block doesn't approve of some of
the art we sell. Or what it raises money for.*

P: *Makes you wonder how he found out about it.*

C: (sneers, shrugs): *Oh please. Nobody over the age of 12 would blow him. He just wants to force us out so he can buy our building.*

Next panel, time has passed, light in cafe is dimmer, a new singer is onstage while Challis and Pharmakon drink and embrace at the table. Next panel, the two are walking away from the closed club, arms around each other's waists, silhouettes retreating under streetlight's honeyed glow. Meanwhile, teen boy from first panel peers anxiously around the alley's darkened wall, a bottle in his hand.

Pharmakon and Challis are in the latter's apartment, seen through the window from outside. The room is on an upstairs floor of an old brick building, over a bodega. Next scene, inside the bedroom, which is hung with Indian blankets and contains more guitars and amps. Pharmakon half-sits, half-reclines, on the bed while Challis drapes himself over him, undoing his zipper.

P: *There's something...maybe...we should talk about.*

C: (still caressing him): *I'm undetectable now. Don't know how it happened. But we'll use protection, don't worry.*

P: (tilting back more, starting to yield): *There's more than one way to be unsafe.*

C: (pulling back gently, though he's already undressed): *Are you religious?*

P: *I believe—I know—there are powers greater than us.*

C: *And what do they think of this?* (Slips off Pharmakon's pants, bends down to draw his erect cock into his mouth)

P: *Nothing—I hope. Oh—please—*

Pharmakon sprawls backward on the bed, grimacing with ecstasy or the effort of holding back the emerald tinge that begins to blossom from his groin to his torso and thighs. Challis, eyes closed, does

not seem to see the tendrils of color. Pharmakon's
eyes widen, as if with fear. About to come, he pulls
out, to Challis' surprise, rolls over and pumps
himself onto the mattress.

C (confused, but making light of it): *I do swallow,
y'know.*

P (muffled, face in the pillow): *Take me.*

Condom on, Challis enters him, his slim body riding
Pharmakon's hard flat ass. Close-up of Pharmakon's
face, hidden from his lover by the pillow and
crumpled blanket. Peaceful smile, closed eyes...and
green skin.

Next panel, time has passed, still night. Challis
sleeps. Pharmakon sits up. The moon is a crescent
through the bedroom window. Quietly Pharmakon gathers
clothes, sneaks out. By the time he reaches his
own apartment, in the next panel, he is staggering.
Fumbling, in a rush, he fills his bath, splashes in
red liquid from the vial. Glances out the window at
the unchanging moon. Caption: *The phase is wrong...
but it's his only hope.*

Dark confused clouds swirl around Pharmakon's dreams
as he lies in the tub till morning, but no visions
come. He wakes, still green-skinned, as daylight
whitens the bathroom window. He applies makeup
heavily to cover his haggard and unnaturally tinted
face.

Next panel, a TV plays overhead in a hospital waiting
room. Pharmakon, in his scrubs, pauses to watch.

Young Female Newscaster: *Greenville High School today
mourns the sudden death of sophomore Sam Weeks, an
honor student who led the soccer team to the state
playoffs.*

Next panel, close-up of TV screen now showing a
school photo of the teen who was lurking outside
Dorothy's.

Young Female Newscaster Voice-Over: *Weeks was found
hanged in his room this morning, an apparent suicide.
Police are asking...*

Evening, Pharmakon's apartment. He is slumped over in an armchair, head in hands, ignoring the ringing phone. Answering machine lights up: *Hey Tod, it's Ryder. I'm not working tonight. Are you—*

Pharmakon rushes out, slamming door, before Challis' message ends.

Next panel, the priest from the protest locks up his office in the parish hall attached to the church. Pharmakon steps out from the shadowed stairwell behind him. Before the man can cry out, Pharmakon claps a hand over his mouth and drags him into the bathroom. Priest is older and smaller, plump and balding, easily overpowered. With one green hand, Pharmakon yanks down the man's pants and shorts, shoves him against the wall and rapes him. Eyes popping, tears streaming, the priest gasps for breath. Tears also stream from Pharmakon's eyes as the green drains out of his grim face.

Smaller man slumps to the floor, eyes open, clutching his chest, dead. Pharmakon pulls the body onto its back, pulls up and straightens pants. Caption: *A heart attack. He'll keep his secrets...*

Next panel, door closing behind Pharmakon, body on floor. Caption: *...I'll keep mine.*

THE BODY ON TOP OF ME was warm and heavy and smelled like vodka. One arm was flung across my windpipe. Talk about having an anchor for my morning meditation. I closed my eyes again, balancing on the edge of oversleeping, and tagged each short shallow breath with an intention for my day. May I inspire the Gateway kids. May I find time to write the next scene for Ty. May I never again drink Jell-O shots off the pecs of someone calling himself Jean-Jacques who is clearly not French.

"Ugh," Julian pushed himself up from where he'd been drooling on my chest. His hangover face was still beautiful, sleepy eyes and pillow-wrinkled cheeks making him look wrecked by the sex we'd been too tired to actually have last night. "Is it morning yet? Which one?"

"Don't give me that. You've gone on bigger benders than this and shown up for a 12-hour studio shoot right after." I kissed his ear loudly, because I was evil.

"Ah, but that was when I was young and single. I'm out of practice."

"Living in your own reality, as usual."

"As long as you're living in it too..." He thumbed the stubble on my cheek. "There's no better place to be."

I sucked his fingertips. Sometimes it was so easy to make him happy, I felt like I'd moved to one of those countries in the Oxfam brochures, where the price of a cup of coffee could feed six adorable children. Powerful, sure, but guilty, not knowing where the limits were. "I'm almost done with my work at Grandpa's place."

"I know, sweet thing. And I love having you here half the week. Waking up together, making breakfast..." He sat up, made a gagging face, flopped back down. "Okay, never mind the breakfast. Hey, I wonder if this is what it's like to be a divorced dad."

"Way too heavy a thought for first thing in the morning."

"Sorry. You had fun last night, though, right?"

"Sure." We'd gone to the holiday party for *Crush*, a new streetwise fashion and culture mag that had thrown Julian a lot of work this year. He was bummed that his turn in *Vogue* had been a one-off so far, and *Glamour*'s suburban stylings were becoming boring. *Crush* let him mess around with digital special effects for that beauty-in-ruins look he loved. I think my comics collection was rubbing off on him, with those impossible anti-gravity poses. *Crush*'s shtick was covering both men's and women's wear in the same issue (gender-matching of models optional), which meant they'd either start a decade-defining trend or go out of business next year for lacking a defined customer base. Or possibly both.

I survived on this alien planet by translating its customs into my home equivalents. A party full of people in oddly proportioned outfits, dropping obscure names with intense adoration and contempt, was like Star Trek fandom with really expensive Vulcan ears. When Jule forced me into some Italian suit that rearranged my butt cheeks like a Cross Your Heart bra, I decided it was part of being a good subbie. Armani nipple clamps? Yes, sir!

"What about you, did Jean-Jacques' posse show you a good time?"

"Not the kind you're thinking of." Jule's voice was muffled, as he'd rolled face-down onto the pillow, ready to sleep again.

"It's okay, I wasn't making a crack. I like seeing you show off on the dance floor." Liquid, all sweat and muscle, flashing in the lightning-shock rainbow strobes. Guys were drawn to him, but I wasn't insecure that a trick could win him away from me. Not anymore.

"I've given up my wicked ways. The only one who gets a piece of this peach pie is—getting out of bed, why?" He tugged on the leg of my boxers.

"New weight-training client, then I have to set up for Cheryl's presentation."

"*Why* do I always date guys with real jobs?" he groaned. "I forgot her publicist rescheduled her for today. Thanks for giving her a slot, by the way. She's really trying to turn her life around."

"Aren't we all!"

"You don't need to. You're Clark Kent. Want to leap over my tall building?"

"You're impossible." I laughed and jumped on top of him. I felt his hardness against my belly, but he was waiting for me to move first, not grabbing after I'd said no. I sank into the warm, soiled bed, inhaling the fumes of last night's drink and crowds. What if this was good enough to be my life? To be me, whoever I was when the work paused—super-nothing, rescuer of none. Then no thoughts but the flooding urgency of hands finding tender places, pulling us together, pumping towards climax.

Afterwards, standing up in the shower by myself, I was hit with vertigo. I chalked it up to the unfamiliarity of chugging anything stronger than beer. Leaning my head against the coolness of the white and black tiles, I blinked and they were blue-green, a kaleidoscope spin of color over color, pink plastic bottle *No More Tears* gone when I rubbed my eyes, only the familiar wire shower caddy tilting under the weight of Jule's shampoos and moisturizers. I shivered in my towel. Just my luck if my life turned out to be a gay remake of *Love Story: Brilliant young man finds love, develops inoperable brain tumor.*

I couldn't put Julian through that, I had to leave now, before I broke his heart...

"Can I pee, already?" Chelsea's answer to Ryan O'Neal banged on the door.

Fuck that, I was going to see Paris before I died. Metaphorically speaking. I opened the door. "What would you do if you had only a year to live?"

"Pee in the shower to save time." He didn't smile, though. "And don't talk about dying or I will murder you."

"I'm sorry. Everything's fine. Wonderful." I kissed him extra long.

But the question dogged me as I blended our breakfast smoothies. Our generation came out in the valley of the shadow of death. That was old news. I'd coped with it the opposite way from Julian and most of our friends, too many of whom were gone now, or facing an unknown future of chronic illness managed with the brand-new drug cocktails. They lived for the beautiful moment. I stubbornly refused. I smacked the Reaper in the eye with my resumé. But did I love any of my work enough to spend my last ounce of juice on it, like Frida Kahlo covering her body cast with painted butterflies? Where was my Paris?

Cleaned up, in his green velvet robe, Julian lounged on a kitchen chair. "What time is Cheryl's spiel? After I process my pictures from yesterday and pick up some new girls' portfolios from Manhattan Model Management, I could take you both out to dinner."

"Three-thirty, assuming she's not late. I'll give you a call. If you have time, would you come to the presentation?"

"You can handle her, darling, don't worry. I don't want to cramp your style."

"I don't *have* a style."

"Well, this is how you get one."

I ruffled his hair, and with my other hand, whisked away the small bottle of rum he was about to splash into his banana coconut soymilk drink.

"C'mon, Peter, I've got to keep my blood alcohol levels, level."

"'Jesus cleanses the temple of our body from the money-changers of addiction,'" I quoted Cheryl's book.

"Jesus also turns water into wine every Sunday morning at 10."

"It's Thursday."

He sighed theatrically. "You poor man. You'll be so horny tonight and wifey will have a dreadful headache. Speaking of which, why were you asking about bucket lists just now? Are you sick? Vertigo again?"

The photographer's eye missed nothing, liquored-up or not. I should have known. "It's nothing. I'm a hypochondriac."

"No, you're not. You never think about yourself."

"Maybe that's the problem. I'm working too hard. I need to meditate more."

"Okay, but if you have any more of those weird spaced-out moments, check it out with a doctor?"

"Sure, hon," I said, but I wouldn't. Occasionally—very occasionally—seeing a shard of *someplace else* from the corner of your eye wasn't a symptom of AIDS, but it *was* an excuse for men with wire-rimmed glasses and flat voices to lock you in a small white room without your belt and shoelaces. Ada wrote a lot of poems about that.

M Y NEW WORKOUT CLIENT at the Ironman Gym was Stacia, a compact thirtyish woman who trained service dogs and therapy animals. She looked off to the side when she talked to you, but she wasn't at all shy, and very interested in hearing about the animals I'd tended on the kibbutz. We agreed that rabbits had a lot more personality than people gave them credit for. As a kid, I'd dreamed of owning a pet, but Dad was allergic to anything with fur. He'd made us re-home the one-eared stray tom that Ada smuggled into Prue's room as an apology present for missing her eighth-grade band concert. Since moving out, I hadn't lived in one place long enough to set down a litterbox. Perhaps Julian and I would become the kind of childless gay couple who threw birthday parties for their tiny purebred dogs, like our friend Frank the drag chanteuse and his partner Stan.

I pumped extra hard on the Nautilus machine after I finished with Stacia. I imagined I could feel my pecs and biceps ballooning instantly like Popeye's when he chugged spinach. A glimpse of myself in the mirror was arousing and strange. There was a man, with a broad hairy chest, full-grown fists with veins bulging around the metal handgrips, determined eyes in a sweaty adult face. A switch in the brain, a moment of translation required to believe he was me. I flicked my eyes away, embarrassed, but the guy lying on the leg curl machine next to me bared his teeth in a silent growl, as if to say he liked what we both saw. In case his meaning was unclear, he also popped his butt up a little more than necessary on the next rep. The man in the mirror had no need for the fears that usually needled me when I got cruised. I smiled in what I hoped was an enigmatic manner and shrugged, promising nothing. Just to be safe, though, I'd wash up at Gateway instead.

Julian had thoughtfully dug up some back issues of *Femme NY*, *Mademoiselle*, and *Allure* so the kids could see Cheryl in her fashion-model prime. Styles from 1991 already seemed laughable to these snappy teens, but underneath their cool pose, they were impressed. I thumbed open a random page to Cheryl's melon-round rear end glistening in a skimpy bikini bottom and in a flash I was—*in Ben's room That's sex She's on his face Ben shoving the wrinkled page at me Her bush swallows him Ben laughs Pretend I'm not gagging Pretend it's news to me—*

I knelt on the floor, head down, acting like I was checking the microphone wires until my latest spell of whatever-this-was passed. Scanning the room to steady myself in the here and now, I noticed that Micah and Ty were the only ones missing—the former doing Christmas shopping with his dad, the latter AWOL. Checking his room was my excuse to take a breather.

I walked in on a mess. Torn pantyhose and crumpled blouses spilled from a trash bag on the floor, with lipsticks rolling underfoot. Ty slumped in the middle of a sheet half-pulled from the bed, picking angrily at his press-on magenta talons.

"What the heck, dude? Did a tornado hit CVS? It's time to come down for Cheryl Kingston's presentation. We'll straighten this out after."

"I ain't a *dude* and I don't need to hear some bitch talking about girls' makeup."

"It's not optional. And we don't use that word about women in this house." I softened my tone. "What happened here, anyway? Quick version."

"Nothing..." Ty muttered, head down. "Just throwing out some shit." His fingers worked at the sheer gauze of a leopard-print scarf, winding, stroking gently, then yanking taut as if to rip it, but unable to.

I took a gamble. "We're not trying to police your style, Ty. We just want to help you become a whole person—the same person all the time, with all of your feelings."

"You gonna wear a dress, Pedro?"

"What are you even talking about?"

He looked up with scorn. "Tai isn't a *style*. She's a person."

"A character you play."

"Pharmakon is a character. Fucking 'concerned social worker' is a character. Everything you do is fake. You're not my friend."

I kept my temper with difficulty. My neck felt rigid. Must have hit the machines too hard. "Whatever else I am, I'm your staff mentor, and I care about your future. Cheryl's been through some of the same things you have, and she's rebuilding her life because she stopped fighting with herself and faced reality. I think you could learn something from her."

Ty turned away again, binding and unbinding his wrists with the scarf. "She's gonna talk about girly fashion shit. I don't wanna deal."

I understood now. "Hurts too much?"

He snapped his head round, eyes blazing. "You couldn't fucking know. I've been trying, okay? The Beckers take me to the movies and museums and stuff. We go places for dinner where I have to wear a suit. Sometimes it's okay and then it fucking chokes me, y'know? Like if your mom made you wear a dress and called you her little princess. You'd wanna die."

"Do you have suicidal thoughts?"

"Oh shut up. If anyone walks out a window round here it's not gonna be me." Tai pointed a fuschia claw in my direction.

"Tai, please, no one—" *will find me in time   Cold floor   Plastic lump of pills   Choking Sick cherry burning liquor Drink drink drink it—*

I swallowed down the dry heaves, began again in a calmer voice. "No one's going to get hurt here. Except Cheryl's feelings, because she's a really special lady, and she wants to meet you."

"For real?" Hope and skepticism fought for the upper hand.

"Yeah," I fibbed, "I told her how much you love being creative with fashion."

Hope winning out, Tai threw on a FUBU sweatshirt, an on-trend gift from the Beckers, rolling down the long sleeves to cover his manicure. We made it downstairs just in time for Cheryl's grand entrance. She was more done-up than when I saw her last at Spiral Gardens, with pale lipstick and some kind of facepaint that looked nude head-on but caught the light with blue and green sparkles. She wore a multi-layered aqua tunic dress over flowing pants that didn't look warm enough for December. The kids drew in a collective breath and murmured together softly, in awe. Dr. Marla put on a big encouraging smile.

Cheryl began by putting us through a short guided visualization. I didn't welcome this respite as I usually would. My mind was playing all kinds of tricks today, and letting it wander while I closed my eyes would be like leaving an unsupervised toddler in a roomful of crystal stemware. I counted breaths, thinking of numbers, resisting the lure of the green glade and bubbling stream that Cheryl described. But then I felt the same heaviness that overcame me sometimes when Julian and I got close, the yearning glimpse of a joy that I couldn't handle. I was both God and Moses, barring myself from the promised land.

I made up my mind that "The Poison Cure" would have an end—a luxury of having no fan base—rather than be trapped in the Dantean repetition of a soap opera or superhero franchise, where the Joker always breaks out of Arkham Asylum, the dead first wife returns just before you say your vows, and Lois Lane never recognizes the Man of Steel's nebbishy other half. Otherwise *my* grandchildren (or dogs) would someday be trapped in an apartment full of incomplete manuscripts, with no room for a mate.

Belatedly I registered the command to open my eyes. Cheryl was reading a passage from *Fit for a King* that I'd skimmed earlier, about consoling her inner child. She said it healed the emptiness inside that she was filling with fame and drugs. It made me sort of uncomfortable. A lot of people would say I acted immature enough already. If I started crying over my old teddy bear (and Mom certainly had Mr. Piggles stashed somewhere), whatever functional adult self I possessed would dissolve into pink goo, like cotton candy left overnight in the car. (Which was totally Prue's fault.)

Glancing around, I saw Tai sketching intently in her notebook. She pushed her sleeves out of the way, no longer conscious of the flashy nails. She... he... *they* were different. I couldn't fail to see it, though I didn't know what to believe about the cause. I saw it in the tilt of her head, how she swung one leg over the other, the assured flick of her hand inking figures into action on the page. Tyler was no Method actor performing these tics for an audience. Both halves were real from the inside.

That scared me, because the world won't let you have two lives. These kids had to fight for just one. Ada thought she'd pulled it off, but Prue and I paid the price during those episodes when she crashed, nothing left for the everyday after the muse's manic soaring. I didn't mind defrosting some burgers and hauling out the overflowing trash, as much as pretending it wasn't my regular labor—the fiction of an impromptu favor I kept doing. But who would Tyler be without Tai, integrated and drab? My stepmother minus her bipolar cycles would be a normal woman, like Barbara, the half of his life that Dad had already decided was not enough.

I was breathing too fast. Was I actually plotting to sneak out of a lecture on sobriety to go smoke a joint? Seriously, Cheryl could talk all she pleased about Jesus, but she didn't have to *function*. No one was depending on her. She could close her eyes and go on her inner journey while someone like Julian took pictures of her in overpriced clothes.

"Modeling isn't easy. You're stuck with your own thoughts for hours while somebody is telling you what to do with every part of your body. Kind of like jail," Cheryl quipped. The audience laughed, and I wondered at the synchronicity between her and my guilty mind. "But jail is better because you can't run away. You have to surrender to Love or you won't make it."

Her voice was sweet and animated, but I saw her hands shaking slightly on the podium. For the first time I considered that she might have gone into this business not because she craved attention, but because it's what she had to sell: her face, and then her story. Regardless, she was brave. I couldn't imagine making the circuit with my mistakes between paperback covers as an example of what not to do. It reminded me of that stupid book Brent had sent Julian, full of pseudonymous confessions from messy lives like ours—hookups, breakups, parties and loneliness—every one ending in either heterosexuality or death.

Cheryl mingled with the kids after her talk, very down-to-earth for a celebrity. Shy again, slipping into boyhood, Ty ducked his head down and tried to stay on the fringes of the small group, but she took his hand.

"What stunning nails. Did you do them yourself?" He nodded, tongue-tied. Cheryl beamed, cradling his long fingers in her once-lovely ones— cuticles uneven, cigarette-burned at the tips. "I really wanted to say in my book that beauty is for everyone, but I kind of only had to *imply* it, because the people who order books for Christian stores would be too upset. They think fashion and makeup are only for girls, isn't that silly?"

"Yeah... uh, y'know... I'm a girl, sometimes," Ty choked out.

Cheryl gestured for her roadie to bring her purse. She dipped into it for a pastel-blue jar, unscrewed the silver lid and dabbed some of her sparkly blue-green face highlighter on Ty's strong cheekbones. Then she handed the jar to him. "Makeup is magic. Wear it whenever you need to remember you're a precious child of God." She glanced around, gauging the group's reaction, and added in a less trippy voice, "But stay safe."

Before she breezed off with her two assistants, I worked up the nerve to ask her out to dinner with me and Julian. "And some friends," I admitted, because the plan had changed since this morning. When I ran out at lunchtime for a salad from the Korean deli, I'd bumped into my friend Kevin, who was uptown today visiting a client. We'd been case management technicians together at Housing Works, the AIDS services organization for poor and homeless New Yorkers. Now he was their community liaison to African-American businesses and charities. He was thrilled to hear of my connection with Cheryl. Kev himself had been homeless when he was younger than Ty, kicked out for the usual God-bothering reasons. He found an unofficial foster home with a houseful of transsexual women who dolled him up as Cindy, Linda, Christy, and

Naomi. He and Julian could trade fashion-model gossip long after I'd exhausted my share of trivia.

I hadn't seen much of Kev this year because his longtime main partner, DeWayne, had a nasty series of bacterial infections that we all feared was the end. Some people want you to drink at their wake while they're still alive, like our Phil, and others isolate themselves, like DeWayne, a closeted high school science teacher who'd put in for a "study sabbatical" as soon as he tested poz. He figured he'd be dead before the Board of Ed noticed he hadn't completed the Natural History Museum's "Amphibians of the World" course, and meanwhile he'd have his privacy. But the newest AIDS drug cocktail had worked its magic—for how long, no one could predict, but meanwhile he was writing his lesson plans for the spring term.

The community Kevin served was on equally uncertain ground with this medical breakthrough, as priorities shifted from end-of-life comfort to finding housing and jobs that a chronically ill person could maintain. He would have gladly headhunted me from Gateway, but my old gig seemed to have gotten harder, and no better paid, than three years ago. Straight people with money were eager to believe the spin that the epidemic was over, turning their attention to diseases of less scandalous parts of the social body.

AT THE END OF MY Gateway shift, I rushed to my apartment to change clothes yet again, envying the convenience of Superman's ubiquitous phone booths. I chose a dark brown collared shirt and matching button-down vest that Julian picked up at a Joseph Abboud sample sale. He said layers were in but ties were out. One of these days I might return the favor and teach him something. He could choose between how to roast a turkey, use a ball gag, or fill out a grant application.

Two blinking messages on my machine were both from Mom. She was at the police station with Micah. Something about a missed visit with his father and shoplifting. The background noise of other phones, arguments, and intercoms made the story hard to follow. The second go-round straightened out some facts. We all knew Barbara was about to recommend terminating Mr. Bonte's rights if he skipped one more date on the court-ordered visitation schedule. As a jazz musician and restaurant dishwasher, he kept irregular hours. When the guy's girlfriend had come for Micah at Gateway, over an hour late, Mom had refused to release the boy to her. A standoff ensued, with some shouting of expletives in Haitian Creole as the woman tried to raise Mr. Bonte on his pager before Barbara could summon the police to haul her away. This much I'd already learned from Gateway staff gossip after I struck the set for Cheryl's presentation. The new information was that the family of three had made it to Macy's, only for the stupid kid to get himself collared for stealing a fancy electric shaver.

The phone rang again while I was listening to the messages. It had to be Mom. My hands clenched, pulling back against the reflex to pick up the receiver. I thought of Julian wearing out his patience with my first-responder lifestyle, and Cheryl's kindness to Ty. I noted with shame my irrational dislike of Micah. Why was I always being yanked in two directions? The ringer shrilled and shrilled and stopped. I took a deep breath into the silence of the few seconds before the answering machine squawked on.

"Peter, it's Mom again. I don't know where you could be. I also tried you at Gateway. I wish you could've helped me stop him from going with that *nafka* Ines. I know he didn't take it, he's covering for the father. Anyhow, as soon as you hear this, see if your father has a friend who can take this on *pro bono*. Love you, Peepers. Goodnight."

I pushed *erase* on that faster than Mom squashing a cockroach, blushing with relief that Jule hadn't been around to hear the idiotic childhood nickname. I would phone Dennis tomorrow, but first I had to learn from the unfortunate Mr. Bonte's example and show up on time for someone I wanted to keep.

Just a few minutes first to settle my head. Carefully I took off my vest and shirt, so no tell-tale smell would attach, and folded them over the back of a chair. From the drawer of Grandpa's desk, I pulled out the cough drops tin with my smoking stuff. As I was about to touch the lit match to the spliff, the phone ringer screamed again. *"What?!"* I yelled, dropping the match on the rug, frantically stomping it out. Disaster averted, but I splashed water on it to be sure. The ringing cut off without a message. A brown spot cankered the faded yellow petals of the woven rose. Not my rug, not my house, not my life. I lashed out at one of the unsorted file boxed with an angry kick. The reverberating pain in my toes cleared my head. The sagging cardboard sides split partway, spilling pages of photocopied Hebrew texts. I tossed them back haphazardly. They were beyond my expertise. A sheaf of looseleaf notebook pages, written in English in Rabbi Saul's tense first-draft scrawl, poked out from the stacks. *Adonai is multiple*, I read. Great, a personality disorder report on the Almighty. Explains a lot. Limping a tiny bit, I got dressed with no more fooling around.

I caught up with Cheryl and the guys in an upscale Greek seafood restaurant in Tribeca, one of those expensively minimalist places with exposed brick beams and little drop-shaped lights on long chains from the ceiling. The center bar area was occupied by a curved banquette of ice chips where freshly dead fish and crustaceans of all kinds were laid out, a dull red and silver rainbow. Tribeca was a long, though direct, subway ride downtown for me, but convenient for Kevin and DeWayne. I welcomed the change of scene.

Cheryl was so sweet and down-to-earth that my pals soon overcame their starstruck stiffness. We joked about our favorite dumb TV shows and what they revealed about us. True to the program in her book, Cheryl consumed only sparkling water, grilled fish and vegetables, but I noticed once more the tremors I'd seen at the podium. Looking from her and DeWayne to the rest of us, I experienced an unsettling time slippage, some of us changing, some not: Cheryl's fading ice-blondeness like soft washed cotton, DeWayne big-eyed and sallow, his neck too thin for his collar, compared to Kevin's shiny brown cheeks and gym-toned body, or Julian's perpetual exquisiteness. DeWayne's next topic of conversation underscored that we were not the same guys who'd wasted our nights on stoner movie marathons and dance clubs with bad beer.

"For however long I've got—longer than we thought, anyway—I've got a new life. I realized, *we* realized, I want to do more for kids than teach them the parts of the cell, which they're mostly going to forget as soon as they hand in their blue books."

"Don't underestimate kids. Kids are wonderful," Cheryl raved. She was fresher and brighter after her trip to the ladies' room. Makeup must be magic after all, though to me as mysterious as the lettering on the golem's forehead that brings clay to life. "One of them could cure AIDS."

I gave her credit for speaking the name, instead of hemming around it the way straight people usually did with us. The guys seemed comfortable with her frankness. Even for Julian, Phil's death was becoming another fact about himself, the new normal, not a bottomless pit that all facts vanished into.

"I don't think I have *that* long," DeWayne quipped. This too was new. He was usually the pensive partner to Kevin's outgoing humor.

"We're talking about becoming parents," Kev explained.

Julian was first to react to this bombshell. "Who's the mom?"

"We both are." Kev and DeWayne pointed to each other simultaneously and giggled.

My boyfriend rolled his eyes. "What I meant was, who's the lucky lesbian with the turkey baster?"

"Oh no, we want to adopt," said Kev. "There are so many children who need homes."

Cheryl tossed back her blonde mane and dabbed her nose with the maroon cloth napkin. "And what about the moms? The ones whose babies are taken away and they never see them again?"

"When we place kids from Gateway, we encourage the parents to stay in touch with the biological families, whenever it's safe to do that," I assured her. Though I couldn't be certain that Quito and Cara, and other kids Barbara had rescued for Social Services before she moved to Israel, had really kept up their visits to the jails, rehab units, and housing projects where their first parents struggled on without them. "Or you could try those orphanages for abandoned girls in China. Ethiopia has a program now too. They're not taking gay couples, but Kev could pretend to be single." My cousin Ben, who was investigating these very options, had asked me to be a character reference for him and Amy. They were the perfect adoptive couple: professional, in love, religious but not crazy about it.

"So, not too different from how we live now," DeWayne came back with the gallows humor. In six years he'd never let his school administration or colleagues know he had a life partner. Having seen too many clients lose jobs and apartments because of prejudice, Kevin was pragmatic and did his best not to resent his man's secrecy. I hadn't asked, and they hadn't confided, how DeWayne contracted the virus while Kev was negative. Most relationships in our community were assumed to be open, whether or not that was true. So maybe it was my own projection that a double life was like a prescription painkiller, something you could start to crave for its own sake, past the healing of the original wound.

"C'mon, you want your kid to lose her whole *country*, not just her mom?" Julian objected. "Culture shock is real. I can't even get decent collard greens out of you Yankees." He poked his fork at the kale salad, untouched next to the spiky remains of his langoustines.

"Could I eat that?" Cheryl reached over.

"Everything I have is yours, my diva."

Later, I'd let my conscience nag me into visiting Micah in the overnight holding cell, where he'd blubber that he stole the shaver to pretend it was a Christmas gift from his dad, because maybe if Barbara and Dr. Marla saw that his dad could provide for him, they'd let Micah go home. Later, the lawyer from Dennis' firm would persuade the juvenile court to deem all those statements inadmissible, and Micah would be fast-tracked into a placement with a big-hearted grandma who took him to her charismatic church three times a week. Later, immigration agents would send Mr.

Bonte back to Haiti, citing a drug-related parole violation that had surfaced when he contested his loss of parental rights.

But that night at dinner, when I still believed in the strings of the system and my ability to pull them, I told my hopeful friends, "There's a kid I want you to meet."

[EXTRACT FROM A LETTER TO RABBI SAUL HAUSER FROM RABBI NORMAN AHRENS, POSTMARKED FORT LAUDERDALE, FL, NOV. 5, 1983]

...I thought long and hard about whether to contact you, since she implied there was some danger at home and she needed to lie low. Annette and Joe are always glad of a visit from an old friend, and their Bethany definitely has eyes for Peter—my silly dream for our grandchildren persists! But I started to worry when it came out that Barbara doesn't actually have custody of the other child, in fact (she says) she took the children on this unplanned holiday to protect them from the girl's mother, that strange woman Nathan got mixed up with. What a tangle.

You and Barbara are like family to us, of course. I respect her judgment as a social worker. So please forgive me for not understanding—if she wants to keep her family together and adopt little Prudence (an odd name for such a wild creature!), wouldn't it be smarter to prove in court that the woman is manic-depressive and noncompliant with treatment, as Barbara insists?

Don't involve Nathan just yet. Between you and me, he's too easily led around by his—etcetera. Call her, or better yet, make it a real family vacation and bring Reyna down to join us for a day or two. I got concerned when I overheard Barbara asking Annette about apartment rentals today. A little bit of mama-bear madness that'll clear up under your steadying influence, as usual...

[EXTRACT FROM A LETTER TO RABBI SAUL HAUSER FROM RABBI NORMAN AHRENS, POSTMARKED FORT LAUDERDALE, FL, APRIL 29, 1984]

..."Next year in Jerusalem!" I hope my card reached Barbara in time for the holidays. What a blessing for her to celebrate her first Pesach in the Holy Land. Bittersweet, though, without the children. I can tell you, that's *not* how we thought all this would turn out. Joe used to tease poor Bethany that Peter's heart belonged to mommy. Now here they are, half a world apart. And you tell me Nathan's thinking of marrying that woman? I think he needs to keep his zeal for unpopular causes in the courtroom and wake up to who the real victims are.

Speaking of Bethany, she just shaved off one side of her hair and dyed the other side orange—without asking her parents, naturally! Something she saw on the MTV. I hope Peter likes the looks of this Cindy Lauper? I'm a Barbi Benton man myself. Did you know she was Jewish?...

[EXCERPT FROM *THE AKEDAH, SACRIFICE AND SANITY* BY RABBI SAUL HAUSER (HEBREW STUDIES PRESS, 1981]

...How do we know what is true? And who are "we"?

Modern man says he knows through his physical senses and reason. He supposes these mechanisms to be constant and identical for all individual units in the factory of mankind. But remind him of the devout millions whose certainties are unverifiable by his methods, and he must either admit his partiality, or grandiosely declare that his forefathers and many brothers are all lunatics, and himself the only sane resident of this planetary asylum.

On the contrary, a people constituted by hearing the voice of G-d, who had no identity till he called them out from among the nations, might well expect His commands to alter their reality again and again, all other scientific or social "laws" being mere contingent guesses at the truth only G-d knows. Greater than reasonableness is the wisdom of Abraham's knife...

[EXCERPT FROM RABBI SAUL HAUSER'S UNDATED HANDWRITTEN NOTES, ASSUMED TO BE FOR HIS MANUSCRIPT OF THE FAITH OF EVE]

"The Three Faces of Eve"—and Eve made in G-d's image??

Tractate Berakoth records Rabbi Ishmael ben Elisha's vision of G-d seated on His throne, praying. And for what does G-d pray? For His mercy to overcome His justice.

The question they dared not ask—to *whom* does God pray?

Shema Yisrael, the Lord our G-d, the Lord is One. But He prays to Himself! "The Lord... the Lord..." Repetition is always significant.

Adonai is *multiple*—seems to contradict Himself and set us up to go against His will (hardening Pharaoh's heart).

But Adonai is *one*—because all G-d's deeds serve a consistent purpose.

God is good. We're not wrong. The command that seems evil *is* evil—and part of a larger good plan. God wanted Abraham to refuse!

And so in Eden—

Can it be that Adonai gives some commands, not because He wants us to obey Him, but to destroy our false ideas of Him—to see if we will value truth and compassion higher than the egotism of being "good" obedient children?

This, only this, is a religion of mature men:

Will we risk even our relationship with "G-d" to do G-d's true will?

As the mother wishes her child to grow to manhood—*and* to stay safe at her breast—which mother will he choose? Once he realizes there are two...he will never know "love" again with the innocence of Adam.

If we say Eve passed the test that Abraham failed—

[rest of page is torn off]

❝I JUST CAN'T RELATE to this. I don't like it. Is that bad?" my cousin Ben whispered to me, standing before a painting of a three-eyed demon astride something that looked like a cross between Winston Churchill and a giant Shih Tzu. We were checking out a Chinese Buddhist art exhibit at the New York Open Center so he could learn something about the spiritual heritage of his future daughter. Right now Amy was sweating over a choice between possible matches, two flimsy folders of guesses about the health and history of abandoned baby girls. Ben and I hoped that a little dose of Quan Yin's equanimity would rub off on him, and failing that, there was always air hockey.

"The Buddha would say to move past liking or disliking. You feel whatever you feel."

"Then why does he have so much swag?" Ben motioned to a more attractive scene in shades of red, jade, and pink, in which a ruby-skinned young Siddhartha sat surrounded by ornate pagodas containing smaller copies of himself. It was a lot of sensory input for a Jew, I admit. Pomegranates on the Torah scroll covers are as fancy as we get.

"I guess Nirvana is boring to paint." I back-slapped him between his tense shoulders. Straight guys should really get over their fear of massage. "Again, Buddha says don't over-think the culture shock. Every religion is freaky. If they'd put accurate pictures in our kiddie Bibles it would've looked like your *Vault of Horror* comics."

"See, Adonai's ban on graven images makes sense."

I yawned in reply. When I stood still for too long, my limbs felt heavy and my head light, as if my consciousness really was slipping free from the tedious specificity of this body.

"You okay? Coming down with something?" He inched away from my imaginary germs.

"Nope, not sleeping well, that's all. Weird dreams."

"About what?"

"Ah, it doesn't mean anything."

"You're doubting Freud? That's Jewish heresy!"

"Come on, I'm up to my neck in psycho-interrogation here. Dad is pushing me to apply for a counseling job. He says I'm wasting my talents babysitting the Gateway kids. But not only do I need more coursework, I'd have to spend half a day taking expensive personality tests. I mean, why more than one? How many personalities am I supposed to have?"

Ben snorted. "The key to acing those things is, imagine the most boring person you know, and answer how she would. I use my mother-in-law. She's never cracked a book that didn't come from a drugstore check-out rack, but she can tell you the life story of her former co-worker's best friend's nephew. And she will." He grimaced, anticipating the drive to Amy's family in Scarsdale after our excursion. Then he sounded wistful. "She'll be the perfect grandma, though. Birthday cakes, new dresses, trips to the zoo. God willing."

We paused by a blue and white porcelain tabletop sculpture of a jolly obese Buddha with ten boy babies tumbling and crawling over his mountainous body. "Why do you want to have kids, anyway?"

My cousin's swarthy angular face darkened. "What kind of question is that?"

"I mean, how do you know whether you actually want something, or you want it because someone else wants it and you want that person in your life?"

"Cold feet about moving in with Julian?"

"Stop answering my questions with a question, you schmuck."

He punched my arm playfully. "You started it, you gotta finish it."

How to explain to my straitlaced cousin, the choice between the warm ease of love and the bracing-cold blade of pain? I'd sneaked out to Bernie's dungeon once more, this time to indulge a rather nasty rape fantasy. I didn't even cum. Yet when I imagined giving it up, I felt... *bereaved*. I was turning away from someone on the old world's killing shore while I boarded a boat to freedom.

The gallery's clean rectangular edges, white walls and blond board floors were a marked contrast to Grandpa Saul's book-lined cave, the nest of scribbled papers that were more organized than before, but nowhere near the coherence his editor hoped for. This thought suggested a safe answer for Ben.

"Maybe I'm making excuses but I feel bad about leaving Grandpa's project unfinished. It's like, that's the story of my life."

"The story...? Which character are you, Adam, the snake, or God?" Ben smirked at my presumption.

"According to Grandpa, we should all be Eve, wanting to know the truth at all costs."

"You and Julian won't last long with that attitude."

"So cynical. No wonder Dad likes you better than me." I paused. "Sorry."

He shrugged. "The truth, right?"

"Yeah...?"

"What I meant is, I'm not defending lying or cheating, but just that it can be better to move on from something that the people in your life, your *good* life, can't handle."

"You got a Las Vegas showgirl in your past, cuz?"

"If only." He smiled, on cue. Flicking his wristwatch face-up, he said, "Uh-oh, there's a roast chicken with my name on it in Scarsdale."

We rounded the corner toward the elevator. A blackened severed head rose up before me, tongue spilling out, fierce white eyes leering at my exposed secrets.

"Peter? Are you okay? Breathe." Ben's face, too close, replaced the vision. I was sitting on the cold floor. Weird.

"Duh," I said, shaking myself off, stumbling upright. "Did I fall asleep for a second? Man, that dream kicked my ass." The grotesque mask of Kali on the wall brought the memories back.

"Tell me about it. Quickly." With a firm push on my arm, Ben sat us both down on the bamboo bench under the angry goddess.

"It was terrifying because it was so familiar, but it wasn't anyplace I could have been for real. I kept thinking 'Here I am again, I've always been here, I'll never get away.' Some kind of med school dissection lab—" I forced down nausea— "but I *knew* the corpses. Not real people in life, people I knew in the dream. This older man's bloody head was in a glass tray, and I remembered that he was my teacher and I'd *killed him*, maybe all of them—and then the head opened its eyes and blood came out its mouth and it *talked to me*." I glanced at Ben. "Asshole, stop laughing at me."

My cousin wiped his eyes. *"Herbert West: Re-Animator.* You pussy."

"Oh, *jeez*." Of course, this scene was straight out of the campy 1980s movie of H.P. Lovecraft's zombie tale, which Ben and I had seen as teenagers. He wasn't done ragging me, though.

"How could you forget? You were obsessed with that gross-fest. Made me watch it on the Late Late Show twice. Remember that Halloween when it came out in theaters, I had to take you because you were underage?"

"Yeah, and *you* cut out to barf halfway through and never came back."

"But you crept back to my parents' house in the middle of the night because you were freaked out."

"I did?" Something dark pulled at my memory, gone. "What was I doing in between? Why didn't I just go home?"

"You said Mr. Jonas from the comic book store was having a party." Ben wouldn't look at me. "Like I said: it's better to move on."

"I guess I already have, because I'm drawing a blank. Probably the first and last time I was blackout drunk."

"Kids, make the safe choice: smoke weed." Ben's fake PSA voice was funny in a rote way, an expected call and response, lacking his full attention, which was preoccupied with the domestic dinner ahead. We plowed through the cutting January wind to the parking garage, where he paced in irritation while the attendant retrieved his black Lexus from the strategic puzzle of triple-stacked lifts. I offered to walk crosstown to my West Side subway line to save him time, but he insisted it was no trouble to drive me a few blocks.

"You're twitchy today. Afraid of Amy's parents, or just their cooking?"

Ben stopped drumming his fingers on the leather steering wheel. He frowned at a bus that pulled out from the curb in front of us, cutting us off from making the green light. "Thirty-fourth is a madhouse. I'm going down to 33rd."

"I can walk from here, really."

"No, it's okay." He sighed. "In-laws are fine. What it is—somewhere out there is a baby, an actual specific baby, who's already watching the sun rise—or whatever-the-fuck time it is in Shandong—already shitting and discovering her toes and growing an aptitude for math and violin music in her little brain cells—and right at this moment my wife is deciding that *this* is our—Oh! Oh, shit!"

A hard jolt, a tinkle and crunch. Turning left onto Fifth Avenue, Ben had scraped fenders with a cab that swooped up to the curb for a fare. White-faced, he shoved me against my passenger-side door. "Quick. Get out."

"What? Why—"

"I took two Valium and I had wine at lunch. If they test me—" He flung his arm across me and pushed the door open, so I had to put one foot on the ground to keep from ass-planting on asphalt. Before I could think twice, I was standing in the cold, listening to the approaching siren, while my cousin had slid over to the passenger seat. The would-be taxi rider, a pale-haired woman burdened with Macy's bags, jabbered nervously in a Russian accent to the traffic cop. His partner was trying to take a statement from the driver, but he was swearing in Arabic at the fool who had ripped off his side mirror. It was shaping up to be a very bad day at the U.N. Security Council.

Another officer swaggered off his motorbike. "License and registration," he demanded. I took the first out of my wallet in slow motion, remembering what can happen to guys (like Ty's late father) who reach for the side pocket too fast, but for the second, I gestured helplessly to the glove compartment in front of Ben. With a glum expression, he found the papers and obeyed the cop's order to step out.

The cop's eyes darted back and forth between us. "This your car?" he quizzed Ben, a trick question since the registration matched the name on his license, not mine.

"Yes, but he was driving," my cousin croaked.

Heat flooded my body. He was really going to put the squeeze on me like this, make me take the fall or be responsible for his misdemeanor charge of lying to an officer. Because his life mattered more, right? *He* was serving God and raising babies. "Fuck you, Herbert," I told him.

"*Sir.*" The officer moved in on me, a warning tone in that one syllable.

In the horror film that was my dreams, I wasn't the mad doctor, no. I was his inexplicable friend, the loyal narrator that the tale requires, his body assisting while his soul protests, as much a zombie as the electrified corpses on the table.

"I'm sorry, officer," I said in a shaky voice. "My cousin is so upset, he doesn't know what he's saying right now. His wife is about to have a baby. He's a good citizen, a cantor at the Park Avenue Synagogue. Please just give him the ticket and forget about what he said. We promise his insurance is good for it."

Seeing I wouldn't play ball, Ben nodded. With a look of disgust, the cop gave us both a moving violation and told us to fight it out in traffic court. The rubberneckers had drifted away, no blood on the pavement to hold their attention, and the cab was also gone, to a repair shop or more likely to keep picking up fares till he too got ticketed for driving without a mirror. Ben tried to speak to me but I shook him off and ducked into the crowd. He couldn't abandon his precious Lexus, so I was safe. What a prick.

R AGE, LIKE A FEVER, quickly ebbed into chill waves of shame as I hunched in my seat on the uptown train. Tight-packed commuter bodies were all that kept me from pacing and twitching as if I could escape my own skin. If there'd been a river, I would have jumped in it. Then I thought of how Julian would miss me and I nearly cried, cocooned in the stale wool heat of my neighbors, the old black lady flipping the onionskin pages of her Bible and the Asian boy nodding to the tick-tick of the rap backbeat on his headphones. Every life seemed so precious to me, unseen, like that baby in a Chinese orphanage who might never know Ben and Amy's loving arms because I picked *that* moment to stop being the family scapegoat. Jackass. It didn't reflect well on me that this guy had been my best childhood pal. I mean, you do think fondly of the kid who shows you your first porno mag, even if it wasn't really your type—

No, that wasn't how it happened. The scene shutter-clicked in front of my eyes. The jolting of the train became the sprung shocks of the white van belonging to Ben's dad, my Uncle Leo. He used to let us bounce around in the back with his electrician's toolboxes, free of seatbelts (life was cheap in 1979). The flutter of pages in my ear was the greasy magazine that 11-year-old Ben dug out from under the seat, with the shit-eating grin of Little Jack Horner securing his plum. A face I imitated—I could feel it stiffening my cheeks—to cover up the dread *familiarity* of the acts in the crinkled photo spread—the dick in the hairy hole, the face mashed into the bush— my crushing shame that I could no longer pretend ignorance of what these parts together meant.

Bing-bong, the train's door-closing bell brought me back like a swat from a Zen master's stick. So what if I had more experience than Ben suspected? Dad must have left all kinds of nasty crap in his home office from those obscenity cases he was defending in the 1970s. Probably I was poking around, discovered Exhibit XXX, and got such a scolding from Mom that I felt gross about sex afterward. There you go, my Garden of Eden moment at age nine. No wonder I had such a hard time bringing myself to explore Grandpa Saul's mystery boxes. Would Eve want to work on an apple farm?

I had to walk off this stress. Instead of going straight to my apartment, I paced across the avenues till I hit Broadway and the tall black iron gates of my alma mater, Columbia. The tiered marble plaza and red brick courtyard brought back the safe, orderly sensations of burying myself in poli-sci textbooks and all-night roleplaying games in the dorm common room. Lights strung from the trees sparkled orange-gold against the dimming gray sky. I climbed the slippery stone steps to the marble rotunda and recalled how I used to stand here and fantasize I was leading a protest at the Lincoln Memorial. This weekend was probably still winter break because the campus sidewalks were deserted.

I tucked myself into a familiar hiding spot between the pillars, where I could sit and look down over the plaza all the way to the temple-like library. A floating sensation took me over, a tempting detachment, as I practiced my meditative breathing. The alternative was to plummet and crash into head-on awareness of decisions unmade, pain not felt, choices I could no longer avoid. Light snow blew into my hideaway, unnoticed till my stocking cap soaked through. Although my legs were cold and stiff, I wouldn't quit, not till I picked a side, this life or nothing. Inside me, something cracked, knife-like ice cleaving into scraping sobs that I muffled with my ski jacket sleeve. I howled through the gag that my fist made in my mouth. Yes, I was broken, I was crazy, I was a loser—and, like the pain-pleasure switch of submitting to the inescapable bondage fuck, at last I was drowned in the peaceful relief of facing the truth.

That left me two alternatives, my current drift downward or its opposite. Sartre said the failure to choose is also a decision—according to Chad, my dorm suite mate, who'd used that line to convince Barnard girls that they'd consented to sex by not leaving his room. I thought about how things would end with Julian, when he realized I didn't know how to love as wholeheartedly as he did. Then—I'm a New Yorker, after all—I'd regret giving up a rent-free apartment for nothing. But I forced myself to picture the other ending, the two of us moving forward through the years, daring to claim a home and a family, like Kevin and DeWayne or my bastard cousin and his hopeful wife—not perfect, but more often happy than not. The vision burned like the sun, with agonizing allure. Since when did I run from pain, if there was a chance of ecstasy on the other side?

Stretching my cramped limbs, I wiped my face and picked my way carefully down the snow-dusted steps to street level. En route to the apartment, I bought a powdered donut and a super-sized black coffee from a street vendor's tin-sided truck. Chugging the whole thing in two blocks gave me a slightly uneasy stomach, but the cocaine rush of sugar and caffeine was necessary for my plan.

I loaded the 5-CD player with Kraftwerk and Devo albums and surveyed the half-opened time capsule I lived in. Gray shadows collected in the corners beyond the glass-shaded circles of lamplight. Grandpa's executor had swung by in December to pack up any valuable antiques for the estate sale, which would cover the maintenance for the next couple of months. Gap-toothed bookcases showed where leather-bound first editions had slumbered, the newly exposed wood making shiny contrast stripes against the dusty shelves. Some wall-mounted china plates and a framed tapestry had left the ghosts of geometric shapes on the parchment-colored paint. Incongruously modern, my new electric shredder dominated the small space between the desk and the green velvet sofa. This bad boy had helped me hack a path to the bedroom closet by devouring several reams of irrelevant lesson plans, tax and insurance records, and business correspondence. Inside the closet with its mothball fumes was a stash of family photo albums and storage boxes from my childhood—school papers, holiday cards, journals— that Barbara must have offloaded on her parents when she moved to Israel after the divorce. I decided to hold off on excavating this crap until Julian was around, so he could say encouraging untrue things about my lumpish middle-school visage. Grandpa's book notes were the priority before my energy buzz wore off.

As I'd previously complained to Jule, the job was impossible, because the rabbi's completed chapters and those notes that were legible fell into two categories: those consistent with the Kierkegaardian argument of his *Akedah* book, that God could redefine right and wrong at any moment; and those arguing the exact opposite, that the God who set up the arbitrary sting operation in Eden was a conflicted tyrant in need of Adam and Eve's courageous defiance to save Him from His dark side. Presumably Grandpa now knew which answer was correct, but I'd need a Ouija board to poll his opinion, and it would put a damper on my sex life to be haunted by an old man who thought Vanna White showed too much skin on "Wheel of Fortune".

I cranked up the music's robotic heartbeat. Repetitive instrumentals put me in a zone where I could act without overthinking, like a videogame soldier in a first-person shooter. I couldn't pause to feel guilty about this responsibility, this military sorting of the huddled stacks of a dead man's life work, this side to the publisher, that side to the incinerator. Though I exaggerated there: the rejected drafts would first molder in a storage unit till the editors decided whether the other version was saleable, or the contract expired and everyone gave up. Then my grandfather's legacy would be those bundles of Polaroids in the closet and a single book defending child sacrifice. And me.

About two hours in, I took a break and stood on my head. Tree pose, Noose pose, Half Lord of the Fishes. The ancient *asanas* shifted the tension from hunching over the closely written papers. Clearing space for a real workout was another incentive to finish this task. Just when my chest muscles really started to open up, a too vigorous Half Moon stretch caught the corner of the desk and spilled my unread mail onto the floor. A postcard from the ACLU fluttered at my feet. The black and white stripes of a stylized flag bore a quote attributed to Thoreau: *Disobedience is the true foundation of liberty.*

I turned the postcard over in my hands, looking from there to the framed photos on the alcove wall, and back again. Closest to me was a vacation snapshot of my grandparents when they were about the age my mother was now. Despite the Florida heat, Grandpa Saul wore a tie and a white fedora. He had my thick build and broad face, in his case solemnized with a salt-and-pepper beard, and Grandma Reyna's dark curly hair was my inheritance as well.

Unwillingly, I thought of Ben, who would not get to read his history in his daughter's face. The sacrifice of Isaac was more than a really bad parenting decision. It was murdering your hope of belonging to a tribe, all because you heard a voice inside you, crazy but true, the originator of your soul. Where did disobedience end? Sure, I could break the family rule that Ben was the prince and I was the valet, but once this beast began to flex its muscles, who else would I lose? Two rectangles side by side, sun-tinted faces, black and white words. Julian always chose people over ideas, but I wasn't Julian.

In fact, the question of rebellion was moot because there was no one to tell me what to do. That's what scared this subbie the most. My fingers itched to hold a joint, but I put the postcard down, and with an exhaled prayer to a nameless deity, knelt before the stack of papers commending Eve's defiance. I would put these in some sort of logical order for the publisher, then box up the contrary files for storage tomorrow.

With the stereo on automatic replay, I lost track of how many hours had passed before I felt Julian hug me from behind. I'd copied an extra key for him without telling Barbara, who was squeamish (as all mothers would be, I guess) about imagining us sharing her father's bedroom.

"My grandfather's dead," I sobbed.

Jule sat back on his heels. "Yes, and—?"

"And I'll never know what he really wanted."

He inspected my pupils. "Are you high, sweetie?"

"I should be so lucky."

"You are. You *are* so lucky. Would you like to hear why?"

"Because I have you?"

"Ahh. You really mean that?" Jule pressed a soft kiss on my lips. I kissed back harder, opening his mouth with my tongue, leaning him backwards over the spread of discarded drafts blanketing the rug. All my pent-up willpower, hedged around so long by the space I made for other people, surged with an unstoppable heat that we could only quench together. Julian fumbled for balance, trying to unseal his lips from mine to finish whatever he'd come here to say, but he stopped resisting when I pulled us down to the floor, my weight pinning his spread body. The hard place in me felt like I'd never wanted him, or maybe anything, as much as I did right now. He gasped, his dark eyes holding steady on my face, and cupped his hands round my ass. I ground my dick madly against him till the painful lightning bolt of my want passed through us and let me go.

As soon as I could lift my dizzy head, I touched his cheek and he gave me a shaky half-smile. I sat up partway so we could breathe easier. "Did you cum?"

The rest of his smile caught up with him. "And ruin my Armani pants?"

"What was I thinking? Here, let me..." I bent my head toward his fly, but he nudged my chin upward.

"Let's say you owe me one. Now go clean up and put on something that screams 'I'm too cool to make an effort.'"

"Sorry I forgot, did we have plans tonight? I was going gonzo on these papers so I could move the hell out of here by next week."

Jule perked up at my mention of a definite date for our union. "You didn't forget, it's a surprise. I was about to tell you when you turned into a sex werewolf. Now you'll just have to wait till after I approve your clothing." He tapped my butt. "Can I help tidy up the library explosion here?"

"Sure, those are just the notes we're not using for the book—dump them in that box by the window."

I showered and put on a pair of jeans with a subtle gray and black camo pattern, a black turtleneck, and over it a lime green T-shirt screen-printed with an ad for a Japanese footbath, with liberally applied exclamation points and cartoon happy faces. My stomach rumbled from a day of disregarded hunger. I hoped our surprise rendezvous came with a side of fries.

"That's the most random thing I've ever seen. I love it," Jule said when he saw my outfit. But his face was shadowed with concern.

"You okay, babe? Was I too—*rrawrr?*" I mimed a wild animal pounce.

"I made the mistake of looking at those papers. Your grandaddy wrote some scary shit. Crazy isn't crazy if God says so? 'The truth is on the other side of the murder of love'—what the fuck?"

"That's why that's the discard pile. For what it's worth, he was a pretty nice guy in real life. He and Grandma had us over for Passover and Hanukkah every year till she got sick, even after Mom left the country. Me and Prue both. He treated her just the same as me, like family."

"I didn't know that. I see why you care about finishing this job. Will a week be enough? I didn't mean to pressure you."

"It's okay. I'm dying for a fresh start." I beckoned him to follow me to the kitchen. "I assume we're going out to dinner, but I need to pre-game."

As I applied myself to a bowl of frozen yogurt with mixed nuts, Jule beamed with the excitement of finally spilling his good news. "Cheryl was so thrilled with the pictures Ty drew of her, as a character in your comic book—Phoenix?"

"Eva Phoenix, right." We'd made up a role for Ty's new diva as a magical mentor who appeared in Pharmakon's dreams to guide him about right and wrong uses of his powers, like a prettier Yoda to his Skywalker.

"She passed them round to her media contacts, including this guy at *The Advocate* who was researching a feature on gay-friendly Christian inspirational writers—obviously she doesn't have much competition in *that* niche—but anyway, he wants to meet you and see some sample pages!"

I nearly choked. "*The Advocate* might publish *me?*" It was like the *New York Times* of gay culture mags, publishing serious political pieces alongside celebrity profiles and pioneering gay cartoonists such as Howard Cruse and Donelan. "But what about Ty? He's underage, he'll need someone to sign off on it."

"I don't know, we'll work out the details with Marco tonight. He must already know that from Cheryl. C'mon, let's hustle."

MARCO SANTINI, *The Advocate* assistant editor for art and comics, hadn't chosen our venue with "business meeting" in mind. Housed in the boxy red brick shell of a deconsecrated church on West 20th Street, the Limelight was a gay nightclub so trendy that no one I knew would admit going there. In a couple of hours there'd be a line out the door and a wall-to-wall carpet of beautiful bodies gyrating in the nave below our balcony table. For the moment, you could still see the floor. Smoky gold spotlight beams criss-crossed the high hollow space, glinting off the lead-outlined stained glass panes of the Gothic windows. An elevated cage awaited the dancers' ascent, made of the same tubular black metal as the dining balconies that had replaced the old church's stone galleries.

At a table so minimalist that the appetizer platter made it tilt ominously, Marco slurped on chicken wings while locking eyes on my boyfriend's mouth. He was around thirty, with olive skin and gelled dark curls that tumbled in a fake-messy way over his forehead. I let him buy us vodka shots as well as my usual one bottle of beer on the wall. I ordered stuffed jalapeños just to make a "poppers" joke. I was breathing fire.

A half hour of flirty bullshit later, during a lull in the disco noise, Marco got down to examining my color xeroxes of our first "issues" of *The Poison Cure*. No way I'd let the originals within range of alcohol spills. Call me OCD but I firmly believe there's no excuse for having only one copy of anything.

"Huh, hmm, very edgy, really different," he talked to himself while skimming the pages. "Ooh, we could get some hot complaints about that one." A sweep of blue light from a rotating strobe showed me he was at the scene where Pharmakon assaults the anti-gay priest. Marco abruptly leaned toward me, our faces so close I could smell the barbecue sauce on his breath. "So the poison thing is like a metaphor for AIDS, right? Like the drug cocktail side effects? That's cool, that's cool, but hasn't it been done already, the gay disease thing, like *Interview with the Vampire?*"

Oh dude, watch me go all Susan Sontag on your ass. "Or you could say AIDS itself is a metaphor for the fear of otherness and contamination that's really universal, timeless. Who isn't afraid of letting a lover see their dirty secrets? What gay kid hasn't secretly rooted for the monster in the horror movie because the 'normal' world is one where we shouldn't exist? What I want to do here is bring that into the open, complicate the idea of good and evil so it looks like our real lives, instead of having to read ourselves into some caricatured bad guy who's predestined to lose."

Marco sat back, nodding. "Whoa. You should write that down."

"Uh, thanks. So are you interested in publishing—"

The editor cut me off with a kingly swivel of his hand in the air to summon a passing waiter for more shots and nachos. I began to be anxious about my assumption that we were on the magazine's expense account. Julian bummed a ballpoint and extra napkins from the waiter, to transcribe anything intelligent I might say in the future. Our conversation paused as the breathy tones of Madonna's "Love Tried to Welcome Me" swelled and ebbed.

"About Tai—" I tried again. One complication among many, my collaborator wanted the female name on our work, saying this was who she became when she made art. I could foresee this raising the bar for social worker approval of the improbable venture under discussion tonight.

"Why's he called Pharmakon? Sounds like he works in a drugstore. You open to changing it?"

"Well no, it's the original Greek term for the poison cure—the improvement that makes things worse. It comes from Plato's dialogue *Phaedrus*, where Socrates argues that oral tradition is superior to writing because writing substitutes a fake symbol for a real interaction. As soon as you put something into words, it becomes a lie, because words don't change but people's feelings do."

Marco was closing his eyes and shaking his head before I reached "Socrates". Jule, on the other hand, was looking at me like I'd come up with the formula for changing water to wine.

"Sorry, man, this thing's gonna go over everyone's head, you know?" the editor said, at the same time as Julian exclaimed, "So *that's* why gay men can't say 'I love you'."

"Guys. Chill. It's a comic book about a slutty musician and a mutant who fucks child molesters to death. Who wouldn't be into that?"

Marco guffawed. "You guys are quite a pair. Okay, I like your spin. Tell me about the kid. What'll it take to get the rights from him?"

My Spidey-sense didn't like that phrasing. The way DC Comics screwed Siegel and Shuster out of the Superman franchise profits was legendary. This opportunity was such a surprise, I'd never really looked into the legalities of taking our little project pro. "Ty's between foster families at the moment. Technically he's a ward of the state. I guess that means his caseworker would have to approve it. Maybe a judge. I can ask—" I almost said, *my dad*— "A lawyer I know."

"But he could just send his work to us on his own, hush-hush, no one cares? Since he's using that girl pen name anyway?"

"Contracts get weird when you're underage. It's not valid unless a grownup signs off, I'm pretty sure."

"*Contracts?* Shit, you try to do a poor ghetto kid a favor, give him some exposure... How long's this going to take?"

That *was* the question on everyone's mind. This guy had no right to the details, but where the gavel would come down on Ty's comics career probably hinged on his foster placement. If Ty was already in a stable home with the Beckers, who were not favorably inclined toward smut or the dual personality involved in its creation, the court would probably defer to their judgment that the *Advocate* deal wasn't in the kid's best interests. If we could get Kevin and DeWayne appointed as Ty's foster parents instead, Pharmakon had a chance to see print.

I lied with a smile. "Shouldn't be more than a few weeks."

Marco swallowed it. He slapped a business card down in front of me, making my drink wobble. "Okay, call me when you've cleared this up. Who wants the first dance?"

Julian pulled out his wallet, signaling the meal was over. I tried not to count how many twenties covered the bill. "Sorry, cutie, but Peter here is the jealous type."

After Marco left us alone, I whispered, "Yeah, I'm real jealous that sleazeballs hit on you instead of me."

"Just so you're not mad I nixed the casting couch?"

"What I really need you to do is blow the Family Court judge instead."

Julian stuck out his tongue in disgust. "Come along home, my selfless public servant."

I hesitated. The crowd noise had amped up, and women and men in skin-tight clothing were bobbing and sweating on the dance floor below, baptized in swirling flecks of light. For a short while, they had no plans, no duties, no memories of a tedious day toiling for someone else's goals.

Whatever religion lingered in the Limelight's walls was still the opiate of the masses.

"I didn't think this was your scene," Jule commented.

"My scene needs an upgrade." I pulled my shirts off, flashing some persuasive chest hair, put the T-shirt back on and folded the hot turtleneck into my messenger bag with the *Poison Cure* pages. "When did you become so respectable?"

"A lady reaches a certain age, she prefers to get rimmed in a clean bathroom."

"Let's dance, at least. This is one of those experiences you want to be able to tell stories about when you're old."

Jule exaggerated his Southern drawl. "And that, Lula Mae, is why Grandpappy is goin' to hell."

"Fuck that brainwashing. Hell is for people who hurt someone, not for the way you love. Your father's the one who should be worried, not us." I bit my lip. "Uh...is it okay I said that?"

"No, I must challenge you to a dance-off to avenge my family honor."

"Ah, this is awesome, my life has become an '80s movie. Bring it, Molly Ringwald."

As we descended the stairs, past shadowed windows of indifferent saints, the warmth of the re-breathed, dance-churned air engulfed us like an ocean. It reminded me of childhood trips to the Brooklyn Botanic Garden, stepping out of winter into the magic of the tropical greenhouse. January could go on without us, with its fat-free resolutions and sad Christmas firs browning on the curbside trash piles. The sound system saturated our ears with the club remix of Belinda Carlisle's "Live Your Life Be Free". I stretched my arms up, tilted my face to the shine and glitter overhead. Julian and I moved together, magnetized, pressed inward by the bobbing and rubbing of the bodies closing in around us.

I believed I could be a whole new person. My stomach cast a dissenting vote. There's a reason I don't do shots, let alone layered on top of chili peppers. I mimed needing a bathroom break, though at first Jule thought I was proposing a different activity. He looked relieved that I only wanted to splash cold water on my seasick head.

Maybe that's why I felt disoriented, I thought, as I blundered around a dark corridor in search of the Gents'. This wasn't the Julian I knew. Romance, commitment, sure, he'd always secretly hoped for those, underneath his mayfly persona. But now he seemed afraid that we couldn't have a happily-ever-after unless we gave up everything that made us different from Mr. and Mrs. Selkirk of Marietta, Georgia. Then again, maybe my boyfriend was on trend, as usual. A new conservatism was leaking into gay consciousness. Now that AIDS was theoretically survivable, fatalistic excess wasn't the only option. Some of these cocksuckers were even voting Republican.

I was overthinking all this to stay awake. My insides had settled but my head weighed the wrong amount. I propped myself against a wall near the entryway to the dance floor, next to a corkboard layered with flyers for concerts, liquor brands, and "alternative" services. *Tarot/Psychic*, read the one closest to me, an eyeball staring from the palm of a hand, flanked by a card with a nude woman dancing inside a wreath, and another upside-down card showing—

—hand over my mouth   too strong   can't breathe

look at his hairy arm   look at the blue ink   it'll be over soon

upside-down horse knight cup

sharp fire ripping inside me   can't move my legs?

you know what he's doing to you   what you are   NO

STOP   be anywhere else   anyone no one

but why doesn't the cup spill?   why—

—gasping with pain ramming into my ass from nowhere, everywhere, rubbery limbs helpless knees shaking feet drumming on the sticky black floor of *what place was this?* Face to the corner of a hallway wall echoing with an endless backbeat, lights in my eyes flashing angry as police.

Wet, pain hot turning cold. Bleeding? If it were only blood... Shame sickening, like that hand stifling my nose and mouth again—or had it, had it just cupped my cheek with words *cute* and *have another*—some grownup drink tasting like nothing great but the burn of pride that these guys wanted me here, at a real party with a fake ID.

Headache, heartbeat gagging my throat. Twitch of terror. Target splat on the floor, pants down what if they came back—unmoving hands moved, touching myself gross like a dead body. I was dressed, I was dry. And so it couldn't be (my mind slid away from the cannonball truth in the pit of my stomach, strobe light slipping down a wall into black) friends of my friend Jonas who had waited for him to go somewhere else in the bar and spread me against this wall and—*NO*—

Hadn't happened. Wouldn't happen. No. Just wait for the pain to stop and then I could go home. How long had I been here? Someone had dressed me in a stupid unfamiliar shirt I couldn't even read. I dragged myself to sit against the wall, bent my head down to hide as feet clumped through the hallway, door slamming on sounds of piss and groaning. Time loop tunnel where I'd fall like a dummy forever, until that man's knight tattoo (*he said he liked my stories, said good enough for Omni*) and the other's bitter aftershave (*dressed as Halloween pirates together kissing Jonas then me with the same tongue*) would shrink to dreams of dreams, didn't happen, couldn't believe. *Flash* of his arm crushing my cheek, *one no the other* stab up into me, my Novocaine legs trembling. Knocking my head against the wall.

No, I was doing that to myself, right now. Bang, bang, awake. Stupid Peter. Horror movie and big-boy liquor. Then somehow I'd hurt myself, slapstick tailbone bruise. Go home and pray Dad doesn't start to care what time I come home. But I smelled—was it me or this place, the stale cum, fear, sweat, drink? I panicked realizing I didn't remember what this club was called. The important thing was to get out before they came back.

Supposed to be spending the night at Ben's. That's right. He wouldn't ask questions because by then I would be sure nothing happened. And in an even deeper level of my brain I wondered why I was good at this, why I knew the location of the switch to turn it all off. That warm pride again, watching myself from above. Cold, though, out here on the street, forgot my coat, wind weirdly sharp for the end of October. Weightless sick with a new fear at the wrongness of where I was, the sudden blank as I tried to remember the right subway line from here (here?) to Ben's parents' home in Brooklyn. I shivered, leaning on the side wall of the club that had somehow turned into a church, where heavy-coated figures lined up to enter even though it was night.

A hand on my back. I jumped. Not one of *them* after all, just a slim twentysomething guy in an expensive-looking wool trench coat that he draped around my shoulders before I could draw another breath. "What's going on? You okay?"

"Just...just waiting..." I stammered out. Fear chased excitement, ambushed by disgust at myself for wanting this again, drunk-stupid and stained by the gross thing that had (*hadn't*) left this burning pain reaching up to my spine. The pretty man studied me with concerned dark-fringed eyes like Matt Dillon's, some probably-celebrity I could almost put a name to.

"I worried when you didn't come back from the bathroom. The guy at the door said he saw you run out here." He tried to put his arm around me, but I shrank away, more scared than flattered that Mr. Rob Lowe Cheekbones here was following me.

"Thanks. It's okay. I really should go home now," I croaked.

"Poor darling. No more shots for you. Come back inside where it's warm. I'll go fetch your stuff from the coat check." He steered my numb body into the vestibule.

More shame, not wanting this cool guy to see—what had I brought here? That dopey rubber mask from the party store, my duct-taped puffy jacket? But I was shivering and I had to get *away*. I dug in my pocket for a claim ticket. As soon as he'd gone, I thought about running, right this minute... except I shouldn't boost this fancy coat...except Jonas' friends might come back and...where *was* Jonas? Why didn't he help me?

I was breathing so fast it made me dizzy. We must have come here without him. That's why. If I hailed a cab now, I could leave Prince Charming's coat behind and not freeze. Check my wallet for enough cash—

Plummeting again, elevator drop, exploding pressure in my head as *now* rushed back in. That was *my* driver's license in the billfold. My treasured photo of me and Julian and Phil on our last camping trip together. My boyfriend's coat wrapped around me, his body's sweet smell of home.

Now I was really scared. I'd stepped out of my life and back in again, without warning. How would I ever stay nailed down?

I leaned my hand against the entryway wall and it didn't go through. That was a start. In the red-lit corridor I caught sight of my face, broad and shadowy and strange, in the mirrored panel opposite. I took a step closer, into focus. Someone inside me saw a strong man from the future, a Jedi hologram, statue in a secret cave. *Help.*

I will, the man in the mirror said to whoever was behind my eyes. And the scared child turned over and went back to sleep, invisible, so I could almost pretend I was alone again inside my ordinary brain. My brain that I hoped was broken in some boring way that I could take a pill for.

"I'm going to the doctor," I told Jule as we waited for a taxi. "I'm getting on meds for these panic attacks and I'm going to meditate more and move out of that damn apartment and do what I want."

"Good! Whatever you need, you know I'm here." He laced his fingers more tightly through mine. Chelsea was the kind of neighborhood where we could do that. I nodded and squeezed his hand. Out of the corner of my eye, I could sense him looking closely at me. I leaned away into the street to spy out our ride.

"Something weird happened back there, didn't it? Not just the drinks and Marco crapping on your art."

Lying was an easy habit that had gotten us nowhere—or somewhere worse—but I didn't know what was true. "I think the club reminded me of a place I went as a teenager, with—" don't say Jonas, he already doesn't like him— "some older guys. It, uh, it turned out to be a rough night."

Jule's face was stern, withdrawn into hurt or protective concern that he knew I wouldn't welcome. "There's a lot you don't tell me, babe."

"I don't have any big secrets. I just think Ben is right. We all have shitty memories. I don't care why we made stupid decisions in the past. The important thing is I'm ready to move forward, finally. With you."

"All right. We'll talk about it more tomorrow."

He touched his fingertips to my lips to cut off my protest—the gentlest movement but for a split second *that smothering hand* stopped my breath, till I recovered the sanity to kiss his hand away and let him bundle me into the waiting cab.

PART II

BESHALACH

JANUARY 1997 — APRIL 1997

The future is the book one must dare to read,
no matter what it says, no matter what death
it may bring to the beliefs and securities of the past.

—Robert M. Price, 1997 Cthulhu Prayer Breakfast Sermon

Blue-green shadows of dusk in Pharmakon's apartment. First panel close-up on a tabletop arrangement of objects like an altar: knife, bowl, blank paper, incense burner, little girl doll, and the stoppered glass bottle where Pharmakon keeps the red liquid for his dreaming bath. The bottle is empty save for a trace of red in the bottom.

Next panel, green-tinged hands pricking finger with knife, writing symbols in strange script on the curling page of paper. Next, Pharmakon's face as he breathes in the spiraling blue smoke, eyes closed.

Next panel, pull back to show Pharmakon draped on couch as if unconscious, as billows of blue smoke blur the scene. His body remains dimly visible behind the blue-white clouds filling the next panel. In the foreground, a regal blonde lady touches her hand to the sleeping man's chest, causing a semi-transparent version of himself to separate from the prone body and begin to stand up. Her gown is made of yellow light, and flame-like feathers hang from her sleeves.

Pharmakon's astral body (bowing, reciting the litany): *'Hail, Lady Eva Phoenix. The vessel—'*

Eve: *Why do you summon me now?*

P (confused, takes a step back, restarts the prayer): *'—the vessel of my dreams has been emptied in your service. Pray refill it.'*

E (holding up her hand to refuse the bottle): *You have chosen otherwise. I do not know that I can help you now...or your human lover.*

P: *Challis? He doesn't know anything about...<u>this</u>. And he won't have to. I can protect him.*

E: *Protect? By choosing another's time to die? That man's life was not given to you to decide. Nor is your own.* (Phoenix's feather-flames darken red as she calls up an image of the priest in his death throes.)

P: *You can't tell me he didn't deserve it! If it's between his life and Ryder's—*

E: (sad face, drooping feather-flames dimming to pale yellow): *This sacrifice will not be enough. Can you not feel it? Each time you are sexual—with anyone— your poison power surges.*

P: *I know that! It's always been that way. So what? Refill the bottle and let me get back to protecting people.*

E: *But you have upset the balance. You were not to touch a man more than once. If there was evil in him, it would return to him and strike him down; if good, you would draw any toxins out and use them to do justice elsewhere.*

P: (holding his head in his hands): *So that's how I cured Ryder of AIDS! The only good man who's ever held me...*

E: *But now the bond of your repeated coupling has built up an energy you will be unable to control.*

P: *You mean, I could hurt Ryder?!* (Phoenix shows him a vision of Challis sickly and green in a hospital bed.) *No! I don't want this power anymore. Take it away—I don't care what you have to do to me.*

E: (gradually turning from vibrant yellow, to flame-cloaked red, to stooped and blackened ash, over the three panels where she shows him these future scenes): *To you—but also to those you can no longer help.*

Phoenix first shows a split scene of the girl from his birthday party vision: shrinking in terror from her father in a darkened bedroom, then running happily through a sprinkler in the park with her mother. The second vision is a 10-year-old boy in a school locker room, looking sideways in shame as he pulls down his gym shorts. This is split with an image of Pharmakon

in the school shower stall with the coach, who
wears the same school colors as the boy's uniform.
The man's eyes are closed and his head thrown back
in painful ecstasy as green spreads up from his
neck. But in the third vision, the coach, older
now, receives an award from the school, while a
teen version of the boy lies on the floor of a filthy
warehouse with a needle in his arm.

P: (covering his eyes with one hand, tryng to push
the visions away with the other): *Please, stop! There
must be another way!*

E: (sadly, with a light touch on Pharmakon's chest):
*Your heart is unselfish still. If you keep your
poison...there is only one more place for it to go.*

P: *I...I'll die, then. But how will I keep him from
learning why? He'll remember me as a monster...*
(Tears trickle down his face.)

E: (once again upright and draped in healthy golden
flame-feathers): I will refill your vessel only once
more. Consider whether it would be kinder for him to
lose you now, rather than some other way.

The two figures fade into the smoke that begins to
clear. Next panel, Pharmakon wakes, sits up, sees
the vial once again filled with red liquid. Final
panel, rear view of Pharmakon standing at the
window, gazing at the full moon.

❝Pick a card, any card," the shrink said.

"I just came in for a prescription," I grumbled. I dug the toe of my black combat boot into the red and blue carpet belonging to Dr. Sidney Katz, disrupting its border of Ukrainian-style doves and flowers. My seven-league shitkicker boots that Julian had bought me to celebrate our official move-in date. He was also replacing my baggy jeans with skinny ones, one pair at a time, under the pretense of reorganizing our newly shared closet. My gift to him, besides my willing submission to the grunge makeover, was a set of camera lenses that I could only afford by selling my mint-condition Watchmen comics back to Jonas at Rogues' Galaxy. I didn't miss them; four months in Grandpa Saul's apartment had nearly cured me of hoarding paper products.

Katz ("call me Sid") raised an eyebrow, as bushy as his head was bald. Sixtyish, with a close-cropped grizzled beard stubbling a thick neck, and an undisguised Lower East Side accent, he reminded me of my other grandfather, Abe Edelman, a retired shop steward in the garment workers' union.

"You don't want to know yourself, there's cheaper ways to get a good night's sleep," he said. "But since you're here…"

"So, what, should I lie down and tell you my dreams?"

"You can if you want to," he said, with a wry glance around the small office. It was a tight fit for our two armchairs, his bookcase and file cabinet, and the glass-topped folding table where he set down a black and orange cardboard box. "I don't really go in for that Freudian power dynamic, but you're the boss here. I just thought, since you're a writer, you'd get a kick out of some creative free-association."

My heart warmed toward him a little. No one had called me a "writer" before. Sure, I wrote things: speeches (words in a politician's mouth), alt-weekly editorials (under a pseudonym), case reports on the kids, captions for pictures of Ty's imaginary world. I nudged the small box toward me. The lid showed a pale, sharp-faced youth wrapped in layers of medieval-looking brown clothes, captioned "The Fool". On the side, white capitals on a black background read *AQUARIAN TAROT*. I pulled my hand back, pushing down the memory of the Limelight poster, the man's inked arm reaching out of the past.

"Too freaky for you? Sorry. I also have angel cards, a mythology art book, or we could forget the whole thing and just talk about why you think you're anxious."

"Nah, I'm not superstitious. I like scary stuff. It reminded me of someone, that's all."

"What about them?"

I forced my breathing to calm. "A guy who...didn't treat me right. I don't know much about him. I don't know why he had a Tarot tattoo and it probably wouldn't help me understand what happened. Anyway, it doesn't look like this style of art, at all."

"That's true, there are many different versions of the Tarot. This one's from the 1970s. I like to use it in session because it has a kind of stillness, a watercolor feeling, like a dream after you wake up."

"You would like my boyfriend. He's very visual too."

Sid smiled. "The photographer, right? Pick a card to tell me about him."

"Just at random?"

"Whatever you want."

Despite my assurances to Sid, this really was freaky, but much better than the sincere interrogation I'd been dreading—the mask of concern, the relentless waiting until I barfed up all the drab humilations of my autobiography. I shuffled and fanned out the face-down cards, their blue and white backs scrolling with stylized waves like a Chinese screen painting.

King of Rods, I read. A classically handsome profile of a man with a bronze eagle on his helmet, gazing intently at a thick green budding stalk that opened into a black-edged blossom.

"Okay, how is this like Julian?" Sid prompted.

"He likes a big rod?"

The social worker chuckled. "Trust me, I *won't* tell you that sometimes a cigar is just a cigar."

With that out of the way, I tried to think seriously. "He's not shy about his looks. He would talk you into believing that a bird hat and a circus tent robe were 'in'. He wants one thing and that's all he can see."

"Say more about that."

"Well, he's staring at this plant, but the most unusual part, the flower, is above his head. He's not even looking at it."

"What doesn't Julian see about you?"

My badness, I thought. *My sickness, my not-right.* But Sid would try to talk me out of that, according to formula, because the goal of therapy was to shrink (haha) your problems down to a size where they could share personal space in the crowded elevator with every other schmuck's problems. Which

I shouldn't kvetch about, because I'd claimed I was here for a pill to do just that.

"I don't even know who I am, so how can whatever he sees in me be real?"

"Okay, pick another card to find out who you are."

I gave him the fishy eyeball. "Why does this work?"

"Is it working?"

"Oy." I put the cards down.

"The thing is, Peter, if I asked you who you are, you wouldn't tell me. And if I told you who you are, you wouldn't believe me. Which is all good."

"It *is?*"

"Sure. You belong to you. You don't owe me any information. And I'm certainly not the expert on you—*you* are. With me so far?" He paused to look at me, and I nodded, unable to speak for the relief that welled up in me, an ocean wave from my throat to my eyes. "So what we're doing here is playing a game with no wrong answers. Whatever card you pick, you're going to see something true, because the meaning comes from something you already know on some level. The Tarot is designed for this, but you can do it with anything—a music video, a magazine, what you see in the clouds. The world is full of help if you're willing to ask."

"I don't want to become one of those guys who finds CIA conspiracy theories in the daily crossword puzzle."

"'Those guys' are usually scared. So should we all be, a little. It's a scary world. They're right that they've lost their keys, they're just looking under the wrong lamppost. But we can try something else now, if you're not into the cards."

I made theatrical hand passes over the deck to lighten the mood, pushing away the hope and fear of some portentous revelation. "Abracadabra, hocus pocus, who am I?" *Nine of Rods*, answered the shiny rectangle of cardstock in my hand. A grim dark-haired youth guarding, or being guarded by, an uneven palisade of those tall mutant plants.

"Tell me something I *don't* know," I muttered.

"All right, what don't you know?" Sid asked, too chipper for his own good. "What's behind that fence?"

I glanced at the clock. Only ten minutes left. Good. "Knowing shit is overrated. We have this idea, this myth, that the brave person should open the box, eat the apple, fight the power. But what if I just want to be happy finally—get on with my fucking life?"

Sid didn't seem inclined to argue. He was so unlike Dad. You're screwing up my transference here, Sid. "How can I help you with that? What's the first thing you need?"

I closed my eyes to think. The first image that arose was the Zenith TV from my parents' bedroom, a hot-breathing clunky plastic box with rabbit ears that we had to jiggle and slap when the picture zigzagged into repeating frames. I needed a "vertical hold" knob for my brain.

"I don't know what'll fix this, but I want to feel more...100% *here*. I'm exhausted from having weird dreams, and during the day, sometimes I have these moments where I get lost in—I don't know what to call it—places I've already been, that aren't here? Memories of stressful shit, but more distracting than they should be. I can't just think it through and snap out of it because it's talking right in my ear. Not literally," I hastened to add. I didn't hear voices telling me I was Napoleon. *Yet.*

Sid nodded and wrote something on a pad. "I can start you on a low-dose anti-anxiety prescription. But we're going to keep talking about this too. Deal?"

"Deal," I said, rising to leave. We both knew it was early yet, but he let it be. He shook my hand firmly as if we'd accomplished something, as if he was pleased with me already.

"Free bonus question," he surprised me. The good old "Columbo" move, the parting shot. "Think about this for next time: what are you most anxious about? As they say in the private-eye novels, no problem is too big or too small."

"You're not taking this seriously, Sid. I think that's a defense mechanism."

He laughed, for real, and so did I. On impulse, I pulled one last card. *King of Pentacles* showed a sensitive-looking man with a goatee. A horned beast, bull or ox, loomed behind him, against a pleasant blue and white sky. The pattern on the king's tunic made a strange trick of perspective, sloping inward like a tunnel, over which floated a huge red circle containing a five-pointed star. An occult symbol I recognized from hair metal videos on MTV "Headbangers' Ball"—cliché but still disturbing, in this strange new world of therapy where no messages could be dismissed.

"There's a hole in his heart and the devil's inside him," I thought aloud, cringing inwardly as the words sounded like wannabe Ozzy Osbourne lyrics. The counselor opened his mouth, but I cut him off. "Well, thanks for a really weird time. Maybe next week we should stick to talking about my mother, right? See you then!"

"Keep a journal!" Sid called after me. Didn't he realize I had no privacy anymore? I couldn't even keep my old high-tops unless I convinced Jule that they were fashionably distressed. It was like fucking a televangelist. Every time he laid hands on me, he hoped for a miracle cure.

[Placement Report on Tyler Wick]

Dr. Marla Fuller, Staff Psychologist, Gateway House
January 28, 1997

Tyler Wick is a 15-year-old African-American/
Dominican youth who has resided at Gateway since
September 1996 en route to a permanent foster
placement. He has applied himself consistently to
his GED coursework and should be prepared to pass
the test next winter if he keeps to his current
schedule of progress. Tyler has a quick mind and a
talent for drawing. While he continues to struggle
with displacing his difficult emotions onto an
invented female character, he has made progress in
therapy in speaking directly about his parents'
deaths instead of escaping into his fetishes. The
staff here are in agreement that he is ready for the
more consistent attachment and authority structure
that a family can provide.

Since November, Tyler has been building a
relationship with Dr. Horace and Aletha Becker, an
African-American couple in their 40s with previous
foster parent experience and a stable income from
Dr. Becker's position as a radiologist at Columbia-
Presbyterian. Recently another candidate entered the
picture, referred by Tyler's Gateway staff mentor,
Peter Edelman. Kevin Clarke, 28, is the African-
American community liaison at the AIDS nonprofit
Housing Works. He lives with his boyfriend, DeWayne
Marshall, 31, a public high school science teacher.
Tyler appears to prefer this match because Mr.
Marshall shares some of his proclivities for cross-
dressing.

Though it is commendable for them to offer him
a home on short notice, Tyler's caseworker from
the Office of Children and Family Services and the
Gateway counselors agree that Mr. Marshall's health
prognosis, as a person with HIV, is too uncertain
to add the responsibility of caring for a troubled
teenager. Even Mr. Edelman, who proposed the match,
is on record as saying that it is in Tyler's best
interest to be placed in a family as soon as
possible.

    Therefore, we recommend that the court approve the
Beckers as Tyler's foster parents.

[Excerpt from emails]

Sent: February 8, 1997, 9:03 PM
From: missionxbrent@aol.com
To: jselkirkphoto@aol.com

Hi Julian—

All heck has broken loose around here! I wish you'd come visit again!

Your dad's campaign is barreling along. Too early for meaningful polls, but folks are voting with their wallets, if the response to our last two begging letters is any indication. I see some real changes in him since we started working together. He's taking the high road in this GOP primary fight, sticking to the issues, even though the other side has gone for the personal smears. It's stressful. We've been praying together a lot.

Mission X-Force has a gig coming up on March 9 at the Prayer Warriors Conference at North Point Community Church in Alpharetta. It's like Promise Keepers but cooler—BMX bike stunts, wilderness team challenges, rad metal music—we're opening for this band called Gladiatorz that won a Dove Award last year. And great preaching, of course. Supposed to be 2,000 men there. Mr. Selkirk and Carter are going. Any chance you'll want to check it out? Could be some great photo-ops! The lead singer of Gladiatorz does this awesome bit on "Thumbs Down for the Devil" where he fights off a flaming lion hologram with the cross on his guitar neck. I don't know how they can do splits in those leather pants, though. With God all things are possible :)

I'm not trying to change your beliefs, whatever they are now, okay? I just have a feeling this could be a nice moment for your family to start fresh, and I wouldn't want you to miss it. We were such lonely kids. I don't know about you, but I'd have done anything to have more bonding time with my dad. When I see some of the families in our Mission X-Force audience, if I'm not careful I could start blubbering like a girl, which is a bad idea when you're balancing a bathtub on your head.

Love, Brent

Sent: February 9, 1997, 2:40 PM
From: jselkirkphoto@aol.com
To: missionxbrent@aol.com

Dear brother in Christ,

You are so gay that your balls are going to marry each other and have babies.

Thanks for thinking of me, but Peter and I will be baptizing ourselves in the salty waters of South Beach that weekend. He and his sidekick have finished the first issue of their comic book and now we're hand-selling it to gay bookstores and nerd conventions wherever we travel. I can send you a few copies to drop off at Outwrite Books next time you're cruising Piedmont Park for Love In Action recruits.

Not that anyone in the state of Georgia cares what I think, but this campaign is stressing me out too, and I don't even give a shit who wins. Did you sign off on that fundraising email that mentioned Carter and Lulu but not me? What kind of passive-aggressive bullshit was that? Reagan had a gay son, you know. Anyway, all you did was show the other side the crack in the family armor, because now I'm being hounded by opposition research flacks who want me to dish about Daddy's wife-beating hobby. I'm not getting involved, of course. If Mama finally wants to be safe, she knows who she can call, and it ain't a politician.

Good luck with your big show. You're an annoying asshole, but you work hard to do impossible things, which I sort of respect. I hope you convict many people of their sins.

Break a leg (preferably Daddy's)— Julian

Sent: February 9, 1997, 8:12 PM
From: missionxbrent@aol.com
To: jselkirkphoto@aol.com

Hey Julian,

I wasn't involved with that mailing. The fundraising guy usually bases them on Mr. Selkirk's speeches to Rotary Clubs and stuff, but I don't know what he might have edited out. Sorry it bothered you. I'd have thought you would prefer it that way, anyhow. Since you don't believe what we believe, why would you want to be included?

Anyhoo, the Prayer Warriors Conference would be a great chance for you all to reconnect. Carter's speaking at a workshop about 12-Step. I'll put aside tickets for you and Peter, just in case.

Love, Brent

Sent: February 9, 1997, 8:23 PM
From: jselkirkphoto@aol.com
To: missionxbrent@aol.com

"We"? I wasn't aware that I made you a member of this family when I stuck my finger in your ass after the 1989 homecoming game.

When was the last time you got some?

Sent: February 9, 9:07 PM
From: missionxbrent@aol.com
To: jselkirkphoto@aol.com

I sucked a guy off at a rest stop on I-75 in October of last year. Before that, my last sexual sin was watching pornography in the hotel when we toured July 4th weekend. Everybody who matters knows about this already. We keep a journal for Love In Action and show it to our accountability partners. It was my program sponsor's idea for me to join the American Values Network and help your daddy. He thought it would give me some positive role models and new friends. I do stupid things when I'm lonely.

Julian—I don't get why you, of all people, are jealous of me?? Anything I have, you could have if you wanted it.

Love, Brent

“WHAT DID DAD SAY was so important that we have to give up the first nice Sunday in, like, months?” I kvetched.

Julian pulled his cashmere scarf higher. “This is nice weather to you Yankees? How sad.”

“C’mon, it’s 40 degrees out, the sky is blue—well, mostly—and we haven’t both had a weekend off in so long. We could have gone rollerblading, cooked brunch together, I don’t know—what are couples supposed to do when they’re not working or fucking?”

“Watch sports? Buy napkins at Gracious Home? Whatever you want, darling. I’ve never had a normal relationship. Everyone in New York seems to be in their own private time zone.”

I pushed his arm playfully. “To hear you talk, you’d think you hadn’t been living here for almost seven years.”

“Yeah, funny about that, it’s what I dreamed of, when I was a tragically cool kid in the suburbs, but sometimes I wish it would just *slow down*.”

“We don’t have to go to—whatever this is, today.” I stopped short, causing a hiccup in the pedestrian flow along West 14th Street. “Look, there’s a Goodwill. I have a sudden urge to buy something with zippers all over it. Help me make good choices.”

Reliable as a cat when it hears the electric can opener, Jule pivoted, but then shook his head. “Ten minutes tops, okay? Ada was pretty insistent. She called me like four times in a row.”

“Oh jeez, this was *Ada’s* idea? You should’ve said so. I’d have bought a crash helmet. Or a ticket to Timbuktu.”

“For someone who works with mental teenagers, you’re pretty freaked out by your stepmama. Is she actually evil, or just, you know, one of those madcap Jazz Age characters who dances on tabletops?”

“Ada annoys me because she’s all energy and no substance, like a—a sandstorm. You’re going along your way when this force out of nowhere sweeps you up, spins you around, and drops you into a glittering oasis that always turns out to be a dry heap of dirt.”

“I know the feeling.”

“Who are *you* talking about?”

“Most people, actually. But it’s illegal to marry dogs, so we learn to live with our disappointing species. Come on, let me buy you something before we go.”

"Can you find me a leather collar?"

He reached up and patted my head. "I promise, we'll cut through Christopher Street on our way home."

I was not a very good dog. I wasn't loyal, obedient, or purebred, though I could be persuaded to wear a leash and a muzzle. As Jule went to pay for something he wouldn't show me, I practiced the anti-stress tricks I'd been learning from weekly sessions with Sid. Savor three deep breaths. Count backwards by tens. Feel my feet on the floor. Remember where I am. It's safe here.

Maybe Julian was right that I dwelled too much on the helpless chaos of the past. Holding grudges was the Jewish version of mindfulness, an outdated survival skill from forty years in the desert with no signposts except the mirage of how things ought to be. I had a real future to aim for instead. The terrifying time slippages had stopped since I went on the anxiety meds. They made me feel a little bloated, a small price to pay, but another reason to be grumpy that Jule and I couldn't spend today doing something vigorous.

We both made an extra effort to be cheerful to each other for the remainder of our walk. I figured something about his family had put him in a sour mood, so he was hoping to play house with Nathan and Ada. Jule came off bitchy a lot of the time because he was so sentimental underneath. He pretended to despise his father (though not enough to air his dirty laundry to the *Atlanta Journal-Constitution*), but deep down he wanted that Hollywood ending where tragic flaws become lovable quirks and everyone realizes they need each other. He'd never admit it but I could tell from the shows we watched. The guy never missed a Dickens episode on Masterpiece Theatre. Living with someone reveals a lot of odd surprises. "I'm interested in the costumes" was the Julian version of reading *Playboy* for the articles.

At the door of Nathan's brownstone, I rehearsed my new attitude. Accept people for who they are—even people who might flip from Tigger to Eeyore mid-sentence. Live in the present. Nothing else is real.

All these good intentions flew straight down the road to you-know-where when Ada flung open the door and a crowd behind her yelled at me, "Surprise! Happy birthday!"

My heartbeat choked me and my body felt numb. For a moment I couldn't distinguish the faces in the room. A party horn's strangled bleat, popping balloons, and the lurching start of inevitably off-key singing blended into a rush of noise. The tremor in my leg turned out to be my pager vibrating. Everybody wanted a piece of me at the same time, as usual. I didn't look at the screen. Instead I shot daggers at Julian. Had he been in on the plot? Didn't he know me *at all*?

Jule also looked surpised, and irritated—at me, of all people—which he quickly covered up with a big smile at our hostess. Ada adjusted her paper "Star Wars" party hat and hurried us into the living room, where a dozen members of our extended family prepared to slice into Darth Vader's buttercream-frosted head. I drew in a deep breath, preparing to extinguish his crown of candles, thinking that my only wish was to get through the day without murdering anyone, which was maybe not Darth's specialty.

A feeling of defeat made my eyes prickle. I craved Julian's touch to reassure me that I was his mutt and I didn't have to win a show ribbon for anybody. But he was apparently mad about something that I didn't have the strength to care about. Also, I kind of wanted some cake. So I sighed, gathered another breath, let its power swell my chest, and blasted out my silent will to the universe.

I want to be heard.

And so did my pager, which buzzed against my hip a second time. I stole a glance while Ada was busy passing plates of cake. Mom's number. We'd had a quiet lunch two days ago on my real birthday, agreeing not to make a fuss about it in front of the Gateway kids, who could have complicated feelings about family celebrations. As did I. A burger at Big Nick's and a gift certificate to Tower Records were more than enough for me, Mom knew. So this call was probably work-related.

As a freelancer who traveled a lot, Jule had given in to the craze for the new Motorola mobile phones, but I wasn't ready for the on-call lifestyle. I pulled him aside from refereeing a debate between Dad and Cousin Ben about the O.J. Simpson acquittal. I only had to overhear a few words to know Nathan would come down on the side of correct procedure, Ben on the side of correct results. Less filling, tastes great. Meanwhile the dead stayed dead.

"Babe, can I borrow your phone? Emergency at Gateway."

"What else is new?" He tossed it to me.

I locked myself in the bathroom, the only quiet spot downstairs. Mom's phone at her Gateway office forwarded to the weekend intake/security guy's desk after six rings. He said I should meet her at the Natural History Museum as soon as possible. It was a popular spot for our foster kids' family outings, since it was on our subway line and housed many gross and scary marvels to delight the toughest boys. The desk duty guy wasn't authorized to give details, but I assumed a supervised visit had gone sour.

Julian was waiting for me in the hallway, mimosa glass in hand. "Hey, party boy. You're missing out on Goth Pictionary. Ada just tried to draw Freddy Krueger."

I motioned for him to hand over his drink, and took a gulp. "You're having a good time?"

"Should I not be?"

"You should've told me this was happening."

"Dummy. How would I have known, when someone doesn't even bother to tell me it's his birthday?"

So that explained his bad attitude. "I don't like making a big *megillah* about it. Somehow it always winds up being about other people's feelings instead of mine."

"Is there ever going to be an okay way to do something nice for you? I buy you clothes, you complain I'm trying to change you. I play diplomat with your family, you act like I'm disloyal. Do you just want to be alone?"

"No! I want to be with you...*just* you." Sweating, my heart racing, I craved another pill but it was too soon. Julian let me put my arms around him. How could he not see that this was enough for me? Not presents, not the spotlight, only his centering touch. "But...please don't hate me...I have to duck out now. Sounds like a foster family visit went sideways."

"Not like this one." Jule pulled away.

"I'm sorry."

He put on his party face again, the resilient smile that reminded me of his mother. "Do what you gotta do, Batman. But you know, for a guy who claims to crave independence, you keep choosing jobs where someone else snaps their fingers and you jump."

The museum entrance on Central Park West was mobbed, as was typical for the weekends. Children clambered over the triumphal bronze statue of Teddy Roosevelt on horseback followed by servile Indians. I needed a breather before I tackled the line at the information desk to see if Mom had left me a message about our meetup spot. As I'd done so many times over the years, I sought out the quiet dimness of the Hall of Birds, drifting back into the 19th century civic majesty of polished marble floors and wide glass diorama windows. Nothing changed in these portals to unspoiled worlds, not since my 1970s childhood, not since the age of the great white hunter-scientists who had shot, preserved, and re-strung these birds in unending flight against a painted blue sky. My falcons were still there, nesting on a sheer cliffside of the Palisades above the Hudson River, three scruffy chicks and a scatter of prey bones, the mother diving down with fresh meat. Impossible not to feel a slight imaginary breeze, the vertigo of real distances. My breath, in and out, expanded into peace.

"This was always your favorite spot."

I jumped at the voice behind me. My mother rose from her bench by the side wall, tucking into her handbag the paperback she'd been reading to pass the time. This also was too much like the old days: me lost in a telepathic conversation with lumps of sawdust and feathers, Mom deep into a Jewish immigrant saga by Howard Fast or Belva Plain.

"Mom! Where's the fire?"

"No fire. Your father's wife is plotting a surprise party for you, can you believe it, and I knew you'd want to get out of it but you'd feel guilty unless you thought it was a work emergency."

"That...was evil, Mom."

"But true?"

I sighed. "But true. Ah, Julian's going to be so pissed at me. I left him all alone there to play Pin the Tail on Chewbacca."

"Oy, you went already? I tried to warn you, but I guess you and your boyfriend sleep so late you don't answer the phone."

That was indeed an accurate euphemism for the morning routine in the new Selkirk-Edelman household. My cheeks reddened. "I'm surprised Ada invited you. I mean, surprised in a good way. Jule thinks it's time we all got over it. Is that okay to say?"

Mom sniffed. "I'm over it. That doesn't mean I have to sit around and have cocktails with the two of them like one of those wife-swapping Martian novels you used to read."

I snickered when I got the reference. "Oh, right, Heinlein. *Stranger in a Strange Land.*"

"It was strange, all right. Ah well, I guess mothers can't be expected to understand all of their children's interests."

"You understand me pretty well."

She smiled and patted my back. "Do you forgive me for finagling you here? Maybe you don't want to stay?"

"Nah, what's done is done. I'd look dumb if I went back now. Let's pay our respects to the grizzly bears."

We strolled through the monumental halls of taxidermy devoted to North American mammals. At the water fountain by the elevator, I gulped my anti-anxiety pill, but not fast enough to dodge Mom's notice. She must have honed her observation skills catching the Gateway kids with contraband.

"What's that? Are you sick?"

I tried to be charitable about her prying. Everyone who loved someone gay in these plague years developed a certain paranoia at the sight of mystery meds. "I'm fine. Just stressed. My new therapist prescribed these to help me calm down and get back on track."

Mom hugged me a little too long. It was kind of embarrassing at my age, but what could I do? When the elevator door opened, I stepped away and wedged myself on the other side of a woman's baby carriage.

The gemstones and minerals rooms were even darker and quieter than the bird tableaux. Tourists unconsciously hushed, as though in a cave or church. Narrow pathways led between vertical glass cases where crystals of misty pink quartz and glittering fool's-gold bloomed from rough chunks of rock. I didn't think I'd ever outgrow the wish to touch them, to join my body to the earth's magic that the city's cement and asphalt kept at a distance.

I caught up with my mother in her usual place, adoring the outsized star sapphire and diamond necklaces on velvet. "Instead of popping those pills, maybe you should stop working so many jobs. You're always running from Gateway to your gym classes and back again. Even when you're not at work, it's hard to get ahold of you. No wonder you're anxious. As Momma used to say, you can't dance at two weddings."

Three, actually—those hours when I didn't pick up the phone, more often than not, I was writing or looking for places to sell *The Poison Cure*. When the happy pills and deep breathing failed, when I gasped awake at 2 AM and gazed at my naked, sated lover sleeping soundly beside me, the only thing that stopped me from rushing out to Bernie's dungeon to be whipped into guilty oblivion was to pick up a pencil and my storyboard sketchpad and write furiously on the couch till I conked out.

"What can I do—I need the money. I've got a fancy man now who likes his vodka and cufflinks."

"Does he, really."

"No, I'm kidding! Jule would totally support me if I asked. I'd feel bad not pulling my own weight."

"I'm sorry we can't pay you more, boychick. Our year-end report just came back from the accountants, and...ugh. Those schmoes in Washington, I don't care if they're Democrats or Republicans, they all think 'welfare' is a dirty word." She cast a longing glance at the sparkling ropes of gems behind glass. "Too bad you're not a jewel thief."

"Maybe in the next comic book. 'Robin Hood and his Mom'!"

She laughed. "It's the kids I feel bad for. Not so much the parents, they made their bed. But someone else always has to pay."

"Don't be discouraged, Mom. You're doing great work. 'Whoever saves one life...'"

"'...saves a whole world.' I know." She shook herself out of the mood. "There is a full-time job opening up in April, when Sheena goes off to work for Blue Cross." Another good one lost to the private sector, her expression seemed to say. "Mostly administrative, but you'd have stable hours and benefits, so you could take night classes toward a social worker license."

I had the sensation that Sid and I had dubbed "the bees"—a buzzing, swarming energy in my chest that I routinely swallowed down or smoked into sleepiness with ganja. *Befriend your bees*, Sid would nag me. *Find out where they want to fly.* Then he'd launch into some trippy extended metaphor about the ecosystem and how the world would starve without pollinators. He was a nut but that was okay, it put us on a level playing field.

"Mom," I exhaled what felt like my last breath, "don't take this wrong, but that scenario sort of freaks me out."

"Birthday blues, not a kid anymore? Health insurance is too bourgeois?"

"Hell no...after you watch your best friend die from the common cold... 'rebel without a cause' doesn't feel like an option anymore." Not to freak Mom out, but a condom or a 401(k) couldn't make safety my birthright. How long would Julian and I stay together, if we were only exclusive out of fear? "You all mean well and I'm grateful, but I feel like everybody wants a piece of me. I—I'm tired of doing jobs that are important to other people."

"You need to *find yourself*?" Dangerous ground here. In Mom's lexicon, that was baby-boomer slang for adultery, my father's side hustle that he'd taken full-time. Oddly enough, Mom was very fond of Prue. "Fruit of the poisonous tree" didn't apply in her court of law.

"Well, Buddhists say the self is an illusion, so maybe not that exactly. But I have to find...something." A clear sky above it all. A perch on the Palisades, like my stuffed falcons, that I (and every kid at the museum) secretly believed came alive when the doors locked behind the humans at closing time.

"Go meditate, then. You look like you need the rest. I hope Julian doesn't keep you out all night at the clubs."

"Ha! Our life should be so exciting. He's another one who's working too many hours. Fashion is a mean business. This month's cover photo is next month's birdcage liner."

"I do enjoy those magazines," Mom confessed. "They're like a fairy tale. So long as you know that's all they are. Poor girls throwing up in the bathroom to be skinny. Even you used to do that. Is that a homosexual thing?"

"What, me? I thought I was legendary for not caring about my appearance.

At least compared to other homosexuals," I ribbed her. Mom's terminology usually lagged a decade.

"Never mind. It's good you don't remember. You're perfect just the way you are. Let's go have a club sandwich at Cafe 82 like old times."

"Good plan. I should stop by the gift shop first, though. I owe Julian a peace offering for skipping out on our day off."

But the hospital-soap odor of the museum men's room sent a sharp fragment of memory into my brain, a *déjà vu* of pills, vomit, fear—intense but quickly gone. Once more I was caught in the slippage between lives, the one I knew and the one that other people placed me in, and I didn't know which one a sane person would choose.

J ULIAN'S—*OUR*—APARTMENT smelled like burnt grease. I heard the clash of pots under running water, but I guess I missed the smoke alarm. "Everything all right, babe?" I called out.

Jule emerged from the kitchen, wearing a sheepish expression and a joke apron (my move-in gift from Stan and Frank) that read "May I Suggest the SAUSAGE" with a cartoon hand pointing downward. "I thought, how hard can it be to stir-fry vegetables, but the teriyaki sauce turned into some kind of *tar*."

"Aw, you didn't have to make anything. I'm so sorry I bailed on you." I kissed him.

"I still wish you'd told me, but I shouldn't have dragged you somewhere you didn't want to go. Consider this your belated birthday dinner—which is probably not going to improve your opinion of the day." He tapped my butt playfully. "There's some meat in the oven."

"Is that a compliment on my figure?"

"It's a free-range chicken—well, formerly free-range, hopefully it's not going anywhere now, but you'd better check on it." Jule cleared a spot on our mail-cluttered foyer table for my museum shopping bag. "Heavy. Did your mama buy you a bowling ball after you rescued the helpless orphans? What was the crisis anyway?"

I sighed. More truth, more bees, let out to fertilize or sting. "False alarm. That's why I feel bad about today. She heard about the party and she was trying to give me an excuse to skip it."

Jule frowned. "Because she doesn't trust you to make your own decisions?"

"I can't say no to something I don't know is happening, right? Yeah, Mom is not totally clear on the concept of my adulthood, but she's okay. She is who she is. Reliable." I took his hand. "Like I want to be. I'm really trying."

"Me too, darlin'. I hope I haven't become too Betty Crocker for you. Do you miss the shallow slut you fell in love with?"

"You're still pretty shallow."

He beamed. "Wait till you see what I bought you. But first, I have to baste those burning thighs."

I followed him to supervise. An eat-in kitchen—with a window, a double rarity in Manhattan—was wasted on that man.

"Hey, do you think I should take a full-time administrative job at Gateway and quit everything else?"

"Lordy, no, within a month you'll be faking your own death and sailing for Shanghai. You'd be bored behind a desk. You need to move, and write. Don't you think so?"

"I do, actually. But I'm not used to following my gut." I leaned against him, enjoying his steady warmth. "Do you ever feel like the people in your life are like pieces of a mirror—they each reflect something true about you, but only a piece?"

Jule considered this. "I don't think I'm as complicated as all that. But what do I know? And more importantly, do we have time for a quickie before dinner?"

"Oh, I want more from you than that. I could give you your present, though."

"For me? What's the occasion?"

"Just being a good guy. No, the *best*."

He carefully lifted out and unwrapped the hefty tissue-papered lump from the museum shopping bag, with an admiring gasp when it opened into two halves of a cleaved rock, their concave inner surfaces studded with amethyst crystals.

"They're geode bookends. Don't forget the card, too."

He found the creamy cardstock slip with typed facts about the geode. I watched his face as he read what I'd written on the back: *For Julian—it might seem like my heart is made of stone, but inside are treasures just for you. Love, Peter.*

Jule closed his eyes, letting the card dangle from his hand. Was he sad? Disappointed? Embarrassed to tell me how lame my poetry was?

I waited, till I cracked. "What's the matter?"

"Give me a sec." He turned away, took a deep breath, passed a hand over his face. When he turned back, he'd managed a smile. "It's sublime, darling, thank you."

"Nuh-uh. It's not the Best Supporting Actress statuette. What'd I get wrong? Do you hate purple? Does it remind you of an ex?"

"It's perfect. I mean it. Thank you." He blinked hard. I wiped his eyes with a rough stroke of my thumb. He flicked his head, shaking me off.

"From the king of bullshit to the queen—I've got no right to call you out, but I will anyway. Last chance."

"Babe, this is going to sound mean."

"Whatever."

"You know how much I long to hear you say...the kind of stuff you wrote here. But it's so unlike you, I'm sorry, that's the mean part, or I'm being a needy bitch and you hate that, but I get worried it isn't real. That you're only saying what boyfriends are supposed to say...or apologizing for something I don't want to know about."

I opened my mouth to protest, but remembered my dungeon adventures. Jule might not know the details but he could recognize the feeling of divided attention, invisible walls. "Yeah, sometimes I fake it till I make it, but that's not your fault. My love for you is always there, even when I can't feel it." My eyes welled up.

So did his. "You're really having a hard time lately, huh." At last he embraced me. I was heady with relief, like waking from a bad dream. Saying the L-word hadn't killed me. What else was I capable of?

I led him over to sit on the couch and took his hands between mine. "Jule, I've got to be honest with you."

"Uh-oh. Should I turn the oven down, or stick my head in it?"

"Nothing like that! I'm just, I've been, uh...I think, I think something's wrong with my head. More than I've told you."

Anxiety tightened his voice. "Are you having headaches? Double vision?" I guessed he was thinking of DeWayne, who was undergoing tests for a possible tumor related to his HIV.

"No, nothing hurts. It's my mind, not my brain—leaving aside *that* philosophical question." He didn't appreciate my nerdy joke, so I pushed myself to continue. "I don't remember events that everyone says happened. And I remember other things that I don't want to, that don't make any sense, coming up at weird times, so strong that I forget where I am." *Or who*, I didn't say. "I feel like a Philip K. Dick character—like I'm going to find out I'm not the real Peter, I'm a cyborg with an imperfectly loaded personality chip."

Julian put his hands on his knees and sat back. "Whew. That's...intense. What does Sid say?"

"I haven't told him, exactly."

"Why the hell not? This sounds serious. *I* don't know what to do."

"What if he has me locked up?"

My boyfriend searched my face for a long moment, with those beautiful dark eyes that could discern a pixel's worth of mood variation between aqua and turquoise, weighing the chance that I was Mr. Hyde on an amnesiac killing spree. "I promise I'll never let that happen."

I let out the air I'd been holding in my chest. "I should make you my healthcare proxy, then."

He seemed equally glad to be back on the solid ground of the mundane. "Yes, let's both do that. This queen of denial doesn't even have one. I assume my family would bury me just to keep up appearances."

"Mine was Kevin, but he's got his hands full with DeWayne's situation."

"Fuck, if it's not one thing it's another. No wonder you're on the panic pills. Me, I fill all my prescriptions at Captain Morgan's."

"We're going to have to have *that* discussion, too."

"Damn—I think I liked you better when you didn't talk about your feelings."

"Most people do."

Jule touched my cheek. "No, I'm kidding. I'm sorry. Whatever this is, we'll deal with it together. It's not fair of me to expect a break from—" He spread his hands wide, shrugged with his usual gracious resignation, running out of words for the threats that hovered over our community like insidious, invisible radioactive fallout.

"Well, maybe I can take your mind off it for a little while…?" I massaged his thigh.

"You think you're excited now, check out what I bought you this morning."

He passed me the small plastic bag from the thrift shop. I was not expecting the contents: two studded black leather cuffs connected by a chain that was perfect for wrapping around a bedpost. "You found handcuffs at Goodwill?"

"New York is a weird place."

I hugged him hard. "Thank you for letting me be…whatever the hell I am."

"Happy birthday, Mr. President," he replied in a breathy Marilyn Monroe lisp, and sashayed into the kitchen to finish dinner.

[EXCERPTS FROM A DIARY KEPT BY BARBARA HAUSER EDELMAN, 1981-83]

11/19/81: I hate hospitals. Everyone does. Even doctors, I bet. They're just in it for the money. Solving puzzles. Does Nathan care about justice or only the sound of his own voice? This is his fault for calling Peepers fat. Peter, I mean—he says he's too big for the nickname. Eleven feels like nothing to a mother. Oh G-d, please let him get older, so old that he has a big white beard like Papa when I'm long dead.

When he wakes up I'm going to smack his face. I never heard of a boy making himself throw up that much. We thought it was just the flu. But Dr. Berkowitz said alcohol, and pills too— He's a kid. It doesn't make sense.

I'm putting him in the Jewish youth group. He needs more wholesome friends that don't sit in basements all night playing dice and drawing monsters on graph paper. Miriam Dorfman's son lost 15 pounds this summer at Camp Ramaz from the hiking and swimming every day. Not that Peepers isn't perfect the way he is. But it'll get Nathan off his back for being "soft". I wonder if he means something else by that. It's all very well for his friends Lew and Dennis, they've got their pinkies in the air, if you know what I mean. But not our son. Leave him alone. He's too young, he shouldn't worry about it.

11/21/81: Peter's home and he'd better accept he's grounded for life. I don't know who gave him the bright idea to putz around with alcohol but we're going to watch who he socializes with from now on. No more trips alone on the subway with Ben. Nathan's sister is going to be offended but, if the shoe fits—

I told Nathan it would help if he also didn't disappear overnight randomly like he does. He promised but I know that pulled-away look on his face. What's so important to him? I'm not an idiot. Men want more of it than women do.

I only wish I'd had a daughter. A little sister for Peter. We would be more of a family then. I'm 36, it's not too late. I know what he'll say, you don't want to risk another miscarriage. G-d damn men. They'll never understand. Mother-love is in your whole body, you bleed for it, you die for it, and if you're lucky and have a child then you have to watch him walk away with nobody seeing that your guts are still connected to him, out there, unprotected.

3/12/82: The youth group has been great for Peter, I was right. They're teaching him to play basketball, lift weights, even. Hiking when the weather is nice, later. I swear he grows overnight. One day I won't recognize him. I'll think, who is that man with the hairy chest and muscles? Fuzz on his face already. He's going to be a big bear like Papa. He got mad when I mentioned it, won't take his shirt off around me anymore. He never had tantrums as a child. Saving it up, I guess. Anger and sex, that's what you get for becoming a man.

My new co-worker, Sally, at the Office of Children and Family Services, is a lesbian. She says it isn't any easier. I think it makes her better with the kids, though. She doesn't look down on the girls or believe the baloney that the boys sling to get out of trouble. You know, I bet a lot of people don't realize it themselves when they're lying. What can you do about that?

I've taken on more hours now that Peter doesn't need me. Also going to the women's group at the synagogue, since I'm dropping him off there anyhow. It's not what I expected, not baking bread and teaching Bible stories. Last week we went to a protest march for affordable housing! Planning a trip to the Holy Land, just us, no families. It's a little crazy but I might tell Nathan I'm going. I haven't had an adventure since—well, never.

6/5/82: Oh my G-d, Jerusalem was amazing. I have chills. It's like stepping into the pages of the Bible. Time doesn't mean anything. The world is just beginning. So dusty, though, hot and noisy, everyone drives like a *meshuggenah*. I thought New Yorkers were tough. These women are soldiers. They don't sit home and kvetch that nobody needs them. They're saving lives, defending their little country against everyone who wants to wipe us out.

I'm going to try to be more grateful for my family. I'm too old to shoot people 5,000 miles away, all by myself. G-d put me here for a reason. Nathan and I have had our problems but we're devoted to making a home for our son. I could appreciate him more. Maybe now I'm doing interesting things, like he is, we can get excited about each other again.

I'm so bad, I left this book for him on the night table, with a *scene* bookmarked. It's something called *The Valley of Horses* that they sent me from Book of the Month Club. Really long, but I learned a lot about Neanderthals and Cro-Magnons. Made me miss being out in the countryside, in Israel. Then all of a sudden there's a bit where these priestesses are showing this boy how to have intercourse for the first time, with everyone in town watching, to teach him how to treat women right. There was a *lot* of detail. I don't know if anyone else was expecting that, but I wasn't. Wonder if the book club will get complaints. Probably from men—they don't like thinking they aren't born knowing everything.

7/26/82: We could've had a nice day. Peter scored the winning basket at his youth group game. I couldn't help it, I was excited and I kissed him, but he pushed me away. Nathan didn't even tell him to be polite. Well, don't invite us to Family Day if you're ashamed of your family. I'm so tired when I think of the rest of my life like this, watching great things happen and sitting on my hands.

The welfare mothers on our caseload have chipped in together to rent a plot in the community garden on Avenue B. Sally and I helped organize it. A little late in the season, but we put some flowers in. Marigolds and pink and purple petunia flats that we found for cheap in a Korean store by 25th Street. Perked right up once we put them in the ground. Everyone was happy as children to see those bright colors, like a surprise party in the middle of a trash heap. If they manage to follow through long enough, we can try tomatoes next year. I'd like to drag some of that Israeli sunshine over here. On the kibbutz we toured, they had eggplants the size of bombs.

1/30/83: Doing my own taxes this year, so proud of myself. Ever since I saw that segment on women entrepreneurs on Good Morning America, I've been thinking I don't even know enough about how our family runs. It's not the same world from Papa and Mama, where her job was to raise us and volunteer for everything a rabbi's wife could possibly do.

There was the sweetest little black girl came through our office, three years old, with all those ponytails like they have. No one but a grandmother who's too sick with diabetes to keep raising her, so she's being taken in by a white foster couple in Mamaroneck. It's going to be strange for her to leave the city and her kind of people. I could make a good home for someone like that. I'm not going anywhere.

Nathan says we can't afford another. Looking at these bank statements, I can see that, but I can't figure out why. Sure, Peter outgrows his sneakers every five minutes, but we don't live fancy. What an absent-minded professor, as Papa used to say when Elaine was daydreaming too much.

Poor Elaine, one bowl of lentil soup from those Hare Krishna crazies and I don't have a sister anymore. To Papa and Mama she might as well be dead as be Swamee Rosebud Moonchild whatever.

Nathan's got our accounts mixed up with something from work— shouldn't these payments for "Trial witness support" have come out of his law office account? I don't know this "Ada Porter". We'd better not get audited. I'm not telling him I'm in over my head. I'll go through it one more time before I look for a new accountant.

2/8/83:

I don't know why he didn't tell me.
I don't know why he had to tell me.

[EXCERPT OF SCRIPT FOR *THE POISON CURE*, VOL. 2, ISSUE 2]

A series of three split-screen panels depict pairs of simultaneous events:

Left: Pharmakon, smiling and holding wine botle, at door of Challis' apartment.

Right: In a brown-tinted hallway with peeling paint, a balding man with a goatee and a sharp black suit bangs on an apartment door. He is scowling and holding a paper with "Eviction" in big black letters at the top.

Left: Pharmakon, inside the apartment, kneels on Challis' Indian blanket, pressing his mouth to the other's naked torso.

Right: Leering, the landlord gestures at his crotch, beckoning to the shocked teenage boy who is feeding his baby sister in a high chair. They are a Mexican-looking family with coppery skin, black hair, and a colorful picture of the Virgin of Guadalupe on the wall. From the doorway in the background, the children's mother stumbles on the scene, opens her mouth to scream and flings out her arm in a "stop!" gesture.

Left: Pharmakon and Challis showering together. The steam-dimmed light and blue-tinted tiles make their skin tones seem identical, with an underwater tinge. Challis' eyes are closed. Both are smiling, relaxed.

Right: The family and their meager pile of furniture huddle on the pavement in the rain. A police car has pulled up beside them. An armed

officer with the white letters "INS" across the chest of his black uniform heads toward the frightened mother.

Full-panel scene, Challis' apartment interior at night. Window shows full moon rising over skyline. Pharmakon stands up from the futon-bed as Challis, seated cross-legged, reluctantly lays down his guitar. Pharmakon's hooded sweatshirt veils his face in shadow.

Challis: *You still cold? You look a little sick.*

Pharmakon: *Long hours at the hospital, I guess. Sorry I have to go.*

C: (wry smile): *Good thing we both work nights.*

Pharmakon frowns slightly, turns away from kiss so his hooded face only brushes Challis' cheek.

Next panel switches scene to landlord reclining on bed, silver flask in hand, in well-furnished room with large TV. He is wearing suit pants, shirt, suspenders, no jacket or shoes. Speaking into the phone: *Yes, 90 minutes. And not the boy you sent last time. Someone...exotic.*

Next panel, split-screen again:

Left: Pharmakon, green-skinned, eyes wide open, lies beneath the waters of his bath.

Right: Challis reaches for his ringing phone.

Full-panel scene of landlord, hoisting unzipped pants, opening apartment door to a shadowy figure. From his height and greenish backlighting, one can guess it is Pharmakon.

Next panel, Challis in his bathroom, slicking back his hair. He has put on a tight-fitting shimmery shirt. On the countertop rests an open bag packed with a box of condoms, purple dildo, lube bottle. Next panel, Challis with messenger bag over his shoulder, knocking on apartment door. He looks surprised when it swings open at his touch.

Next panel, Challis walking carefully through darkened living room, searching for client. Groaning and rustling sounds come through the cracked-open bedroom door. Challis thinks: *Didn't tell me it was a three-way. I better get paid extra.*

A loud cry. Bedroom light goes out. Challis crouches behind leather sofa, watching bedroom door. Close-up on his face sweating with fear.

A tall figure crosses the room. Moonlight reveals Pharmakon's face, now normal skin color. Challis gasps.

C: *T-Tod? Did you—did you track me here?*

P (face distorted in shock): *Ryder—No!* (Glances toward bedroom, grabs Challis' arm) *Get out. Quick! You were never here.*

C: (pulling away with effort): *No. You know what I do. Either deal with it or fuck someone else. Don't try to save me by stealing my clients!*

P: *Save you?* (masking his confusion as an idea strikes him) *Yes, right, I'm sorry. No one's here, so let's go home and I'll make it up to you.*

C: *Bullshit. I heard you two going at it. Now I won't be able to pay my rent this week unless—* (As he speaks, he strides to the bedroom door and pushes it open.)

Next panel, the goateed man is lying dead on the bedroom floor, face distorted in a final spasm, a faint greenish glow outlining his splayed form.

C: *Oh my God, what happened to him?*

P: *Aneurysm. Let's <u>go</u>.*

C: *Are you kidding me? He's fucking <u>radioactive</u>.* (But he lets Pharmakon push him out the door and steer him through the apartment.)

P: *It'll subside in a moment. Look, these things happen. I've seen some weird shit at the hospital.*

The important thing is, let's not be around when somebody finds him.

Next panel, Pharmakon and Challis outside, in the shadow of the apartment building. Shielded from street view by dumpsters in an alley, Challis crouches with his back to the wall, hands on knees, sweating and seeming about to faint. Pharmakon steadies him with hand on shoulder.

Next panel, Challis straightens, looks searchingly into Pharmakon's face, which is sliced with sharply angled shadows from the moonlight and seems almost alien.

C: *What—what are you?*

P: *I'm your lover.*

C: *You brought me back to life...and you take life away, too.* (Backing away, face changing with fear and anger) *He isn't the first one, is he?!*

P: *Rapists. Child abusers. Killers. That's all they are. Why do you care that there's one less murderer's cock you have to suck?*

C: *What I do, doesn't hurt anyone! You don't get to judge, you...you...UGH.*

P: (seizing his shoulders, forcing their faces together): *I don't want to live this way! You have to understand...it's either them or me. Or you.*

C: (frightened now): *What do you mean? Are you in some kind of...* (dropping to a whisper) *vampire mafia?*

P: (downcast): *No. There's just me. And I don't know...what I am.*

C: *But you're...human, right?* (shaking his head) *I can't even believe what's happening right now. Last time I saw something like you, I was tripping on peyote with Granddad.*

P: *Maybe you can tell me what to do, then. Because I don't remember anything. Not how I got this way, or when...if...it'll ever end.*

Pharmakon's shoulders slump. A greenish tear slides down his face. Challis hesitates, then pulls him close. A dark cloud drifts over the moon.

C: *There's got to be a cure. If you promise to stop...we'll find another way.*

P: *I won't look the same. Soon...I won't be able to touch you at all.*

C: (half-smiling): *Hey, I have lots of ways to play safely. That's my job, right?*

P: (pulls back): *Then why didn't you protect yourself the first time?*

C: (shrugs): *Hazard pay. And before you ask—I'll be more careful, but I can't afford to quit.*

P: (turning away): *Neither can I.* (Challis grabs his shoulder, forcing eye contact.) *Ryder, don't you see? There's so much more at stake than just us. I <u>save</u> lives. In the hospital, and on the streets. People who have no one to help them but me. Crimes no one sees...or believes.*

C: *But how do you know they're guilty? What if you're wrong?*

P: (uncertain, ashamed expression): *I have dreams... visions. There's a goddess...*

C: (frowns, shakes head): *A lot of our people have been wiped out by true believers like you.*

P: *You think I'm just a monster.*

C: (embracing him again): *I want to keep you from becoming one. Please, Tod, let me help. You saved my life—now it's my turn to save yours.*

Like Hell when the Mets win the World Series, paradise sometimes freezes over. A rain cloud was following us around the Miami area today, not the best conditions for hawking comic books. Julian was being a very good sport, not grouching about the extra money we'd wasted on renting a pearly-white convertible when we couldn't put the top down. So far we'd dropped off consignment copies of *The Poison Cure*, Issue #1, at one genuine comics store, a New Age gift shop with a book called *Gay Astrology* in the window, and a combination adult bookstore and tobacco emporium. Sometimes a cigar is *really* not just a cigar.

"Hey, the Sunshine Galleria mall is coming up. Can we take a lunch break?" Jule asked.

"Should I drop you off and come back? There's one more store on my list."

"You just want a chance to drive the Pimp-Mobile."

"Nah, I'm having fun pretending you're Detective Sonny Crockett and I'm a Russian prostitute who's secretly a CIA double agent."

Jule smirked. "Typical Pisces."

I flipped through the zodiac love signs guide while Jule swung the car into the mall parking lot. *When Pisces get scared, they may lie about silly things to distance themselves from the relationship.* "I can't believe you bought this. What would your Sunday School teacher think?"

"It's only polite to purchase something, since we're asking the owner to sell your book, and I'm not spending twenty bucks for a rock to balance my chakras."

Once inside, the calm sterility of the mall softened my Marxist defenses against the addictive cycle of cranking out, craving, and discarding stuff. We sampled the Ruby Tuesday's all-you-can-eat salad bar and strolled past the display windows.

"Jule, what's this 'Tommy Bahama' brand—hot, or not?"

"Pretty hot right now. See something you like?"

I pointed out the short-sleeved button-down, made of breezy mint-green cloth like a Hawaiian shirt, with a pattern of small pink cephalopods waving their suckered tentacles. "That one would go over well at the comic-con tomorrow. Cthulhu goes on spring break!"

"Kuh-*who*?"

"H.P. Lovecraft's alien god. You don't know Cthulhu?"

"Does he want a personal relationship with me?"

"No, the whole point of the Mythos is that the gods don't give a shit about us, except if you accidentally wake them up, they'll eat you. So I guess you could say they have very strong interpersonal boundaries."

Jule raised an eyebrow. "I know all about your tentacle fetish. Go try it on, if you want."

"Problem is, Cthulhu's safeword is unpronounceable by human tongues." As was the jaw-dropping price of the shirt, I discovered. Julian wouldn't let that stop me. I liked what I saw in the mirror—someone unusual, daring, pushing the edge of good taste but able to laugh at himself. Maybe that could be me. "Nah, I can't afford this."

"Consider it your belated Valentine's present, or birthday present, or if you hate both of those, an early birthday present to myself because I get to look at you picking out clothes with an actual label."

"But you already covered this trip—"

"Flyer miles."

I hugged him. Florida was still the South and I didn't want to be harassed by rent-a-cops watching us kiss on security camera. Another problem it was easy to forget amid the sealed-in uniformity of chain stores. "I love your generosity, but don't you ever worry about saving up for the future?"

"Not to be a downer, but I don't count on it one way or the other. I've got skills, I won't starve. But you're here *now*. We can enjoy life now."

By the time we'd finished spending Julian's money, the sun had reappeared, promising a steamy afternoon. The moisture-heavy air wavered in the rays striking the blacktop. We tried keeping the car top down till Julian decided his hair was looking too sweaty. The last and biggest bookstore, which I'd saved for the end so I could refine my spiel, wouldn't take my comics at all, either on consignment or for free. I felt offended and disappointed to an absurd degree, considering I'd only embarked on my so-called writing career three months ago. Maybe Julian's approach to life was raising my expectations too painfully. He expected to be sipping champagne with supermodels in Paris, and he was more or less right. On the other hand, I believed we could live long enough to start a Roth IRA, which was a kind of optimism he could use more of.

Our evening accommodations were in the sort of place we would have called a "motor lodge" on my childhood road trips to the Jersey Shore. A two-story strip of stucco walls with blue wooden doors lined up along a concrete terrace. Inside, the usual formica bathroom fixtures, seashell prints, and faint mildewy smell coming off the wood-paneled walls. But we forgave everything because we could hear the ocean from our window. The back door opened onto a minimal patio of weathered gray boards with steps that went right down into the sand.

I sat outside in the dark while Julian showered first. I had to go down some way before the parking lot lights faded behind me, letting me make out a thumbnail of moon and a few stars blinking through the humid clouds. I was going to wash up soon so it didn't matter if I got my pants full of sand. The water tickling my toes at the shoreline was borderline warm enough for a swim despite the day's rainy start, but I drew my legs up close to me after a few minutes, somehow feeling agitated by its teasing touch.

Lovecraft had lived by the water all his life, and feared it, as much as he loved his history-haunted city of Providence. He spent his days obsessively imagining the cold, devouring, "mongrel" creatures that pressed in at the edges of fragile rationality. But he didn't move to the desert. His characters pretend they don't want to know the truth, but they do. With no Jehovah to punish you in the name of love, there's no greater pleasure-pain high than discovering you're not the center of the universe.

Eyes closed, I sank my full weight into the sand, letting its bumpy sharpness anchor me in my body as my mind spun out. I pictured a soft light traveling from my feet to my crown, sealing in my energy so no one could steal it. I was just nervous about tomorrow, my first time tabling at a convention. I'd be sharing a booth with two guys I knew from a listserv. One of them had created a trading-cards game about gay elves, and the other one made his own chainmail.

The rush and retreat of waves gave a rhythm to my breath. Still on the shore, I was floating, rocking. I curled into the peace of being small. The cosmos went about its business overhead, a scatter of stars that knew nothing about Cancer and Pisces and their 63% intimacy styles compatibility rating. Something skittered over my bare foot. I heard my mother's voice: *Where there's one cockroach, there's more than one.* I sat up and slapped at a tangle of crusty seaweed the tide had flung across my ankle. Embarrassed, I returned to headquarters.

IN THE MORNING I emailed Tai from my laptop to tell her how the "book tour" was going, focusing on the positive aspects. I let Ty use the girl persona online with me when she needed to resurface, figuring it was a safer outlet than stealing Mrs. Becker's pantyhose. I was starting to be able to tell, even before I read the signature line, who I was talking with. Tai made art and took no shit. Tyler played the rebellious clown but longed for a family who wanted him. He'd tried to explain once, in Gateway support circle, what the shift felt like: *My clothes are wrong. My body is wrong. I look down and expect to see something that isn't there.* And Dr. Marla had scribbled some crap like "depersonalization" and given him the same pills I was on now.

Could two minds get along in the same brain? I asked myself as I looked in the mirror at the man in the Octopus Shirt, an easygoing muscle bear who just couldn't wait to meet new goofball friends and invite them to play in his make-believe world.

"Jule, have you ever pretended to be someone else, to do something that scared you?"

"My first year of college, I got into bars with a fake ID that said I was James Dobson. They don't focus on the family too closely at Trapdoor."

I laughed nervously and held him tight. "You always make me feel better."

"You'll be fine, sugar. Don't over-think it. Remember what it's like to be the guy on the other side of that table. What's he feel? What do you want him to feel?"

"Aroused?"

"*Now* you're thinking like an artist."

"Seriously though—the best feeling is, when I read something and discover that I'm not the only freak out there who's had this fantasy. Like there's a story that puts my weird feelings into a shape I can comprehend."

"I guarantee you, people are not that complicated. Whatever you've felt, there's someone who's felt the same way. Trust me, I'm in advertising."

"But what if I can't find that person?"

Jule looked a little hurt, but quickly wiped the expression off his face. "Gotta start somewhere. Now change into your short-shorts and let's go."

"I didn't pack any—oh, jeez."

From his suitcase my boyfriend produced a fitted white pair that would have attracted a lot of whistles at Fleet Week. "I've been reading up on the Dom/sub lifestyle, and I'm pretty sure it means I can order you to wear this."

"That's only if it's 24/7. Submissive in the bedroom doesn't mean I consent to it in real life. We'd have to draw up a contract."

"Perhaps we could start with an...*oral* agreement." He grinned like he was the first person to make that joke. New kinksters are so cute.

"Like, right now?" He nodded and pointed to the floor. "Let me take this off first, I don't want jizz on my new shirt."

He sighed with satisfaction even before my lips closed around his cock. "Ah, I've taught you well."

I convinced a post-coital Julian that it wasn't necessary for me to dress like a gay drug dealer's houseboy, so he wore the shorts himself to attract attention when handing out my postcard flyers on the convention floor.

TropiCon turned out to be a small-time operation compared to the cons I'd visited in New York and San Francisco. These amateur gatherings spring up all the time and either die out after a few years or develop a following, depending on whether the organizers have connections with any famous headliners and aren't too baked to remember to call them. We occupied two of the smaller ballrooms and a half-dozen breakout rooms on the third floor of the Miami Beach Convention Center—an enormous, low-slung, gleaming white building with cut-out portholes and squares punctuating the façade, a sleek modernist update of the Art Deco proportions of South Beach's classic hotels. It was like the honeymoon stretch limo of buildings.

"I think this was where our church youth group went to a Billy Graham crusade over winter break," Jule said.

I could still be shocked by reminders of how deeply he'd been embedded in that world. "Was it...good?"

"You know me, I'll take my hope where I can get it." He looked sorry he'd brought it up. "You're lucky, you don't care about being part of anything."

"Yeah, like a penguin doesn't care about flying—can't do it, why think about it?"

Actually I did feel right at home in that hall of hopeful misfits, each hawking their Vampire Lestat fanfiction zines or hand-stitched steampunk corsets, but I kept it to myself so Jule wouldn't regret his lost salvation. The visible gay content was limited to our table and some fan art of Xena and Gabrielle kissing. However, Jule soon caught on that nerd girls are less vanilla than average, and steered a number of them to sample the dangerous charms of Pharmakon and Challis. In my reckless new persona, I flirted with any passing guy who seemed indifferent to the bowling-ball boobs of the space vixens on the posters at our neighbor's table. Sexy fairies, sexy vampires, sexy slime monsters—straight guys had a limited imagination.

Landis, the elf cards guy, sold a pack about once an hour, usually to some chubby, furry young man who looked around sheepishly first, as though worried that a taste for twinks with butterfly wings would mark him as too unmanly even for this crowd. These customers stole longing glances at my comic, which I'd flipped open to the spread where Pharmakon kisses Challis back to life. They were afraid to meet my eyes till I (as Octopus Man) greeted them in a relaxed deep voice and smiled at them the way Julian smiled at me. Then they would fork over a ten-dollar bill for a signed copy, sometimes rushing off without their change.

Jule dropped in on this scene mid-day. "Out of postcards. How goes the empire?"

"Marketing is great for getting laid," Landis said, with a wink at me and a flick of his long bleached hair.

"Thirty-seven, thirty-eight, thirty-nine," muttered Ronan, grumpy at being interrupted in hooking his metal rings together. A witty film critic on the listserv, he was mostly nonverbal in person, using his third of the table as a live manufacturing demonstration. We handled his customers in exchange for unlimited dried fruit and beef jerky sticks from his overstuffed orange backpack.

"How about I take over for awhile," Jule said. "Wasn't there a panel discussion you wanted to hear?"

I checked the schedule. "Yeah, if I hurry, I can grab a bagel and catch 'Monsters in Love: Why Heroes Aren't Hot'."

Landis stood up when I did. "I have to go to the bathroom. These decks sell for fifteen, the full-color ones for twenty-five, and they're limited edition so write the copy number on this form before the customer walks away with it," he directed Julian.

"Got it, Tinkerbell."

As intended, Landis didn't like that. I faked interest in a display of D&D dice till he stalked off.

A bathroom break wasn't a bad idea. I went around to the single-occupant one tucked behind the exhibitors' room, which was further away but had no line. I was startled when a slim figure darted in behind me. "I've been waiting for you," Landis rasped.

"What is this, James and the Giant Peach? Let a guy pee in privacy."

"I don't mind watching."

"Gross, dude. I'm with somebody. Go away."

"C'mon, you were literally flashing your tits at my customers all morning. So to speak."

You see? a small voice in my head yelled at an absent Julian. *This is why I don't try to look good.* But a new, stronger voice in there rumbled, *We can take him.*

"Take"—fuck, punch, or some combination of the two? That was all the guidance I got. What would Julian do? *Protect the shirt.*

I tried out a sneer, channeling Jafar from "Aladdin". "You couldn't *handle* my kink."

Landis's bravado cracked a little. "T-try me."

"Wellll...you asked for it..." I stalled. "Turn around, away from me...now drop your pants..." Slight hesitation, but he actually did it, lowering his unbuckled cargo shorts to the tile floor with a clank, revealing loose-hanging gray boxers. I cast about for the next step. "Now, uh, take off your sock—" because of course he was wearing white tube socks with his sandals—"and put it, ah, tie it around your mouth."

"Aw c'mon, what—"

"Uh-uh. Talking leads to punishment."

He complied, with much grumbling and hopping around, because his pants were around his ankles. This kind of thing went much smoother in the pornos. His hard-on tented the front of his boxers. So that's why he wore them so large. The elf was skinny but he was hung.

I'd been prepared to leave him there, half-undressed on the dirty floor like an idiot, and sneak out before he realized I had no endgame. But now my own dick chafed against my fly, heavy with unpredictable tension.

"Blegh. Unf?" he prompted me through his gag.

"On your knees," I ordered, before I could think twice. I pushed his head down, to show myself that I meant it, I was committed now. His hair was limp and dry. Not like Julian's silky waves, at all. I wanted him because I didn't want him, because he was gross and today I was the kind of guy who ate raw meat.

Landis, on the floor, fumbled between his legs, rubbing the cotton bulge. Should I forbid him? No, I wanted to see. It was long, all right—like a daikon radish. Despite the sock in his mouth, he was smirking, proud of his secret weapon. I shoved my crotch into his face and unzipped. His eyes widened. He mimed the offer of a blowjob. I didn't usually like those, but I didn't like him either, and here we were.

I untied the sock, since his hands were kind of busy, and pressed his head to the wall with my pelvis. He made a bit of a choking noise but didn't stop jerking off so I figured he was okay. As soon as his tongue slid around my dick, though, I felt like I was being sucked into a black hole. My heartbeat thudded in my ears, a thousand pounds of undersea pressure. For a second I was afraid to pull out, afraid of teeth, though his lips and tongue were working me smoothly without a scratch.

Looking down at him brought me back to myself. He was sitting with his skinny legs splayed out, pumping it like a twelve-year-old with an underwear catalog in his mom's bathroom. I pushed his face off me, my palm on his forehead, making him knock his head against the wall. We both breathed hard. Recovering the arrogant twist to his smile, even as he rubbed the bump on his head, he said, "Hey, do me next—" His words were cut off because I aimed a stream of cum at his face, grappling my dick with less pleasure than the mere need to be done.

"Now, go. I still need to pee," I said, hoping he couldn't hear my voice tremble.

Landis wiped his eyes with that versatile tube sock. "*Troll*," he muttered. But he cleaned up quickly and left.

Once I was alone, I heaved into the toilet. My legs shook. I felt terrible for Landis, who'd probably been humiliated his whole life as an effeminate nerd in an Ohio public high school. Why had I done this to him? And more to the point, what would he tell Julian?

I snuck in late to the panel discussion about villain fandom, more for an alibi than because I cared to listen anymore. The audience was mostly women processing their feminist guilt about crushing on the Phantom of the Opera. I decided not to be the kind of asshole who brought up Foucault.

The scene at Booth 386D was much as I'd left it: Ronan weaving his armor, Landis brooding and flipping his hair at potential elf-fetishists, and Julian escaping into the Fashion Week issue of *GQ* from the airport newsstand. The stack of our comics had shrunk, a good sign. After-lunch sales traffic would be sluggish, as most folks had already made the circuit of our small room. In another hour I'd be giving the issues away to spare the effort of re-packing them. It wasn't about the money anyhow. Before the bathroom encounter, I'd felt grateful and excited to be here at all, as a member and not just a fan. The sourness in my stomach had spoiled that too. I didn't detect any unusual tension between my table-mates, but just for pre-emptive damage control, I made myself lean over Landis with a sly smile, teasing him: "Have some fun back there?"

He jerked his head up, regarding me with a mix of fear and fascination, like a girl in a Dracula fanfiction. I recognized that feeling—I was usually on the other end of it. "Uh...yes?"

Putting my hand on Landis's shoulder, I remarked to Julian, "I just wanted to take a piss earlier, but this player somehow found the only other attractive homosexual at this con, and...I had to wait quite awhile for the bathroom."

Jule raised an eyebrow at Landis. "I had no idea this was a spawning ground for your species." He got up to offer me his seat. Elf boy looked relieved, so peace was restored to Middle Earth.

We only sold one more copy for cash, and two others (while Julian was off at the cosplay contest) to a guy who passed me a Ziploc baggie of 'shrooms under the table. He was unloading his leftovers for virtually nothing because he wouldn't risk passing them through Customs on his flight home to Toronto. I was packing up to leave early when a woman in a Hello Kitty skull tank top came up to me. I recognized her from the monster panel, though I blanked on her name. "Hey," she said very softly. "I bought this earlier." She touched her palm to the box of my unsold copies.

"Thanks. I liked your panel. Sorry I was late."

"It's okay. I didn't notice." She gathered her breath. I saw tears in her eyes. "I read the part where Tod cures Ryder... My brother died of AIDS last year. The cancer was everywhere."

"I'm so sorry. I lost my best friend to it in '95. One of my other friends, we think the drug cocktail is working, but it's so soon, no one knows for sure."

She bowed her head. "I've just never seen...our story...in comics before. You'll give them a happy ending, right?"

One more thing that was beyond my ability to promise, yet I longed to say yes, and mean it. "I hope so. The characters kind of do what they want. They're both pretty screwed-up guys."

"That was the whole point of my presentation, though. Monsters show us that love doesn't have to be earned by perfection. We find grace in the mess." She gave a self-deprecating half-smile. "You can tell I'm a seminary dropout."

"That's inspiring, what you said." I hoped I could remember it well enough to tell Julian later. If only I'd taken notes. "Sorry I was spaced out when I saw you before."

"Ah, I expect it at these things. I pretend I'm touring with the Dead."

"I won't say 'I don't inhale', but this time—well, I was stressed out by— some guy who wasn't taking no for an answer." *That guy* who had turned out to be me.

"Creepers—another scourge that no con is without." She curled her lip in disgust. "This is really going to be the year we start that all-female con at Hampshire. I'm an adjunct there—modern lit and women's studies."

"Hampshire College in Amherst? My sister's an undergrad. Prue Porter. Look her up—she's a geek like me."

"Excellent. Here's my card—I want to subscribe to your next issue. Send me the bill."

I pocketed the card, stealing a glance at her name: *Professor Andrea Vargas.* "Thanks a ton, Andrea. My co-creator, Tai, is...well, legally she's a boy, but sometimes she's a girl. Could she come to your con?"

"Oh, man. That's a whole other can of worms, no Freudian metaphor intended. One more reason it's been such a challenge to get our event off the ground. But I'll push for an inclusive policy. You ask me, we all need to stick together."

I felt better after meeting Andrea. The warmth inside me returned, and with it, that not-unpleasant restlessness almost like arousal, or hunger when it's still mild enough to be enjoyed: the story awakening, itching to lead me somewhere unexpected and right.

Julian reappeared, digital camera around his neck, and showed me highlights of the costume show: a sleek, silvery Storm and mascara-eyed Wolverine, a burly hairy-legged Wonder Woman with her lasso thrown round a Hobbit. "See, I knew you'd find something that was your speed here," I said. "Maybe next con it'll be you walking the runway."

"Perish the thought. What would I be?"

"You always reminded me of the fox from Disney's 'Robin Hood'—I had such a crush on him."

"The day I let you turn me into a furry..."

"I know, it's a great idea in theory, but it must be really hot in there."

"Just like the preacher said."

WE ENDURED THE HIGHWAY traffic jam back to our hotel so we could unload our materials, freshen up, and take turns checking mail on my laptop. The electronic word was less intrusive than phone calls, but less respectful of normal business hours. I had my doubts about the creeping advance of the always-on-duty culture. But I kept my critique to myself, rather than force Julian to admit out loud that he was worried about his dad, who'd been struck with chest pains and shortness of breath while stumping for voters at a business leaders' golf outing last week.

I lay facedown on the bed in nothing but my boxers, flipping through that dumb astrology book, while Jule chuckled and muttered "As if!" at someone's AOL Instant Message. *Cancer can be somewhat traditional about love, which Pisces doesn't really understand.* I was too much of a socialist to believe in Fate. I wouldn't settle for a cosmos where people were locked into their social roles by the orbits of unfeeling planets.

"'Pisces' need to connect and feel love is larger than any role that humankind makes for love,'" I read aloud. "So get off the computer."

Jule clicked the window shut, but not before I'd peeked over his shoulder to see the handle of his dialogue partner: *missionxbrent.* I flopped on the bed with an exasperated sigh. Jule climbed next to me and stroked from my chest to my navel. Too gently. I wished he would scratch me, mark his territory.

"Hey. Stop moping. I was just checking a message from a client and he popped on there. Apparently this IM thing lets your friends see anytime you're logged in. Kind of creepy."

I dragged his hand to my nipple, pressed down hard to give him the hint. "Fuck him or block him. This isn't difficult."

"Life isn't that simple. I feel responsible for people, and he's one of them. Besides, aren't you always saying that gay culture will never mature unless we can have nonsexual friendships?" He pinched my nipple, but the delicious shock of sensation didn't distract me. Getting what I wanted from him made me feel stronger, clearer.

"Responsible how? All you do is make fun of him and wave your unavailable hellbound booty in his face."

Jule sucked on my other nipple, cradling his head on my arm. My breath quickened. His hand crept downward, hinting, not rushing my reward. At last he said: "Truth is...it was easy to hate him when I hadn't seen him since high school. I'm working overtime to put those walls up again, but then he says something so fucking naïve that I'm in *pain*. I want to ask him, *why* are you still praying to God to take away the *one thing* that saved us from blowing our brains out? What could be so important that he'd throw away what we had—if it ever meant anything to him in the first place." He sat up, wiping his eyes with his forearm. "Sorry. This shouldn't be your problem."

"Your problems are my problems."

Unsure (as I was) whether I'd made a complaint or a vow, Jule fingered my waistband. "Well, I see one problem we can both enjoy solving."

"Bite me."

He withdrew his hand. "Okay fine, you're still mad. You want—"

I crawled onto him, leaning across his lap. "No, I meant, *bite me.* Spank me, pin me to the floor. The tender and seductive thing is great, but sometimes I'd love to feel you—just—*Hulk out* on me."

Jule didn't say anything. My face burned. My stomach felt shivery. In a smaller voice, I asked, "Are you really turned off by that?" *By me.* His body was hard to read: slumped shoulders, but a bulge of arousal, his thighs held taut in the way I knew from spending so much time between them.

Looking out the window at the darkening sea, he said quietly, "It's not that. I'm afraid...I'll be *too* into it, and hurt you and not be able to stop."

I wanted to tell him I knew he'd never do that. Not like other men. Not like *me.* Instead I just said, "Look, babe. There's two ways we can play this. One: you can periodically suck Brent's dick to Amy Grant music and make him cry, while I'm at the dungeon getting fisted in a sling. Or, two: we can try to be everything to each other, which means you learn to play safely in my world, a little bit, and in return I'll...I don't know...go to church with you and let you replace all my clothes."

I ran out of breath, stopped, waited for his reply for what felt like a million years. But when he opened his mouth, I was afraid to hear it. So I started up again: "It's a lot, I know, but...you say you want to be closer to me, you want me to let you in. So...this is it. This is the person you're getting into."

Julian hesitated, studying my face. "Wow. Pushy bottom alert. You're a man of many personalities."

"Guess that means we're already polyamorous." But neither of us could pull off a joking tone. Chills of shame swept over my bare body. Only crazy brains switched around like mine did. Even the guy who loved me most—let's be honest, the only one who ever had—thought my Batmobile wasn't running on all cylinders.

"You're right. Those are the choices... I'm going for a swim to think it over."

In silence, I watched him change into his turquoise Speedo—so perfect against his skin, which held a hint of bronze even in winter. After a decent pause for privacy I went out to stand on the sand-speckled planks of the patio, in time to see his lithe body disappear into the waves. Night comes early in March so the sky was black, too dark to see where it met the water at the horizon. The exterior lights of the motel and its neighbors cast a glow sufficient for safe swimming if you didn't drift too far out.

Jule wanted to be alone. Or to face the fact that he was always already alone, in a relationship with me. Well, the mighty Atlantic had room for both of us. The incoming tide surged over me, warm (barely) and salty, pushing against my steady strokes like a persistent sparring partner. But soon the deeper water buoyed me up, and I rolled onto my back to float. Between the groundlessness below and the illusion of starry dots on a flat black map overhead, I could lose all sense of distance and gravity.

Brent's life, for Julian, raised a terrible question: was there something that mattered more than love, the love we knew in our bodies? And somehow I'd brought us to the same brink—for what? Not fear of God, but a driven instinct my Hebrew ancestors might have recognized, a possibly profane, possibly ridiculous version of their quest into the wilderness. Being broken apart made me whole.

"Are you *skinny dipping*?" The water under me rocked with the motion of Julian swimming nearby.

"Go big or go home."

"That seems to be tonight's theme."

I submerged again and treaded water alongside him. "Did I spoil everything?"

He paddled closer. His body heat warmed the water near me. "You told the truth. I guess we needed that."

"We don't have to play rough tonight."

"You're right. I don't *have* to do anything. Because I'm your dom."

"Avocado."

"Oh, suck my balls—not now, dimwit, you'll drown." He flicked water in my face. I splashed him back. Suddenly he ducked below the surface and pulled me under. Though I outweighed him, Jule lifted regularly at the Ironman Gym to maintain his circuit-queen figure. This time he had the advantages of shock and his grip on my nads, exerting painful pressure when I tried to struggle upwards. Green starbursts popped behind my eyes. Frightened heartbeat and throbbing dick were one and the same adrenaline rush.

Probably it was only a few seconds before he pulled us up. I gulped air. He panted, eyes bright, and tugged me forward. "This way. Under the pier."

Between our motel and the shuttered boat-rental shop next door was a shaky-looking wooden dock, with the cracked hull of an abandoned orange canoe caught on a spar at one end. A stray edge of plastic drew a shallow scratch down my shoulder as I let Jule drag me through a gap between the pilings. He pushed his hand against my chest to make me lean back on the tiny strip of tide-washed grit beneath the shore end of the pier. If I spread-eagled my arms around the closest pilings, I could keep my head and chest above water. The sea floor fell away sharply under my legs.

"Ouch, these damn rocks." Digging his knees into the sand on either side of my head, Jule straddled my face. I choked down my laugh because the next moment he was fucking my throat harder than he ever had. Bruised lips, throat raw, I entered that sweet semi-conscious state where oxygen is scarce, sucking and curling my tongue around his shaft, and trying to banish the worry that my stiff dick bobbing in the water would lure some hungry crustacean. His balls slapped me in the face as he grunted and pounded to a gush of release. My arms burned with muscle fatigue. The waves lapping my cock were agony, I was so ready. Julian clambered off me, not looking me in the eye, and hoisted me up to lie facedown on the sand strip. I cupped a hand over my junk to avoid the scraping pebbles, but he pushed it away, so I had to pop my ass up to stay off the ground. Two spit-wet fingers shoved roughly inside me were all it took to bring me off.

I closed my eyes for uncounted seconds and opened them in the humid dark, not knowing where I was. *[Jonas—]* I saw his face over my shoulder in the strobe lights of the club. My body on the floor, weak, inflamed. *[Knight of Cups overturned—]* Tasted salt, sweat, my own sickness rising from my gut. *[Hand on my shoulder, Jonas—]* No, that wasn't real. The lights were only the reflection of water rippling on the underside of the boards. I was outdoors, cold.

I crawled up onto the dock. Out in the waves, another pair of motel guests were enjoying an evening swim. I hunched over and crossed my arms in my lap, regretting my naturist enthusiasm.

Julian jogged down the beach toward me, bearing towels and the shorts I'd shed on the patio. I gladly pulled them on and we wrapped ourselves in the three skimpy bath towels the motel provided us. Sitting side by side, he put his arm around my shoulders. We watched the sky. A point of light detached itself from a constellation, blinking red tail-lights as it turned toward some distant airport. Jule picked grit out of a scraped patch on his knee.

"Was that what you needed, sugar?"

I blinked away the after-image of impossible faces from the past. Just us two, surrounded by the beautiful standoff distance of sky and ocean. Whatever risks I'd taken were my choice. "Oh yeah. It was everything. But...didn't you like it too?"

"Unfortunately, yes."

"Look, it's only a scene. It's not our whole relationship."

"So what you're saying is, slave in the sheets, mysterious and elusive in the streets?"

"That sounds more glamorous than my actual life, but sure."

Jule pressed closer to me for warmth. "We could try it."

But I had to push my luck. "You really think it's realistic for us not to fuck anyone else for the rest of our lives?"

He tipped my chin toward him with his fingers, teasing. "Hey, hey, now you're spending your life with me?"

"I don't know. Just wondering what's the endgame."

"How about, not dying?"

"That's not a good enough reason."

Jule kicked one foot in the water with a quiet rhythmic splash. "No, it's just easier to say than the truth."

"Which is?"

"That it kills me that there's a part of you I can't have."

"I'm not a roast chicken. Nobody gets to 'have' all of me."

He laughed. "Touché. But for real...it would bother me to think we hadn't even tried to do better, we just gave up before we began, because gays can't sustain anything except Liz Taylor's career."

"There's a flaw in that logic somewhere, but my ass is too sore to keep sitting here talking about it."

"Get used to it, slave." He reached under the towel to pinch me.

"That is a *problematic* word coming from a white boy from Georgia."

"You picked me."

That I had, though I'd fought against it, from the moment we'd met in the Ironman locker room four years ago. I could see how, after dating a porn performer who'd died of AIDS, Jule might be hoping for a more grounded experience with a nerd like me. As for me, I envied his cheerful selfishness, which paradoxically coexisted with his generous acceptance of most people's flaws.

In a subdued mood, we dressed for a casual dinner. Jule grimaced listening to his cell phone voicemails.

"It's my brother. He's taking a fearless moral inventory."

"You need to call him back? I'll wait."

"I'm not prepared to relive every noogie and Indian burn of 1979 on an empty stomach."

"I suppose we should go see him at that men's prayer thing on the way home."

"Yeah, we're doomed. I'm sorry. I promise, it'll be better than Disney World—and twice as fake." He passed me our *Access Miami* book. "Now find us someplace with unlimited shrimp and margaritas, and I'll let you drive the Pimp-Mobile home."

[Email exchanges]

Sent: March 6, 1997, 10:51 PM
From: wicked80@hotmail.com
To: man.solo@earthlink.net

Pedro—

Having fun in the sun? Winter sucks. Make for L.A. when I age out, find me a "Pretty Woman" Richard Gere boyfriend.

I checked out some botánicas on the Lower East Side for the next scene. First place the guy *stared* at me, like I was taking pictures of his shit just to steal it. Bitch please, I wouldn't wear these shoes if I wanted to hide.

You think that stuff does anything, for real? Candles and magic words? I know what I'd wish, how about you?

—Tai

Sent: March 7, 1997, 8:37 AM
From: man.solo@earthlink.net
To: wicked80@hotmail.com

Good morning Tai—

Don't envy me, it was pouring yesterday! Good news, we talked a few stores into carrying *TPC*. Whatever happens, I feel good knowing that it's a real thing in the world now. These daydreams in our heads are something that other people can share. "It's alive!" says Dr. Frankenstein. That's a kind of magic, right?

About the other kind, I don't know. The fairy tales always say it comes with a price. You wouldn't want to have to marry a frog, or climb up a mountain of glass, for example!

Ever read "The Monkey's Paw"? I'll get you a copy.

How's it going with the Beckers? You don't talk much about them. Hope you can be patient with them—you're an unusual kid, but they want to understand.

May the Force be with you— Peter

Sent: March 7, 1997, 5:11 PM
From: wicked80@hotmail.com
To: man.solo@earthlink.net

Dude, a frog would be good next to some guys I've done. You don't know shit about price. Walking on glass is what I do when they make me be the wrong one. Name, body, clothes—I want to switch when *I* need to, not b/c Dr. B is home or not.

Aletha's alright. We paint together. She bought me some kids' books by this Faith Ringgold lady who draws real black families in the hood, having fun, being beautiful and all that shit. I acted like I thought it was baby stuff but she knew better.

But I never see anyone in those books like me. "Girl-Boy." Parents would burn that one.

Sometimes I'm so fuckin tired I want to give up, but I got a plan—

Girl in my last foster home was sick of the mom making her drink nasty-ass diet shakes instead of food, took a dishwasher job at Shun

Lee Palace where they don't check age, found some girls let her sleep on the floor for cheap rent, and she got the judge to let her out of there at 16. I forget what it's called. Could you look it up?

Besitos—Tai

Sent: March 7, 1997, 10:22 PM
From: man.solo@earthlink.net
To: wicked80@hotmail.com

Hey there Tai—

The word you're looking for is "emancipated". When you're 16, so pretty soon now, you could ask the Family Court to declare you legally an adult. You'd have to show that you had a stable living situation, a way to support yourself, and be able to finish school while you're doing it. But I wouldn't rush into this if I were you. I know the Beckers cramp your style somehow, but with them supporting you, you can concentrate on building your academic record so you have a shot at Cooper Union. A GED won't cut it. Trust me, school is tough enough when you're not also cleaning out deep-fat fryers at midnight.

I'm going to put you in touch with a teacher at Hampshire College (where my sister goes) who loved our comic book. I met her today at TropiCon. She said Challis reminded her of her brother. Made her cry!

See, we're doing something important here. Representing. Got to play the long game, OK? Keep yer head up— Peter

Sent: March 7, 1997, 10:40 PM
From: wicked80@hotmail.com
To: man.solo@earthlink.net

No grease traps for me, Pedro—already talked to Mr. Jonas and he said he could use me part-time to stack shelves and keep track of orders, like you did. If I'm for real about this emancipation, he'll ask his friends for more jobs for me. See, your girl knows how to get by.

That's cool about the professor. Does she want me to draw her? What character should she be? Your new script is cool. What's the potion going to do to Pharmakon? Let's not kill him yet. I'm sick of that tragic homo shit.

—Tai

Sent: March 8, 1997, 4:03 AM
From: man.solo@earthlink.net

To: wicked80@hotmail.com

Dear Tai—

I've been up for hours stressing about what to tell you. I think the best thing is to explain most of it in person. I'll be back in a couple days, let's grab some dim sum at The Cottage and figure out a better plan for your future.

Basically all I can say right now is: Don't get too cozy with Jonas and his friends, especially when I'm not around. We'll find another way for you to support yourself.

We're flying to a Christian extreme sports conference in Alpharetta so Julian can enjoy (??) some male bonding with his dad and brother. How much Red Bull will I have to chug to stay awake?

Manly hugs— Peter

Sent: March 8, 1997, 7:47 AM
From: wicked80@hotmail.com
To: man.solo@earthlink.net

I was on the street longer than you been working for your mama. You think I don't know who to watch out for? Fuck you for acting like I got nothing to sell but my ass. Mr. Jonas believes in my skills even if you don't.

—Tyler Wick

Darkness smothered the packed hall, where moments ago plumes of white smoke had obscured the flash of screaming electric guitars. The pop-crack of gunshots echoed from all sides. Their split-second white light revealed men in black bodysuits crabwalking across the stage in a sniper's crouch. It was too dark to see if any of the hundreds of men in the North Point Community Church auditorium flinched, struck by combat memories more wounding than the blanks the performers were shooting. Spotlights again bathed the black-bearded man atop the crystal platform, who continued his sonorous recitation, in a tone halfway between a sermon and a spoken-word poetry jam: "HE...strikes swifter than any army... HE... lifts you higher than the greatest victory..." The snipers scattered into the wings, and a half-dozen basketball players leapt into the shining circle of switched-on stadium lighting, their lithe dark limbs passing and dunking the ball in a dancing blur of movement. "HE...is the one... HE...is the SON."

A final explosion of smoke jets around the platform, and the crowd cheered, a sound ragged-edged with the release of tension, like when the tie-breaking home run sets free the exhausted overtime crowd. An unseen chorus struck up a pop-music praise song, the cue for a sea of those one-handed waves to undulate across the room. Julian nudged me and said in a low voice, "There you have it, the Kingdom of Heaven: masc 4 masc, no fats, no fems."

"It *was* thrilling, sorry to say, but LARPing Mortal Kombat is a weird way to celebrate the Prince of Peace."

Jule sighed. "Delicious, right? So much testosterone. So much certainty. I could just *bathe* in it and never come up for air." His expression hardened. "Now imagine growing up here and having that dangled in front of your face every day, feeling all the passion they want you to feel *and more*, and the more it excites you, the more you understand why it'll never be yours."

I patted his back just once, the most straight-acting way I could think of touching him. "Jesus doesn't belong to them, you know. These are just puzzle pieces you can put together whatever way you need. Leather Queens of the Sacred Heart, why not?"

"That's not what I'm talking about." He left his seat and squeezed past me into the aisle. "I'm going to pick up a schedule so I can find my brother."

"Should I come?" I called out, but my words were lost in the murmurs of the dispersing crowd. I wandered in the direction of the exits, rubbing my aching temples. Ty's emails had cost me a sleepless night. My throat closed up when I thought about torpedoing my friendship with Jonas over some fragments of decade-old memories. But then chills of shame fevered me— how could I ignore my duty to protect the kids? My responsibility for Ty didn't end when he left Gateway. If anything, our bond had grown stronger. I felt all alone in this, because I couldn't ask anyone's advice without talking about my first sex with Jonas, which they'd rush to judgment about and trample over the last little flower of happiness I was safeguarding in the memory by keeping it private.

So I had less than usual patience to spare for Julian pouting about his flamboyantly damned soul, like Lord Byron in khakis and loafers. (We were lucky that white evangelicals' revival meetings were dress-down—a nod to the egalitarianism of total depravity, perhaps—as we'd had no time or money to shop for church suits for this impromptu extension of our trip.)

I went up to wait for him by the registration tables in the lobby, which were covered with flyers promoting Christian variations on every possible extracurricular activity for men, from 12-Step groups to wilderness expeditions. I kept my brain out of sleep mode by watching the people around me for *Poison Cure* character ideas. But this line of thought reminded me of Ty, with a jolt of guilt that maybe I'd done wrong by treating him as a creative partner—unthinkingly encouraged him to believe he was an adult. I was about to seek out a phone to call my mom when Julian resurfaced. He touched my shoulder gently, a discreet apology. "Hey, would you come to this workshop with me? I'm betting Carter will be there because he mentioned the guy's name in his message."

I looked at the text box he pointed out on the schedule. *Wounded Warriors: Healing for men abused as children.* "Wow, that's intense. You guys are brave to try and come together over this. Are you sure I should be there, though? It doesn't apply to me...and I don't want to make Carter uncomfortable."

"I'm sure it's a 'Don't Ask, Don't Tell' kind of situation. In every way."

"I don't know, what if they make us go around the room and share why we're here? My parents were dysfunctional, but in a normal, Woody Allen kind of way. Nobody ever hit me or anything like that. I mean, I remember a lot of rectal thermometers, but it *was* the 1970s."

"Just say you're not ready to talk about it. Should be easy for you."

"Well...okay, I'll try. I want to be there for you." To take the focus off me and my privileged childhood, I asked, "Do you know what your brother wants to make amends about? Are you going to forgive him?"

"Oh, the usual shit that straight boys do. Make-believe fighting that hurts a little too much. Taking Daddy's side in the family war. He was just doing what he had to do to survive. I stopped taking it personally a long time ago. He doesn't care about the important things in my life and vice versa."

"That's sad. I hope it changes."

"You think Jesus can make me love real estate and heal him from the sin of wearing plaid pants?"

"There's more to both of you than that."

"True, we both like football and Cindy Crawford, though not exactly for the same reasons."

"Drop the cynical queen act. Twenty bucks says you'll be crying like a baby in the next hour."

"Making me cry is no great accomplishment. All it takes is two fingers of vodka and Judy Garland singing 'Have Yourself a Merry Little Christmas'."

"'Make the Yuletide gaaaaay...'" I crooned off-key. Jule put his hand over my mouth.

"Shush. Round here, we say the Yuletide is struggling with same-sex attraction."

We found the right breakout room, a repurposed classroom for the church Sunday School, with a paper taped to the door that read "Wounded Warriors: Kris Anders, Living Waters Ministry, Lake Forest, CA". About twenty black plastic chairs were arranged in semicircular rows facing a wooden podium and projector screen. The crowd was shaping up to be standing-room-only very soon. I was shocked that this many guys were rushing to admit they'd been beaten—or worse, since Jule often said spanking didn't count as abuse down here unless you had a hospital bill to show for it. I shuddered, as if the body-snatchers' disguise had been lifted *en masse*, and these big men with their dad paunches, beards, biker tattoos, or business suits reverted to their true form as a pack of soiled, bleeding, cringing little boys. What a fucking great time to have run out of my anti-anxiety meds. We won't talk about why—but if an extra pill now and then kept me from toking and cheating, don't tell me it wasn't therapeutic.

At the front of the room, Carter was standing by his seat and glancing around for someone he knew. He saw us and waved us over, pulling Julian into a hug and shaking my hand with enthusiasm. "Hey, you made it! Brent said you might, but I thought you'd just stay out there taking pictures and making fun of everything."

Jule fluttered his hands over his heart. "The word of truth! I feel so *convicted.*" I wondered if Carter could tell he actually meant it. "Nah, I...I think what you're doing for yourself is great. You should be proud."

Carter tugged his keychain out of his pocket, showing us the attached metal charm. "Check it out, four months sober."

"Awesome," I said. I imagined measuring my life that way, a daily self-deprivation so great that only the smallest time horizon was bearable. It made my teeth ache. "How are Stef and the boys?"

"Haven't ditched me yet, praise Jesus. I'll tell them you said hi. She really liked you—and for once I don't have to be jealous!" He elbowed me in a friendly way, and I was willing to laugh with him. I knew all about having a hot partner who seemed too special to put up with your mess.

"So who is this guru we're hearing today? Is he going to make me bang on a drum and talk about my inner child?" Jule asked.

"You've never been to a 12-Step meeting, have you?" Carter responded. We shook our heads. "Julie, you should try Al-Anon. I went to a few of those too. It explains a lot. Like, the way it seems people keep screwing you over, letting you down, but what's your part in it, how are you picking the same role you had in the family? 'You' meaning 'me', sorry."

"Carter, I do believe that's the first time you've said 'sorry' to me when Daddy wasn't dragging you over by your shirt collar. This is truly a born-again moment."

"So, *you* going to apologize to me for telling Fat Gina I was into her in eighth grade? They were drawing gross pictures of us on the boys' bathroom walls for a month."

"Really, of all my cruel deeds, that's the one you hold a grudge about? She was a nice girl. Not my fault you didn't have the guts to date someone unpopular."

The moderator began urging the lucky people with seats to take them and the others not to block the aisles. Carter whispered, "Anyway, what I was going to say is, this thing today should be kind of like Al-Anon but for, you know, all kinds of bad childhood stuff." The row had filled up while we were talking. The guy next to Julian and Carter offered to find another place so I could sit with them, but I assured him I'd be fine by myself in the back. The brothers could use some privacy, I told myself, staking out a patch of carpet where I could lean my back against the wall.

Kris Anders, fortyish, with a trimmed beard and neatly blow-dried wave of hair over a craggy forehead, had the kind of face you see on grizzled henchmen in a swords-and-sorcery movie. His eyes were squinty but warm. His voice was instantly intimate, relaxed and sure of the space that our stories were about to fill. Not *my* story, I thought, strangely distressed, as if I'd ever had the illusion of belonging here. I was burdened—damaged— like these men, but by something intangible, untraceable to another's crime, a dark cloud that the preachers here would call a demon and my world would call a chemical imbalance in the brain. My problem wasn't Jonas but my attraction to Jonas, born looking for an abyss to throw myself into. Which was a ridiculously teenage thing to say about myself. Maybe a career in the funny papers was all I was fit for.

Anders was saying something actually rather sensible about the father wound, our often unmet need for loving connection with a model for the man we should become. Without this, we felt inadequate compared to our culture's superficial, unfeeling images of manhood. He could have been describing the Ironman Gym. We could find a guy in the back pages of *Gay Downtown* to play daddy for a couple of sweaty hours, and savor being held by someone too wise to die at the age our friends had gone. I warmed inside, hating myself for it, when I recalled Jonas' patient interest in my juvenile fictions, his faith in the man my parents couldn't see in me. As for his touch, it survived only as a few shivers of painful wonder, the shock of parachuting out of a plane into the wide, dangerous world of men.

"You've been ashamed all your life. It's okay. *It's okay.* You don't have to be ashamed here.

"You've done great deeds to cover it up. Corner office, fancy cars, beautiful kids, community service, deep prayer life. But you know you're a fake. Right?

"Well, congratulations—you're human. I want you to turn to the brother next to you and say that to him. Say it with love. Because the truth is, we're all fakes. Only Jesus is the real deal. You—*you!*—are no more broken than anyone else."

The guy next to me on the rug, a slim late-thirties suburban dad type in a Mr. Rogers cardigan, gripped my shoulder as he told me I was human, tears filling his pale blue eyes. Others around us were hugging or doing a kind of fervent arm-wrestle handshake. I said my line, fighting equally strong desires to fall into his arms or take a scouring-cold shower. *Please see me, please don't.*

Anders kept on: "You've believed the lie of pride, that being wounded makes you less of a man. But our Savior was wounded too—wounded for love of us, to take away every speck of dirt that we fell into in our weakness. Right here, right now—every one of you is clean, no matter what secrets you carry. You can let it all go."

I had that sensation you get before fainting, sinking in too much gravity, vision melting into green like the cake in "MacArthur Park". Was it even necessary to keep probing for what was wrong with me? What if this sweet dizzy relief could be mine, as easy as declaring it so, and then choosing it day after day, like an alcoholic refusing the cup of self-loathing? *Or Brent—* But I wouldn't go down that road. I didn't have to buy Uzi-toting heterosexual Jesus to benefit from Anders' advice and release the murky past.

My eyes sought out Julian up front, but he didn't see me. His face looked pale and miserable as he supported his weeping brother's heavy torso. The air was so wet with emotion I feared the ceiling would sprout mold. They were going to hurt him, these stupid people, they were going to strip his haute couture armor and sink their hooks into his soul. Fuck all of them and their promises of ordinary happiness; sorry, Lois, it's back to the Fortress of Solitude for me.

I stumbled stiffly to my feet, but it was too late. Jule crumpled into his brother's embrace. I couldn't interrupt this rare moment of rapport between them. Cardigan Man touched me again, his palm between my shoulderblades like a Norman Rockwell doctor soothing a nervous child.

"Hey, take a deep breath, buddy. You'll get through it. We all will, praise God."

"Through what? I don't think I belong here—" I wanted to spill out my whole jumbled history to this bland stranger, trusting that he would finally make sense of it. Which meant he was probably a con man and a serial killer. He was right about one thing, though—I had to stop hyperventilating.

"The first time I came to one of these, I ducked in the door and right out again, like a kid in a dirty bookstore. Took me another couple of tries before I could admit it. My wife still doesn't know." Sadness wrinkled his smooth face.

"Admit...?" I repeated dumbly, skin crawling as I anticipated some unwelcome confession of pay-per-view wanking.

"That I'm an incest survivor." He said it as straightforwardly as he might have said *I'm a dentist*.

"No, you don't understand—I'm not here for me. I'm with my boyfriend because his dad beat him up. But he doesn't need me, so I should—I've gotta go."

Only when I'd fled the crowded room, found a niche in a dim hallway beside the water fountain and folded myself into it, did it dawn on me that I should have said "Sorry" or even lied "I'll pray for you" (the Christian equivalent of "that sucks") to the man who'd offered me his worst secret. I was a real shit.

I dug through my pockets on the slight hope that a mislaid anti-anxiety pill remained from my stash. In the inner pocket of my jacket I touched a lumpy pouch that I withdrew with shaking fingers. It took me a moment to recognize the shriveled brown things in the ziploc as the 'shrooms that Canadian guy had traded for my comic. Poison cure, for real. I reasoned that a little nibble at the Mad Hatter's tea party would mellow me out to be more available to Julian. If I knew nothing I saw was really happening, nothing could freak me out. That's the impeccable logic that got me through Columbia University in five years. I chewed the spongy, earth-flavored pieces and washed them down with metallic-tasting water from the bubbler. Better save some for Julian in case he agreed that Brent's Mission X-Force show would be enhanced by psilocybins.

Based on my limited experience with hallucinogens, I would be coherent for another hour, maybe. I sidled up to the door of Anders' workshop so Jule wouldn't miss me on the way out. Unless they had left already? I cracked the door open just a little. No one seemed to notice me. Anders was leading the standing men in a version of the children's song "Jesus loves me, this I know" with a tacked-on chorus that went "He loves me just as I am, he loves me just as I am" seventy billion times in a row. I edged inside. The repetition got into my head, making me sway with the crowd. What if I said it, just one time? Whispered it under my breath? Would it be like one of those horror stories where a scholar reads the forbidden name of an Elder God and never again escapes its pitiless all-consuming regard?

He loves me just as I am. Tears burned my eyes because there'd never been anyone I could say that about. Who was "he"? Certainly not my grandfather's empire-shattering, son-sacrificing Yahweh, and not the mournful hippie on the cross that these guys claimed to worship. I didn't want his martyred love that was never unconditional in the end. In the darkness behind my closed eyes I visualized a doorway, another exercise that Sid had suggested I use when I had an attack of feeling trapped. For whatever weird reason, the first image that came up was the pillared archway of an Italian Renaissance courtyard at the Metropolitan Museum of Art, where Mom would take me for a peaceful outing on school holidays. I used to carry on long conversations in my head with the alabaster statues of Bacchus and Flora, hearty giants with jolly smiles and fruiting wreaths around their long hair. *He loves me just as I am.* My lips moved soundlessly.

The song fell apart into competing conversations, the business of wrapping up. I opened my eyes to the hubbub, leaning against the wall to wait for the Selkirk brothers. Eventually they pushed through to find me, Carter looking wrung-out but satisfied by the emotional marathon, Julian more subdued and almost protective of his big brother. I assured them I hadn't minded my back-row solitude. Carter half-heartedly offered to stay and endure the conference's boxed lunches with us, instead of driving to Arby's with Daddy Selkirk and his political hangers-on. But Julian gave him his blessing to depart, promising we'd stick around for his sobriety testimony on the main stage after the Mission X-Force show. "I dunno how they roped me into doing this—I feel like I'm on freakin' *Geraldo*."

"Would it help to imagine everyone in the audience naked?" Jule offered.

"I'll leave that to you two."

"You have my word, I'll be out there undressing them with my eyes—for you."

The brothers gave each other a fist-bump and parted. As soon as he was out of earshot, Jule muttered to me, "You'd think we hadn't just soaked our hankies at a sermon that said homosexuality is caused by bad men touching our little boy butts."

So that's what I'd missed when I was off taking care of my head. "I'm glad Carter can let the bullshit go in one ear and out the other. He just wants to be your friend, I think."

Jule sighed. "I guess he's not as much of an asshole as he used to be. This whole come-to-Jesus circus has done something good for him."

"Are you afraid it's catching?"

He didn't answer directly, but brushed his shoulder against mine, leaning into my touch. "There's a lot of people from normal families who turn out gay too, right? Weren't you always hot for He-Man and the Masters of the Universe?"

"Define 'normal'."

"Okay, *safe*, then—where the hand that patted your head today wasn't going to bruise your backside tomorrow."

"I don't know what goes on in anybody else's family. But why does our existence need to be explained? Why are there straight people?"

"To be fruitful and multiply, thus saith the Lord."

"Yeah, and most of them are shitty parents, otherwise Anders would be out of a job."

That won me a half-smile. "Did I ever tell you, I love you for your mind?"

I risked a hug. "Jule...do you love me 'just as I am'? Like that dopey song said?"

"Darlin', I don't always *know* who you are. But I love everything I do know. How about me?"

"Yeah. For sure."

"Then I don't need anything else," Jule said fiercely. "Except one of those horrible turkey sandwiches they're handing out in the Manna Room."

MY SURROUNDINGS were becoming a little fuzzy around the edges, though I could chalk that up to fatigue and too many people breathing the same air in a crowded lunchroom. The Magic Marker pink and yellow hues of my ham and cheese wrap might simply attest to the scarcity of natural foods below the Mason-Dixon line. It wouldn't be the worst thing in the world if the Canadian had stiffed me on the edibles. Readers were readers, after all; I wasn't in comics to make money. I didn't realize I'd laughed till Jule asked me what was funny.

"Nothing, I'm just happy to be here," I covered. That didn't come out right. "I mean, that you could be with me. Not alone."

"Yeah, I don't know how I'd bear it otherwise. You want something to laugh about, come on, let's watch Brent wrap his hands around a nice thick crowbar and make it his bitch."

I gulped soda past the gelatinous lump in my throat. The ginger ale fizzed on my tongue like sweet stinging hailstones.

On the main stage, the evangelist's crystal platform had been replaced by stacks of bricks, boards, and metal dumbbell plates. Bulky men in black tank tops and silver basketball shorts were warming up with squats or slowly rotating their bullet-like heads on thick necks. Brent was gathering up an armful of iron bars with no more effort than a gardener clearing twigs from the lawn. His new crewcut was unflattering. The recorded music overhead sounded like Aerosmith till I caught the words "sanctified" and "lamb" between the shredding guitar licks.

Finding a good seat wasn't as easy this time. We had to settle for a side view between a balcony support pillar and a tower of amplifiers atop a black-curtained platform that presumably concealed the tangle of power cords. It didn't stop Julian from staring at Brent's bulging quads as he gave a piggyback ride to a man lifting two large barbells. Kicked boards disintegrated in a hanging cloud of dust like a newborn galaxy exploding, seeming to pick up burning sparks from the shifting spotlights. The sound of bricks crumbling, once begun, never stopped cascading, till I could feel pebbles rattling around inside my eardrums. The crowd bellowed their devotion, but the man in the center was completely folded into his agony, teeth gritted in a red-faced grimace, contorted over the bar he was trying to bend, like he was taking the worst shit of his life. I held in my laughter for fear I wouldn't be able to stop—I'd bubble over, liquefy, like the metal that at last collapsed into a snake-bend that satisfied the giant.

Julian was almost as sweaty as the victorious stuntman, who was now panting in the arms of a fellow performer as the latter slapped him on the back. "Welcome to the sexual frustration variety show," he whispered to me.

"Not necessarily..." I rubbed my leg against his groin. The friction of cloth on my skin felt feverishly sensitive, as if a mouth would open anywhere he touched me, letting him penetrate at will.

His mouth made a silent O of shock. When he was able to reply, he sounded breathless. "Where?"

I shook my head, out of ideas. In this chemical state of mind, I might give directions like *Under the second toadstool to the left, where the talking bunny lives.*

He refocused on the stage, where Brent was balancing two audience members on either end of a plank across his shoulders, and I was afraid I'd screwed this up. But then Jule nodded and motioned for me to follow him. In the dark pauses between explosions of light, he led us to slip behind the amplifier tower, and then into the curtained space under it. I crawled in carefully atop a nest of cords that gave off a heated plastic smell. The structure vibrated with the chainsaw rumble of electric guitars. I hoped I wouldn't pass out. When his soft lips found mine in the blind darkness, I relaxed, cradled in his arms. He guided my fumbling hands to his unzipped fly. Jule was massively hard, I was less so but his reciprocal touch eased my tension. He bit down on my lip, groaning into my mouth as I rubbed him off. He scraped a fingernail down the length of my dick and I shuddered, the electric shock of sudden desire almost simultaneous with its easing. We held each other, damp and shaky, hidden in our sanctuary.

Everything was muffled in a black blanket, closing off air and sound. We could be spinning in a space capsule. I palmed his cheek, wet with tears, to remind myself which way was down. "We can't be the only ones who've ever done this," I said. A theory was on my tongue-tip, a conspiracy of desires provoked just to trap us in shame, but the words slithered away into the coil of snakes we lay on.

"That's for damn sure. But we're the only ones who aren't going to feel guilty about it," Jule replied, with a bravado I hoped was sincere. I tried to smile but my lips seemed to be made of wax.

"Better go...wash up..." I mumbled, holding onto my face so it wouldn't slide off. I smelled the ocean salt of his body on my sticky hands.

"Sshh. Fuck." He bumped his head on the platform and winced. "Music's stopped. I can't go. I'll miss Carter's thing. Hurry up, bring me back some damp paper towels. I'll wait for you over there, by that Gladiatorz concert poster." He pointed through the curtains at a blur of red and gold stripes in the distance.

"Stay...here?"

"No, they might strike the set. Go—just my luck, I'll have to shake hands with my whole family like this." He pushed on my back to speed me along.

The white light bouncing off the bathroom mirrors and tiles was like paint flung in my eyes. People do this for fun, I marveled, people *choose* to feel this awful, and I was one of those people. I wanted to cry. I stuffed the baggie with the remaining 'shrooms into a pile of used paper towels in the trash. This was the end. I stared into a row of mirrored men washing hands at the long sink. In the middle was a broad-shouldered Bacchus with crinkles around his eyes and a flowing curly beard like Scrooge's Ghost of Christmas Present. I hoped that was me but it didn't seem likely.

When I returned to the auditorium, everything was backwards. It's because I was facing the other way, I reasoned, but it didn't help me decide whether our meeting point was on my left or my right. People searching for seats bobbed along the aisles in all directions like balls looping through a conveyor belt. Too tired to resist the flow of bodies, I slumped into the nearest open seat. Just for a moment.

Introductions, or something. Mushy electric keyboard music. The preacher with the pointy black goatee from the opening montage recited the Twelve Steps, adding more Jesus along the way. Julian could try to find me, too. I checked that my pager was on. Low-battery piece of crap. Why couldn't I have nice things? He was right. Enough of my hair-shirt lifestyle. Carter muttered his amends, his script brushing the microphone with a thump. He was changing for his wife and kids. He'd been afraid to show weakness, drinking to be brave. He was my brother, sort of—he was just like me. Except that *he* wasn't high as fuck. I would've rushed to Julian, to apologize for everything, but I had to wait for the floor to stop rippling.

As Carter mumbled through the second page of his notes, the preacher took advantage of one of his "ummm"s, clasped his shoulder, and addressed him with forceful bonhomie. "That's a powerful testimony, friend. Tell us—do you now know the love of the Father?"

Knocked out of his routine, Carter stuttered, "Y-yeah, you bet, I've been praying every day to stay clean, and here I am."

"Have you received his forgiveness?"

"I, uh, sure hope so." My skin itched with sympathy. The anxiety worms were writhing inside both of us, in anticipation of an error about to be exposed.

"Then are you ready to share that unearned gift with another sinner who needs it?"

"That's what I'm doing h—"

Sweetened keyboard riffs drowned Carter's lagging response, as the preacher's attention and the spotlight swung to another man emerging from the wings. Daddy Selkirk. I thought Carter looked surprised by the staged confrontation, but the shifting lights were curtaining everything before my eyes in deep-sea blue. When the older man opened his mouth, lurching forward with arms outstretched, all I heard was the jagged squeal of microphone feedback. No one else seemed to have trouble understanding. The air darkened from blue to purple. The crowd whispered and swayed. The preacher couldn't stop smiling and wiping his dripping eyes.

The band of sound tuned in suddenly on a few clear words, startling me: "—forgive me for not being a better father, I wasn't myself when I drank too much and hurt—" They leaned into each other, faces gleaming wet. The scene no longer purple but red. The father clutched his heart and panted, his tongue spooling from his mouth like a Chinese New Year dragon. I shook my head hard to snap back to my senses. Daddy Selkirk sobbed into the microphone on Carter's shoulder: "—ask God to make me a new man—" Where was Julian? Why wasn't anyone apologizing to him? Maybe he couldn't accept redemption because of what we'd done. I had to find him, tell him I'd let him go, so he could stop hating himself and belong to God. The thought tore a hole through my center. If I looked down, would I see my ribs shatter like the bricks Mission X-Force had crushed with bare hands?

But I plunged back into the crowd, fighting upstream to where I thought he was, till I realized every direction looked the same and perhaps I wasn't moving at all. A commotion surged behind me like a breaking wave. I couldn't look or I'd be sunk. Clinging to a support pillar, I gasped with relief when the lights brightened to a soothing gold. This was a ridiculous situation I'd put myself in. I should just go drink a huge bottle of water and lie down in the rental car till this spectacle was over. Now where was the commissary again? On the lower level, past the exit door near the foot of the stage...

Heading that way, I noticed another praise band had assembled and the Selkirks were gone. Harp and flute tones lazily rose and fell like the background music in a spa. I wound up in a line of people shuffling slowly toward something that was happening around a huge silver chest, or tub, up at the front. *Come and drink, be made new,* the musicians crooned. Maybe they were handing out water bottles like they do at raves so people don't pass out. I couldn't see. Some of the folks ahead of me were wailing or shaking. Was I trapped in that book Grandpa Saul had shown me, my people's history, the showers that weren't showers? Terrified now, I wanted to step out of the line, but I'd shrunk down like Alice in Wonderland, a caterpillar in a forest of trampling legs. Hands pushed me forward, up the clanking steps to the rim of the metal tank. Huge hairy arms embraced me, warm and wild as a grizzly bear. I saw my Bacchus, his beard sweet-scented with wine, and reached for him with a gasp of joy—right before I was plunged into freezing water that blasted the breath from my lungs.

I drowned but I couldn't die. Water thrust hard fingers in my booming ears, invaded my nostrils as I pressed my lips tight against gagging, and licked, licked, *licked* below at the crotch of my soaked pants. It was underneath, inside, everywhere. If only I didn't move...but it moved me. Moved me against *someone* who was in here with me, stuck to me by the wet pressure—no, who *was* this place, airless and pulsing and alive. Blue world turned purple again. Purple of her tentacles latching onto my prick, her red salty mouth pulling and *pulling*—

I screamed bubbles, the black explosions in my vision clearing to blessed white light as the giant's hairy arms lifted me into air. I clung, dripping, to his broad chest, blinking like a baby at the glow that backlit his crown of curls.

Three voices clamoring around me at once:

"There he is!"

"What the fuck—" That sounded like Julian.

"Arise to new life in Christ!" the Hairy Dude boomed, and pushed me down the stairs.

Brent caught me before I pitched forward on my face, and handed me off to a pale and wide-eyed Julian. His panicked expression frightened me. Had he seen her too, clinging to me in the tank? Was she still pursuing me? "Jule, help me...*raped*..." I rasped the forbidden word, feeling the cold water smack my chest, ready to stop my heart.

"Oh my God, who—when—"

I pointed a shaking finger behind me. "The Sea Witch! She's in there. If the Ghost of Christmas Present hadn't pulled me out—" I stopped, hearing my rubbery lips spill out words that made no sense in translation from image to sound.

Jule grabbed my face roughly and peered into my eyes. "Are you—are you fucking *high* right now?" Receiving no reply, he shook me so hard I thought I might vomit. "Answer me! My daddy's *dying* and you're tripping balls in the motherfucking baptism tank?" he yelled.

"Whoa, step back." Brent pulled us apart.

I staggered toward Julian again, both of us trembling. "I—I'm so sorry. Whatever happened, let me help—"

"No! I'm sick of your craziness! It's *your* fault I wasn't there with him!"

I reached for him anyway. A sharp crack of pain snapped my head back, lights exploding behind my eyes. I fell to the floor, clutching my bleeding nose.

Someone was wailimg: "Oh God oh God oh God…" Was it me? My mouth didn't feel like it was moving. Half-opening my one unswollen eye, I saw Julian kneeling and rocking, his head in his hands, as two bouncer types in Mission X-Force shirts took hold of his shoulders. Brent motioned to them to stand down. Over the drumbeat of agony in my head, I heard him directing Julian: "Give me your hotel address, I'll get him safely home, you go to your daddy in the hospital."

I must have blacked out then, because the next thing I knew, I was lying across the backseat of an unfamiliar car, my bruised face resting on the gravelly lump of a melting baggie of crushed ice. An Atlanta Falcons stadium blanket was draped over my wet clothes. I wished to return to unconsciousness but I wasn't that lucky. I felt filthy from the touch of the creature in the tank. If something so horribly tangible was imaginary, what was real? Did it have to be real that my Julian had punched me in the face? I prayed not, but I knew there was no answer to such prayers, no matter how many times I was drowned and reborn.

MORE BLANKNESS, another fall into the gaps between. I didn't see the darkness coming, I was just gone. Woke up lying on the ceiling, no, the floor was upside down, with my face in the fire and my body on ice. I raised the cement brick that my head had become, and saw He-Man from the Masters of the Universe stealing my shoes. "Hard times," I said, tasting blood when I tried to laugh.

"Praise God, you're awake. I made coffee, it'll sober you up. Do you have a concussion? How many fingers am I holding up?"

"Slow the fuck down," I groaned. It was just stupid Brent. "And stop touching me, you repressed Moral Majority pervert." I was proud of the way that sounded, like something my dad would say on his radio show. I never wanted anyone to touch me again.

Brent propped up the back of my head with one hand so he could tilt the styrofoam cup of bitter instant coffee to my mouth. "It's not good for you to be shivering so much. You should take off those wet clothes and have a hot shower."

"That's what you want. That's what they all want." But now that he'd mentioned it, my skin felt dreadfully clammy, and I craved nothing more than to peel off every clinging layer, to be hard and pure as bone. I dragged myself unsteadily to a standing position, leaning on his shoulder till I could trade it for the neutral support of the hotel room wall.

"I'll stay out here, of course. Once you're safely in bed, I'll go, if you prefer. Though I'm worried, uh...Julian wouldn't want you to be alone like this. Should I see if I can reach him at the hospital?"

"Why is he..." Time slipped, words danced away from questions too big for them. Who was sick, who was in danger? Weren't we all?

"Mr. Selkirk had a heart attack. Carter and Julian went to the emergency room with him. That's why I brought you back here in my car, because Julian missed the ambulance. We were searching for you in the auditorium and..." Brent left the rest unsaid, waiting for my reaction, but I didn't have the energy to care about the old man—a dictator of a foreign country, as far as I was concerned.

"Listen, Peter, I'm sure Julian's really sorry. I mean, *really*. He'd never want to hurt you."

I clung to the wall, my only friend. "Sorry...for what? For fucking you?"

"No, for...don't you remember?"

The fire in my swollen face spread tendrils into my whole body. *"Remember?* Who am I? What is the purpose of everything I do, everything I've ever done? To *not* remember—"

I crashed into the bathroom and slammed the flimsy door shut. But of course I remembered. It was still happening. His fist hitting my face, his cries of grief... Propping my arms on the sink, I raised my head to look at my black eye and blood-crusted nose (not broken, luckily) with a sick sense of relief, of rightness. Which was insane. Memory on top of memory, a new problem to shove a worse one down into its watery grave. By now I'd sobered up enough to be aware that Ursula from "The Little Mermaid" couldn't literally have been at the bottom of the Prayer Warriors' repurposed hot tub. But I had confronted something old, and awful, and real.

Naked, I froze when I reached to pull aside the shower curtain. Pure panic banged in my chest. I couldn't go in there. I sank to my knees. "Oh, Julian, oh, Julian..." I sobbed quietly. I couldn't bear this without the grounding of his simple, steady love. A love that was another way I'd tried to destroy myself? I couldn't be sure. I could only let this false life break, helpless as a little boy again, crying for my mother like a dying soldier.

Brent knocked tentatively on the door. "Peter? Are you okay?"

"Go away," I forced out, his annoying presence breaking the spell, as I automatically turned on the shower full blast to silence him. Legs shaking, I stepped into the hot steam. This water didn't frighten me after all: it was moving, alive, with pockets of air in it. I could speak into its thunder and not have to hear myself.

"Something very bad happened to me," I told the walls. They waited, without judgment, for the half-truth to echo, till I was ready to complete it. "Someone...did something to me...a long time ago. And I will find out what it was."

My plan to sleep off this unwelcome decision was stymied by Brent not budging from the room's one chair. "Please go, really." I sat on the bed.

"Can I pray with you first?"

"That's gross, please stop."

"How about snacks? You look like you're gonna faint." He held pout a two-liter Orangina and a bag of Slim Jims. "Brought these up from my car. I always keep a calorie stash in there because I'm on the road a lot."

My hollow stomach reminded me I hadn't had dinner, so I accepted. We munched our junk food in silence till the room phone rang. I shook my head. Brent picked up anyway. It had to be Julian. I dreaded what was coming: his guilt, my disintegration, the choice neither of us could handle making tonight.

I could only hear one side of the conversation. "How is Mr. Selkirk? Praise God... Yes, he's here, he's fine..." *Fine* was not how I would have described the combined sensations of a hammer hitting my eye socket, panicked shivers, and a lingering belief that the floor was rippling, but I was in no mood to correct him. Longer pause, Brent trying to interject into a flow of words on the other end. "No—no, don't say that—you can't do that. As long as you're alive—*please,* Julie—there's no sin that Jesus can't forgive... What? No... please, Julie, please pray with me. Here we go, repeat after me: 'Lord Jesus Christ, have mercy on—'"

Staggering up from the bed, I smacked my hand down on the phone console, cutting off the call. "You have to stop. You're breaking him."

"But he needs—he was going to—"

"Leave him alone. Understand? Never talk to us again."

I startled at the glimpse of a man in the closet door mirror: red-eyed and bloody, white-knuckled, twisting Brent's wrist to make him drop the receiver. It was me. We fell apart. Brent sighed in defeat. "Promise me you'll forgive him. That's all."

I lay down again with a groan. "I thought you wanted to split us up."

His smile was sad. "Forgiveness isn't the same as putting things back the way they were."

Once I was alone, I was almost sorry I'd kicked him out. The light hurt my eyes but the darkness smothered me. Sleep would show me something I couldn't bear to see. Nothing would ever be the same—and yet, this was how it had always been. It was like finally turning round to look at someone you knew had been walking beside you all along. Your soul, your smarter brother. *There you are.* There I was.

And all of us were in danger. I hugged myself tight, trying to keep everyone inside from tumbling out. I couldn't shake the belief that something was creeping up on me under the covers. Too old (and dizzy) to check for monsters under the bed, and feeling like an idiot, I accepted that I couldn't lie here one more second. I spared a moment to curse the rest of America for not being New York, where you could lose yourself on a crowded sidewalk at any time of night. Here, below my sealed-up window, I saw only an asphalt island of obedient parked cars under surveillance spotlights, a square-clipped hedge, the highway beyond. Wrapped in a blanket, I huddled in the chair, wishing I had a shotgun to lay across my knees, as if I knew how to use one. The fire extinguisher was unavailable behind glass. The heaviest portable object I could find was the iron in the closet, so I clutched it on my lap—the kind of ordinary talisman that, in a Stephen King novel, would turn out to be uniquely effective against my own personal demon. Fight madness with absurdity, why not?

I didn't think I would sleep, but time skipped ahead somehow, tangled my thoughts in choking seaweed, lost hours in the dark. White light invaded the haze. A cloudy morning was forcing its presence through the curtains I'd left half open. Julian, in his undershirt and briefs, was sitting on the edge of the bed, looking haggard. When he saw I was awake, he flinched back and put his hands up like a man being stopped by police. I realized how I must look, still wielding the iron like an old lady who hears a burglar downstairs. "I-It's not you I'm afraid of."

I saw doubt on his face, like he knew what was between us couldn't be fixed that easily. "How's your head?"

My head? Crowded, insane, hurting like fuck—where would I even begin? Instead of words, wild laughter, escalating to sobs. My reaction scared him. Well, let him be scared. Let him follow me to hell, because that's where I had to go.

And he did come over, cautiously, kneeling at my feet, touching my hand as if afraid I would break. He could barely meet my eyes. "Peter...I promise. Everything's going to change."

Despite what he'd done, his closeness calmed my fear, if not my anger. "It already has."

He heard the end of us in my voice, though I hadn't meant it that way. At least, I didn't think I had. Maybe it would come, but not today. I couldn't bear it.

"What I did to you—" he choked up. "The last thing I ever wanted was to be like Daddy. I understand if you can't forgive me..." He covered his face with his hands, muffling a sob.

"I don't know. I want to. I hope so. But I can't think straight right now, okay?" Irritated, I rubbed my aching forehead.

He knew better than to touch me. I was spinning, ungrounded without him, disgusted with him, with the part of myself that had pushed him to the brink. Everything I'd believed about our love could be as false as my happy, hazy childhood memories.

"Whatever happens...to *us*...I'm going to change. Pray, get counseling—"

I shook my head, then regretted the motion. "Not here, not this brainwashing that makes you hate yourself."

"I *should* hate myself, after laying a hand on you." Jule regarded the offending member like he was going to take Jesus literally and cut it off.

"That never helps. Maybe you wouldn't have done it if these steroidal fanatics weren't trying to come between us. And I do mean *come*, in Brent's case." How I longed to believe my own reassurances, that the fury that possessed my lover was alien to him, easily exorcised by leaving.

Julian sighed painfully. "This place is agony for me, but there's something missing in my life that they have. It shouldn't be just a joke to you. Not that that justifies what I did, at all—"

"You better fucking believe it."

"I thought Daddy was dying! He apologized to Carter but not me, and I was afraid I'd never have the chance, because we were fucking under the bandstand instead."

"And you think his apology is worth anything? That it matters more than you and me? He's a *politician*, on a stage."

"If there's no hope for him, there's none for me."

"You're not like him."

"That's what we're going to find out, isn't it?" He laughed without humor. "Among other things."

He looked at me curiously, for the first time awakening from his own misery to wonder about my part in tonight's disaster. "What did happen to you back there? Did I put you in a situation that freaked you out? I'm sorry. I thought you didn't have any buttons for this place to push, not like me."

"I thought so too. But in that workshop...I literally felt I was going to die of fear." I tried to push down the memory of that stifling sensation with a joke. "If I hadn't popped those 'shrooms, I'd be your dad's roommate in the heart attack ward."

He took my hand, stroking the back with his thumb, and this time I let him. "Fear of what? Not God? I thought you didn't believe in hell."

"Let's say, rather, I disagree as to its location."

"Seriously, Peter."

I could only slow my heartbeat by attuning my breathing to his gentle touch. Fuck my life. If the first of the Twelve Steps is admitting you're powerless, I was definitely addicted to Julian.

"Jule...I remembered...at least, I think I did...I might have been hurt when I was younger. Like, you know, *touched*." I couldn't say that clinical term because that would make it real, the name-spell that summons the demon.

He let out a little cry. "Oh my God—I hope that's not true."

This suddenly enraged me. "Don't say that! What, you'd rather walk away thinking I'm just a fucked-up stoner who didn't love you enough?"

"No! Please, don't send me away."

"Go or stay—I have bigger problems than you right now! I've got nothing, don't you see? Not even myself. But if I have to do this with nothing, then I will. I have to *know*."

"You don't have to go it alone. I would do anything for you. Tell me what you need."

"I wish I could." Exhaustion overtook me. I sank into his arms, willing my mind to stop racing through the possibilities for our future. "I guess I should start by being more honest with Sid. And with you."

"First, don't hurt yourself. True confessions can come later." Jule laid his cheek against my chest. "God—when you figure out who it was, I'm going to kill him."

"I can attest to your mean right hook." Jule stiffened. "Sorry—too soon?" I asked.

"Nah, I deserved that." A lopsided grin, though his eyes were wet. I gave in and stroked his hair. As they say in the Tarot...stick with the Devil you know.

[EXCERPT OF SCRIPT FOR *THE POISON CURE*, VOL. 2, ISSUE 2]

```
Early morning on a narrow city street of small
shops jammed together: locksmith, coffee shop with
dingy yellowed windows, check-cashing outlet, and
a building with a blue awning reading Botánica and
an eye-in-pyramid design painted below the front
window. Tall, trim, elderly person in Western-style
embroidered shirt and jeans unlocks the botánica and
```

pushes up the metal window gate. The elder has white hair in a ponytail, an androgynous bronzed face with high cheekbones, a leather cord necklace with an amulet.

Next panel, interior view of botánica, looking towards door, over the shoulder of elder sitting behind back counter. Shelves are closely stocked with tall votive candles in glass jars, hanging plastic packets of herbs, painted ceramic and metal statues of Mary, Jesus, and saints. Larger versions of same in window. Challis enters.

Elder: *Ah. Ramon. It's been a while.*

Challis (approaching, looking uncomfortable): *Ryder. I'm Ryder now.*

E (almost smiling, but eyes are grave and piercing): *You are many things...to many people.*

C: (trying to grin): *That's business, right? Gotta drive volume.*

E: *Your mama and Luis left their new address. In case you ever came to see me.*

C: *That's not what I'm here for.* (pocketing the folded paper) *But...thanks.*

E: *Come, sit and drink first.*

The two sit at a small folding table in the back of the store. Elder pours two steaming cups. Silence, both looking at Virgin Mary votive in center of table, rather than each other.

E: *Who is he, and what trouble is he in?*

C: *How can you tell?*

E: *I know the look of a heart carrying another's burden. And with you, it'll be a man.*

C: *Yeah, Luis made sure the whole neighborhood knew that when he kicked me out. No stepson of his was gonna be a maricón.*

E: *His words don't have to be yours.*

C: *Same old, same old. Nah, I've got a more interesting story for you. This guy I'm seeing, you won't believe it but—* (leans head on hands) *Who am I kidding? I can't even describe it. I must be crazy.*

E: (stops him from leaving, with a palm-up gesture): *Then talk about something else. Your music? Your health?*

C: (in a whisper): *I'm...I'm <u>cured</u>.*

E: (eyes wide): *How is that possible? No one—* (looks heavenward) *What I do here...no one really believes it has that much power, not even me. The candles, the herbs, they give you hope, ease some pains, let you know that <u>el Espíritu Santo</u> hasn't abandoned you. That's something. But—a plague is a plague.* (touches amulet, the way another person might cross himself)

C: *It wasn't your St. Sebastian candle. It was <u>him</u>—my boyfriend, Tod.*

E: *He's a doctor?*

C: *No—a monster.* (sardonic smile) *Look, I wouldn't believe it either, if I hadn't seen it—felt it—myself. He's—I don't know what he is, but his touch can suck the evil, the sickness, out of you and put it into someone else. Someone he says deserves it more. Y'know, like cops and Republicans.*

E: (concern replacing excitement): *This is very bad. Black magic. You cannot make another pay your price for you.*

C: (raising voice, angry): *No? What about Jesus? And why is it <u>my</u> "price" to cough myself to death because some rich fuck didn't wear a rubber and I needed a place to sleep?*

E: *Jesus healed, he didn't kill.*

C: *Tell that to the priest who told me I'd burn forever.*

E: *Neither of us believe that, Ramon, so why are you here? Something in your heart knows this can't go on.*

C: *I want to cure Tod. Can you help me?*

E: (taking the young man's hand): *Tell me more.*

C: *The poison builds up in him, every full moon. If he doesn't release it into someone else, he's the one who will die.*

Frowning, the elder goes to examine the shelves, passing from the cheerfully painted Christian trinkets at the front of the store, to dustier, darker shelves up high in the back. Here there are animal claws on leather cords, knobby roots twisted in jars, bird bones and papery coiled snakeskins, and bottles of dark liquid.

E: (still facing the shelves): *And what would <u>you</u> give?*

C: (toying with a hand-sized plaster crucifix with bloody paint): *My life wouldn't be enough.*

Close-up on the elder's hands crushing a falcon skull with a pestle in a stone bowl, then pouring in a reddish powder, then a golden liquid that causes the mixture to give off fire-hued clouds of steam.

E: *Love is harder than death. Love asks you to give the beloved over to his own destiny.*

C: *Which is <u>what</u>?*

With a silent shake of the head, the elder merely offers the bowl to the hesitant Challis.

C: *So do I drink this stuff, or—*

Suddenly the elder cuts Challis' hand with a knife seemingly pulled out of thin air. When his blood hits the mixture, it instantly cools and turns clear as pure water. While Challis, shocked and angry, wraps his hand in his jacket, the elder calmly pours the liquid into a crystal bottle with a stopper, puts it in a brown paper bag and hands it to the young man.

E: *You'll know what to do with it.*

The elder resumes position behind the counter, as if to signal that their business is concluded.

C: *Th-thanks. What do I owe you? (tucking bag under arm, fumbling for wallet with un-injured hand)*

E: (shakes head): *Just call your mama.*

C: (cocky attitude returning): *Is it too late for me to pick death instead?*

But when he looks toward the counter for the elder's reaction, no one is there.

THE AFTERNOON WAS MINE. Taught a 6 AM yoga class, back-to-back weight-training clients all morning, forced down a salad for lunch because I had no one to cook for. No one to come home to. I hadn't meant to exile Julian to the couch, but I flinched and jerked awake whenever his body brushed against mine, and then he'd cry because neither of us could forget how he'd hurt me. So we lay awake in separate rooms, missing each other. It was a whole new level of loneliness when he flew back down for his dad's heart surgery. I hadn't appreciated it at the time, but his presence out there in the living room had felt protective, like a guard dog keeping evil spirits from my threshold.

Phil had died in this apartment. I wondered what he'd make of the mess that his best friend and his lover had created for ourselves. Probably he'd tell me to forget the past, have hot and nasty make-up sex, and concentrate on becoming a comic-book celebrity. He would've pretended not to understand my problem with Jonas. Phil was all about the hustle, even though it killed him—but who was I to blame anyone for trusting the wrong person? Last night I'd lit a Shabbat candle, popped open a can of Phil's favorite beer (Pabst Blue Ribbon, gag me now), and pulled a Tarot card on the chance that he had a message for me. *Knight of Cups, reversed.* I winced. Phil was nothing if not confrontational. Guess that hadn't changed in the afterlife.

So after lunch I took the train to Rogues' Galaxy in Brooklyn Heights. The store was busy on a Saturday, with weekend dads trying to restrain their sticky-fingered spawn from ruining the new issue of *Spider-Man*, and adolescent boys wandering too casually past the X-rated shelf, standing lookout while their friends took turns sneaking a peek at Gilbert Hernandez's *Birdland*. Swap it for *Tom of Finland* and they could have been me fifteen years ago. The curling laminated sign taped to the bookcase— "Stop! You must be 18+ for this section"—might even have been the same one. Strange to think of adulthood as the end of yearning. Thanks, "Kake," but I can have all the cock I want now, and possibly more—a wish whose fulfillment revealed how childish it was, like all-you-can-eat jellybeans.

I leafed through an *X-Men* anthology but discovered I wasn't in the mood for more punching. A little boy next to me was enjoying *My Little Pony* till his father brusquely snatched away the pink and purple magazine. Ashamed, he hid his incipient tears with a scowl. I picked up the offending object and pretended to read it, to make him feel better. Friendship *is* magic.

Jonas had a new assistant behind the counter, a college-age girl with burgundy-dyed hair and a fine array of face metal. She directed me to find him in the stockroom.

"Hey, kiddo—I was going to call you. We sold the whole stack of *Poison Cures*. Or else they got shoplifted, which is also a good sign." He shoved the last box onto the wire rack, wiped his dusty hands on his skinny jeans, and took a closer look at me. "What's with the shiner?"

The bruise from Julian's fist still discolored one side of my face. If I was a cartoon character, my eye would be cross-hatched in purple. "Walked into some equipment at the gym."

"Must've been pretty well hung to put your eye out."

"Could someone just fucking believe me for a change?"

Jonas held up his hands in mock surrender. "Hey, you like it rough, I don't judge. So tell me about your other adventures. How was TropiCon?"

I was grateful for the subject change. I remembered why I used to confide in Jonas. Unlike my cross-examining parents, he knew how to sit next to me quietly, smoke a joint, and wait for me to talk. If I never did, that was okay too. Maybe he really hadn't known what his friends did with me. He let me handle things my own way.

"The convention went okay. A few people even wanted to subscribe, so I guess we'd better do another issue." I tried to relive the exhilaration of meeting my fans. "There's a real untapped market for gay comics. DC and Marvel are never going to give it to us. We shouldn't settle for subtext forever."

"Damn right. No one else has ideas like yours, Peter, I always said so. I was just talking about you and Ty to a guy I know at *New York Press*. We should all have lunch."

I nearly said yes outright. The paper he was talking about, a would-be rival to *The Village Voice*, published surreal cutting-edge cartoons (most of which, frankly, I didn't understand). "Look, Jonas. I appreciate what you're doing for Ty—"

"No problem-o. Talented kid, needs a place to be himself—or herself."

"But, uh, there was some stuff that went down, when I was his age...that I've been feeling kind of uncomfortable about."

"I won't tell him that we messed around, if you're worried about it getting back to your mom."

"That's not it. I just mean...Ty's younger than he thinks he is. And, and I guess I was too."

Jonas lowered himself to sit on a crate. Concern replaced the glint of amusement in his eyes. I felt rude towering over him, so I dragged over another box seat. "Peter, what do you think happened between us?"

For a moment I was afraid I'd imagined everything, and I couldn't breathe. But hadn't he just admitted it? "We fucked. Right over there. My first time—I was thirteen."

"Were you ever afraid to say no to me?"

"N-no. I mean it was a surprise, but—" What had it really felt like? The memory was a jumble of pain and pride, hot breath on my neck, cold metal where my hands were braced on the shelves. Had I wanted it in my body or only my mind?

"Then don't over-think it. That's how *they* get to you." He tapped his temple with a forefinger.

I laughed too loud, nervous. "Who—aliens?"

"What we used to call 'The Man'. The voice of society that tells you who you can and can't be. Like making Ty choose between being a boy or a girl. When you were born, two men making love was a mental illness. Send a poor scared kid to a shrink to hook up electrodes to his goolies."

"That's like Julian's friend. I don't know about electrodes, but the church taught him to torture himself, and Julian too."

"And now he's doing it to you."

"I didn't say that."

"Come on, I can see how possessive he is, and probably scared of not being normal, like we all are in this fascist country. Your work with Ty goes to some pretty dark places, kiddo. Can Julian handle it?"

"I didn't come here to talk about him." I'd almost lost track of what I did come for. "Ty's really set on being emancipated, and he's got it into his head that working at Rogues' Galaxy is the way to do it. Before I can defend this to his social work team, I need you to promise you'll, uh, keep things professional."

"Relax, Peter, I won't make you lose your job. But don't infantilize your co-creator. Ty trusts you because you trust him, or her, to know what's true for them." He leaned in close to me, almost as if for a kiss, which had never been part of the intimacy I remembered. "It doesn't matter how anyone else sees it. When you tell yourself the story of your life, what made *you* happy?"

I closed my eyes and swallowed hard. I smelled the familiar chewing tobacco on his breath. The Knight of Cups reversed flashed into my vision, ink on skin, my body pinned to the wall. "Do you remember taking me to the Halloween parade in Greenwich Village?"

"Sure I do." He chuckled. "You were so freaking tall already, you made a perfect Frankenstein to my Elsa Lanchester."

"Who were those friends of yours that took me to—I think it was the Limelight?" The memory had come to me in that notorious club, so I took a guess that it was the scene of the crime.

"Man, I hardly remember who was there, it was such a wild night. Not a lot of fifteen-year-olds can say they got in on the ground floor of *that* place, I'll tell you."

"Tall blond guy, Tarot card tattoo on his arm?"

"Oh! Alex—no, Alan, Alan Raines. Great sci-fi scriptwriter. AIDS, two-three years ago. Very sad. You could've learned a lot from him."

"I'm sorry." I said it automatically, but I was sick with happiness that he was dead. Wanted to picture him shriveling and sweating his life out—maybe at the same moment Phil was breathing his last—wanted to imagine that my own body had poisoned him, though I was, and always prayed to be, HIV-negative. "Hey, Jonas—that night's kind of vague to me, but I think I ended up being—I think I had sex with, with Alan and somebody else, that was not—that wasn't what I wanted. Were you...around?"

His eyes narrowed with caution as he chose his words slowly. "I did follow you to the club for a little while, to make sure you could handle yourself. You were drinking like you were trying to embalm yourself, Frankie-boy."

"That doesn't sound like me. You sure it wasn't somebody else in a monster suit?"

"Well, you were rather throwing yourself at those guys, maybe you wanted to impress them with your hollow leg." Jonas' smile faded. "Why are you bringing this up after all these years?"

"Dunno, rethinking a lot of things. You know, therapy, quarter-life crisis, whatever." I was suddenly anxious to get out of there. The musty odors of cardboard and newsprint thickened in my lungs and my head felt fuzzy.

Another concerned look, but he didn't reach out to touch me. I had liked that about him, back in the day. He didn't act entitled to handle my body, outside the time (times?) we'd fucked. Yes, there had been others. I remembered that now. I'd spent most of my fourteenth year in Israel with Mom, exploring whether I belonged there. But it had proved too much for me: the dust, the prayers, children wearing bombs and young men mowing them down with tanks, claiming the soil with each other's blood. When I returned, tanned and hardened with farm work, Jonas had looked me over, flicked a glance toward the stockroom, and had me on the floor, a rough cleansing. And then we simply went back to doing inventory, no questions asked, no drama.

"Earth to Peter?"

"Yeah, sorry. Lot of memories in this place."

"I was saying, I'm sorry you got in over your head. I think we all see ourselves in the next generation, can't help it. You regret some of those wild times, so you want to protect Ty from the risks you took. And I—" Again that far-off stare, a soft weariness creeping into his voice. "I grew up in the Midwest, did you know that? Grand Rapids. Furniture factories and Dutch Calvinists as far as the eye could see. Pop bought me Superman comics to teach me to act more like a man." He snorted. "But when he caught me jerking off to Clark Kent, my next present from Santa was an ass-whupping and a dose of Thorazine. Rather have a drooling zombie than a faggot son.

"You were too young to understand this before, but I'll tell you now: watch out for picking guys who feel too much like home. I met your dad through this lawyer dick I was seeing who wanted to turn me into a white-picket-fence gay. He had a Republican boner for me because I owned my own business before I was thirty, never mind that my business was selling *Little Annie Fanny*. Anyway, forgive the villain monologue, my point is that I didn't want *you* to grow up tamed and ashamed. But I should've realized you're not me—just as Ty's not you."

"No, he's not—he has someone who'll look out for him without expecting dick in return."

"This, again? Ty and I are *not* fucking, and it wouldn't matter if we were, because I only promote work I admire—or can sell. You two are winners on both counts. Have more faith in yourselves, if not in this old man."

"Ty has too much, that's the problem."

"Jealous?"

Uncertain shame pierced me like an icicle, warring with hot anger, an uncontainable storm. "What—no! Fuck off!" To deflect my fists from where they wanted to land, I shoved over a stack of cardboard boxes that spilled a landslide of shrink-wrapped *Archie* comics.

"Hey, hey, Incredible Hulk, chill out." From behind me, Jonas laid his hand on my shoulder, and I went motionless as a golem with the words of life erased from his clay forehead. Instead of re-enacting the rest of that memory, he kept it zipped, holding still until we both calmed down.

"Sorry," I said. "I've been having a hard..."

"Life?"

"Yeah." I laughed nervously.

"Pour it all into your art, kiddo. It'll get better."

Promising him we'd have the next issue ready this month, I beat a retreat. With no destination in mind, I walked fast to clear my raging emotions.

Gentrification was polishing off the scruffy establishments where I'd blown my teenage pocket change on the weekends. Mr. Souvlaki had become a men's hair salon with black walls and silver swivel chairs, and a computer store replaced the Everything Yogurt where I'd read Asimov paperbacks with a jumbo milkshake at my side. At least the Promenade was an unchanging oasis: wrought-iron fence, benches mostly empty on a windy March day, the choppy steel-gray river, Wall Street skyline flashing back the intermittent sun from mirrored windows.

I'd reached the streets' end, nowhere to run. The water whispered in my ears. I gripped the railing, gazing down. Rather than think the next thought, remember the next real feeling, I could fall. I squeezed my eyes shut, heart pounding. To be afraid once, and then never again…

It would kill Julian, though. He'd blame himself. He'd never survive this. I prayed to the trees, to the wild man-god who'd pulled me out of the tank, anyone who was listening. *Get me through the next seconds, turn my feet around.*

I made it as far as sitting on the bench. That was something. There was someone beside me. If I turned to look, I wouldn't see him. He'd only stay if I stared straight ahead at the piers, the screaming gulls, the blue city haze. Then I could see how young he was. Scuffed white Reeboks his mom bought him. Nicks on his upper lip from trying to shave the feeble black hairs that sprouted in odd patches like sidewalk weeds. His body still soft but overnight grown big, musky, capable of secret pleasures that sometimes scared and disgusted him. He was worried about his algebra homework and nuclear war and whether he'd ever get to see the series finale of "CHiPs" since his dad's stupid girlfriend had videotaped "Masterpiece Theatre" over it.

If he looked at me, what would he see? A tired man in a sweatshirt and no-name jeans, pushing thirty, working two jobs with no benefits and one with no pay, and sporting a black eye from the last guy who fucked me. *It's my fault,* Peter-13 would tell Peter-27. *If I hadn't let Jonas do it… If I hadn't liked it even a little bit… If I hadn't forgotten that something else happened…we wouldn't have turned out so bad. Right?*

"If you need a bus pass to get to a booty call, you're too young," I retorted, aloud. A passing jogger ignored my demented muttering. God bless the inventor of the Walkman.

Peter-13, and all those below him, nascent souls in the cavern of my memory, plunged into terror. I shook helplessly. Saw his pants pulled down, saw a grown man's body cover his—*my*—unformed one, my solitary skin, hungry for touch, finding its heat twinned and merged with the burn of shame. *This is what you desire, this is what you are.* Our first, deepest lesson.

I held in my bowels the pain he'd been so proud to keep secret. Even now he repelled my care. He prickled at any tenderness that could rip open our grief. But we were stuck together till death. Was Julian, at this very moment, wrestling with the same impossibilities? *For God's sake,* he would say to me, *don't throw yourself off a pier dressed like <u>that</u>.*

That voice compelled me through the glass doors of Salon Onyx, where, a half-hour and a week's rent money later, I emerged looking like the broody member of the Backstreet Boys. My only directions to the scissor-wielding queen had been "modern, but not trying too hard." Now my black curly mop was shaved straight around the sides, just a small puff remaining on top, spiked with gel. It didn't scream "gay," which was good, but it clashed with my schleppy clothes. They'd be next to go. Peter-13's confidence in me ticked up a notch.

At home, I deleted several attempts to reply to Julian's emails, before simply writing: *Got my first good haircut today. Come back and take a picture before it grows out. I hope your dad pulled through okay. xo P*

His daily messages to me had been long and serious, describing the family's preparations for Mr. Selkirk's heart surgery, and always ending with another apology and I-love-you's. I hadn't known how to respond. Was it good news that Carter was taking him to Al-Anon meetings? I didn't trust anyone south of New Jersey to offer help without a side of self-hating Jesus juice. But I no longer had the energy to save him from salvation.

I consigned half of my already meager wardrobe to trash bags for donation to Housing Works. *Sweat pants are not clothing:* thus saith my boyfriend. My remaining color palette was mostly black, gray and camo, plus a few cartoon-character tees. Might as well work on Julian's guilt and have him buy me some better-fitting dress shirts for work. With the boy-band makeover and the projected expense of printing the next issue, I'd be eating bulk rice and beans a lot this month.

Housing Works made me think of Kevin. Our friendship had been strained since Gateway nixed his application to foster Ty. I could use the donation as an excuse to see him. I shouldn't have defended their decision when he got mad. DeWayne's migraines weren't cancer, thank God, but a side effect of his HIV meds that they still didn't have under control. Of course they deserved a normal future, which to them meant having kids, but life with Ada had shown me the challenges of being a teen with a health-impaired parent. On the other hand, Ty would be a hundred times better off with them than running to Jonas. Each step I took made a bigger mess. With apologies to

Peter-13 for such a childish solution, I decided it was time for some help from my mom.

Another crisis week at Gateway. Two girls fighting over the dividing line between their crap in their shared room, a weaponized hair dryer, security guards and stitches. A trespassing mom screaming about black genocide because we'd placed her son with a white couple on Long Island while she was supposed to be getting clean from crack. One bright spot when Cara passed her Regents exams with high scores. Her placement was underway with a middle-aged single foster mom, a pediatric nurse—another white lady, a trend that made the activist in me uncomfortable, but these were the people who had the resources and bureaucratic endurance to adopt a stranger's child. As far as Mom and Dr. Marla were concerned, Ty was a solved problem, and a precious black family success story to boot. There was no chance of reopening the case unless I grabbed time outside of work.

I took Mom to dinner at a kosher dairy restaurant she liked on the Upper West Side. Cheese blintzes put her in a nostalgic mood. She fussed that she was gaining weight and made me share some of her dish.

Before I could raise the topic, she had another agenda. "Boychick, did you and Julian break up?"

"No, why?" I asked warily. I hadn't told anyone about our fight except Sid.

"Black eye, new haircut that says 'I'm on the market'?"

"I told you, I had an accident at the gym."

"Peepers—" she patted my cheek, staying clear of the tender fading bruise. "I've been a social worker for over 25 years. You don't think I know what a punch looks like?"

I went rigid, heat spreading up from my collar to my shaved scalp. "It's—it's not what you think. Things are...complicated."

"If this is a *sex thing*—" her turn to blush— "I don't need to hear details, but you shouldn't keep doing this to yourself. We've lost so many of you boys to that disease. It's your duty to live."

I swallowed hard to force back tears. "I'm sorry to worry you, Mom. This has nothing to do with that. Jule and I did have a-an argument, but it was my fault for not being honest with him."

"Not you too." Solicitude edged into irritation in her voice, as it so often did.

"What does that mean?"

"Believe me, there were times I could have gladly hit your father over the head with a frying pan, but wanting and not doing is what separates mankind from the apes. Remember that next time a pretty young thing walks by."

"Ha—I could care less. It's usually Julian they want, anyway. And we're cool with that. No, he was mad because I was under a lot of stress, and I got high, and wasn't there for him when his dad almost died."

She laid her hand on my arm. "What is all this stress you keep telling me about? Do you need money? Ask me now, while I'm still drawing a paycheck."

"Oh no, is Gateway in trouble?"

"I don't want to put you in the middle."

"That's where I always wind up, though. So, shoot." Classic child-of-divorce stuff, Sid would say, if I bothered to talk to him about something so cliché.

"That friend of yours with AIDS lost his teaching job so now he's making noises about suing us, of all the nerve. Says we 'outed' him by doing the background check for the home study."

The blintzes turned to lead in my stomach. No wonder Kevin and DeWayne were avoiding me. They must be wondering whose side I was on. Join the club. "And did you?"

"We make every effort to preserve confidentiality. But the kids' interests come first. Nobody's entitled to a child if she can't take care of her."

The pronoun switch confused me, but I chose to hear it as a sign that Mom was finally open to acknowledging Tai's reality. "I'm sorry to hear all that about DeWayne. Let me try to smooth things over with him—please don't go into battle mode yet. But while we're on the subject, I wish you and Dr. Marla would reconsider how important this boy-girl thing is to Ty. We don't have to understand it, to see that he's willing to risk just about anything to be...all the people he is inside."

But Mom was already shaking her head. "A normal person, a healthy person, doesn't split his life in two to avoid his feelings. Ty should grieve now or he'll only suffer later, and blame it on someone who doesn't exist."

My hands trembled, rattling the silverware against my plate. I gave up trying to cut the food I had no appetite for anymore. "But...what if the life he's been given isn't big enough to hold all of himself at once? Whose fault is that?"

The elderly waiter flicked the bill onto the table as he shuffled past. Mom fished in her purse for correct change. "Men who feel entitled to more than one life end up leaving women with only half of one."

"So this is about Dad."

She snapped to attention. How had I forgotten that she could get angry? The wax mask of her face, emptied of tenderness? I knew that look from the terrible season of my parents' falling apart.

"If we're going to talk about your father—you knew what he was doing was wrong, or you wouldn't have brought me the proof."

"What? What proof?"

"The book of love poems dedicated to him, the photos of the child he'd been keeping from me?"

"*I* did that?"

"Don't you remember? If that *meshuggener* boyfriend gave you a concussion, he's going to be hearing from me."

"I'm fine, Mom, really."

"You are *not* fine, boychick. You're losing perspective at work, you're forgetting things, and I'm worried you're living with someone unsafe. Are you and Julian taking those party drugs I hear about? Is that it?"

I longed to unburden myself to the one person I could still count on to have my back, whatever her reservations about my lifestyle. But if I told her how badly my brain was broken, she'd never trust my judgment about Ty, whose needs had to come first. "No, I—I think that time in my childhood was so rough, I let the details slip away."

"I'm sorry. I did my best."

"You're the only one who did." I took her hand, warm and sturdy like mine. "And now you're being the best mom you can for the Gateway kids, and I know sometimes that means making unpopular decisions. But Ty isn't hurting anyone by dressing up. Not even himself. Think of it as...play therapy. If he needs to outgrow it someday, he will, in his own time."

"You have a good heart, Peter. Someday I hope you go back to school for a counseling degree." She gathered up her jacket and purse. "Let me think about everything you said. Meanwhile, if you have a little more time, I've got some things for you in Papa's apartment."

Grandpa Saul's former home was nearly stripped bare. The high wooden bookshelves built into the living room wall held only some accordion folders of papers salvaged from the vanished desk. A fold-out couch, too threadbare to resell, sat on an island of darker wood flooring where the Oriental rug had lain. I plopped down there while Mom fussed around me. "I can't make you instant coffee because there are no more cups, but I keep some diet iced tea in the fridge."

"Wow, the estate sale guys didn't waste any time. What did you want to show me?"

"The closet's full of photo albums, personal things that I don't have room for at Gateway—Papa and Momma's travels, your baby pictures, some of your aunt Elaine you never met, special moments like that. I thought we could go through them to see what you want to keep, before I winnow out the rest."

"Sure, I can take a look. Not tonight, though. I promised Frank I'd come see his new cabaret act." And possibly confer with him—a/k/a "Miss Anna Bollocks"—about how to explain Tai to the people who didn't want her to survive.

"I'm so glad. Here, bring one home, to start." Mom led me into the master bedroom, our footsteps echoing in the hollowness of a space without furniture. Four worn divots on the floor mapped the ghost shape of the old brass bed.

She hadn't exaggerated the scope of the job. A tilting stack of albums filled the closet from floor to ceiling, propped against another stack of cardboard file boxes with yellowing handwritten labels. I pulled out an album bound in fake baby-blue leather that was flaking away at the creases, and balanced it on one arm to flip through it. Mom peered over my shoulder. "Aww, look at those chubby little *pulkies*."

I stifled an embarrassed groan. Though I might be Batman in my own dreams, in hers I was that curly-haired two-year-old running through the park sprinkler, soaked plaid shorts drooping low on his dimpled legs. How small, how far away he seemed.

But who was that young woman in the background, smoking a cigarette by the swing set? Long straight black hair, a *film noir* actress's body language, that pose of mannered relaxation that reminded me of—

"Mom, is that—" I pointed to the figure, at a loss for words. "Is that *Ada*?"

She curled her lip. "That's her all right."

"But why? I thought she wasn't in my life till, you know, everything came out."

"She was one of those grad students we used to rent the basement apartment to. Money was tight when you were a baby. I insisted on staying home with you as long as possible, but your father had invested a lot of hours in a couple of cases that didn't pan out, and I had to fill in as support staff at his office, unpaid of course. A little free babysitting from the person downstairs—it wasn't how I wanted it, but we had to keep a roof over your head."

The picture blurred before my eyes. "Dad always said he met her when she was a witness in an employment discrimination case he won against City College."

"That's how it started. Then she moved in when that nice boy before her—I forget his name, Tom or Tim—started his medical residency. She was with us maybe a year before she moved upstate for work. *Feh*—what does it matter? Now she has my whole house."

On impulse, I hugged Mom tight, an awkward move with the album under my arm. She threw both arms around my neck and kissed my cheek. That was a bit much, at my age. I wriggled free. "Maybe I should never have told you."

"What can you do? At least now Prudence has one normal parent, such as he is. And she has you for a big brother. Lucky girl."

I nodded, my thoughts elsewhere. I loved my half-sister, an oddball like me, with none of her parents' arrogance. Whether she'd still feel the same about me, once I started mining these albums for more clues to my aversion to Ada, was another kettle of sea monsters entirely.

[EXCERPT OF SCRIPT FOR *THE POISON CURE*, VOL. 2, ISSUE 3]

Interior of small casual nightclub, wide-angle view. Foreground, a sign reads *Singing Contest Tonight—8:30 PM.* Background, Challis on stage with guitar. Audience is enthusiastic. Split panel, simultaneous action separated by diagonal line, bluish color scheme and fading lines to indicate a dream sequence: close-up on a floral rug with a doll lying down, a tipped-over box of crayons spilling out, and a sketchpad. A child's hand holds a green crayon over the paper.

Next panel, Challis, smiling, shakes the emcee's hand and accepts a bottle of wine with a blue first-prize ribbon tied around it. A middle-aged white man with sharp, handsome features, dressed in a good suit, looks on from the audience. He is drawn with more color and brighter lighting than the rest of the onlookers to show his significance for the next scene. Split panel, the dream has changed to show the girl's hands giving her now-naked doll a bath in the kitchen sink. Part of her drawing is visible on

the fridge, showing a green human-shaped stick figure
in a sort of fighting pose, but the figure's adversary,
if there is one, is outside the frame.

Next panel is only the nightclub, no more dream
sequences. The suave older man approaches Challis with
a confident, seductive air. He is clean-shaven with
dark hair graying at the temples.

Man: *Ryder, is it? Congratulations—great show. I'm
Jared, by the way. Buy you a drink?*

C: (eyebrow raised, flirtatious half smile, holds up
wine bottle): *Thanks, but—*

J: (laying hand on his arm, intimate, possessive):
*No, I insist. Save that fine Cabernet for your special
someone. I can tell a real love song when I hear it.*

C: (appraising him again): *I know a lot of special
people.*

Pleased with the banter, Jared sits down at the bar
next to Challis, leaning close enough that their arms
brush together.

J: *So what do you do to keep the lights on, besides
win talent shows? Man cannot live by wine alone—
unfortunately.*

C: *Oh, you know, freelancing, odd jobs. You?*

J: *Neurologist, University Hospital. But I also have
some property investments around the city—including
the Blue Velvet Club.*

C: (awed): *Wow, that place is <u>legendary</u>. One of my
guitar teachers, Rico Pacifica, he used to say playing
there was the highlight of his career.*

J: (perhaps too big a smile): *Oh, sure, Pacifica, I've
heard of him. Well, I'm only one of the investors, but
let me see what I can do for you. Call me—<u>soon</u>.* (tucks
card into Challis' pocket)

Next panel, Challis is in his bedroom, which is lit by
the full moon shining through the open window. He sets
down the wine bottle on the nightstand. Pharmakon,
his skin a normal color, is sprawled out in bed, sound

asleep. He opens his eyes partway and stirs when Challis kisses his cheek.

P: (struggling to sit up, holding his forehead): *I hadn't slept...in so long...I'd forgotten what it was like.*

C: (sitting on bed so Pharmakon can lean on him): *The potion's working, then? You feel all right?*

P: *I-I think so. I was having a dream...*

C: *So you can still do that? See people who need help?*

P: *No, it wasn't like that. I was a child. There was no one else. I was happy...I think.*

C: *Good, then you can take care of yourself, for a change. Like I'm going to do.*

P: (spotting the wine bottle): *Looks like you had a successful night! Shall we celebrate?*

C: *Tomorrow, for sure—reached my limit.*

P: *That's not the celebration I had in mind.*

He unzips Challis' fly and strokes him to hardness. Next panel, they are entwined on the bed, giving each other head in 69 position. Pharmakon is naked. Challis has taken off his pants but was in too much of a rush to bother with his socks and shirt. There is no green anywhere on the men's skin.

Next panel, morning in same apartment, Challis in bathrobe and Pharmakon in scrubs at breakfast table. Challis is pouring the botánica potion into a water goblet for Pharmakon to drink. Pharmakon holds out his hand, ready to receive it. He is not green, but in the morning light, he looks thinner and tired, with lines under his eyes, his color scheme subtly washed out compared to Challis.

Next panel, hospital emergency room. Foreground, young woman with heavily bruised face and torn clothing is wheeled past on a gurney, clearly a victim of violent attack. Background, Pharmakon, pushing a cart of medical equipment, pauses to watch with an expression of helpless sadness. His thought bubble: *Without my dreams...who else is living a nightmare?*

Next panel, Pharmakon sitting in hospital cafeteria with coffee, leaning forehead on hand, eyes closed, spiral marks above head to indicate dizzy spell. Tall blonde woman, seen from behind, crosses in front of him to bus her tray. When she turns, he jerks upright in shock: he, and the reader, see that she has the exact same face and hair as Eva Phoenix, though in modern business-casual clothes (blouse, cardigan, slacks, gold necklace).

Next couple of panels show Pharmakon tracking the woman, at a discreet distance, through several wings of the large hospital, as indicated by the signs overhead for different departments. Finally she checks in at the nurses' station for the ICU. Close-up on her conversation with the nurse at the desk. Both look sad.

Woman: *No change today?*

Nurse: *I'm sorry.*

W: *I brought her a new chapter book, <u>Ballet Shoes</u>. I believe...I <u>know</u> she can hear me read to her.*

Next panel, Pharmakon tries to follow, but is collared by a cross-looking doctor who needs some supplies from his cart. Off to the side, the nurse and her co-worker are talking about the blonde woman, who has walked away towards one of the patients' rooms down the hall.

Nurse #1: *What a devoted mom. So sad.*

Nurse #2: *How long has she been in a coma?*

Nurse #1: *I'd have to look it up, but before my time, so...at least a year.*

When Pharmakon looks around again, the woman is gone. His pager is going off, so he must stop searching for now.

New scene, evening, Challis pushing open the door of a small building wedged between an art-house cinema and a French restaurant. The sign says *Blue Velvet Club* in light blue script on black with a silhouette of a sax. Guitar case strapped to his back, he walks through the glamorous, crowded lounge area to a shabbier back hallway with scuffed white walls. A bulletin board plastered with overlapping flyers and business cards suggests there are many musicians competing for attention here.

Challis knocks on an unmarked black door that is opened by a skinny, bored-looking older man in rolled-up shirtsleeves. Inside the room, the man chews on a cigar while Challis sings passionately, his posture as expressive as his listener's is indifferent. Next panel, audition over, Challis holds out his hand but the manager doesn't bother to shake it, closing the door with a curt nod: *We'll let ya know.*

Next panel, outside the club, Jared waits in an expensive-looking streamlined black sedan, holding open the passenger door for Challis, who climbs in, looking glum. A panel of silent driving, Challis with head hung low, Jared focused on the road, but with a small confident smile. Next panel, Challis speaks without looking up.

C: *Thanks for the opportunity...I'm afraid I didn't make much of an impression.*

J: *Don't jump to conclusions. Marty's an old grouch, but he's got the best nose for new talent. Was he recording you?*

C: *Yeah, I think there was a camera—figured it was for security.*

J: *He's gotta show that tape to his headliners, see if anyone wants you to open for them.*

C: (brighter expression, wide eyes): *So I could still have a chance?*

J: (taking one hand off the wheel to squeeze Challis' inner thigh): *You could.*

Car pulls up in front of white apartment building with manicured flower beds out front. Challis turns head, raises eyebrow, in surprise at the unexpected detour.

J: *Forgive me, I did say I'd drive you home but my place is on the way—are you free to come up for a drink? Unless someone is expecting you right away...?*

C: (putting on his professional seductive smile): *I'm not free...but I am available.*

Next panel, Jared in background, seen through doorway into kitchen, pouring drinks at a stainless steel counter with gleaming pans hanging overhead. Challis in foreground, appraising his surroundings. The living room is furnished with antique upholstered armchairs, a chandelier, bookcases holding medical texts, a gilt-framed diploma from Harvard Medical School to "Dr. Jared Morgan".

C: (thought bubble): *Sure beats hustling in the park—safer too. I hope Tod sees it that way...*

Next panel, Jared and Challis laughing and drinking on the sofa, knees touching. Next panel, colors are dimmer, as if through a haze; Challis leans back, eyes closing, while Jared looks alert as before. Next panel totally black.

Next panel, a tilted oval slit in the blackness, indicating a glimpse through the eye of someone just waking up. The slit shows a hand, in Challis' skin tone, locked to a bedframe by a metal cuff attached to a chain. Next panel, Challis, naked and lying on his stomach, rears up in shock and cries out, his pain depicted with a jagged starburst of white light behind him, as a whip strikes his back. Wider view in next panel shows Jared on top of him, wearing rubber gloves. The bed is the only furniture in a windowless room the size of a walk-in closet.

J: (pushing into him, smirking): *No one can hear you, whore...so relax and enjoy it...one last time.*

C: (sweating with fear, gritting teeth): *C-condom?*

J: *I'm no fool—I won't leave a trace.*

He pushes Challis' face into the pillow and wraps his hands around his prisoner's neck, choking him while he fucks him. Challis' face starts to turn purple.

Next panel, close-up on the glowing screen of a
Motorola phone in a corner on the floor. Next panel,
Jared looks over his shoulder and scowls at the
continued ringing. Next panel, he stands and listens
to his message with a shocked expression, while
Challis struggles weakly in his chains, which we now
see are attached to both hands and feet.

J: (menacing): *I'll finish you later.*

He locks the door behind him, taking the phone.
Challis slumps on the bed, weeping.

C: (thought bubble): *Pharmakon could have found me—
but I took his powers away! If it had to be him or
me...No! I made the right choice...*

Close-up on his face, eyes closed, wrenched with
grief.

C: (thought bubble): *Tod—if you can hear me
somehow—I LOVE YOU!*

BENT OVER A SKETCHPAD, Tai bobbed her head to the beat of her portable CD player as the Metro-North commuter train rattled toward Connecticut. From the rhythm that buzzed through her headphones, I deduced she'd put Tupac Shakur's "So Many Tears" on repeat. The Gateway kids' obsession with the rap star had gone into overdrive since he was gunned down a few months ago—only 25, two years younger than me. I fidgeted in my cushioned seat, re-reading *The Case of Charles Dexter Ward* with only half my mind on the labyrinthine depths of Lovecraft's prose. Irrelevant, maybe, to excavate ancestral horrors when your generation's main concern is dying young. I followed Tai's sightline to a middle-aged businessman across the aisle, a trim and sharp-featured character who was absorbed in scrolling through columns of figures on his laptop. On the sketchbook page, he was engaged in the far more interesting activity of strangling Challis while our hero was naked and chained to a cot.

Catching my look, Tai made an annoyed sound and flipped the sketchbook shut. I tapped on her CD player to indicate I wanted to talk. She pushed her headphone off one ear.

"Not to stifle your creativity, but maybe some details should wait till we're off the train?"

She rolled her eyes, plugged back in, and started a fresh page. I waited to see that she was drawing Pharmakon this time, and that he was fully clothed (for the time being) in hospital scrubs, before I made a fresh attempt on my book. And here I'd thought Tai had absorbed my message about being discreet. On casual inspection she looked like a typical urban teen boy in a hoodie, jeans, and black and red Air Jordan 12's courtesy of Dr. Becker. The costume jewelry rings and subtle streaks of glittery bronze eyeliner were my clues to today's gender. Though I definitely did not want to talk about underwear with Tai, there was probably a lacy bra under there, too. I only hoped she'd come by it honestly.

When we pulled up to the platform at Stamford, Tai stuffed all our things in her backpack, and we walked to the diner a few blocks away, where Cheryl Kingston had promised to pick us up. She was out here doing promotional work for Nutra-Joy, one of those mail-order vitamin drinks that supposedly cured everything from obesity to impotence for

$40 a bottle. She might have an internship opportunity for Tai—Julian's doing, since I wouldn't have presumed on my slight connection to the former celebrity fashion model. Let it not be said that I was avoiding being at home when Jule returned from Georgia. I simply couldn't send Tai alone into deepest Connecticut to sell suburban white ladies their joy juice.

While Tai demolished a Lumberjack Breakfast, I dared to ask, "So about that scene you were sketching with Challis—why do you think the story needs to go in that direction?"

"Why shouldn't it?" she replied through a mouthful of pancakes.

"Well, first of all, your humble co-author has no idea how we're going to get him *out* of there, since we took away Tod's super-powers?"

Tai made a grim face. "Who says he gets out?"

"Oh come on. Fuck the tragic gay trope. Nobody reads comics to be told they should give up and die."

She chewed this over. "People do, though. Die, I mean."

"Like Tupac?" *Or your parents,* I thought, but knew better than to say.

"Working the street, shit happened sometimes...it was close."

This chilled me. I knew the statistics but I'd tried not to think about what Tai might have endured. I had to act low-key or she'd clam up. "I'm just glad you made it out. I'd never stop you from working out your bad memories through your art. I know I feel lucky I can do that. But—"

"What bad memories *you* got, Pedro? Must be some crazy shit to come up with Poison Blowjobs Man."

"Well, if I could answer that, I'd know how to finish the storyline. But what I was about to say was, *The Poison Cure* has turned out to have some, uh, pretty *adult* themes—some people might say it's weird, like not appropriate, for a 15-year-old to be creating this, especially with an older man. So I felt I should check in with you, every so often, to make sure I'm not crossing any lines."

Tai grinned devilishly. "Got no lines to cross." Seeing I wasn't taken in by her bravado, she asked, "Look, you're not into me, right?"

"No! You're like my kid brother, or sister."

"Yeah, and I'm not feelin' it for you either. So we're cool." She undermined this by adding, "Though that grizzly face you're rocking doesn't look as dumb as I'd expected."

I rubbed my new beard growth self-consciously. "Watch your mouth, young lady."

Soon afterward, Cheryl picked us up in her silver Audi. I sat in back, grateful for my leather jacket because the car's heater was feeble and musty. Cheryl embodied professional elegance in a dark grey knit dress and silk scarf with a peacock-feather pattern. To cover Tai's shy silence, our hostess miraculously found a Latin pop station, filling the car with the energy of our home streets as we drove past empty off-season golf courses and sprawling office parks.

Nutra-Joy HQ was a two-room cubicle farm on the second floor of one such building, a far cry from the sun-kissed farmhouse and berry fields depicted on the bottle label. But Tai seemed pleased by the brief tour: the kitchenette with bubbling spring water and free energy bars, the posters displaying Cheryl's smiling face next to a glass of the purple potion, and the well-dressed older black woman who came out of her office to greet us, not skipping a beat at Tai's unconventional get-up.

In no time, Cheryl herded us out again, with the promise of a surprise before our return train. Since Tai apparently would have bought the Brooklyn Bridge from her, it fell to me to ask, "So what exactly is Tai's job going to be, and how much does it pay?"

"It's minimum wage," Cheryl confessed, "and she'll be doing a lot of things, really. When we get mail from customers, she'll pick out the ones that say nice things, pull out quotes for our brochures, and send them back a coupon. Oh, and I promised our sales reps that if they sign up a certain number of new people, I'll send them a personal letter with my advice for cleansing your life. So she can write those."

"I get to be you now? Cool! What should I say?"

As much to me as to Tai, Cheryl said, "Don't worry, it's all from my book—I made up form letters you can use, so it basically is like a letter from me, only we know it's impossible for one person to do all that, of course, with touring and recovering from—taking care of my health." Now that she mentioned it, her features did look strained, less vibrant than on the poster. "And I could see from your comic book what perfect handwriting you have."

Her anxious eyes met mine, and I shrugged, conceding the argument before it began. Not for me to judge the morality of fake celebrity mementos as rewards for selling a fake product. Maybe the joy juice even worked sometimes, though I was suspicious of any claims of a single cause for all human ills.

Our surprise was a detour to a Vietnamese beauty salon where Cheryl treated herself and Tai to matching lavender nail polish jobs. I submitted to a mani-pedi to keep the good mood alive, needing no translator to apprehend the old woman's disapproval of my gnawed-on cuticles. Julian would hardly recognize me tonight.

At first Tai sat warily upright in the padded chair, her eyes darting around the room, while the manicurist painted on the first layer. I squared my shoulders like a bodyguard. Cheryl turned up the wattage on her supermodel smile, beaming good vibes at the other clients to draw their attention away from our unusual companion. Tai soon forgot her self-consciousness in the warmth of Cheryl's charm, which was somehow sweeter for being faded around the edges. As her top coat was being applied, I caught Tai preening in the mirror, tossing back invisible locks of long hair. She waved one drying hand at me like a queen on parade.

I saw Cheryl's manicurist pressing her hand flat to counteract a tremor in her client's half-painted fingers. Anxiety on Tai's behalf, withdrawal, Nutra-Joy sugar rush?

"Thanks again for making this opportunity for Tai. It's a big weight off my mind," I told her. "Maybe, if she works from home, and can pretend to be you on the days she feels like a girl, she can be more patient with her foster parents and stay put till college."

"I do hope so. Kids shouldn't be out on their own so soon. I started modeling at Tai's age, and I sure wish I'd had someone like you to protect me." Her hand twitched, and the manicurist rapped her knuckles to signal she should keep still. "Peter, could you do me a tiny favor, since I'm not allowed to move? There's a prescription bottle in my purse, would you get me two of the blue capsules?"

While the beautician jabbed at my toes, I rummaged through the bag till I identified the correct vial (there were three), placed the pills on her tongue, and held up her Evian bottle to her coral-pink lips so she could swallow. "They're to help me focus. There's so much *paperwork* involved in being a writer, I'm not used to it." She blushed.

"Are you happy, Cheryl?"

She drew in a quick breath. "Oh—goodness, I can't remember the last time anyone asked me that."

I waited, but she didn't say more. "That's too bad."

"No, I really believe that true happiness is in the big picture, you know? Like the earth in that photo from space. The earth is life, it's everything we need. Down here it may seem like things aren't always bright, there's darkness and storms, but the earth is still turning in the right direction." She broke into the guileless smile that launched a thousand Nutra-Joy bottles. "Recovery is kind of like that."

"Reminds me of that Bette Midler song: 'God is watching us, from a distance...'"

"Oh, so pretty." She crooned "'Some say love is like a river...'," a different song, but one I knew well, and somehow I wound up singing and giggling with her, till Tai asked what the hell kind of old-people crack we were smoking.

The station was much busier for our afternoon ride home. Tai slipped her rings into her hoodie pocket and wiped off her eyeshadow with a McDonald's napkin. I didn't know if this meant he felt like Tyler now, or a self-preservation choice in this suits-and-pearls crowd. Either way, to avoid embarrassing him, I pretended to shiver on the platform and pulled my gloves on, giving him an opening to do the same. "Gotta pee," Ty mumbled, ducking back into the station. Some instinct made me go in after him. The commuter rail ran every 25 minutes, so it wouldn't be a big deal to miss this train. I hovered in the doorway of the men's room while Ty stretched out his purple-nailed fingers under the hot air dryer, unconsciously imitating Cheryl's graceful gestures.

Two cops blocked our exit. Hands on their holsters, they ordered us to step aside in opposite directions.

"Hold on, officer. What's the matter?" I asked, trying to keep my voice level and low, though sweat prickled my body. What *were* those damn pills of Cheryl's? Had the beauticians narc'd us to avoid deportation to Ho Chi Minh City?

My cop didn't answer. Meanwhile, Ty's officer had grabbed his thin wrists roughly in one meaty white hand, inspected the manicure with a sneer, and pinned Ty against the wall with his other arm across the youth's neck. Protest died on my lips as Ty's wide, frantic eyes signaled to me to keep quiet.

The officer on my case didn't touch me—yet—but planted himself much too close to my face. The sleeping weight of the gun hanging at his hip magnetically drew every other thought out of my brain. I didn't expect I'd ever enjoy a police porno again.

"State your business and your destination!"

"Um, I'm bringing him home from a job interview. His foster parents live at—" I stumbled over the address, recalling the street but not the building number. To compensate, I volunteered Dr. Becker's name and the hospital where he worked. The cop wasn't writing any of this down, which didn't seem like a good sign.

"What is your companion's age?"

Did I detect a sarcastic emphasis on the word *companion?* I wouldn't rise to the bait. "He's fifteen. I'm his youth mentor at the group home that he was just placed out of. You should call the Nutra-Joy company in Stamford, they hired him as an intern today." The cop made no move to confirm this. I glanced in the direction where I'd last seen Ty but he and the other policeman were gone. Now I was angry as well as scared. "Look, you can't just hold us here without probable cause. I have a legal right to know the charges—"

His hand twitched toward the arsenal of clubs and cuffs on his belt. "Quiet down, sir, or I'll have to restrain you." The tone was nowhere near as polite as the words. Still with his eyes boring into me, the cop radioed his partner, who returned several excruciating minutes later, without Ty. I was too worried about him to be embarrassed when they frisked me and examined my wallet. The Gateway staff ID and Nutra-Joy coupon must have convinced them of my alibi for whatever crime they suspected, because they shoved the documents back at me and departed, not before firing off a warning that "you'd be better off keeping your boy on the other side of that state line."

Praying that Ty hadn't been arrested by another member of their squad, I ran through the bathroom and then the hallways, calling his name. I found him slumped against a wall in the far corner by the service elevator, cradling his bleeding hand in his lap. The side of his face was swollen and dark. I didn't think twice before gathering him into my arms. He shook and sobbed like a child.

"Fuckin' pigs," he mumbled into my shoulder. "Fuckin' white motherfuckers ripped 'em off."

I examined his injured fingers. One of the nail extensions had been torn off completely, leaving puffy raw skin beneath, and two others were cracked below the cuticle line, jagged and painful-looking.

With his other hand, he smeared his wet eyes. "Least it wasn't my drawing hand. C'mon Pedro, get me the fuck outta this place."

I helped him to his feet. "God—what an outrage. I'm so sorry I couldn't protect you."

"Ain't dead yet."

"I'm sick of settling for that! What did they even want, do you know? They wouldn't tell me anything because they knew it was bullshit."

Ty seemed about to retch, but gathered himself up and spit on the marble floor instead, his commentary on suburban Connecticut. "Tried to make me admit you were pimping me. But I didn't do nothing, I swear—I just went in there to pee. This guy with a briefcase was scoping me out at the urinal, then you came in and he must've thought we looked weird together, with my nails 'n shit, 'cause I saw him whispering to the cops right before they grabbed us. Fuckin' profilers."

The ride home was interminable. Ty leaned against me the whole way, looking anywhere but at me, keeping up a proud pretense that we were forced into contact by the crowd of commuters. I counted my breaths, meditation-style, but they synchronized with the clack-clack of the wheels' relentless pace. I'd learned my lesson about overdoing the anti-anxiety pills, though. Actually I'd soured a bit on the whole concept of dosing myself into tranquility. Too many real reasons to be afraid.

Arriving at Grand Central, Ty was at a loss. "Man, I'm gonna catch hell if I show up at home looking like this."

So the Beckers' place was *home* now. "I'll call them to say we're stopping at my place for dinner first. Julian will know how to clean up your manicure."

Relief warred with fear of being unwanted. "Nah, he's gonna want to get you alone, rub that beard on his—"

"We'll have all night for that," I said firmly.

J ULE'S EYES SPARKED with surprise and interest when he opened the door to me. "Rowr—who's that mountain man?" But he waited for me to take the first step forward. I felt a rush of sadness that after all these years, he still wasn't sure how I'd receive the affection he constantly offered. Nor was I. But a second later, I crushed him to my chest. Here was safety, my body told me. I didn't understand how that could be true. So I did what I always do and shoved someone else's problems between us.

Briefly, I explained our run-in with the Stamford police. Ty let Julian hug him and examine his damaged fingers. They set to work with bandages and nail clippers while I prepared the salad and grilled chicken that I'd bought for us the previous day. By padding out the salad with some beans and nuts, I could stretch the supplies to accommodate our teenage guest's appetite. No doubt he'd help himself to a second dinner at the Beckers' later tonight. We avoided discussing the incident over our meal, letting Julian catch us up on the news from Georgia. Mr. Selkirk had come through his heart surgery without complications and was persisting in his State Senate campaign. To counteract charges that he was too old and feeble, he'd roped Julian into taking publicity photos of his father doing rehab exercises with the Mission X-Force team.

"And you're cool with helping elect this goober after how he smacked you around?" Ty asked with his usual tact.

"The voters of my fair state are never going to elect Ralph Nader. If not Daddy, it'll be someone just like him. This way, the more he's in the public eye, the better he treats Mom and Carter. It's all about triage, princess."

Bitsy had sent her son home with a tin of her sticky pecan cookies that we enjoyed for dessert. Jule dared to ask about Cheryl's internship. Ty's enthusiasm for the project had vanished. He studied his bandaged hand glumly. "I don't need this shit. It didn't make no difference, you know? I was playing by all the rules, but they can still shoot me down in one second. Life's gonna be that short, might as well do what I want, when I want."

Jule leaned his chair back, considering this. "That's not the lesson I would take from today's events, not at all. Cheryl is a very, very kind white lady with the practical life skills of Tinkerbell, who should have known better than to send you into Rotary Club territory dressed for the Mermaid Parade. That is no reason to reconcile yourself to an early grave because the world can't handle your fabulousness."

"*I* should've known better. Ty, Julian's right. You're not selling out by thinking strategically about when and where to show the most vulnerable part of you. I screwed up. Like Jonas said to me, I only wanted you to feel proud of what makes you different."

"Pride won't stop a bullet, Pedro."

"No, but it might keep you from jumping into its path," Jule replied quietly. "My first boyfriend died at 24. He wasn't careful because he couldn't believe guys like us had a future. And not a day goes by that I don't see these straight assholes walking around like *of course* they're going to get married, start a business, have kids, die in Florida and go home to Jesus— and I just want to scream in their faces. But instead I wake up every day and take pictures of pretty things so we can remember that the world doesn't completely suck."

I clasped Julian's hand. He so rarely spoke about his grief over Phil, instead of pushing it away with a defensive quip. Ty muttered, "Sorry."

"No need to apologize, sweetheart. Stay angry at the right people and you'll stay alive. And do whatever Cheryl asks, unless it involves accepting unmarked packages from strange men in an alley."

When Mrs. Becker came to pick Ty up, he explained his injuries by saying he'd slipped on the marble staircase at Grand Central. He accepted her comforting hug with more grace than usual. I told her about his new job with Nutra-Joy and he didn't contradict me. He'd already said he wasn't quitting Rogues' Galaxy because comics were his life, but at least we'd reduced Jonas' leverage over him.

That left Julian and me alone. On the couch, he clicked the TV remote through two-second intervals of a dozen programs before settling on the M2 music video channel with the sound turned low. I lowered myself onto the other side of the couch as The Verve Pipe's "Freshmen" pleaded their innocence.

On the third or fourth hypnotic repetition of the chorus, I encircled Julian's chest with my arms, from behind, an invitation for him to rest on me in our usual TV-bingeing position. He lay back slowly but his body stayed tense. I heard him draw a deep breath, as if holding back tears.

Another sad song followed, one of Jewel's over-played ballads. Somebody find this VJ a new girlfriend immediately. "Tell me something," I said.

"What?"

"Anything. What's wrong with my beard. How is your father going to balance Georgia's budget. Whatever you've been doing this week." The past seemed marginally easier to discuss than the future.

Jule turned away from the screen, resting his cheek on my chest. I felt his breath on my skin, the warm weight of him over my heartbeat.

"Well, I've been going to Al-Anon meetings with Carter. I think his sobriety's going to stick this time, except someone might murder him like the husband in 'Chicago' because he's chewing gum all day to calm his cravings. But anyway, in 12-Step they tell you not to blame other people for your choices. That's why I agreed to work with Daddy."

"And with *Brent*?"

"I can't refuse to forgive him—either of them—and turn around and ask for grace for myself."

"From me, you mean." I noticed he hadn't confirmed or denied my suspicion that Brent had offered some southern comfort. Honestly I cared less about the cocksucking than the brainwashing afterward.

"From God. I don't even deserve to ask you." He bowed his head in his hands to cover up his tears. "I'm sorry—I thought I'd done crying before you came home, so you wouldn't have to take care of me instead of yourself."

I gathered him into my arms. "You're a moron, and I could absolutely take you down in a fistfight, so I'm willing to take the chance that it won't happen again."

"Thanks...I swear it won't." He sniffed.

I kissed his soft hair, inhaling his scent, remembering, with a shiver of fear and gratitude, that I'd come way too close to the dark waters that would have severed us.

When we couldn't put it off any longer, we went to bed. I wanted him near me, not out on the couch, so I wouldn't forget what was good between us. But as soon as we were lying side by side in the dark, my exhaustion turned to panic and I knew sleep would be a long time coming. Sensing my restlessness, he reached for me, and I let him caress me so his feelings wouldn't be hurt. Arousal followed its own script, not requiring my will or decision for friction to build toward release. I felt better when it was over, the familiar smell of our bodies together letting me pretend the clock had turned backward, to a time before we knew too much about ourselves.

[JULIAN: 12 STEPS]

My name is Julian S. and I'm a
(camera)   (homosexual)   (sinner)
   (son of the South) (violent lover)   (bruised child)
(undetectable widow)   (lucky negative)
   (teasing brother)   (snob)   (sissy boy)
(beloved)   (disappointment)

1

We wrestled like atoms in the heart of a star. How much we had to split ourselves to give light to others. How we would burn. If you constellate the lines between us a certain way, you could see lovers. With the naked eye, a scatter of broken glass. Our lives had become unmanageable.

2

I've come into the ring. I turn my gloves over. Who made the ropes? Who holds us apart? He knew the score, when the first brother's blood spurted on the ground like seed, twin to the first desire, the first waste. I've come to believe.

3

Let *father* be my broken umbrella. Let *mother* be the rain. Poor collapsed sharpness. I turn my will over. On the reverse side I read where I was made.

4

Searching and fearless is the eye of the camera on a baby in the crook of his father's tree-trunk arm, two faces blooming with the rosiness of colic and smooth whiskey, the father's eyes half-closed like he's caught the melody of a distant piano. The inventory will pile up, its price unknown.

5

The exact nature of our wrongs is a flaming hoop, and penitence is the tiger who jumps through it again and again in the same spot, a diversion for whoever pays the most.

6

Are the stumps entirely ready to be removed? The trash houses pulled down? I prayed for this, like all weak boys in a bullish country, for my father's growling machines to flatten and rebuild me into that split-level where Jesus dwells.

7

And I asked for the mirrors to be taken away, from the ceiling over the bed, from the rear view, site of my shortcomings and long goings. Instead I was given to reflect on the sight of you, longing for me, a river mapped with bruises.

8

When you made a list of all the muscles to be taxed and torn into the strongman you would distantly become, you didn't include mine, how I would hold you in my arms like a stone and walk into the water.

9

So I will take a picture that leaves nothing out, the upside-down rainbow of my mother's face, my father's hands that dig too hard into what he would hold together, pilings driven into slippery clay. Wherever possible, shovel.

10

No inventory without an inventor. Who swirled my life in his bottle? Whose paired heat collided into my blast pattern? The tree of gratitude and blame bears stone fruit. No re-admission, says the flamer at the gate, but you don't have to stay here, either.

11

Strike the set, I'm going home. Prayer: an empty closet. You're not there even when you're there. But if you are, how will I bear it?

12

I believe what you have forgotten. Let the meteors scream. We have tried to carry this. Let the stars fall elsewhere tonight. I am trying again.

“I'm sorry, but I'm not increasing your dose,” Sid told me. As he had last week, and the week before that. I rubbed my shoulder, aching from the bodybuilding boot camp weekend I'd unwisely signed up to teach, and repeated the reasons why my anxiety demanded some extra milligrams.

I had my first-ever case of writer's block on *The Poison Cure*, just when Ty finally seemed resigned to life with the Beckers and was ready to crank out a new issue in time for GalaxyCon in May. My friend—at least I hoped we were still friends—Kevin was quitting Housing Works for a better-paying job at a public relations firm, now that DeWayne was unemployed and fighting for his disability payments. There was no more talk of them becoming fathers. My plea for them to drop the complaint against Gateway met with a chilly reception. They were in mediation now, as far as I knew. Though she wasn't supposed to say anything, Mom told me that in the worst-case scenario, she would put up a couple thousand of her own money to settle with them before Gateway's reputation was ruined. Under this pressure, all of us at the group home were working more intensely than ever to make progress with the kids, demonstrated by the number of placements finalized, standardized tests passed, and behavioral health classes completed.

“But I don't know, Sid, my heart's not in it anymore,” I complained, shifting in my chair to accommodate my stiff neck. “What the hell do I know—or any of us—about what's best for these kids? We might just be delivering them to a better class of axe murderers.”

“Do you listen to the kids about what *they* want?”

“Sure, sometimes, but when I was their age, I wanted to fuck forty-year-old men and join the Israeli Defense Force. And I was considered a gifted child.”

“It sounds like being right is very important to you.”

“That's a banal observation.”

“Agreed.” Sid smiled. “One of my ex-boyfriends used to say, ‘Would you rather be right, or happy?’”

“And?”

“And the truth is, we can't control either of those things. Whatever you aim at, sometimes you'll be sad, and for sure you'll make mistakes. So what are you really trying to avoid?”

I rested my head in my hands, studying the floor. Beards required a lot of landscaping to stay on the right side of the spectrum between "Renaissance courtier" and "maniac in a log cabin"—as Julian never failed to remind me, with his cabinet of lotions and clippers—but stroking the chin whiskers was a good way to pretend to be gathering wise insights.

"Have you had any more of those memory fragments, or intense dreams?"

"Maybe a couple," I confessed. Those moments that plagued me were like trains barreling toward me out of another dimension, a sudden streak from an unnoticed angle of vision, speeding past before I could make out the scenes through the windows. They didn't run as often as the IRT, but the constant possibility kept me on edge. "But now that I understand what they are, I can just let them pass through, like you're supposed to do when you meditate—twigs floating in the stream of awareness."

This was a phrase from the relaxation tapes I fell asleep to, on the nights when Julian wasn't home. One of his Fashion Institute of Technology classmates had co-founded a dot-com that sold high-end clothing brands over the Internet, with a digital assistant (think Kate Moss crossed with Microsoft Clippy) to give you "advice" on your personal style. Jule was considering their offer to become art director, with payment mostly in shares of the company. At the moment he was spending many late evenings hanging around nightclubs to snap paparazzi pics of the rich and semi-famous wearing the brands that Shooz.com sold. I'd gone with him to a rock concert at CBGB's once and hung around for the after-party with his colleagues, who memorized NASDAQ figures to the second decimal place and said things like "Print is dead."

Sid only said "Hmmm."

"Are we being passive-aggressively Freudian today?"

"We can talk about the Oedipus complex, if you think you have one." Sid's wide-eyed sincerity dared me to call his bluff.

"Eew, no. I just mean, all this digging around for things that might not have happened is making me paranoid. I can't relax when Julian touches me because I keep second-guessing myself. It feels right to be with him, but I ask myself, am I seeking out victimization again? Am I sick because I can only get hard when I'm in handcuffs? I'm so fucking tired of looking for what's wrong with me, I'm dying to switch off the questions and just *be*. I wish I could unscrew the top of my head and throw my brain away."

Sid's gaze softened. "You're in a lot of pain."

"Yeah, and from what?" I felt like a failure for crying in therapy, even though that's what I was paying for. My tears felt performative, a forced legibility, someone's proof that I could be reduced to the most basic drives.

"Do you want to find out?"

"That's the Magic 8-Ball question, isn't it? Should I pop that pimple? Pull out the ouija board and discover the family curse?"

"Nonrational tools *can* help when your brain is at an impasse." Sid unboxed and shuffled his trusty Aquarian Tarot. "Pick a card. What's the worst that could happen if you don't pursue your suspicions about your past?"

I cut the deck and drew out the card that sent a charge of energy to my fingertips. *Eight of Cups.* The scene pieced itself together from clashing shades of red, aqua, orange, and black. A cloaked, androgynous figure turned its back on the golden goblets stacked in the foreground, bowing toward a horizon of stony mountains beneath a blank white sky. A waning moon, oddly colored pink and yellow, hung overhead.

"Ah, the blank page, every writer's enemy," I said.

"Where do you see that?"

"In the sky. He doesn't know what comes next. He's got a lot of good things behind him, but he can't have them anymore. Or he doesn't want them, like when you're sick to your stomach and can't eat—you had too much of your favorite food and threw up, so now you hate it." I was frustrated with this sad-sack card. My dad would say it represented my inability to get my shit together despite the many advantages I'd been given. But I didn't see how my functionality would be improved by reliving suppressed horrors—if such existed.

Sid inferred from my silence that I was ready to move on, unlike the dude with the cups. "And what's the worst that could happen if you uncover the truth about your past, whatever it is?"

Second cut. *Queen of Swords* was the legend below the imposing figure in hues of pink, russet-brown, and silver. She met the viewer's gaze directly, her white face somehow both pensive and bold, framed in flowing chestnut hair. Full-blown roses clustered around her sword hilt. The sky behind her billowed pink like a storm at sunset.

"She knows what she wants," I said.

"Do you?"

"Justice," I said instinctively. "She reminds me of the statues, I mean. She's a warrior princess—Wonder Woman."

"How do you feel about these two cards, side by side?"

"I don't agree with them. I don't understand why she's so much happier knowing the worst. Unless the point is, there's nothing to uncover and

I'm just scaring myself." I turned them face down and jammed them back into the deck. "Fuck this voodoo shit anyway."

"All right, fuck it," Sid agreed, in the mild, cheerful tone he adopted to drive me mad. "Tarot is a mirror. There are others. Whether you have a song stuck in your head—or you have the same argument with three different people—you're going to keep seeing a certain pattern everywhere in the world until you see it in yourself." He glanced at the clock. Our session was nearing its end. "If you knew you had only a short time to live, what would you do?"

"I'd say, thank God," I blurted out.

That wiped the bemused expression off his face. "Now I'm seriously concerned."

"Don't worry. I'd never do that to Julian."

He didn't look reassured. "Is Julian a wise person, do you think?"

"Not particularly." But I said it with fondness, as his modesty in this regard was refreshing next to my family of intellectual show-offs. "No, I take that back. He may have lousy impulse control, but he sees through to the heart of things when I over-complicate them."

"And does he love you?"

"Yes...so much..." Damn tears again.

"Then I'm giving you an order. Two, actually."

"Yes, sir!" A dom-sub relationship with my therapist was the final piece I needed to make my life a complete freakshow.

"First, you will call me, at any time of day or night, if you find yourself planning to shorten your lifespan. *Capiche?*" I nodded. "Second...when any part of you is in distress, wondering 'should I remember or should I move on,' you'll treat that part the way Julian would treat you, with love."

I was scared of how this made my heart ache. "Minus the punches in the face, I take it."

"Has that happened again?"

"No. I forgave him. I think it's over."

"Then trust yourself and find out where that belief leads."

We both fell silent. A few minutes remained in our session. I closed my eyes, reaching back for the certainty of the sensations in the Prayer Warriors tank, that horrid engulfing touch, the shock to my sense of where self began and ended... I gasped, doubled over.

"Breathe," he instructed. "One, two, three, four..."

"How can I live with this?" I whispered. "If this much almost kills me... it'll only get worse, the more I know."

"It's only a memory, Peter. You lived through the real thing—"

"If there *was* a thing—"

"The *alleged* thing, when you were smaller and weaker than you are now. It's coming up at this time because you're finally strong enough to process it. How's your spiritual life?"

"On a scale of one to ten from Richard Dawkins to Mother Teresa... confused." I meditated daily, I lit Sabbath candles, I prayed to a muscle bear from a drug-induced hallucination...you know, the usual.

"Beliefs don't matter. Make up any image that helps you tap in to spiritual protection. And you need community. Shame isolates, healing connects. Before you go, let me give you contact information for a support group I researched after last week's session."

"No way—I mean, thanks, but I'm not going to sit in a room full of women with daddy issues and describe a psychedelic octopus sucking my dick."

He failed to suppress a laugh. "This is a *men's* group. Not as easy to find, I grant you, but there's something for everyone in the five boroughs."

"I stand corrected—a room full of Christian masturbation addicts who hate fags because Father Flanagan gave them private catechism lessons."

He pushed the memo over to me. "Time's up, Peter. Take it or leave it."

"You're making me reconsider being submissive."

"Hey, I never said transference would be fun." And the bastard winked at me.

Home for spring break from Hampshire College, my kid sister was playing guitar tonight at Caffe Sha Sha, an Italian pastry shop and open-mike venue in the West Village. Nathan and Ada were in New Orleans for a conference on law and pop culture, and wouldn't return till the following day. Julian had another meeting with the Shooz.com guys, who preferred to conduct business at Chelsea Billiards after 8 PM when their day jobs turned them loose. I expected to be the family's sole representative until Mom invited herself along. She had a last-minute interview with a potential foster family at the end of the day, so I promised to save her a seat.

The crowded little place was an old-style sweet shop with marble floors, those uncomfortable wire-backed café chairs, and long curved glass cases displaying glazed fruit tarts and creamy éclairs on paper doilies. Not seeing anyone I knew, I found a small high-top table in a corner near the stage, and sipped a coffee ice cream frappe while skimming the book I'd brought in my messenger bag: *The Echo Room* by Ada Porter. It was one of her early chapbooks, out of print, borrowed from Dad on the pretext that it was time I tried to understand my stepmother better. He gladly loaded me down with three poetry volumes and a critical anthology to which Ada had contributed an essay about sexism in the public reception of the confessional poets. Her thesis, as far as I could infer from the academic jargon, was that alcoholic male writers are seen as tragic and heroic, while suicidal female writers are dismissed as hysterical. "A man's life is allowed to be a sacrifice to his work; a woman's is collapsed into it." Was I so predictable, then, examining her art for clues to her enigmatic psyche?

The Echo Room had a black cover with a multiply-exposed image of an antique white porcelain doll head, each iteration smaller and more blurry, receding in a line behind the foreground figure. The poems seemed to be conversations among different girls who might be the same person, like switching make-believe games with a toy that doubles as the action hero, the tea party guest, the bedtime comforter. Bad things happened to them, as they do to toys: chewing, breaking, undressing, indelible dirt. Sometimes the girl speaking was the one who did it, split the plastic baby from crotch to head-seam, sank Teddy in the green-slimed pond. Confession disguised as cliché? If this was the bathos I'd be soaking in at Sid's trauma support group, count me out.

I left my table to help Prue and her friend Aisha haul their sound equipment to the back of the room. Traveling performers know not to rely on a venue's AV system. All the hopefuls at tonight's open mike were cluttering the stage area with their portable amps, guitar cases, and wires. In the short time since December holidays, my sister had outgrown her skater-punk camouflage. For tonight's showcase, she had put on a black sweater, super-skinny dark green tartan pants that matched her eyes, and Doc Martens with electric blue laces. Full-figured Aisha dared a crop top with black jeans, platform ankle boots, and a long baggy red plaid coat. She was a handsome girl with a resonant laugh, and I wondered if their easy camaraderie was something more than friendship. My sister's more mature look brought out the resemblance to her mother, formerly masked by her tomboyish scruffiness. Against my will, I felt alienated from the person I saw emerging. Unfair, I knew, and probably sexist too. Still, the subtle changes in Prue made me even more unsure of her allegiance.

Aisha went to wait in the long line for coffee and cannolis. Prue, being vegan, only wanted a green tea, but assured me they'd gorged themselves on faux spare ribs at Vegetarian's Paradise 2. Her gangly figure had always belied her big appetite. "Ooh, don't start with *Echo Room*, she hates that one," she said.

"Why? I thought it was, uh, powerful." Making my skin crawl had to count as a superpower.

"Well, it's essentially an Anne Sexton knock-off, you know, all that Gothic fairy-tale incest stuff."

I made a choked noise in my throat. How could she drop *that* word so casually, like a poisonous spider landing in the middle of your dessert plate?

"Was Ada...I mean, what do you know about her history?"

Prue wrinkled her Frida Kahlo eyebrows. "That's one reason she moved away from that style of writing—she was sick of people treating her work like therapy session notes, when she intended to give voice to women's collective experience."

"So it *isn't* autobiographical?"

"Why do you care?" She heard herself and modulated her sharp tone. "Sorry, I'm just used to you pretending she doesn't exist."

"No, I'm sorry if I've behaved that way. I'm going through something strange that I thought maybe she could shed light on. But obviously we don't have the kind of relationship where I could ask her, you know?"

"'Much madness is divinest sense,'" Prue quoted cheerfully.

"That's a change. You used to think 'much madness' meant another day of stealing convenience-store Pop-Tarts for dinner while your mom wrote an epic in the bathtub."

"Why are you starting shit with me?"

"I'm not—I'm trying to be honest about our life, so we can both have a better one from here on out." Prue continued to scowl, so I changed the subject. "Never mind, tonight is about you. I want to hear what *you're* writing."

She smirked. There was my kid sister again, with the chip in her front tooth from one of our unwise skate park stunts. "My songs should be easy to understand: cops are pigs, meat is murder..."

"Shit, you mean I can't eat a cop? There goes my Pride Weekend plans."

Naturally that would be the moment Barbara arrived at our table. She kissed Prue's cheek first, then mine. When Aisha returned with our desserts, my mom pre-empted introductions by saying, "I'm Barbara, Prue's stepmother. And you must be her special friend...?"

Prue groaned. Her companion laughed it off. "Aisha. Prue and I were roomies at band camp last summer. She's crashing with me and my girlfriend this week. We're rehearsing to cut a demo CD."

So that was that. We chatted while the opening performer put across an angsty Pearl Jam song, followed by a spoken-word poet with lively riffs on loving her body and demanding respect from men. Just graduated from

Hunter College, Aisha worked as a go-fer at NBC Studios with a side job as a sessions musician at small gigs around the city. Ever hustling for her kids, Mom invited her to speak at Gateway as a role model. "I dunno, I think I'm too poor to go around inspiring anyone for free," Aisha said, but with a chuckle to take the edge off.

Mom switched her attention to probing my sister's summer plans. Prue was waiting to hear about an internship at an Internet startup here in New York that was developing a new search engine. MIT coding camp was a longshot second choice. Barbara said she was very proud of her.

"The full-time starving artist lifestyle isn't for you?" I teased. Obviously, Nathan and Ada would never let her suffer any real insecurity.

"No way. I'm going to earn good money so I don't have to depend on anyone. Then I can write any songs I want."

Barbara gave her a placating smile. "Well, you're blazing a trail for other women, showing them that computers don't have to stay a man's world."

"Actually, it was black women mathematicians at NASA who put a man on the moon," Aisha interjected.

We fell silent to respect the airtime of the next guy on stage, who read three handwritten pages from his post-apocalyptic novel. Then Prue and Aisha went up. Call me biased but they were the best act by far. Aisha sang Tracy Chapman's "Heaven's Here on Earth" with Prue on guitar, followed by a duet version of "A Change Would Do You Good" by Sheryl Crow, and then two of my sister's original songs. Contrary to her joking description, they weren't angry rants but thoughtful ballads with fertile imagery about our planet and the wounds that humans had left on her. During her song "Birth Chart" I could almost feel the tug of those energetic lines connecting me to the temperamental stars, fitting my fragments into a larger mosaic of darkness balanced with light.

An elfin young woman with long light-brown hair came over and kissed Aisha at the end of their set. Prue hugged her and introduced her to us as Willow, Aisha's girlfriend. Out of politeness, we all stayed through the next musical act. The couple invited my sister and me to go clubbing with them in Alphabet City, but Prue said she'd rather catch up with me somewhere quiet. Taking her hint, Barbara left us with motherly hugs all around.

"You want to see where I'm staying, or hang out at your place?"

"The former—I'd better not disturb Julian. He shot a big feature for *Glamour* today and he probably just got started on the photo editing."

"Okay, then be prepared for cats."

There were four—theoretically, since I was told that Murphy lived under the sofa and would draw blood without compunction if a human disturbed him. Reilly, his portly gray-striped brother, made biscuits in my lap till my jeans were well punctured, then settled down for a meatloaf-shaped nap. Stroking his warm fur made me feel contented. Prue liked the picture we made. She refilled the food bowls for the other two, a yellow tabby and a long-haired tortoiseshell, and brought us some herbal tea. I had permission to smoke up but she wasn't interested in sharing my joint. "I prize being the only clean-living person in this benighted family."

"Fine, as long as you let yourself have some kind of fun."

"What do you mean, didn't we just spend the evening listening to grunge rock and dystopian fiction?"

"Yeah, barrel of laughs. Your set was beautiful, though."

Her expression softened. "I won't quit making music. But I'm not one of those people who thinks you have to give 100% of your lifeblood to one thing or else don't bother."

"I feel ya." The girls' cozy apartment made a good case for a settled lifestyle. Tea and cats, overflowing baskets of spider ferns around an old upright piano, a wall-sized painting of rounded blue nudes with spirals on their bellies dancing along an abstract swirl of deep orange and purple. But this wasn't Prue's home. "At the risk of sounding like my mom, I thought Aisha was cool, and pretty cute. I was hoping you'd make room for someone like that in your busy mad-scientist life."

"You are *definitely* hanging around Barbara too much. Dad isn't bugging you and Julian for grandchildren, is he?"

"He was barely interested in us, why would he care about Generation 2.0?"

Prue snorted. "Gotta roll the dice again to get that future Supreme Court Justice in our lineage."

"Nah, for that he has Cousin Ben's little Mae, destined to be the first Jewish Chinese senator from Brooklyn." The yellow cat tiptoed along the back of the sofa and sniffed my hair. I reached around to pet her, but Reilly sprang up and hissed at her, and she darted away.

"Poor Lena. She's a new rescue and the others bully her."

"It sucks to be the odd one out."

"I'm not." Prue glowered, resembling Dad when he made a passionately opinionated closing argument. "Don't be so transparent, Peter."

"Ha! No one's ever accused me of that before."

"Look, I've tried sex enough, okay? Boys and girls both. What can I say, it was nice sometimes, but I can take it or leave it. Like rollercoasters—fun but not something to organize my life around."

"That's weird." I thought aloud before I could stop myself.

"You *would* say that, dick-brain."

I weighed my next words. The giant cat slowly blinked his golden eyes at me. I'd read somewhere that this was a friendly greeting in feline language, so I blinked back. My heart rate steadied. "I only meant, I've started to wonder if there's some reason I can't get close to people. Something that taught me to be afraid."

"Other than Dad's stellar relationship skills?"

"Nothing so normal. This goes deeper. It's in my body, like a force field I can't see or name, that flares up to keep me separated from everyone."

Was I imagining that she edged away from me, as one avoids the muttering man on the subway? "That sounds like a poem you should write."

"Me? I'm not Ada—I mean, I don't have any talent in that direction."

"Fuck talent. That's our real family curse—be special or prepare to be replaced. Do you need more explanation than that?"

Was it true, was I going crazy to make myself more interesting than all the other aimless children of divorced baby-boomers? "I'm always special to Julian, but thinking about that makes me want to jump out a window."

"Well, you don't *have* to pair-bond. We're not endangered penguins in the zoo." She shot her finger at me. "You need feminist consciousness."

"I need Doritos."

"We have seaweed chips...?"

"You would."

Dried *nori* sheets were salty enough but otherwise a poor substitute for the stoner's signature dish. I sneaked bits to Lena, who'd ventured over again, attracted by the fishy smell. Her little pink tongue rasped my fingers.

"If she barfs, you're cleaning up." Prue came over with two large paperbacks from the hallway bookshelf: *The Signs Reader* and *On Lies, Secrets, and Silence.*

"Great title. Could be my autobiography."

"Read Adrienne Rich's 'Compulsory Heterosexuality and Lesbian Existence'. Just ignore what she says about penises."

"Prue, do you ever remember pieces of scary scenes that don't make sense?" I asked desperately.

"Are we talking about me, or you?"

"I don't know...both?"

"Because my childhood was weird, no shit, but I'm not cool with anyone sticking a diagnosis on me because I don't match the Standard Girl Operating Manual."

"Just me, then." The cats had reached a truce and were each nestled against one of my thighs. How lucky they were, with their simple needs. "There's something about myself that I'm missing, that I need to find out, but I don't know if it's a brain problem or...someone did something...to mess me up."

"Like I said, you don't need to blame anyone for being yourself. Don't buy into that story where you're the designated pack mule and family screw-up." My sister took my hand in hers, which surprised me because we weren't a demonstrative family.

"Is that how they see me? 'Maw, that boy ain't right?'"

"Not Ada. She believes mental illness is a social construct." Prue snickered. "And you're right, I didn't used to defend her ups and downs, but I have a bigger perspective now I'm in college. You know, the social model of disability? Is something wrong with me, or does the world need to change? Society puts certain people—like women, like artists—under stress and then blames them for breaking."

"That doesn't mean they didn't do anything wrong," I blurted out.

"Wrong, to whom?"

I was afraid to answer. She dropped my hand. "To you? Dad's the one who broke up your perfect family. Barbara would've stayed, you know, if he'd given her custody of me and kicked my mother out in the cold."

"Well, when Mom met you, you'd just come out of foster care from Ada's last hospitalization. She wanted to give you something you never had, a parent who shows up for you."

"And what does Saint Barbara say about your bad memory stuff?"

"Oh, I couldn't ever tell her!" The very thought jolted me like a cattle prod. I felt shaky and nauseous, tasting the ocean in my mouth like a nearly-drowned man. Or maybe that was just the seaweed snacks.

Prue's expression softened. "I just want to be here for you now, Peter. You're my big brother, and that's awesome, no matter how we ended up here. I really don't want to relive the past."

I gave her a quick hug. My heart was still racing. "And I wish I could *stop* reliving it. Prue...don't tell *anyone* I said this...but I think I was touched in a bad way, when I was a kid."

My phrasing sounded juvenile to my ears, but I couldn't make my mouth form the more specific, terrible names for it. They all seemed both too clinical and too lurid, words you'd hear on a daytime talk show between floor-wax commercials.

"Oh, no. Oh, shit. I was afraid you were going to say that."

"Why? What do you know?"

"Nothing! Stop interrogating me. God, you're just like Dad sometimes." Prue wasn't the weepy type. When she was upset, the color stood out on her sharp cheekbones and the rest of her face went pale. "Wait...you don't suspect..."

"I have no fucking idea."

"It wasn't Ada!"

"How do you *know* that, Prue? Really?"

"Because—because women don't do that!" she spluttered. "They've done forensic studies and everything. Read Judith Herman's article on incest." She held out *The Signs Reader*.

"Forget it—I see where your loyalties lie." I sprang up from the couch, disturbing the warm feline huddle. Lena snagged a claw on my pants in protest. I rubbed her velvety head with my thumb, fighting off an attack of vertigo by narrowing my awareness to this one sensation that wasn't wrong.

The cat padded along behind me to the apartment door. Prue rushed after us. "No, Peter, wait! I didn't say I don't believe you. I mean, I do. But it scares me that maybe whatever you remember could get mixed up with your grudge against our parents."

I gave her a hard look. "I can't protect your feelings anymore, Prue. If I don't get my brain unstuck...I am literally going to die."

She threw her arms around me. "Don't even—I can't lose you," she pleaded, her small voice muffled by my shoulder.

I shuddered, and detached myself. As I closed the door behind me, the last thing I saw was her green eyes, wide and solemn as the tabby's, luminous with tears.

[EXCERPT FROM *THE ECHO ROOM* BY ADA PORTER (SARGASSO PRESS, 1975)]

WHAT LITTLE GIRLS ARE

made of
butter snow
velvet syrup
(and a gull's eye
and a queen's axe)

made
pillow friends
fast
with jelly kisses (and

cliques of rosaries)

maid of
air teacup
teddy princes
(and all torn
buttons and meats)

maid
of porcelain families
in backless homes
(and the kitten-worried
doll's trunk)

made off
with a dog's back a frog's net
jet swan lucky
step through the glass (and
imagine the ring)

Medea

Drop stone out of my body blood.
Soft head stone fontanel rubbing smash.
In this stone womb I am womb.
Am I. Again.
But ever drugged stirrups spread.
Though empty.
Again drop bird drop egg or wing now or never.
And nowhere to fall.
So drop me drop you now the truth is.
Mine to eat.
Your twin that sank back into my red sewer.
Cut flushed bent folded unchosen.
But you I chose rock paper stone scissors skin.
You scraped kissed put to sleep only at dark.
Mornings that hit your eyes were my eyes.
Torn paper my story right to unwrite.
To tear to match paper doll to doll Caesarean.
So the heart is out of you too.
Is that so.
Stone.

[EXCERPT OF SCRIPT FOR *THE POISON CURE*, VOL. 2, ISSUE 3]

Silhouette of little girl's head and torso in profile against full moon in black sky. Next panel, lady's hand turning tap to fill bathtub. Steam rises from water. Bathroom is clean and pretty with blue tiles and shell-shaped soaps in a dish.

Next panel, a crayon drawing in progress, seen through perspective of child at her desk. Window over desk shows moon. In the drawing, a tall bright green stick figure shoves a large red figure away from a huddled group of smaller ones. Either the green person's fingers are unusually long, or the curly lines entwining the red figure are rays of power emanating from its adversary.

Next panel, mother bends close to girl, nudging her from chair. No faces visible, heads cut off by top of panel. Mother's hands are the same as in bathtub panel. As she approaches, girl flips drawing over to blank side and shoves it aside in a hurry.

Next panel, scene is blue-washed and semi-transparent, a dream beginning to break up into waking. Montage of fragments: faucet streaming hot water; lady's hand extended, shiny with soap foam; child's naked torso twisting round to turn her back on viewer.

Next panel, Pharmakon sleeps restlessly, frowning, as last image of dream fades out above him: the girl glimpsing her face in the foggy bathroom mirror, eyes and mouth wide with fear. She appears about six years old, with short wavy blonde hair.

Pharmakon startles awake, sits up in bed, hand clutching chest as if catching his breath from a bad shock. Soap-bubble-popping lines above him indicate the dream evaporating. Next panel, he reaches over Challis' empty side of the bed, peers at clock, which reads 4:33 AM. In a pose reminiscent of the girl's silhouette, he stands at the window, watching the full moon fading in the light of dawn. With a worried expression, he thinks: *Ryder said he'd come right home after his audition. Something's wrong, I feel it!*

Next panel, he glances furtively at small locked box on his beside table. Thought bubble in pale-washed colors depicts his memory of Challis' warning: *The botánica owner said, if you take the cure, you can't use your dream potion anymore—it could kill you!* Nonetheless, Pharmakon opens the box and takes out the vial that still contains a little of the red potion. Tormented, he thinks: *There's enough power left in me to _feel_ danger—but I _can't see it_!*

Next panel, he races to the bathroom with the vial, thinking: *Must hurry—before the moon disappears completely!* Next panel, he writhes beneath the waters of the tub, bubbles rising from his nose, in contrast to the meditative stasis of his past dream-immersions. Mere flashes of detail emerge from the green haze of his vision: a hand chained to a bed; a Harvard Medical School diploma, the name too blurry to read; the face of a dark-haired older man whom we recognize as Jared.

Pharmakon sits bolt upright in the tub, gasping like a nearly drowned man, water streaming from nose and mouth. Eyes squeezed shut, he hones in on one image, thinking: *That face—he was the doctor who stopped me from following the woman who looked like Phoenix! What does it mean?*

Pharmakon staggers out, pulls on his scrubs, leaves apartment. His skin now has a greenish tinge.

At the hospital, Pharmakon pushes a cart through the corridor leading to the coma ward, head bent, trying to avoid notice. As soon as he reaches an empty hallway, he looks around, abandons cart, breaks into a run. Arriving at nurses' station, he waits till the staff are preoccupied with their computer screens, then slips past into the hallway where he last saw Phoenix's double. A spasm makes him clutch his head. Green-washed panel split by jagged line shows the fragmented images flashing through his mind: Challis' face contorted in pain; clearer close-up of diploma such that "J~~ M~~" name is almost legible.

Next panel, Pharmakon peers through each doorway, hoping for a clue about why he was drawn back to this place. Gazing down at unconscious old man in hospital bed, Pharmakon frets: *I feel nothing—except time running out!*

At the next-to-last door, he jumps back in shock. Lying in the bed is the little blonde girl from his latest dreams. He enters cautiously and closes the door. Next panels dwell on features of her room, as he would see them. Greeting cards tacked to bulletin board show that several months have passed: Christmas, Valentine's Day, birthday, Easter, Halloween, a group card from teacher and schoolchildren reading "Get Well Soon, Samantha!" Dying flowers stand in a vase next to fresher ones on her windowsill.

Pharmakon skims chart at foot of bed, thinking: *Traumatic brain injury, coma*...poor child. He notices the corner of a small framed picture that's fallen under the bed and returns it to a spot on the bedside table. He is stunned once again to see Phoenix and the girl together, a smiling mother holding her shy child close. There is a small crack in the glass. He thinks: *So she is real—in this world too? How is it possible?*

Next panel, Pharmakon gently bends over the child. Her face looks angelic in repose. His is furrowed with inner conflict, thinking: *I can cure the innocent as well as poison the guilty...but it might be the last thing I ever do.* Hazy memory image of a lovers' kiss between him and Challis. Next panel, memory bubble pops, and Pharmakon leans forward with expression of painful determination and kisses child's forehead.

A bolt of green lightning passes from her to him, flinging him backward. She starts to have a violent seizure. Monitors go crazy with lights and beeping. Pharmakon scrambles to his feet and flees the room. Next panel, he has ducked into a supply closet, trembling as he holds his green hands before his face. From outside comes the loudspeaker of the PA system: *Paging Dr. Jared Morgan...code blue...paging Dr. Jared Morgan...*

Pharmakon clutches his head as two images appear
to him: Challis' face turning blue from the hands
gripping his throat, and a closer view of the
diploma where the doctor's name is finally legible.
Next panel, he dives for the computer at the nurses'
station. The staff have all left the desk to run
toward the girls' room. Small stacked panels show
Pharmakon first typing a password, then pulling up
the hospital directory, close-up on Morgan's home
address. Green finger dials phone. Voice bubble:
*Hello, 911? Reporting a fire at 55 Riverstone
Avenue...Apartment 3A...come quick!*

Dropped receiver dangles from cord off edge of desk.
Pharmakon slumps to floor, unconscious.

"Why is this night different from all other nights?"

Everyone around the Passover seder table at Aunt Nora's home in Brooklyn could have given a different answer. For eight-year-old cousin Justin, her oldest grandchild, the answers to the Four Questions that he sounded out in his early-reader's monotone were illustrated right there in his cartoon Haggadah: we eat matzoh, we dip parsley in the saltwater bowls of our ancestors' tears, and so on. For his four-year-old brother Noah, it was an excuse to stay up late, the charm of which was wearing off as he squirmed on the lap of his mother, Ben's sister Michelle. For baby Mae, it was probably the first time she'd seen this many white people in one place. Not knowing any better, she was taking it rather well.

With her arrival, Ben and Amy's wandering in the desert was over. The new mom's glow was all the makeup she needed to brighten her washed-out face and carelessly pinned hair, the marks of sleepless nights with a nine-month-old whose body was slowly learning that this stranger was family. They were practicing something called attachment parenting, which meant Amy wouldn't unstrap the baby carrier from her chest without a really good reason; peeing and sleeping didn't count. She was going to have killer abs when this was through.

Subdued but smooth, Ben led the service, Aunt Nora and Uncle Leo having passed the torch to him to celebrate his new status as a *paterfamilias*. My job was to sit next to him and discreetly tap the page number if he dozed off with his eyes open and lost his place. So far it hadn't happened, but we were only on the first of the four cups of wine. *Four of Cups*, I thought, coincidentally the card I'd drawn this morning from the new Tarot deck Prue had bought me as a peace offering. It had medieval-style illustrations in a palette of primary colors, cheerier than the Aquarian. A dark-haired person in a tunic sat cross-legged under a tree, brooding or meditating, while, unseen or ignored, three cups waited on the ground and a disembodied hand from a cloud offered a fourth. I had no clue what it meant except that I would be wise to go easy on the Manischewitz.

This was not a problem for Julian, who was preaching the gospel of Al-Anon to my mother at the other end of the table—or possibly encouraging her to shop at Shooz.com, his other main passion of the moment. Yes, that's right, in a move that would surely win me the Nobel Peace Prize if

I wasn't assassinated first, I had persuaded Nathan's family to include his ex-wife in the celebration. Of my three parents, Ada had actually been the most relaxed about this. Barbara was conflicted for awhile, though she'd gotten along well with her former sister-in-law. I sometimes thought she missed my father's extended family more than the man himself. But it was either this or the Chabad Lubavitch community seder in Williamsburg. I had to discourage that relationship before she started picturing me with sidecurls, a plump wife in ankle-length denim skirt and tennis shoes, and thirteen solemn children. Those guys were the evangelicals of Judaism. It was all fun and games till you realized you were trapped in a time machine programmed for 19th-century Lithuania.

Someone with a similar nostalgic vision had created Justin's comic-book version of the seder prayerbook, which was narrated by humanoid goats dressed like the cast of "Yentl". My young cousin regularly tugged my sleeve for help deciphering a difficult word in the captions. Between the instructions for the seder, the relevant Bible stories were dramatized in the style of an action comic. I hoped he'd fall asleep before the slaying of the firstborn. But maybe normal kids didn't connect those dots to themselves; they raced happily through the battles assuming they held the victor's sword.

The eight-year-old was briefly impressed that I was a real live comic-book writer, but I sensed I had lost him with my explanation of *The Poison Cure*: "It's about a mysterious man who, ah, kisses bad guys and makes them die."

Justin squinched up his face. "Why would anyone do *that*?"

I mentally ran through some age-appropriate ways to share the beauty of human sexual diversity, and settled on: "Well, it's easier on the knuckles than punching them."

Ben listened in on this exchange with a demeanor that could have been either brooding or too tired to move his face. I snapped my fingers at him. "The lights are on, anybody home?"

"No, I couldn't find a Shabbos goy to turn them off."

We shared a chuckle. No one in our family had been that orthodox in their ritual observance since my grandmother's generation.

"So, are you being a good feminist dad and sharing in the midnight poop-wiping?"

"Not so much. She's not a bad sleeper, matter of fact. Amy's more worried when she *doesn't* cry. I read, in these orphanages, the babies learn not to bother because no one comes when they call."

"That's so sad."

"Yeah, you see why Amy's doing it by the book, to make sure there's an adult glued to Mae at all times so she knows she's loved."

Something in my cousin's tone made me ask, "But you're not so sure? You miss your, um, couple's alone time?" According to Prue, this was Dad's one piece of sex-education advice when she and Ada came home from her first OB-GYN appointment at fourteen: don't marry your baby and leave your husband out in the cold.

"Oh man, forget about that, neither of us have the energy to jerk off until 1998. To paraphrase Henry Kissinger, sleep is the ultimate aphrodisiac." We laughed. Then he lowered his voice, more serious: "I just don't know what I'm supposed to feel...what any of us are supposed to feel. When I touch Mae, with nothing in my heart, does she register that as love just the same? Am I less of a stranger if I touch her more? When I hold back and let someone else cuddle and change her, because I don't know what I might do wrong, how I could hurt her—that's from love, too, but nobody will recognize it."

"You sound like me. Sometimes we know mentally that we love someone, right, but we can't seem to get it across in a way they understand, and then it's a short step to scaring ourselves with the possibility that we don't have any real feelings. But you do, I'm sure you do."

"Of course. Of course." A tight smile, but his eyes were misty.

"Hey...it's not politically correct, but you can tell me...are you having trouble warming up to her because she isn't yours, biologically?"

His shoulders relaxed. "That would be the obvious reason, right? I've asked myself many times, but I was pretty sure I made peace with it three years and two failed matches ago!"

"What an ordeal." People who knew nothing about adoption often clucked about "so many children who need homes," but those were the older children, the angry and odd ones who fetched up at Gateway from shelters and street corners, not the brown-eyed babies that Amy dreamed of carrying.

"You have no idea, Peter—the stress of turning your body and mind inside-out to be judged by bureaucrats you'll never meet, trying not to have anything but 100% normal American dad thoughts, in case you let the wrong thing slip out—it could be I'm just tapped-out from the process and I've got nothing left in me to enjoy the rewards." Ben sat back, nodding as he surveyed the gathering. "But look at this family. Look at us, all together."

The great hope of the next generation chose that moment to grab a blob of magenta horseradish in her tiny fist, stuff it in her mouth, and blort the unexpectedly spicy food, along with the contents of her stomach, all over Amy's coral sweater set. Mother and child both burst into tears.

"Maybe the enjoyment phase doesn't start till she's no longer a body-fluids time bomb?" I ventured.

Surprising me, Julian was first on the scene to unstrap the squalling pink-streaked bundle from Amy's chest so the weary mom could go freshen up. Mae wore a simple swaddling wrap that even a guy could remove. He wiped her chubby face and belly with wet towelettes passed by a bucket brigade of female relatives. Bouncing on his arm, Mae soon calmed, returning to her usual silent watchfulness. Julian smiled at her, wincing a little but not pulling away when she used his finger as a teething ring.

Ben gave my boyfriend a grateful thumbs-up. Resuming his ceremonial role, he announced, "All right, people, it's time to quit kibbitzing and get through the Ten Plagues so we can eat our brisket!"

Jule raised the hand that wasn't being drooled on. "Pardon me, but I think I smell something...less appetizing. Can you supply a field dressing?"

"On it." Ben went over to a white wicker cabinet that held diaper-change supplies. My mother drew her arm around Julian and the baby, taking charge. Using the floor as an impromptu changing table (since Amy was still in the bathroom, perhaps acquainting herself with Valium and a power nap in the tub), Barbara demonstrated how to clean the baby's privates.

An iron band constricted my heart as I watched them. For a few instants my vision narrowed to a black tunnel. Green pinpoints of light squirmed and popped around the edges of the scene before me, breaking it up each time it almost became clear. Ben was holding the baby's legs in the air while my mother guided Julian's hand with the wet wipe. With every stroke on her body, my heartbeats banged more frantically, willing this one to be the last.

I fumbled for my water glass, to dip my fingers in and splash my face, but they came away red, my brow sticky with the wine I'd dunked them in by mistake. When I dared glance at the group on the floor again, everyone was gone, re-seated around the table for the rest of the pre-dinner ritual. Trembling, I dabbed the plagues on a saucer with my stained fingertip: hail, blood and darkness.

No cause to regret the fleshpots of Egypt at the Kipnis family table. Accompanying Aunt Nora's famous brisket was a potato kugel from Michelle, another one (better, in my opinion) from my mother, Prue's vegan bean salad, and bottles of Baron Herzog kosher rosé selected by Nathan. The kids could look forward to those boxed treats that were a novelty of the season, pasty macaroons and jelly rings that were more satisfying to play with than to eat. Julian and I had contributed a fruit trifle from his mama's *A Table to Celebrate* cookbook, adapted with non-dairy whipped cream. Of course he had no idea how many peaches equaled two cups, so we wound up with a double portion of potluck dessert and a little more left over for a decadent breakfast.

Jule took the extra dish over to Kevin and DeWayne's apartment as a peace offering on my behalf since Kev hadn't returned my recent calls. He reported back that Dee didn't leave his bed much, more from depression than illness, at loose ends since losing his teaching job. My boyfriend prescribed a makeover and a road trip. "We'll just drag him out of there," Jule told me. "Come along next time. Don't wait for an invitation."

"Is that what you learn in 12-Step, to force your amends on people?"

"There's no time for bullshit quarrels, is all. You remember how we all came together for Phil. They need you, even if they're too pissed-off at life to admit it."

Seeing the unlikely harmony of our broken and blended family at the seder, I could begin to hope that any rift could be healed. But the comfort of tasting my mother's holiday cooking was mixed with unease about my weird panic attack during Mae's diaper change. Did I feel the walls of marital commitment closing in? Was Julian, of all people, going to make another sortie into hetero-normalcy by proposing that we become dads? It wasn't a wholly unattractive prospect...for some future me who had put all his mental marbles back into the bag, and, oh yes, regained the ability to tolerate a hand job without feeling that Satan was munching on his testicles. I didn't want to be the first client to take an express ride to the psych ward from the jerk-off room at the fertility clinic.

Aunt Nora served Passover dinner buffet-style so folks could move around and mingle after sitting through the lengthy service. It also lessened the pressure to create a perfect seating chart that separated all family combatants. One could discreetly find a more congenial companion at halftime. The kids especially appreciated the chance to escape the table. Noah ate a piece of fruit and seven jelly rings for dinner and fell asleep on the couch. Justin enlisted his father Dave, Ben, and Prue to act out the battle scenes from his Bible comic. And I found myself squeezed onto the loveseat with Ada, immobilized by the plate of meat and potatoes on my lap. We smiled awkwardly at each other. She was smart-looking tonight in a black silk jumpsuit with a wide shiny red belt and matching high heels.

"Barbaric," she commented with a wry expression, gesturing with her wineglass at the mayhem in the center of the living room, where Justin was drowning the Egyptians in a Red Sea made of couch cushions. "Not that there's anything wrong with that. The blood and gore was the only interesting part of Catholic school."

"That's right, I forgot you weren't raised Jewish."

"No matter, one baseless guilt complex is much like another. Irish, Jewish, either way it all comes down to sexual shame and potatoes."

"Well, one out of two ain't bad." To my surprise, I liked my stepmother's bluntness and bracing wit. Our legs were lightly touching but I felt no charge, none of that telltale shiver of the curtain between reality and the hidden past.

"Prue tells me you're starting to take your writing seriously."

"If you consider comic books serious..." I replied, hoping to head off any mockery. I worried about seeming childish next to my peers in the family. Dave and Michelle were doctors, Amy was the school representative for her teachers' union, and Prue's music was only a diversion from her future as a software mogul. Rather like Ben, who'd once dreamed of opera stardom till a sudden attack of piety or pragmatism in his early teens put him on the cantor track.

"Why not? Genre has no inherent value. A hundred years ago they warned young girls that reading novels would addle their brains. Now the schools force-feed it to them."

Thus encouraged, I told her a bit about Challis and Pharmakon's latest plot impasse, the looming deadline of GalaxyCon next month, and even a hint of Ty's identity crisis. The latter issue piqued Ada's interest because, she said, her current poetry manuscript was about "problematizing the assignment of gender to natural and technical phenomena in the Western literary tradition." What she meant, though don't quote me on this, is that we stereotype civilization as male and unspoiled wild nature as female, particularly those natural features that seem more submissive or soft. "But I want to ask, how is a mountain's hardness and remoteness like a woman? In what ways is the ocean male?"

This turned my inner map of symbols upside-down, for sure. "Hmm... because the ocean wants to conquer the land? It's greedy for treasure ships, like a pirate?"

"Brilliant!" Ada clapped her small hands. "If I use that, I'll credit you."

"Thanks—now can you solve *my* plot problems?"

"Uh-uh. Writing isn't about fixing messes. Lean into the weird. That's what I tell my students. They're so young, they're still worried about going crazy. Especially the girls. They've absorbed this pseudo-Romantic notion that you find art by sticking your head in an oven. When actually it's very boring to be mentally ill. I'm open with them about that. What I say is, when you're lost in a dark wood, just keep going. There'll be something worth writing about on the other side—even if it's Hell."

"That's so helpful," I said, sincerely. Maybe, despite everything I'd believed about her, she was the one who could help me understand. "Ada, I think I'm—"

But her mind zoomed past the gap where my words could have taken root. "For instance, in my poem 'Cave/Man'—that's 'cave-slash-man'—I'm re-valuing the subterranean space not as womb but as male withholding of emotion, the walled-off hollowness..."

Inwardly I sighed. This was Ada, consistently mercurial. Perhaps alone among my family, she wouldn't be afraid of the strange ways my mind worked (or didn't), but the bridge from there to emotional support could be washed out in an instant. Besides, I did *not* want to hear about any attempts to explore my dad's cave.

Now Ben and the women were rounding up the kids for the back end of the seder ritual. Recovering momentum after the dinner break was always hard. Noah beat out his big brother to find the *afikomen* behind a large potted aloe vera and was rewarded with a $10 bill from Uncle Leo, while Justin received the consolation prize of a bag of macaroons. "Why do I have to share? Noah isn't sharing his prize," the older boy whined.

"Because money isn't bad for you, but sugar is," Michelle shut him down. I doubted I'd be able to parent with such simple certainty—or at all, really. My stepmother and I had too many jagged edges in common.

When we were back in our seats, Ben poured the last of the good wine into the extra goblet set aside for the Prophet Elijah. Dad sprang up to open the door for our invisible guest so he could sneak outside for a cigarette. More than one of the adults was flush-faced and sleepy-eyed from the heavy meal and sweet liquor. Side conversations murmured along while Ben zipped through the closing prayers. With more enthusiasm than harmony, we chimed in on the old tunes "Dayenu" and "Had Gadya". Ben offered me the remainder of the prophet's wine. "I switched to grape juice after cup number one—have to be up early tomorrow for my 8 AM bar mitzvah boy," he explained. As cantor, he was tasked with prepping the congregation's 13-year-olds to chant their Torah portion.

I nursed the light, sweet drink with small sips that warmed and calmed me. The party was breaking up. My parents said goodbye to me separately and went home without killing each other. *"Nes gadol haya sham,"* I said under my breath, unseasonally but aptly: a great miracle happened there. Waiting for Julian to finish his conversation with Leo, I thumbed through the comic-book Haggadah that Justin's parents had left behind in their haste to bundle the cranky kids into their SUV. Four cups, four questions, four children with a single trait that defines their place in history.

The wicked child asks, "What does this service mean to you?" He says "to you," but not to him. By setting himself outside the community, he has denied what is fundamental. You shall say to him, "It is because of what the Lord did for <u>me</u> when I left Egypt—for me, and not for you. If you had been there, you would not have been redeemed."

In the half-page image below the text, a wailing child thrashed vainly against the restraining arms of glowering Egyptian guards, as he watched his whole clan follow Moses away across the burnt-orange sands. Not a single one looked back.

I pushed the book aside and went to help Amy clear the table. Ben intercepted me. "Do you want a turn to hold the baby?"

I didn't, but it would have been rude to refuse. She was lighter than I expected, but dense with warm life energy, like a tiny sun. Her feathery black hair gave off a scent of mingled lavender shampoo and pee that was strangely endearing. I was holding a real person who would be lonely and take a shit and get mad when Stuart Little's bird girlfriend broke up with him. My eyes watered. Ben threw his arm around my shoulders. "I know, right? It gets you right in the *kishkes*."

"See, you have nothing to worry about. Catch up on your sleep and let Mae work her magic."

"Sleep, what's that? You offering to babysit, cuz?" Ben teased.

Aunt Nora swooped in. "Oh, Peter, how sweet—we can always count on you. Ben, before you all go, I almost forgot to give you this clipping from the *Times* arts section. Did you hear about Mr. Schecker? What a shame."

Ben froze. He seemed to have forgotten what to do with his hands. Aunt Nora held out the newspaper page, perplexed that he didn't take it. I caught sight of a photo of a square-faced middle-aged man with a goatee, charismatic in a broody German philosopher sort of way. I only read the first word of the headline, *Remembering...*, before it was flicked out of view.

"What about him?" Ben finally said.

"He passed away last month. Only 53. Liver failure. You have to wonder... Anyhow, they interviewed some of his students who made it big." She turned to me. "Mr. Schecker was Ben's voice teacher in the Juilliard summer program when he was in junior high. We bought private lessons for a couple of years after that. He was so disappointed when Ben decided to attend the Hebrew high school instead of Performing Arts."

"He was a bachelor, Ma. I couldn't have this family if I was a spear carrier at Lincoln Center." Ben tried for a joking tone, but his voice trembled strangely. He hesitated between taking the baby or the newspaper, chose the latter, and was at a loss for what to do next.

Amy nudged him. "We'd better start driving, hon, Dr. Weissbluth's book says we have to establish a consistent bedtime." She restored Mae to the pouch on her chest.

Ben snapped out of his trance. "Ma, could Amy and the baby stay here tonight? That way I won't wake them up when I go to my early meeting. I'll swing by and pick them up later."

Amy was as happy to stay put as Aunt Nora was to pamper her new granddaughter. Uncle Leo pressed a shopping bag of leftovers into Julian's hands before he and I walked out with Ben. "Whew, glad that worked out, I need some alone time to reset my brains after all that family togetherness," my cousin said with excessive good cheer. "Speaking of which, Peter, I had a great idea for a guys' weekend escape. Did you know there's a Lovecraft convention in Providence this August? We could go to the beach, watch gross-out movies, maybe find a real horror publisher for your cartoons. You too, Julian, if you're interested."

"Oh no, I never know what to wear with tentacles. Thanks but I'll let you have some homicidal male bonding on your own."

Ben laughed. "Cool, I'll call for two tickets tomorrow." He pulled first Julian, then me, into an intense hug. "You guys will be great dads someday. Don't give up."

As Julian and I rounded the corner towards the subway station, it hit me how tired I was. I thought of asking Ben for a ride, rather than wait for the infrequent M train to Manhattan. But when I looked back, his car was already gone.

THE DAY AFTER THE SEDER, I was taking a break between my afternoon mentoring sessions to organize Gateway's art supply closet when the front desk volunteer brought me up an urgent message to call my dad. I let myself into Mom's office to phone him back on a more private line. Daytime chats with my workaholic father were unusual. At best, I thought, he wanted me to see him on TV in the next 15 minutes. At worst, Prue had been arrested again for liberating rodents from a medical research lab and I'd be driving to Massachusetts to bail her out.

When my father's receptionist put him through, he didn't speak. All I heard was hoarse breathing. "Dad, what's wrong, are you sick?"

His voice, when it finally returned, was a cracked echo of his normal baritone. "I...it's...Leo called me. I have to get over there, but I can't seem to...I don't know..."

I didn't immediately recognize the sounds on the other end as my father crying—he never had, before, in my presence. "Dad! Are you having a stroke? Can you touch your nose?"

"No, damn it, it's not me! I wish—if there was a God, it would've been me, or..." He gulped. "Ben...car crash, early this morning."

"Oh no, oh no." Unforgiving memory reeled back to the moment we left my cousin in the shadows of the trees over Aunt Nora's stoop. However much I spun that image from every angle, no streetlight beam exposed a clue on his dark face, no rewind changed our casual unknowing parting. "Stay there, I'll come get you and we'll go over together. Do you want Mom...?"

"Please don't, Peter, not now. Ada will be done teaching soon, I'm sure."

Trembling all over, I sat down and stared at the silent phone. My mind was so blank that I had to look up the familiar number for Julian's photography studio, and left him a voicemail where I forgot to include my aunt's address. He'd find his way back.

Ben, oh Ben. I should have held Mae longer. Julian and I should have thrown you the gayest male baby shower in history, and you would've made fun of us but secretly been grateful you weren't alone. I never showed you the new episode of *The Poison Cure* or asked you—instead of Ada, what was I thinking—how I could be like the writer guy in *Misery* and unchain my characters from the plot logic of certain death. Sure, you were often a dick to me, but that was an older cousin's prerogative. And I, like Aaron on the Exodus from Egypt, had grumbled and was now in agony.

My father had never looked old to me before. He was bent over like a soldier with a gut wound. I drove his car from his Brooklyn Heights office to the house where, less than 24 hours ago, our family had seemed complete. He didn't speak until we parked. Then he wouldn't get out. I knew how he felt—as if we could keep Ben suspended between life and death, like Schrödinger's cat, by not opening the door to his sobbing wife and mother.

"The police called," Dad said in a voice barely above a whisper. "He was coming off the Henry Hudson Parkway—slammed into the wall holding up the overpass. They don't know why."

I shuddered. "God, poor Ben. Was anyone else hurt?"

Dad shook his head. "No other cars. No blood alcohol. I have to believe he fell asleep at the wheel."

"But he went home. He had the whole night."

"You've never been a parent. One time I walked in on Barbara conked out on the bed with your nappy still in her hand and you sitting there naked in your own shit. Let's go, I can't take this anymore."

The sleep deprivation theory was shared by grim-faced Uncle Leo. The women were too wrung-out with grief to say much. We were the first shift. Michelle and Dave would come in from Jersey later that evening, and Amy's mom was on her way. Dad held his crying sister while Leo worked off his restless emotions by searching for black cloths to cover the mirrors. Mae woke up and howled in her baby swing. Was this the first language she would learn from us? I picked her up, since Amy could hardly move, and checked for wetness. Too bad she didn't come with an instrument panel. She quieted right away, just wanting to be cuddled. Amy slumped against me on the couch.

"I should have done something...I took all the midnight feedings I could... why didn't he sleep?" she moaned.

"Amy, do you think Ben might have been...a little depressed?"

She shot upright, indignant. "Of course not! He was overjoyed that we finally found our baby. She'll never know how much he loved her," she sobbed again.

I held her hand. "Yes, he really did. I just feel terrible because, well, last night he told me he was struggling and I'm afraid I minimized it because I wanted everyone else to be happy."

She glared at me with red-rimmed eyes. "Ben *was* happy. Parenting is hard, that's all."

"So everyone tells me."

Her tears spilled over as she gazed at her daughter, no doubt yearning to hold Mae but unwilling to wake her by pulling her off my lap. "It's the greatest love you can ever know. It's worth any sacrifice."

The pressure in my chest was due to more than the baby's slumped head—perhaps the same crushing weight Ben had felt, lying awake with fears of damaging this little life, then driving bleary-eyed to his morning duties. Or perhaps this was the selfish way I grieved, digging for reasons where there were none.

Mae whimpered and kicked. I was oddly reluctant to let her go. She wasn't anyone's security blanket, mine least of all. But nonetheless we mourners would pass her around, taking from her innocence some substitute for the hope we had lost today.

PART III

BEREISHIS

MAY, 1997

Remain mysterious;
Rather than be pure, accept yourself as numerous.

—John Ashbery, "The Double Dream of Spring"

Fireman's gloved fist pounds on apartment door marked 3A. Split panel: in the shadowy locked room, a bruised and weary Challis startles at the sound and cries out: *Help, help!*

Next panel, one fireman says to the other: *I don't smell smoke. You hear anything?* The second shakes his head: *Nah—better not be another prank. Damn kids.* Next panel, a curling, faintly inked speech bubble issues from the door like a wisp of smoke: *...help...* The first fireman rears back to kick the door in, shouting: *Fire Department, we're coming in!* Meanwhile a white policeman mounts the stairs behind them.

The three men charge into Dr. Morgan's living room through the broken-down front door. Split panel, Challis on other side of locked room's door, screaming for help. One fireman rattles the knob while the other searches the apartment for signs of fire, looking irritated. Challis calls out: *I can't unlock it! I'm trapped!* Next panel, fireman with hood over face, axe in hand, stands in doorway of locked room that he just broke through. The policeman is a dark silhouette behind him. They look imposing and menacing. Challis recoils for a moment.

The fireman with the axe, now with his smoke hood off, looks confused and slightly repulsed by the naked man chained to a cot. *What the hell is all this?* comes the cop's voice from behind him.

Next panel, cop enters room, showing his face for the first time. He has a blocky, powerful build and square jaw with flat line for a mouth. Seeing him, Challis thinks, *Oh no.* The fireman says: *No fire here, officer. And I doubt this guy could've pulled the alarm.*

Challis directs his plea to the fireman: *I don't know how you got here, but please, set me free. The doctor drugged my drink and...chained me up so he could...* He blushes in shame, eyes downcast.

The cop smirks, saying: *I've seen this <u>spic</u> before, down at the station. He's a hustler. Probably tried to roll Dr. Morgan and got a taste of his own medicine.*

Challis' protest is cut off by the cop leaning on his face with a rough hand as he unpicks the locks with a tool from his belt. The fireman shrugs and walks off: *He's all yours.*

Next panel, cop tips Challis out of the cot onto the floor, barking: *Put your pants on, pretty boy, I'm taking you in for solicitation. And this time I'll make it stick!*

Challis scrabbles around, his limbs stiff and bruised, but can't find his clothes. The cop, losing patience, drags him out handcuffed and wrapped in a sheet.

Split panel, one side Challis on the jail's pay phone, the other side a tall black man with close-cropped dyed blonde hair, lipstick, and earrings, answering the phone behind the counter of a coffee shop: *Dorothy's, how may I help you?* Next panel, the barista is in the staff bathroom behind the bar, wiping off his makeup. His earrings sit on the edge of the sink. Through the open door behind him, we see a butch girl with a denim ball cap now wearing his apron to serve the customers.

Next panel, the barista, in a conservative blazer and tie, hands over the bail money to the bored officer at the desk. The officer searches the shopping bag of clothes he brought, then dumps them at Challis' feet in the cell. Next panel, out on the street, Challis in a too-big overcoat slumps against his friend, who wraps his arms around him.

C: *Thanks for bailing me out, Mal.*

M: *That's what family is for, baby. You want me to put you in a cab home, or come back to the House of Dorothy so I can feed you?*

C: *I'd better go to the hospital to see Ryder. He'll be worried because I didn't come home last night. We'll come by Dorothy's later, maybe.*

M: *Mmm, okay, but get some sugar in you, baby, or you'll go into shock. And call me tonight if I don't see you. I don't like knowing that mad doctor's on the loose!*

C: (attempting his old carefree grin): *He won't dare try me again. I can escape from a locked room--I'm a brujo!*

Next panel, in the taxi, Challis sits with head tipped back and eyes closed, his pain and fatigue evident. He thinks: *I hope what I told Mal is true...but anyway I can't wait another minute to tell Ryder that I'm safe, and I love him—whatever he is!*

In the hospital lobby, Challis anxiously straightens his borrowed clothes and brushes back a loose lock of black hair, using his reflection in the sliding glass door as a guide. At the reception desk, he asks the young woman at the phones: *Hi, can you tell me what shift one of your orderlies is working today? His name is Tod Gift.*

The woman tap-taps her computer keyboard with a puzzled frown. Full panel of silent waiting. Next panel, she looks up and says: *I'm sorry, we don't have anyone on staff by that name.*

Challis (doing a double take): *That's impossible! He's worked here for...I don't know how long. Months, anyway. Did he quit?*

Receptionist: *I don't have that information, sir. You'd have to speak with Human Resources.*

C: *Wait, I remember he was working in the AIDS ward, with Doctor...*

In a thought bubble, Challis calls up image of himself in hospital bed, wasted-looking and frightened. Asian doctor with kindly expression stands over him.

C: *Doctor Gregory Lin. Can I speak with him?*

R: *You'll have to go up to the infectious diseases ward, ask the nurses' station to page him. Fourth floor, northeast—*

C: *I...I know where it is.*

A series of three small panels creates a montage of Challis' inquiries. First panel, Dr. Lin says: *I'm afraid I don't remember anyone by that name. Do you have a picture of your friend?*

Challis (hanging his head in embarrassment about the scene in Jared's apartment): *I did, but I...lost my wallet last night.*

Second panel, Challis stands over a desk, growing agitated, as a seated woman in a business suit says: *We have no record of anyone by that name ever working here.* The frosted glass door in the background reads *Human Resources*, seen in reverse since the characters are inside the office. Third panel, a security guard silently shakes his head in response to the question Challis must have asked.

Next panel, Challis, barely able to stand upright, lets himself into his apartment, thinking: *Good thing I gave Mal my spare key! This day has been unreal. Maybe something will make sense after I've had some sleep.* Though the small interior space we see in the next panel is dark and empty, he still calls out: *Tod? Tod, are you home?*

Receiving no answer, Challis flops down on bed, ready to pass out. But when he turns his head and glimpses the framed photo on his nightstand, his eyes open wide in shock. Next panel, he sits hunched on the edge of the bed, holding the picture, brow wrinkled in disbelief and fear. In his thought bubble, two memory images side by side: Challis and Pharmakon posing in front of a park fountain, arms around each other, while a bystander snaps a picture for them; then, a photo of that same pose of the two lovers smiling at each other, in the frame that Challis is holding.

However, in the next panel's close-up on the picture in Challis' hand now, the photo is different. His own position is identical, but he is alone. In the space where Pharmakon would have stood, there is only the backdrop of the fountain and the park. On the other side of the fountain, in the background, a small child is playing. It is Samantha, the girl from the coma ward.

"Why do we take photographs? Why isn't it better to forget?" I groaned, addressing the stiff rectangles of faces that spilled from the mildewed shoebox on my bed.

"I take them to pay the rent, but if it's any comfort, most of them will be forgotten as soon as next month's issue comes out." Julian breezed in from the living room, where he'd been unpacking equipment from the morning's shoot. "It's a nice surprise to see you before tonight—wish I could hang out, but I have to feed oysters to a venture capitalist. Franklin has a lunch meeting at his real job and Toby can only speak in binary code." These two charming characters were Julian's partners in Shooz.com, who were planning an IPO for their startup.

"I canceled my gym clients again. I'm sorry. Amy is making a scrapbook so that Mae can know about..." I choked up, wiped my eyes. "About her father. Because Ben *was*, even if only for a little while. Anyway, as you can see, I'm a wreck."

"How could you not be." He sat down and held me close. "You should wait till tonight, we can go through these together."

"That's sweet of you. It's okay. I've got to deal with it sometime. There are some things I can only work through when I'm alone."

Jule frowned. "You still think there was more to it than a tragic accident."

"I can't help feeling I missed some clue. He would drop these weird hints about how we should put the past behind us, but *what* past? Why say anything, unless he needed me to ask—and I didn't?"

"Darling, it's natural to wish we had control over terrible things. Why don't you give Sid a call?"

"Not everything is about me being crazy."

"I didn't say that."

"You don't have to."

"Well, assuming your cousin *was*...a little upset, and not as careful as he should've been...what do you think he'd want you to do for him now?"

"Ben always wanted me to make his life look better than mine. And I did. And here we are." I brushed aside a sliding pile of photos.

Jule kissed my forehead. "Come to lunch with us. You must know more about finance than me. I've seen you reading *The Economist* in the bathroom."

"It's okay, babe. I don't need a babysitter." I tried to say it kindly, but he looked hurt.

"If you change your mind, we'll be at City Crab in Union Square. At least to start. I don't know what those people do for fun—thank the Lord it's too early for the strip clubs to open."

He left soon after, but the question I'd posed to him hung in the air like the musty smell of the box from Grandpa Saul's memorabilia closet. Why did we believe we'd want this Polaroid evidence that once we'd been young and now were not, once a family and now split by divorce and death? This box dated 1976-78 contained too many (well, really *one* would be too many) first-grade class pictures of me looking glum in a mustard-hued argyle vest, and more relevantly, a set of summer vacation snapshots from the Cape Cod beach cabin our two families had rented for a week: Leo and Nora, Nathan and Barbara, Ben, Michelle, and me. I had loved the ocean then, or so my younger self told me, kicking up his heels in the white surf, holding a glistening-wet shell to his cheek with delighted anticipation of the messages his own blood would whisper in his ear.

I smiled at a shot of eight-year-old Michelle pushing her plastic horses through an obstacle course of sandcastles with the focused scowl of a Preakness jockey. Once we'd established that neither Ben nor I wanted to play the baby in her game of house, she had mostly withdrawn into a girl-world of pony dramas and unflattering diary entries about us. As the youngest, I'd had to choose my make-believe roles carefully to avoid losing status. Regardless, it would usually turn out that Ben was the pirate and I walked the plank, Ben the explorer and I the cannibal sacrifice buried in the sand, suffocating and impatient while he walked back and forth over my mounded form and pretended he couldn't find me. I learned to flip the script by making a slapstick of my victimhood, wailing and flapping around like Abbott and Costello meeting Frankenstein.

Nobody blinked an eye at pictures of naked children in the '70s. Like a less cute version of the Coppertone ad, someone had thought it hilarious to capture me crying with my swim trunks down around my ankles, with Ben in his birthday suit capering in the background. In a flash I was there again, throat stinging from the ammonia of seawater and tears, the burning scrape of sand in all the places it shouldn't be. I was frightened, and doubly ashamed, both for having been that loser boy, and for still caring about it when I was a grown man and Ben was dead.

Dread hit me in the chest when I turned over the next picture, an innocuous-seeming shot of a cabana on the beach at sunset. There was no reason this unpopulated scene should remind me of the closed door before the jump scare in a horror movie. But my body replayed a sweaty scuffle of boyish limbs, bruises and a soothing hand, self-disgust at babyish wetness down below. Nothing else came to me, though I strained with closed eyes for a clearer memory. No, one thing, a scent, sickly-sweet but consoling, of the extra-powerful suntan lotion Mom had slathered on to defend against wrinkles.

That was it for that trip, the remaining pictures not relevant to Ben's grieving family, dumped back in the box. I put on a Bauhaus CD, lay back on the cleared bed, and lit up a joint. Don't tell me Mr. Julian S. was drinking mineral water right now with the Shooz.com investors. In that world, you showed you didn't have an alcohol problem by consuming too much of it.

The droning instrumental opening to "Bela Lugosi's Dead" put me into a smoky trance. I tried to be willing to receive, not analyze. The musical buzz dampened the inner voice that nagged me to stop dissecting the dead past for knowledge no one wanted.

My drifting mind snagged on the more recent memory of Mom and Ben changing Mae's diaper. Time and again I touched that live wire, sprang back, crept up to it once more. Perhaps it was the tragedy of his last time holding his baby that made the scene so hard to approach in hindsight. But I hadn't known what was coming for Ben when I panicked at the seder. I thought of his characteristic way of bullying me but keeping me close, more complicated than just the firstborn prince's need for a foil. We'd been similarly torn between the rewards of wearing a mask and the longing to drop it. He carried guilt, too, for what I'd never know—his warnings to leave the past alone, his fear of harming Mae—

I sat up too fast, nausea surging. *Was that his confession?* Had he done the forgotten thing that broke me?

I slapped my face hard. That was unthinkable. I hated myself for speculating about him for my own purposes, when he'd never be here to defend himself again. Maybe Julian was right that I was only trying to avoid grief by blaming someone. If Ben was a perpetrator, I wouldn't have to mourn him.

Anyway, where would a nine-year-old learn to do...whatever was done to me? Everyone in the family adored him. His parents were still married. No one would have left him unprotected like the Gateway kids, like Ty. He wouldn't have had feelings that he tried to wipe out with a handful of sleeping pills and a 50-year-old bottle of Cherry Heering—the most disgusting liqueur known to man, which is why no one bothered to lock it away, which if I'd known, I wouldn't have thrown up all over the guest bathroom and (according to Dad) nearly given my poor mother a heart attack when she found me passed out in a sticky red puddle. What can I say, it's hard to be Sylvia Plath when you have an electric stove.

Without work, the afternoon dragged, so I went to Gristede's and bought ingredients for shepherd's pie. I could be very productive when I was avoiding writing. There would be no new issue of *The Poison Cure* in time for GalaxyCon, though I'd made a nonrefundable deposit to share table space with a gay 'zines publisher I'd discovered in the St. Mark's Place bookstore. What ailed me these days was too nebulous and all-encompassing to be fixed by an imaginary sexual vigilante. The Beckers had given Ty permission to join me for a couple of hours, strictly conditional on the math Regents exam scores we were anxiously awaiting. His science grades were still subterranean, but I had a plan for that.

While the shepherd's pie was baking, I phoned Amy to tell her I was on my way with food and photos. She was home on maternity leave—now doubling as bereavement leave—from teaching this term, though without Ben's salary, she couldn't afford to be out for long. Her mother was urging her to give up the Upper East Side apartment and move in with them in Scarsdale. It made sense, but I was pained by the accelerating fragmentation of our family. How long before this mother and child, with no blood ties to us, stopped thinking of Ben as a strong enough thread to bind us together?

Amy hadn't mentioned that my father would be there when I showed up. Every time I saw him, since Ben's death, I was struck by how haggard he looked, how vacant his gaze was. It grated inside me like shrapnel, a cold hard feeling that I knew was wrong but couldn't expel.

Amy thanked me distractedly and waved me toward the freezer. "You're very kind, I'm sorry, but I have so much and I have to force myself to eat..."

"It's best when it's fresh," I said half-heartedly, already giving up when I saw the fridge packed with jars of homemade baby food and matzoh ball soup. But Mae cast her vote in my favor, making sign-language gestures for hunger when she smelled the hot casserole.

I sat down with Dad in the living room while Amy was occupied with feeding her daughter. He had various papers spread out before him that seemed to pertain to insurance and death benefits. "I promised her I'd go over these, as a lawyer, but I can't think straight about any of this...losing him..." He sighed. "You can take a look, right?"

"I'll try, but it's not really my area of expertise."

"Didn't you handle that stuff for your friend Phil?"

"Yeah, but he died broke. Less paperwork. Family kicked him out."

"Ugh, how anyone could do that to their kid..."

I patted Dad's arm. "Leave this alone for now. Look, I found some nice vacation photos for the memorial scrapbook."

Dad managed a wavery smile at the Cape Cod pictures. He laughed, a little too heartily, at the one of Ben pranking me naked. I meditated a second time on the sunset landscape, but dredged up no clues from the deep, just the same ominous mood.

"What happened in that cabana, Dad?"

"What should happen? Your mother and Nora kibbitzed, we changed our bathing suits, and whenever one of you kids got teased too much, you'd run in there and cry." He sounded impatient at being interrupted in his nostalgic reverie. Taking the picture out of my hand, he added, "If you're looking for answers, you won't find them here. Or anywhere. As my old partner Lew used to tell his wrongful-death clients, 'I can win you compensation, but I can't give you meaning.' And then he died."

"I'm sorry. It's all so unfair. But when I found this picture, I got a weird scary feeling, even though there's nothing in it. So I just had to ask."

Nathan straightened up from his despondent slump and looked directly at me for the first time in our conversation. "Don't make me worry about you, Peter. It's not healthy to search for patterns that don't exist."

"The time for you to worry about me was a long time ago," I muttered.

"What's that supposed to mean?"

"Nothing." I made a move to stand up, but he stopped me.

"That's right, nothing. You need to grow up and get over your resentment. I can tell you one thing these papers say—" He stabbed the sheaf of insurance boilerplate with a cross-examining index finger. "Amy and her child won't get the money they need to live on, if there's rumors floating around that Ben crashed on purpose. Nothing will bring him back to us, so why does it matter to you?"

"So you *do* think I might be right, but you don't care." A tingling, buzzing sensation filled my ears as I realized I was daring to argue with the man who'd made Chief Justice Rehnquist stammer.

"I care enough about Ben's memory to protect him from your jealousy. You're acting like your mother now, hunting for damage in people so you can play savior."

The buzzing was killer bees, an angry cloud streaming out of the hive toward freedom. "Yeah, go on telling yourself what a disappointment I am, so you can feel better about fucking your crazy girlfriend while I was being raped by your friend Jonas and his pals."

I had the satisfaction of seeing his face turn pale, then red. "This isn't the time for this, Peter," he said tightly.

"When *is* the time, Dad? When do you ever want to hear the truth? There's always someone you care about more than me."

That was the wrong thing to say. The wrinkles of fear on his face smoothed themselves out into the concerned, controlled expression I knew too well. "I gave you a lot of freedom when you were growing up because I *did* care. You were born gay, obviously, but I wasn't going to fuss over you and make you a sissy." He gave me his version of a brisk, manly slap on the thigh with his small hand. "Now let's be strong for Amy and Mae, all right? You and I can hash things out with Jonas when we're feeling...a little clearer." Hopelessness hazed his eyes again, his speech losing momentum to his disbelief that bereavement had an endpoint. Oh fucking Absalom.

"*Strong* is for those bald kids on the telethon. I'm losing my mind here, Dad, and Ben had something to tell me—"

"Whatever you're bickering about, can you please not? I can't take this now," Amy cut in sharply. Mae, in her arms, was placidly eating a fistful of mashed potatoes.

"I'm so sorry. I'd better go. The photos are all done," I said, stumbling toward the door. To avoid meeting my father in the elevator, in case he left too, I ran down the fire stairs—all eleven floors. Tears blurred my view of the steep gray cement steps repeating endlessly below me, as I faced the fact that I might never be allowed near Mae again. Out of all that I'd so recently lost, strangely that hurt the most.

WHEN I GOT HOME, towards dinnertime, I was sore from working out too long at the Ironman. It's hard to do angry yoga, which I guess is the point. So I'd switched to beating myself up on the leg press, kicking the platform away from me again and again like a tethered but unbreakable horse. Two teen boys were watching me, the kind who swing their arms wide and bang down their weights extra loud to make their gangly bodies take up more territory. They weren't cruising, it turned out, but interested in training with me. Amateurs are impressed by misery.

Collapsing at our kitchen table, I wolfed down half a bowl of leftover stew before sparing a thought for Julian. I didn't feel like cooking more today; maybe I'd change into nicer clothes and take him out somewhere to celebrate his debut as a tycoon.

Jule was sitting on the edge of our bed, head in hands. Nearby on the night table were an empty glass and an unopened bottle of Captain Morgan rum.

"Hungover already? Oh—this is serious," I corrected myself, as he lifted his head at the sound of my voice, and I saw his tear-swollen face. I sat beside him, so close that our legs pressed together, and put my arm lightly around his shoulders. "What happened, babe?"

His dark eyes were dazed and wet. "Daddy's gone."

"Oh my God." *I'm sorry* would have been too simplistic. *Were* we sorry? Whatever this news meant to him, I wouldn't judge.

Not asking any questions, I let Jule breathe into my chest, the hitching breaths of someone who was almost all cried out, for now. "I have to go home. The service. Day after tomorrow."

I rubbed his shoulders. GalaxyCon would have to wait till next year. "Of course. I'll book our plane tickets. Who are we staying with, or should I find a hotel room?"

He turned away from me, looking ill at ease, and reached for the liquor bottle. His fingers hovered around it, then he dropped his hand. "Fuck."

I had the feeling he'd gone through this routine several times before I arrived. "Can I get you some food? A smoothie or something?"

"No...I'm already full of oysters and existential dread. That's enough going on down there."

My own gut was heavy with a more abstract grief for another fracture in our families, whatever the flaws of the lost. Mr. Selkirk might well have mocked our faggy tears, a tenderness he hadn't known how to accept. "Was it his heart?"

Jule nodded. "Golfing with the Chamber of Commerce guys. Hot day, walking uphill, et cetera. An eminently respectable way to go out." He gave a sardonic laugh that sounded more like a sob. "Carter called me, and I called Mama, just now."

"How is she taking it?"

"She's devastated, actually. They were still in love—or that's what she's going to tell herself, from now on."

"Poor Bitsy. I should bring her something. What would keep well on the plane? Economy Candy makes amazing chocolate macaroons."

Again that pained, awkward look. "Listen, Peter...I'm going to take this trip alone, if you don't mind."

"Alone? Your dad's dead—this is *important*! And you don't want me there? What the fuck?"

He was nervous but he made himself look steadily at me. "You've been through a lot. We just lost Ben. Another funeral could set you off. And Mama would prefer...well...no excitement."

"What am I, a glitter bomb? *Everybody* knows we're gay. This isn't about her delicate sensibilities, admit it."

"Don't yell at me! He was *my* father and I have a right to handle this my own fucking way. That means I go home, listen to some pious bullshit, drink horrible O'Doul's with my brother, and try to help Mama envision a future without broken arms. I can't deal with anything more complicated than that."

"You still blame me for missing out on his come-to-Jesus moment at Prayer Warriors."

Jule's silence was sufficient answer.

"He would never have accepted you. It was all for show. Now he's gone but you're still letting him and his white Republican god come between us."

His voice was level and sad. "I'm trying to have faith...but you're making it hard."

Great, *now* his anger-management program was working, and I felt like an asshole. "Sorry," I muttered. "Let me help you get ready for your trip."

He fell back against the pillows with a dramatic sigh. "Thank you, darling. Now please take away Captain Morgan before I suck him dry."

Jule and I tiptoed around each other the next morning, using work as a way to interact while saying nothing meaningful. He phoned his clients to reschedule their upcoming shoots, and I performed my morning yoga warmup on the floor nearby. Shame and blame whispered along my nerves, and I held them there until my muscles' burn made me release the pose and everything with it: all the chatter of *but I can't help being...* and *he shouldn't have...*

After teaching my morning classes at the Ironman, I had blocked out some writing time for *The Poison Cure*, but instead I showed up at Gateway, hoping they'd find some odd jobs to calm my mind. Let's be honest, I needed my mom.

I discovered her picking up trash in a rubble-strewn lot behind the Gateway building. The burnt-out townhouse that once occupied it had been bulldozed last winter, but whatever project was planned for the site had stalled, the yellowing work permits peeling away from the board fence that was succumbing to graffiti tags and lumber thieves. Two teen boys from Gateway were nailing together a large rectangular frame on the patch of ground that had been cleared of broken glass and bricks. Hammer blows sounded an off-tempo backbeat to Puff Daddy's "Can't Nobody Hold Me Down" on their boombox.

Mom wiped her brow with her sleeve and smiled at me. "We're making a community garden! Feel like helping? Extra gloves, over there."

I suited up. The afternoon had grown cloudy and cool. Some good outdoor hard work was the cure for my nervous shivers. "Nice—I didn't realize we'd bought this lot."

She elbowed me and murmured, "Shh—I learned a few things from marrying a lawyer. Act like you own it and in ten years you do. And if they kick us out sooner, so what, we'll have some flowers and maybe our picture in the paper—'Homeless Harlem Children Stand Up to Real Estate Mogul'."

"Genius, Mom. That's the *kibbutznik* spirit."

So we hauled trash bags and spread dirt in the raised beds that the boys built. Mom pressed marigold and gerbera daisy seeds into finger-holes in the soil. I took off my sweaty canvas gloves to rub some soft brown loam between my fingertips, savoring how it yielded, smelling the promise of summer.

"Come, have a bite before you go," she urged.

"Thanks, but I'm so gross and muddy."

"Then shower."

"That would feel great but I didn't leave a change of clothes here."

"Well, you should."

"Ah, Mom, I'm scattered all over the place, I wouldn't know where to hang my hat, if I even had one."

"Good idea, I'll buy some gardening hats for everyone, we don't want skin cancer."

I had to laugh at her maternally protective one-track mind. We compromised by bringing out folding chairs and sodas so we could relax in our new paradise. The kids had gone inside for Dr. Marla's social skills group. Mom and I watched the patch of sky between the buildings turn the hazy lemon-gray of late afternoon, and talked landscaping plans till she noticed my anxiety returning to distract me.

"Mom, am I crazy?"

"Of course not. You're just a sensitive boy. Who's been telling you that?"

I hesitated, ashamed to be making trouble between my parents again, but I needed someone to take me seriously. "Ben's death hit us really hard. Dad especially. He's such a wreck, you'd think he lost his own son."

Mom made a noise that could have meant sympathy or disapproval. I went on, "So maybe I'm being callous by bringing this up so soon, but I loved Ben too, and the way I express it is by telling the truth about how he really felt. I wish I'd listened to him better when he was alive. He was struggling with depression, or bad memories, or something. I would have wanted someone to acknowledge that, if I were in his shoes. But everyone else says I'm paranoid."

"I believe you, boychick. Ben was a troubled kid, God rest his soul. I didn't like how he bullied you when you were kids, but your father told me not to interfere. Said you had to learn to handle things like a man, whatever that means—I'm not seeing *him* out here slinging 20-pound bags of cow manure."

"Did you love him, once?"

"Love?" That ambiguous clucking sound again. "I loved who he seemed to be. The future he was going to give me. Women didn't have many choices, in my generation. Not like you. Never settle—don't be star-struck by someone who's going to keep you in his shadow."

"It's okay, Mom. I'm not a spotlight-seeking kind of guy."

"You're too modest. What are these men like, the ones who are selling your boyfriend on their get-rich-quick scheme? Does he invite you out with them?"

I wasn't ready to talk about my latest exclusion from his life. "They're a lot like his fashion industry friends, only not as well-dressed. I don't know how he stands it. He says Casual Friday is going to kill us all."

"As long as clothes are the only thing they're casual about."

"I see where you're going with this, Mom, but I honestly don't mind if Julian has a little fun without me. We're not in each other's pockets. As long as everyone plays it safe and tells the truth, we're cool."

"Hmph. Men and women are different, that's for sure." She didn't sound as though the difference was to our credit. "Well, I hope that works out for him, but meanwhile you have to feather your own nest."

She didn't need to spell out the rest of this disagreement. If Julian struck Internet gold, I could develop my comics-writing career in earnest, instead of squeezing it in between dog-walking, teaching senior yoga, and other odd jobs unworthy of a man nearing his third decade. Meanwhile, despite my protests, Mom was holding that full-time administrative job open for me as long as she could. She wouldn't understand that my chopped-up schedule suited my chopped-up brain. I couldn't stave off flashbacks for eight whole hours, five days a week, in a shared office. Could I truly blame Jule for deciding he couldn't rely on me in a crisis?

"I *am* losing my mind," I confided.

"Don't put yourself down. I have faith in you. If anyone doesn't agree, stay away from them."

"Thanks, but..." My words came out on a thin thread of breath, all I could force through the weight on my chest. "I know Ben wasn't okay because...I'm not, either. I keep remembering bad feelings that I can't explain, like being afraid all the time when I was little, and...being touched in a way that was gross and made me hate myself…made me want to die?"

"That's impossible, Peter." Her face went blank and cold. "What are you saying, that I could have let you out of my sight, let someone hurt you? How could you think I'd neglect you so badly?"

"No, no, I'm sorry, Mom, I didn't mean it like that! But—" My stomach gave that anti-gravity lurch, but there was no turning back. "How do you explain what I'm going through?"

She stood up, slapping the dirt from her slacks. "Maybe you're right, this environment is too traumatic for you. This is why you should go back to school. We all got this out of our system in first-year abnormal psych class, everyone worrying that that week of weird dreams they had was early-onset schizophrenia." I got up too and she gave me a perfunctory goodbye hug, adding, "Take tomorrow off, clear your head. Sula will cover your mentoring sessions and you can pick up her test-prep shift the next day. She needs the experience. And please, promise me you'll stop letting your father drive you crazy. He always had to be number one and that meant everyone else around him must be damaged goods. Of course that would be scary and confusing for an imaginative boy like you."

I followed her out through the gap in the boards, pulling down the flap of sagging chicken wire that served as a gate. From outside, no one would guess that a miniature kibbutz was springing to life behind those unsightly barriers. I closed my eyes and the rushing traffic before me became the sea whispering with its cold tongues, and I the boy on the bare burning sand, so close to walking in and letting the waves cover me.

[EXCERPTS FROM A DIARY KEPT BY BARBARA HAUSER EDELMAN, 1984]

5/10/84: I wasn't expecting paradise every day, but I've never shvitzed so much in my life. After a whole morning planting vegetables, I must be getting sunstroke because I hear Momma's voice in the clucking of the strange birds in the olive trees: *stop slouching, it makes you look fat, can't you fix that hair.* Unspoken but underneath: *can't you be like Elaine, neat little sister doll.* Thinking of her today because I saw a woman in rags selling droopy flowers at the open-air market and wondered if my sister's still out there pushing beads and daisies at some airport. If this woman, a white woman, also came here love-struck for God or a Jewish guy and couldn't find her way back.

Love. What's *love*. A pretty story for two people who wanted something more than their promises and their children, and may they enjoy *that* as much as they deserve. But Peter—

I hope he understands someday that it killed me to leave him. They ganged up on me, said they'd overlook my taking Prudence away (like she didn't need to be rescued from that woman who I wouldn't leave alone with a straight razor??) if I didn't fight for my son. Why Nathan wanted him all of a sudden, I have no idea. Someone to do the dishes while they think deep thoughts.

Nobody in that family cares about Peter like I do. He promised to come here for the summer as soon as school's out. Such a time I had, getting Nathan to agree. In social work school they made us read Freud, or somebody like that, who said mothers who love too much turn their sons into homosexuals. Maybe that's his father's agenda— keep him away from me so he can teach him to be a normal man who likes titties and world domination. If there's such a thing as paradise, it's a place where you can protect your child's innocence and he doesn't hate you for it yet.

5/21/84: I saw myself in the mirror tonight and I almost cried. I'm going to wrinkle so fast in this sun. Fading hair, fading youth. Of course these potato-sack clothes make sense for fieldwork, but I don't have the body underneath like these college girls who come here on a Birthright trip to flirt with the soldiers. Out in the grass and the soil I forget myself in the good growing smells. It's satisfying to work hard. But what will I have to show for it, a bunch of grapes? I'm afraid men can see I'm all used up.

I gave Nathan my last chance. He can't deny it. We could've been a family still. Was it for nothing I looked the other way when he ran around? He couldn't do this one thing for me, to understand why that woman was different? I told him loud and clear: It's because he gave her something he wouldn't give me. The child I wanted.

Papa always said, children are the greatest treasure. Flesh of my flesh. G-d's promise. Then he'd hug me so hard I thought he'd swallow me up! He didn't let most people see that side of him. It was our secret.

I hope this land loves me back.

[Julian: One Less]

Your heart stopped, Daddy.

No one has asked me to speak. They know your song. In the land where we'll never grow old, you're fifty-nine forever. That is, if anything spoken at Roswell Baptist Church of Marietta should be taken literally, which today I'm pretending to do.

Mama can't find fault with our appearance. Me: charcoal double-breasted suit, royal blue shirt and tie. Carter in standard black, discreetly sweating. I've begun to worry about him as one worries about a man, not a boy: blood sugar and apoplexy, not frat-party blackouts, as the fate we pray he'll avoid. My small nephews are stowed somewhere cheerful, too young to look down into the satin-lined box and understand that the cold man dressed in his Sunday best will never again buy them popsicles or tickle them till they cry. No motherly stains today on Stef's high-necked black dress with white pinhead polka dots. And no Laura Sue, at all. My sister is bouncing in a Jeep down a Ugandan road, surveying death in bulk. Or maybe she's asleep, done praying for us. I don't remember the time-zone difference.

Family man. Pillar of the community. Really, could this preacher be any less imaginative? How many pillars could one community need? Daddy wasn't a fan of walls that weren't load-bearing. Waste of money.

He was strict, my brother says when his turn at the podium comes. *He made me who I am.* I assume Carter means this in a good way. Or wants us to think he does. Those of us who don't care to understand. Bless their hearts.

No, he's actually going to share a touching memory. Carter's not a good liar, a difference between us that I exploited to prank him many times, like the closeted little bitch I was. Those sniffles are for real. Talking about Daddy's hand over his, teaching us how to hammer a nail—I can feel it too, its calloused warmth, the greatness we longed to shelter in, to be enclosed in the promise of big fingers wrapped around little ones. Hot sun, cool metal, and the sweet sawdust air of a half-built house. And my body fills in what Carter doesn't say, stomach-shivers and pounding headache, expanding beyond the moment's ideal snapshot to the tense movie of two thirsty children striking crooked nails and prying them out with blistering hands around the hammer till Daddy was satisfied.

I look around. No one here to hold my hand. I'm in the second row behind Stef and Mama. Next to her, Memère, up from Savannah, dozes grouchily under her black-veiled hat, with her houseboy and folded wheelchair by her side. He's obviously gay but won't flirt with me. On the other side of the aisle, Daddy's immediate family is represented by portly Uncle Curtis and Aunt Louella, whose shiny black skirt is a bit too short for the occasion, but I admire her individuality. She enjoys life a little too much for my mother.

My paternal grandfather, Mr. Joe—he prefers "Mister" to "Grandpa" so the ladies won't think he's over the hill—is in a back pew somewhere with his third wife, having crept in late as usual. He's camouflaged by the crowd of well-dressed mourners from the Rotary Club, the Georgia Homebuilders' Association, the American Values Network, and other colleagues and campaign operatives. The lady next to me, a tight, shapely late-thirties brunette with russet lipstick, was Daddy's liaison, or whatever you call it, at the Greater Atlanta chapter of the Republican Party. Justine something. I had to work with her a few times on photos for his campaign. Fat tears spill down her cheeks, though her makeup still looks ready to deliver the six o'clock news. I don't know why I can't be more sympathetic. Well, actually, I do.

Mama rises, shaken and reluctant, graceful even now. My brother helps her up the steps, returns heavily to his seat, his face red and shiny. I clasp his shoulder from behind and he eagerly crushes my hand in his, the gesture once more flooding me with the memory he shared. I know the meaty weight of his fingers is not Daddy's because of the trembling. The old man never wavered with a handshake or a belt. I'm afraid none of what we cherished was real, and it's like little Carter and Julian are dead too, the ones who believed.

There was too much of him not to share with this world. She gave him to the people. Against her protective wishes, she blessed his climb. Up the hill till he tumbled down like a golf ball in the weeds, white and lost. You'd think we were talking about a war hero instead of a guy who lobbied against wetlands protection laws. Despite myself, I understand the moist gleam in Mama's eyes. Each time, after the bruises faded, steadfastness became a point of pride, her complementary strength to his confidence that there was no landscape he couldn't remake. Then he'd make her glow again, and the sounds behind their door at night would change, still almost like weeping, but not.

I get it. I've been horny for brutes too. One of them's sitting by himself three rows down, kneading the back of his thick neck like Mission X-Force piled one too many bricks on it. The difference between me and Mama is, no preacher's wife is going to show up at *my* door with a casserole when it all goes wrong.

The man in the casket frightens me. I know the clichés about the dead: That they look natural, or not. That they might be sleeping. That this tailored and powdered waxwork on the pillow, so like them but not, brings their absence home. None of that is true. My father is more himself than ever before. Immovable. Cold. These eyes will never open on me. Nothing I do will start his heart beating.

I take my place in the receiving line with my mother, brother, and uncle. Mr. Joe decides he's infirm and sits on the bench behind us at the rear of the sanctuary, while Memère is wheeled to the other end of the line. When it's Justine's turn to give us the sympathy handshake, Mama holds her fingers limply for the briefest of moments, like something a lady wouldn't deign to touch but is too polite to wipe off. Brent hand-wrestles me into a bear hug, gripping me with real emotion. I'm surprised by how I sink into his arms, and don't indulge too long, aware that I could crumble prematurely.

Outside, waiting to sort ourselves into the cortège, Mr. Joe asks to bum a cigarette off me, as he's done since I was twelve. I've never smoked. He inquires after my sister, and remarks that she's too pretty to waste on the Africans. This, too, is part of the routine. Mama and her college friend Linda are sniffling over memories of the night she met my father, when the two girls heard his barbershop quartet perform at the state fair. From what she used to tell me, Daddy and his pals had two great years playing church socials and veterans' benefit suppers, but then he had to take over Selkirk Builders when Mr. Joe had a little disagreement with the IRS, and there was no more time for music. I heard the story in pieces over the years because Daddy would always turn the TV up loud or something to change the subject.

Earth spatters on wood. His face is gone. Now only objects will stand in for its memory: a box, a photograph. My feet are unsteady on the spongy turf. Carter leans on my shoulder, this huge man with a scrunched-up crying face like a baby's. Mama nestles into his side. Memère made us memorize a lot of poems the winter that Mama ran away with us, when I was eleven, the one time I really thought we'd get free. *After the first death, there is no other*, it's true, the rattle of dirt on the box is static in your ears forever. I choke, I blink, and it's my boyfriend Phil in there. I'm crying for him. Alone among all these people. It was a secret then and it's a secret now.

I thought this would be the easy part. I was wrong. The minute I step into our parents' house—fear. Only the reason for fear is missing, for the first time and all times after it. So the terror has no caution to muffle it, like a marble ricocheting around in an empty tin.

Subdued tea party vibes from the mourners filling the parlor. Roses in cut-glass vases waft a ladylike perfume through the smells of melon balls and tuna salad. A pyramid of silver-framed family photos decorates the end table that holds the guestbook. I sign it to prove I was here. You never know what they'll say about me, if I sodomize my way into an early grave.

Al-Anon says don't be bitter. Peter would tell me to eat something. I haven't let myself think about him all day. How I've fucked everything up. I still don't know if it would be better or worse with him here. Maybe I needed to let myself be as lonely as I am.

I accept a mini egg salad sandwich from a waiter's tray. It's paste in my mouth. It's the sickly-scented wax blob of the lipstick Daddy made me chew and swallow when he caught me and Laura Sue trying on Mama's makeup together. I gag and spit it into a paper napkin.

The Rotary Club has delivered a wreath, a blue and white behemoth like a tourist boat's life preserver. As they wrangle it into the parlor, a chair tips over. My stomach clenches, and I see Carter flinch at the sharp noise. We must be remembering the same thing. No particular evening, too many to count. What set him off: a child's over-tired backtalk, sibling squabbles, disappointed tears. *I'll teach you to be tough,* he'd say. *I'll teach you respect.* If we cried out, we got double.

"I hate those fucking chairs," I murmur to my brother. "Remember? Sitting on that cane seat after Daddy got done with his belt? Like your ass was on a waffle iron."

"Oh, man." He winces. We're both quiet for a minute. "Well, that's in the past now."

"Mama's finally safe."

"*I* was always here to watch out for her."

"We all did the best we could," I retort. My throat aches as I contemplate my parents' wedding photo in its new frame, on display for the occasion, the vertical rip near the bride's train barely visible where it's been taped over from the back. I won't cheapen myself by bragging how I took the blame, though my skin stings with the memory of the glass I picked up bare-handed. Now I see why I keep blanking on Justine's name. I'm mixing her up with the other big-haired brunette who dropped Daddy off that night in her convertible, foolishly close enough to be spied from Mama's window.

"It doesn't matter anymore, Julie. Leave it be."

"How are you over it already?"

"That's not how I'd want to be talked about when I'm gone. That my wife and kids are better off with me dead."

"Carter. *No.*" Nice thing about 12-Step, it's made my brother all mushy. I can touch him—a manly side-hug, at least—and he won't call me a sissy anymore.

Mama is equally not in the mood for an honest conversation. She's wearing her hostess personality, all chiming clockwork. Only occasionally a blank, frightened look comes over her: where will she go without him to wind her up, shove her forward? She sends me off to fetch a fresh mint julep for her mother. Memère offers me a sip, as she always did when I was little, and pulls me into a conversation about recent movie adaptations of her favorite novels. We concur that Helena Bonham Carter's sex scene in "The Wings of the Dove" was painfully anachronistic.

I want to leave already. I want someone to acknowledge what's happened. I itch for it like Carter must crave the sweet burn of the hard stuff that everyone else here is knocking back, draining Daddy's liquor cabinet like morticians pumping fluid out of a corpse. I'll be one of them if I don't get out. Go up to my room and call Peter.

I sit on the edge of the bed for a few seconds before realizing that I can't stay here either. Can't wrap myself in the same candlewick bedspread I huddled under to muffle the noise of fists on flesh. I re-pack the few items I took out of my carry-on bag and sling it over my shoulder. Mama will be upset, but she has her mother here. I no longer have to evaluate her companions for their skills in defensive weaponry—though Memère did once crack Daddy's collarbone with her silver-handled cane when he tried to take Mama back before she was ready. I love that old dame.

I slump over the wheel of my parked rental car in our driveway. A blue Buick with a Jesus-fish bumper decal has blocked me in. The car's stifling, artificial-pine-freshened interior closes in around me. I hate my father for being dead, for escaping.

I've been banging my forehead on the steering wheel, hoping the pain will finally make me cry, for some time when there's a knock on my window. I roll it down. It's Brent.

"Sorry, I didn't know you'd need to pull out. I'm leaving now."

"Why so soon?" They can't possibly be done in there. So many deal-makers in one room. Whoever Daddy's political heir is, I guess it's not us two faggots.

Brent shrugs—more of an embarrassed dodge, really. Same way he did in our high school locker room, laughing at his loud friends' pussy jokes, meeting my eyes for only a split second so they wouldn't notice. "You want company?"

"Not here.

"Five Napkin Burger?"

"Fuck, yes." I'm starving like a werewolf all of a sudden. We drive off, my car following his, though I don't need to watch his tail-lights because I recall every turn of the road to our old afterschool hangout. Curly fries and pickle chips and a medium-rare patty thick enough to sprain your jaw on. Novelty license plates and Bulldog pennants tacked to the walls. Pitcher of beer, though I never drink this stuff at home. I'm in Al-Anon, not AA, right?

Brent rubs his neck some more, cracks his knuckles. It's more than awkwardness; he looks like he hurts. I'm about to ask but he says, "Peter's not here?" Like that isn't obvious.

"I told him not to come."

"Lucky."

"Me or him?"

"Both of you." He sucks the ketchup off a French fry. I remember the first time I saw him do this, my astonishment that it meant exactly what I hoped it meant. "You protect each other."

Now that's a punch in the chest. "I don't think we're going to make it." The worst thing is out in the open now. The generic honky-tonk from the overhead speakers sounds like moaning, each chord a shower of breaking glass.

"Aw, man. You can't believe that."

"If I wanted to hear pleasant bullshit, I'd have stuck around for Mama's red velvet cake." I gulp the cold bitter drink that made me feel so sophisticated at sixteen. "My father was a shit, okay? Sorry if you saw his good side and you miss him, but I turned out like him. You were at Prayer Warriors. You know." Relief liquefies my muscles. Brent *does* know. He saw the worst thing I ever did, the way I flung violence from me, out of my once-innocent body into another still more undeserving.

"God forgives you." His eyes are so blue, younger than his face.

"Fuck God. Why did God let Peter be molested?" This news shocks Brent. I should lower my voice. Peter would cringe. But none of these people know him, or remember me.

I expect Brent to haul out one of his Christian just-so stories, but he only takes my hand in both of his and says, "I'm sorry."

"You never used to touch me in public," I blurt out.

That sheepish head-bob again, but he doesn't let go. "We're not kids anymore."

I pull away first. "Never mind, let's talk about something else."

We try to take an interest in each other's lives, filling the space with talk about his get-out-the-vote project for the American Values Network and my photo shoots for Shooz.com. My highlights tour of the past few months sounds empty to me, though, and I realize it's because Peter isn't in it. Am I reading too much into Brent's subdued tone, or has he also lost some of his enthusiasm for the gospel of lower capital gains taxes? (A subject I might actually have to take an interest in, if our dot-com beats the odds. Now I *do* feel old.)

The level in the pitcher goes steadily down. When we run out of beer, I'm leaving, I vow to myself, taking smaller sips. Brent chugs his drink with more aggression than pleasure. He always had the metabolism of an ox. Just to keep the conversation going—all right, and also because his neck muscles are distracting me—I ask about his Mission X-Force gig. A shadow passes over his face. He swallows hard. Not helping with the distraction, Brent. My cock hasn't forgotten what we did under a stadium blanket in the back seat of your daddy's car, a detour through the woods on our way home from Glee Club rehearsal. Those trees are lumber now, their land subdivided into cul-de-sacs on streets named Walnut and Pine.

"I...I'm not on the team right now." He looks down at the wet rings on the wooden table. "Came out of a lift wrong, tore my shoulder muscle."

"Ouch, that sounds awful. When can you go back?"

"Doctor found other stuff that's messed up, too. My knee cartilage is fucked." He scrubs at his face with a paper napkin. "Guess we always knew this lifestyle had an expiration date, huh?"

I nod sympathetically. One more student athlete dead in the trenches. "Smart that you transitioned to a political career, then."

Brent shakes his head, scowling. "You'd think. You'd think. A career scripting robo-calls and fundraiser postcards. But you know who gets to be a convention delegate? Who's in line for a job at the Statehouse? That woman your Daddy was fucking—God rest his soul—"

"Bless his motherfucking heart," I intone solemnly.

Brent chuckles. "You're something else, Julian."

"Yeah, you too."

"That's the problem." His lips are set in a bitter line. "I did everything right. I lead a godly life. I don't give in to my sin nature. But it's not enough."

"For them, or for you?"

"Jesus said his burden was light. Why isn't it light?"

"Oh, babe." I lean across the table and kiss him on the lips. I must be insane. He cups the back of my head to hold me closer.

It's second nature to us both to let go quickly, scanning the perimeter for imminent violence. Torn shoulder or no, I'd lay odds on Brent to win a bar fight. I realize I'm not worried that he'd abandon me this time.

"I forgive you for what happened in high school," I tell him.

His eyes well up. Sometime while I was gone, Jesus told Southern men that it's okay to cry. Well, fuck me for being ahead of the curve. There's only grit in my eyes tonight, the gravel of school sandlots where pummeling boys held me down, telling themselves they were nothing like me, that righteous violence was what made them hard. After the first time, I learned not to run home right away. Not until I could smile with a split lip.

"I've done everything wrong," Brent whispers.

I interlace my fingers with his, under the table. It's too easy, this going back in time. "Nah. We were just told the wrong way to be good."

The waitress comes over to swap out our empty pitcher. I answer for us: we're done. We linger by our cars. I say something about finding a motel. He doesn't have to ask why I'm on the run. Instead, and we all know I walked right into this one, he says, "D-do you want to stay at my place?"

"Get in the car. Let's talk."

I slip into the backseat of his Buick. The Chick-fil-A wrappers and musty Atlanta Falcons blanket are a turn-off, to be honest. He turns on the air and lets the car idle, climbing out of the driver's seat to slide up next to me. By "talk" I apparently meant sucking on his tongue. His hot mouth tastes like beer and ketchup. His body is heavy in my arms, inflated with muscle.

I pull back, guide his head to rest on my shoulder, stroke his cheek. His lip trembles. "Sweetheart," I say, pressing my hand to his breastbone, trying to feel the life throb beneath those hulking pecs. "Trust Jesus, and get the fuck out of this place."

I don't wait for his excuses to dribble out. I kiss the top of his head, return to my rented Chevy, swing onto the road back to the Selkirk demesne.

Our post-funeral house is neat and empty. The catering elves have whisked away every dropped sandwich crust and lukewarm gin-and-tonic. The memorial display of photos of Daddy has been cleared off the end table. I assume the hideous wreath was banished to the garage, unless she made Carter take it for Selkirk Builders' office.

A high-pitched, vibrato wail issues from Daddy's den. Memère is watching "Live from Lincoln Center". I keep her company for a little while. *Ah, fuggi il traditor...* She gives me a bull's-eye candy and says Mama took her tranquilizers and went to bed at 7:30. Memère still has all her own teeth. Our family has good genes. *Il labbro è mentitor, fallace il ciglio...*

Back in my room, I phone Peter, at last. I'm prepared for him not to answer—not sulking, but you know Peter, somehow he finds a way to be naked and chained to a wall when I need to talk about our relationship. But he picks up on the second ring.

"I miss you. I'm sorry," I tell him right away.

"I'm sorry too! Do you need an emergency rescue visit?"

"God, you're so sweet. No, I'm flying home tomorrow morning."

"I'll pick you up at LaGuardia."

We talk about nothing much. The day's tension ebbs. My surroundings fade like an old Polaroid, his voice the only thing that's real. He says goodnight, but I have to tell him something. "I didn't fuck Brent."

"Why not?"

I try to find the words for what happened between us. "There's a lot of ways to love someone."

A longer pause. His voice is small. "*I love you.*"

"And I love you more than anyone. No matter what."

"Me too, Jule. To the end and back."

I barely keep it together for a goodnight kiss, hang up as soon as possible, because everything inside me is breaking down and floating away. I heave sobs into my pillow, safely suffocated as my cries always were in this room, the beaten boy's terror and the youth's gasping self-exploration, both forbidden. I moan the way Daddy's ghost never will. He wouldn't come back here.

I'm equally sure I can't sleep another night in this bed. After washing up, I bring my pillow and blanket downstairs to the big sofa in the parlor. Orchestral chords echo from the den, soothing as distant thunder overhead. *A cenar teco m'invitasti, e son venuto.* I fall asleep to the music of the Commendatore dragging Don Giovanni to hell.

Baker's chocolate, butter, and weed: recipe to heal a friend, if not a friendship. I'd decided I couldn't put off visiting Kevin and DeWayne any longer. Now Kev and I were shoulder to shoulder in the sky-blue kitchen of their apartment on St. Nicholas Avenue, communicating in brownie recipe directions, while his partner lay wrapped in blankets on a deck chair on their tiny terrace, with Marvin Gaye's "What's Going On" turned up to full volume on his portable stereo.

"Could you preheat the oven? We should finish these before Ty arrives," Kevin said. I moved to obey, but slowly, parsing the tone of my friend's words for any pain or resentment when he spoke the name of the kid who'd almost been theirs. But it was Kev who'd proposed that we come today, on our way to GalaxyCon at the Javits Center, in the hope that together we could lure DeWayne out of the house.

No better time to raise the subject that made my heart sink. "Kev, I'm sorry I screwed things up so badly, with the home study and all."

"You didn't make this world." He cracked another egg into the glass mixing bowl.

"No, but I led you to trust people who—" Even now I hesitated to speak badly of Barbara, or the imperfect haven she was trying to keep afloat. "Who treated you differently than they've treated me."

He chuckled without much humor. "You think, if you were an HIV-positive, occasional cross-dresser, your momma would hand you one of her precious orphans and say *Mazel tov?*"

"Between us, she might not approve of everything I am, but she's always on my side against the rest of the world. I thought she'd do the same for you, or at least give you a fair shake."

"Speaking of shake..." He passed me the handheld mixer. "Act like a top for once and beat those eggs stiff."

I set it aside. "Seriously, I need to make this up to you somehow. Did you call my dad's friend, the employment lawyer at Aronson and Sturges? Because he—"

Kev put his hands on his hips. "Man, would you stop trying to fix us? We never wanted that. Just listen, just *be with* us. Don't run away from what you can't cure, because there's no place far enough for that."

"Oh, Kev, I'm sorry."

"Dumb-ass." He hugged me. "Now mix."

We busied ourselves with readying the hash brownies for the oven. As I started washing up, he remarked, "Couldn't afford Bob Sturges anyway. You want to ask Nathan's opinion on which of the low-income legal clinics sucks the least?"

"Maybe the call should come from you. Dad and I are kind of on the outs since Ben died."

"Your cousin, Ben? Damn, what happened? Didn't he just have a baby?"

"Oh, God, you don't know..." I slumped against the counter. Telling myself I was here to give support, not take more from them, I tried to keep the story brief, but all the events of the past month spilled out, along with tears, invited by Kevin's warm, patient silence. DeWayne, swathed in a burgundy silk dressing gown with monstrous lotus blossoms, wandered in to refill his coffee mug. Kev glanced at me for permission to explain my disintegration, and I nodded. I couldn't bear to say it all again.

"Peter is having some kind of abuse flashbacks and his cousin might have killed himself and no one believes him."

Kev's bluntness rang like a bell through the fog that had enveloped my mind for so long. It was simple, it was all so terribly simple when I stopped trying to salvage anyone's good opinion of me. Did I say a bell? No, that sound was the ring of the axe on the chopping block, severing *now* from everything I'd clung to in the past.

"Shit...what can we do to help you?"

"Oh, no, you guys, you have your own stuff to deal with—that I made worse—"

"That's not how friendship works," Kev said sternly. "Right or wrong, we don't write each other off, because nobody's gonna look out for us if we don't."

DeWayne said "Uh-huh" to that a couple times and asked if he could hug me. His body wasn't as frail as I'd feared. Kevin made it a threesome, stretching to get his arms round the both of us, as the shortest one of the bunch. I sweated in the huddle, as the oven heated up the tiny kitchen, but it was a good discomfort, reminding me I was alive.

"What you can do..." I mused over a steaming cup of black French roast. "Just tell me I'm not completely crazy, I guess. Tell me whether any of this is worth pursuing, or if I should stop before I fall off the edge of the world."

"Once things start to fall apart, there's no stopping 'em," Dee said, with a hint of bitterness. "The secret's out, you can quit running."

Kevin glowered at his partner. "What Miss Congeniality is trying to say, Peter, is that there's no way to prove yourself to folks who don't want to see it.

Your true friends will stand by you. And as for running—" He gave Dee an affectionate swat on the behind. "You better run and fix your face, you skanky ol' queen, we got company coming."

"I'd like to fix my face right on your ass," Dee leered. But, seeing that Kevin was serious, he went to get dressed, grumbling at every step.

Ty soon arrived, sporting a shiny black and gold warm-up jacket that showed how the Beckers were sparing no expense to make masculinity worth his while. The saunter went out of his step when he saw DeWayne seated at the table with Regents biology exam prep books in front of him. Pre-empting the kid's complaints, I said, "Here's the deal: you're going to work at least half an hour with your *new tutor* so you don't make me a liar to your foster parents, then we'll all dress up and go to GalaxyCon."

"I'm not sure I feel up to—" Dee began.

I cut him off. "Dee has a fantastic Maleficent costume he made out of duct tape and choir robes, that he can't wait to wear again." I heard Kevin snicker.

"Damn, you had to remember that?" the reluctant witch objected.

"DeWayne collected some interesting-shaped chocolates that Halloween."

"Shut your mouth, there are children present," Kev mock-scolded me, and slapped Ty's hand away from the plate of brownies he was bringing DeWayne. "These are for medicinal purposes. The rest of you get the plain ones."

"Even Pedro?" Ty rolled his eyes at me and mimed toking.

"As your responsible adult, I'm on the clock here, so yes, I'm abstaining."

Seeing he was outnumbered, Ty buckled down to memorizing the Krebs cycle. Kevin and I went into the bedroom to root through Dee's plastic tub of costumes and accessories. A minimalist, Kev morphed into Geordi LaForge with the tried-and-true combination of wraparound shades, a two-tone sweater, and a tie tack pinned upside-down over his left pec. I had brought a jar of green face paint to play Pharmakon, but Kevin objected that my character wasn't famous enough yet, which I pretended to take offense at. He tugged a wig over my head, a woman's glamorous coiffure of long wavy red hair. "Poison I-vy-y-y," he sang.

"With a beard?" I couldn't see myself as a woman, let alone Gotham's most gorgeous eco-terrorist.

"I can gussy you up." Seating me on a stool before the bathroom door mirror, he washed and lathered up a razor with a flourish, shaved my chin smooth, and layered on my new face with fierce black eyelashes, emerald glitter shadow, a wicked red glossed mouth, and a dusting of some kind of cough-inducing powder over my green-painted skin.

Only the anxious tilt of my eyebrows was still recognizable. "I look like I sucked blood and it didn't agree with me."

"It wouldn't dare!"

When I laughed, I saw *her* in the mirror: not beautiful, not delicate, but the Great Mother, the fearsome sculpted Athena in Nashville's replica Parthenon, her gold tresses big as hooks that could lift a girder, her bulging painted eyes that transfixed you forty feet below.

Caught up in the transformation mania, Ty and DeWayne clipped leaf shapes out of green trash bags to tape to my clothes in a winding pattern. The three guys circled me, measuring and making small adjustments. "Feels amazing, huh?" Ty asked.

"It's...really something." I wasn't ready to describe what I'd glimpsed and felt. Add it to the long list of things too precious to expose, mint-condition comics of my life that could never be handled and read.

In less time than I would have imagined, Tai emerged, summoned forth by a few well-practiced swipes of eyeliner pencil and blusher brush. She threw on a platinum-blonde wig and declared herself Storm from X-Men. Maleficent appeared next, and then Kevin, as the least freakishly dressed, was deputized to hail a taxi.

I wasn't upset that the guys had avoided lengthy discussion of my traumatic disclosures. Tai's presence made discretion necessary. But when we reached the con, Kev pulled me aside behind a booth of Marvel fan art they were browsing. "Hey, if you ever need a place to hide out from the family drama for awhile, you let us know. The House of Clarke-Marshall welcomes all survivors."

"Thanks for believing me, and...and not asking any questions."

"People who hurt kids are good at convincing you that up is down. Wait around for proof of your gut instinct and you might wind up dead. If my parents hadn't kicked my queer ass out, I might still be trying to persuade myself that putting a roof over my head was the same as love."

"You're very wise. Just don't let my problems stop you guys from reaching out, too. I might be insane but I still make good soup."

Kev fist-bumped me. With the aid of the numbered map in the convention program, we found the table where I was supposed to be hawking *The Poison Cure*, walking slowly as Tai took in the dazzling distractions of her first con. I set down my heavy satchel of comics with a grunt of relief. DeWayne was even more ready for a rest, so he and Kev picked out the panels they wanted to attend and planned where we'd meet up later. Tai was excited to help lay out our wares, but soon became restless when we weren't flooded with customers. I couldn't fight her tourist fever, so I turned her loose with a 50-dollar bill and strict instructions not to shoplift or hook up with anyone in the next hour. "Racist," she said, poking her tongue out at me, before sashaying off.

Meanwhile I befriended Bastian, a reedy white boy in expensive Goth attire, who was sharing my table to sell his zine *Slashrr.* The covers had a cool silver-on-black design and the spines were bound with duct tape made to look like crime-scene "Caution" tape. Inside it was mainly movie reviews and slash fanfiction. It would not have occurred to me that Worf would bottom for Q on "Star Trek: TNG". My wig wasn't the only thing making me sweat. The convention center resembled a greenhouse and the glass walls had the same effect on a sunny May afternoon.

Bastian was impressed with Pharmakon's story and urged me to write a regular feature for his zine. "Anything you want—just make it gay. We need more original content."

"Thanks, maybe I will. No pay, I guess?"

"Not to quit your day job over—I mean, sorry, but I lose $10,000 of my uncle's money every issue."

"On *what?*"

"The usual stuff—letterpress printing, distribution, copyright infringement insurance—that was Uncle Felix's idea. He works for DC Comics."

"Wow, I'd love to write for them someday!" Words I'd never have dared speak before this year.

"Nah, they're too fucking corporate. I did a summer internship there. It's just like any other cubicle farm. Five-page HR memos about what posters you aren't allowed to hang up. You're always Clark Kent, never Superman."

"Well, I spend half my days pumping iron and the other half teaching fractions to juvenile delinquents, so I don't expect the glamorous life."

"I'll pass your book on to Uncle Felix. It really is fine stuff. But don't say I didn't warn you! They won't let you write anything this sick for a mainstream property."

"All the better to protect my secret life. Seriously, thank you."

Right after that, we experienced our first customer rush, as nearby panels ended and people spilled into the hallways. Many copies were handled and a few purchased, as usual. I hoped Tai would return in time to savor the thrill of meeting our readers face-to-face. Though our entire market share was in the triple digits if we were lucky—a mere eyelash on the head of the 50-Foot Woman that was comics fame—every person who opened the pages of *The*

Poison Cure made Pharmakon and Challis a little more real, tethering their airy world in the net of shared belief.

Tai returned pushing DeWayne in an aluminum-frame wheelchair with a stack of books on his lap. "I saw this booth called 'Con for All' where we got lost in the big exhibition hall on the way in. They rent chairs and hearing aids and shit so you old folks can have a good time," she cracked.

"One of the meds makes my feet go numb," Dee apologized.

"Great thinking, Tai. Very considerate," I said.

"Nah, I'm just making him carry all the porn I bought." But she wheeled DeWayne into place beside our table as carefully as if he were really Queen Maleficent on her throne. Their costumes attracted a few more fans to browse our wares. Tai worked the corridor, flirting with likely prospects and extravagantly handing out the pricey advertising postcards that Julian had insisted I print up. He was a true disciple of the spend-money-to-make-money philosophy. The cards invited readers to join my email list to find out when the next issue was available—something I would've liked to know, myself.

Dee tilted his head back in his chair, tired but content. "I'm dropping the lawsuit."

"You sure? I'm glad, but... Why can't *everyone* get justice, not one versus the other? I was so pissed about what Dr. Marla said about you guys. She totally twisted my words around."

"I bet. No, I settled with the school—it wasn't enough, but I don't have the energy to do more. I've been in this twilight zone since the diagnosis—not so close to death that I can go out with a bang, but not well enough to believe in anything big in my future." He paused for breath, settling his robes around him like an elderly duchess. "That's what hurt the most, that's why I was so hot to bring Gateway down. They looked at me and saw someone who was too sick—in every sense of the word—to deserve a family. Someone broken."

I wrapped my fingers around his. "You have a family—us. It doesn't look like a Hallmark card, but it's real."

He squeezed my hand weakly. "Truth. But I'm tired of this life. The church taught us to 'not see as the world sees,' to remember our people are beautiful and worth something. But at the same time, all I hear is I'm good enough to sing in the choir, but not to preach the word. Good enough to help other people's kids—until I wasn't—but never to have my own. How long am I gonna be able to fight that?"

"Don't leave us, Dee."

"Naw. Someone's gotta teach that sassy kid that 'organelles' aren't a 60's doo-wop group."

The kid in question, having run out of postcards, came back to our table to skim issues of *Slashrr.* "Ooh nasty, 'Sherlick Holmes and Dr. Wetson'."

"Why don't you staff the table and give Peter a chance to browse," DeWayne said, in a tone that made it clear it was more than a suggestion.

"Yes, *Mother.*" Tai flipped her platinum tresses and draped herself across a chair. I put my Poison Ivy wig back on, noticing with surprise that I felt shielded, rather than marked out, by my garish drag. Beware the Queen of the Freaks.

On the way home, we had a little argument about where to store Tai's purchases of *Big Loads* and *Wet Ink.* "Your foster parents might not let you hang out with me again if this is what you bring home," I reasoned.

"If they didn't want porn in the house, they shouldn't have taken in a 15-year-old gay kid," Kevin said acerbically.

"You'll leave it with us and you can read it when you finish your practice test," Dee said.

"But no whacking off in our bathroom, that's inappropriate," added Kevin. "Save it for your spank bank. It'll be good for your memorization skills."

"You guys suck," Tai muttered.

"Show some respect, missy!" scolded DeWayne, smacking the kid's hand just like a church-lady grandma.

It seemed prudent to bring Tai back to their apartment to remove our feminine costumes and makeup. The mojo seemed to go out of the kid with every swipe of the washcloth.

"It hurts to go back to boy mode before you're ready, huh?" I asked.

Ty grunted. The switch was thorough, that's for sure.

"Do you think our comic is good, Pedro?" he eventually spoke up.

"Sure. It's rough but it's real. Nobody else is telling a story like ours."

"I don't think anyone's gonna take us seriously."

"Come on, we sold almost all our copies, and got a bunch of new names for our mailing list."

"Yeah, but so did your *Slashrr* dude with his 'Buttman versus Two-Facial' crap. These folks I saw today, man, they're *real* artists."

"So can you be. You just have to learn and practice."

"Stay in school, fool?"

"You know it."

His shoulders slumped. "Pedro, do I really have to live with Dr. Harold and Aletha?"

I put my arm around his thin body. He relaxed against me like a child.

"They're good people, Ty. They'll put you on the right path. I believe you're talented enough for Cooper Union, but just in case they don't have a spot for you, the Beckers can afford to send you to a good college where you can study art professionally."

"Easy for you to say. You're not anybody's community service project. You've always had *real* parents."

His dark brown eyes held all the need and insecurity that his defiant body wouldn't show. My pulse throbbed in my temples. Did I owe him the truth about my childhood (whatever *that* was) or would that be too much for him to carry?

"The people who love and protect you are your family," I said. "Some folks are privileged to have that from the beginning, and some of us have to go find it for ourselves. But you *will* find it if you hang in there."

He nodded once, not making eye contact, so we could both pretend he was too tough to need this reassurance. I saw who Ty could become—the loving man, the strong woman—if we could only keep him alive and moving forward, a fate not even the best parents could guarantee. Then I turned to the mirror to wipe off my villainess makeup. Watching the flesh tones re-emerge from the streaks of vanishing green, I imagined a painter's hand turning back time to his first sketch, this barely formed face that I would claim as mine.

[EXCERPTS FROM A DIARY KEPT BY BARBARA HAUSER EDELMAN, 1987]

6/12/87: I think I'm going to break it off with Avram. I don't like his beard. No, that's not the reason. I'm being childish. Well, what does he expect, the man is six feet tall, anyone would feel like a little mouse with him climbing on top of her. Nathan didn't always know what he was doing, but I could stop him doing it, with one hand tied behind my back!

I got caught up in the dream, that's all. Repopulating *eretz Yisrael* with G-d's people. Does that make me Sarai? The woman who laughs at miracles. I only had one, and he's 6,000 miles away.

Babies are raised in common here. I'm not sure how I feel about that. When everything is yours, nothing is yours.

Still, it's beautiful helping Yasmin, that girl from Michigan who just gave birth to a perfect little son. She came here pregnant and alone, so brave. Watching them sleep under the blanket she wove for them, his tiny mouth on her nipple. *That's* the greatest joy a woman's body can know. And the greatest terror—I used to wake up at night certain that I would kill Peter, roll over on him or something, I guess—those ridiculous things your mind does in the dark hours, when the whole world is dead except for you and him.

I'm flying to New York this week for Peter's high school graduation. I hope Avram doesn't expect to come. He is an impressive big fellow to have on my arm—me, at 41, ha!—but I don't have to be serious about him, just because of what we got up to. Right? It's a new world. Don't tell Papa.

MILLIONAIRES IN GOLF SHIRTS, models in crotch-skimming little black dresses, software geeks, and eager marketing interns with loosened neckties mingled in an effervescent crowd in the rooftop garden of the Four Seasons to toast the Shooz.com IPO. A large, soft man wearing a short-sleeved rugby top flung one arm around my shoulders and with his other hand snagged a drink from the miniskirt-wearing waitress. He presented it to me, though I was already holding a half-empty Corona. It looked like Windex in a martini glass. "Are you a gay? I love the gays."

I could hardly deny it, dressed as I was in a sleeveless black T-shirt with the company logo—a hot pink high-heeled shoe atop a mousepad—and low-rise pants that showed my happy trail whenever I raised my arms.

"No, really, I do, I do. You guys know how to shop."

"Julian picks out all my clothes."

"That's what I'm talkin' about. He's gonna make us rich. My last venture was a real dog." He elbowed me. "Organic pet food delivery service. 'Rover Come Over: for the rich shithead who's too busy to take care of anyone.' That wasn't our real slogan, of course."

"Hey, I had a dog-walking customer who used that. Red box, flying bone logo?" It had resembled a dick with wings, actually. "Was it a success?"

"Nah, shipping costs bit us in the ass. Glad I cashed out in time. My cousin, who came up with the formula, he believed in it too much. Now he's working in a health food store. You can't get too attached in this business. You want self-expression, play fantasy football."

That was more risk than I was comfortable with, outside the bedroom. "How do you think Shooz.com will fare, really? What's our biggest weakness?"

"Shh, not here—don't spook the money men." His roving eyes focused on a pair of pocket-protector types in serious conversation beneath the giant pink shoe-shaped piñata, which (according to Julian) was rumored to be filled with real gold coins, thanks to the generous line of credit Franklin had secured from Citibank. "There's a guy over there I need to schmooze. Stay pretty!" My companion slapped my butt in farewell, spilling my drink.

I brought the untasted concoction to Julian, who was stealing a moment of solitude behind a potted tree to survey the glittering arteries of Manhattan below. "What is this?"

"The kingdoms of the world, darling. Worship the shoe, and the shoe will provide." He took a small sip. "Specifically, it has provided you with a variation on the Bombay Sapphire martini."

"Should I drink it?"

"That depends—do you want to remember anything about tonight besides the pattern on the bathroom floor?"

"I think I've forgotten enough of my life already."

Jule nodded approval and deposited the potion on the tray of a passing waitress. She and her leggy co-workers wore fishnet stockings, a tiny apron, and a Shooz.com mousepad as a sort of rear-end loincloth instead of a skirt.

"Is this our life now?" I asked.

"That is the question I have been pondering in my heart." Jule put his hand over mine on the terrace railing. "Things are moving too fast. Now our family is talking about *selling* Selkirk Builders, can you believe that? With Daddy gone, Carter wants to jump on an offer from this construction conglomerate that has franchises all over the South. The three of us kids would get a distribution, which Lulu will blow on mosquito nets and sneakers for the heathen children, just to stick it to the old man's memory."

"And you're wondering whether to plow your share into—this?" I gestured at the extravaganza around us with my too-warm beer.

"Yep, Franklin's fingers are itching to get ahold of it already. Wouldn't it be funny if I was the one in our family who made a killing in business?"

"Do you enjoy it, though? More than regular fashion photography?" I was pretty sure I knew the answer.

"Well...I'd enjoy not being spread so thin. So far they've only paid me in stock options. Hustling for photo assignments on top of that is giving me stress wrinkles." He patted his perfectly smooth face.

Screams erupted behind us, simultaneous with a sharp cracking sound like a baseball bat hitting a home run. Julian jumped. I wheeled round to see the guests clustered under the piñata, squealing with anticipation and laughter as Toby inexpertly pursued it with a golf club.

Out of breath from the scare, Jule griped, "That dork is *ruining* an expensive seven iron."

"Who even brings one of those to a cocktail party?"

"For all I know, they're giving out the damn things as party favors."

I was mesmerized by the spectacle of the young businessmen, with flushed faces and rolled-up sleeves, taking turns swinging their weapon of choice—another club, a silver-handled umbrella, a plastic bat—at the spinning pink prize that danced crazily away from them.

At last the dog-food man, with the practiced stance of someone who'd spent many hours networking on the links, dealt the papier-mâché shoe a death blow. "Hole in one!" someone yelled, inaccurately, since we'd all seen that par for this course was at least seventeen. But not even Toby was in the mood to be pedantic. All past troubles were forgotten in the scramble for the gold coins that spilled from the shoe's broken-off heel. The waitresses and arm-candy girls stood outside the fray, perhaps envious of the men who palmed the scattered treasure, but certainly aware it would ruin their alluring image (and expose their underwear, or lack thereof) to crawl around on the floor.

Effervescence changed to argument when one guest after another discovered that the reward for which he'd soiled his suit pants was only foil-wrapped chocolate. Julian shook his head sadly. "Let the record show, none of this was my idea."

"Look on the bright side, they're wasting less of your money than you thought." I retrieved a coin that had fallen into the potted plant near us. "Here, have some dessert."

Jule accepted it without enthusiasm and felt around the edges for the foil seam to unwrap it. Frowning at his lack of success, he bit down on it lightly. "Hey, this one's real."

"Whoa—do you think it's a sign?"

"Nah, I doubt God gives a shit about my stock portfolio."

"Depends which god you're talking about."

"That it does." He tucked the coin into my front pants pocket. "Oh praise Jesus, fashion people." And he pulled me away in the direction of the friends he'd just spotted. By this point in our relationship I understood my role was to look brutish and mysterious, like the dumb chauffeur in "Sex Dwarf", and let his colleagues check out my ass while they debated whether horizontal stripes were in and vertical ones were out. It was a turn-on for both of us, imagining them imagining his ownership of me.

I only hoped I'd be able to follow through, tonight. My other self kept pushing me out of my body when I most wanted to give it to my lover. Perhaps soon I could make these memories an inert fact, a long-ago bereavement that no longer shocked—as Mae, someday, would tell Ben's part of her life story. As I would never tell his part in mine.

So there I stood, sweating like the virgin daiquiris Julian passed around from the open bar, acting interested in Wonderbra model Eva Herzigová's diet plan—"honestly, if she lost any more weight, she'd be *anti-matter*!"—and stretching oh-so-casually to show off my abs and make Julian breathe heavily. Toby popped in to ask me whether a mint-condition first issue of DC Comics' *Return to the Amalgam Age* would be a good investment.

"This is just my opinion, but crossovers are kind of a desperate gimmick—it wasn't very good, but it wasn't so *bad* it was good, know what I mean? So no, I don't think there'll be a lot of collector demand for it."

Why was everyone looking at me? Had I talked too loud? Should I have known that this was not a cool question to answer?

"Yeah, yeah, you're right!" Toby enthused, waving his hands. "Hey, here's another thing about comics I want to know. Why are businessmen always the villains? Except Batman, but he's just filthy rich, he doesn't actually *do* anything for a living. Why can't we have a hero who, like, does something *productive*, like Hank and Francisco in *Atlas Shrugged*? Would you want to write that for me?"

I thought back to those overheated nights reading a thick Ayn Rand paperback under the covers at Ramaz summer camp—wanting to impress the self-assured older boy with beautiful eyelashes who'd loaned me his highlighted copy, but distracted from arguments for the gold standard by boner-inducing visions of John Galt's nude electroshock torture. "Only if, one, you pay me in advance, and two, I can make it gay."

I'd meant it as a joke, but the group made enthusiastic noises. "Sure, sure!" said Toby. "Rand never liked women anyway."

One of the fashion boys, a brand manager with spiked blond hair and black plastic eyeglasses, like a starlet playing the ugly duckling at the beginning of a teen makeover movie, chimed in, "Listen to Pete, he's the future! Nerd culture is *in*. We have to redo the Hugo Boss shoot. No neckties, I don't care if that's what they sell, I want sleeves rolled up, outer space in the window, something computer-y in the air—a city, but like, from the 23rd century. What should I look at, Pete—Flash Gordon? What's hot now?"

I burst out laughing, too surprised to be polite. This guy was my age but sounded like my grandfather. "Dude, that was decades ago! Ever heard of *Watchmen*? Frank Miller's *The Dark Knight*? Or if you want something less dystopian, try Jodorowsky and Moebius, *The Incal*."

I caught myself mid-lecture and shut up, cheeks burning with an old memory of being *that kid* who took too long to realize nobody cared. But the guy was scribbling notes on one of the shoe-shaped promotional notepads that most of the guests had been using as drink coasters. And Julian was smiling, not mocking and indulging me (though I searched hard for signs of this), but apparently pleased with my unlikely celebrity.

Jule motioned me over when he saw Franklin headed our way. "Darling, I'm going to make myself scarce before he gets his hands in my pockets. You stay here and sweet-talk Toby into funding your libertarian porn."

"No, it's okay, I'm with you."

Inside the dimly lit cocktail lounge, I pressed him to the wall with a forceful kiss. "That's for being the most generous person ever."

He knew just what I was talking about. "It's not hard to be proud of you." Softer kisses heated us up as our bodies pushed closer together. "Mmm, I'm ready to run my train through your tunnel."

"Where?"

"Not here, alas. The men's room is exclusively for snorting cocaine and the women's for throwing up."

"Express to 23rd Street, then."

Naked from the shower, I shivered as Jule ran his fingers down the fading bruises on my back. I was grateful he was touching me at all. When he'd come home from Georgia and spied the fresh wounds of my latest dungeon visit, he'd postponed our make-up sex, supposedly to spare me pain, but mostly to hide his own. *Wasn't that our agreement?* I'd wanted to shout. *Would you rather I lied to you, again?* But I lacked the will to make a principled stand for an indulgence I enjoyed less and less. Besides, when I gave in to my compulsion to visit Bernie's, I'd wrongly assumed Jule was drowning his sorrows in Brent's ass.

Now he overcame his squeamishmess to touch my mottled flesh, even to test it by pressing his fingers firmly on the sore spots, so that fresh pain sparked along my muscles. I whimpered. He grazed the nape of my neck with his teeth. "I'm glad you don't mind it anymore," I gasped.

"Oh, I do." His voice was sweet and dark as the rum he'd temporarily sworn off. "I want to be the only one who marks you."

My dick ached, suddenly ready, all of me gathered up into one clean, singular need. I reached down to stroke myself but he grabbed my wrist. So good to pretend I couldn't break free, to strain away till he was forced to dig in and squeeze as hard as he could. I gritted my teeth. He pushed me face-down onto the bed with his other hand on the back of my head. "Stay," he ordered. I rubbed my hard-on against the sheet but a light stinging slap to my rear quickly commanded me to lie still. I heard him rummaging in a drawer. Soon afterwards he roughly bound my hands to the bedframe with a pair of velcro fabric cuffs, the kind that cyclists use to keep their pants legs out of the spokes. Their faintly luminescent traffic-cone-orange hue created a prison fantasy vibe that a very politically incorrect part of me enjoyed. That part had to wait for relief, though, as Julian's hand crushed my face into the pillow whenever I squirmed. He lifted himself off me. I gulped a relieved breath, then made an embarrassing high-pitched noise as something small, hard and slippery with lube was wedged between my ass cheeks.

"Hold still, my little piñata." I understood more a moment later when he smacked my buttocks with the flat of his hand, so hard I jerked against the restraints. I clenched my cheeks around the object as the unrelenting blows kept coming. He'd never laid into me like this before, making my skin burn and my eyes water. I let out a cry like a skydiver plunging through the blue. He was my parachute, bindng me, holding me up.

My strength gave out, my thighs aching from the effort of holding myself taut, and with one final slap the thing fell out of me and pinged against the bedframe. Jule triumphantly held up the gold coin, a little less shiny now. "Jackpot! Time for my reward."

Not gently, but taking his time, he slid his fingers inside me. Kneeling above me, he forced my legs apart. His hand was on my neck, his thumb pressed against my throat. Then his cock was in me, grinding, pushing. He growled in my ear. Though I was more ready than I'd been in a long time, it hurt, a sharpness in my gut when he went deep, the old bruises pulsing under his weight. I clenched around him, trying to drop into the liquid darkness where my body dissolved in the pleasure of being used.

Instead I split in two. My body bucked like an unbroken horse, out of my control. The burn as he filled me up, pierced through to the spot that couldn't help but send electric twitches through my limbs, the friction on my dick trapped in his hand—it was too much, above and below me, pressing me into nothingness between them. And my treacherous body begged for it anyway, high on destruction while my mind screamed. There was a word... there was a sound...a sound that would make it stop, but I couldn't hear it in my head. *Nothing. Nothing makes it stop. You're too old to believe in those tricks anymore.* Shuddering, the cold sweat of fear joining the heat of agonizing arousal, I whimpered, "No, no, no..." till my body bled out its passion in a sticky flood. And still it went on. I twisted in my restraints and saw him braced above me, head thrown back, eyes dilated with his own need, seeing nothing else as he finished in me. "No, no," I croaked again, but my voice was lost in his last deep groan.

I gave up. As I always had. Lay immobile, a body under a body. Waiting for something else to happen so I could forget this too.

The ripping sound of velcro separating. My numb arms flopped onto the bed. A voice from far away, at the other end of the tunnel of my consciousness: "Wow, you were right, that was *beyond...*" Light fingers on my face found the evidence of my leaking eyes, a worse exposure than the stained and crushed opening below. "Peter? What's the matter?"

That probing kiss on my moist cheek, so gentle, so repellent—I jerked upright, shoving him off me. Dizzy from the sudden motion, I fought against the green-black haze on the periphery of my vision. "You should've stopped! I didn't want it, I didn't!" I half shouted, half sobbed.

He leaned in to caress me, but I slapped him away. Remorse and defensiveness warred on his face. "But—I'm sorry, but—I thought that was part of your *thing*, what do you call it, the *scene*? Pretending I was, uh, ravishing you?"

"I didn't want it!" I shrieked. If I repeated it loud enough, maybe I could drown out my body's mocking objections, the ugly reminder of how arousal had betrayed me to the invader.

"I'm so sorry—" He tried to touch me again, but I yanked the top sheet off and wrapped it around my dirty nakedness. I stood up, pulling away from him. Now he looked annoyed. "But how was I supposed to know? You came like a fucking firehose. Why didn't you say 'avocado'?"

"Why the fuck would I say that?"

"That's our safe word, remember? Babe, c'mon—" He scrambled off the bed. "Come sit down, you're just freaked out, I'll get you a glass of water and we can talk about what went wrong. I'd never, ever want to hurt you."

"No, I'm never letting you touch me again!"

I ran into the bathroom and latched the door. I had to scrub him off me. The shower water was still cold but I stepped in anyway. My heart skipped a beat with the temperature shock. Soon I was numb to the stinging chill, a dull background pain to complement the compulsive scrape of the washcloth between my legs. I had to shed every cell that had responded with a *yes* when I meant *no*. The first bloody line my fingernail drew along my thigh clarified everything. I repeated it, desperately, but the high faded faster than any scar, leaving only another scratched graffiti no one could read.

Through it all, Julian knocked on the door, pleading, "Peter...just let me in...I'm scared for you. I'll do anything to make this right."

"Go away! Go away, or you're going to find me dead."

A moment's silence. I bent over the sink, sucking in noisy breaths. *Crack*— the door was kicked open, the metal hook ripped from the plaster. And I saw my father's face, disgusted, then blank with forced forgetfulness, retreating. Dizzy, I sank to my knees. Julian leaned over me. "Hold still, I'm calling the doctor. Or Sid? Do you want to talk to him first? I really think you should."

"No. Nobody." I staggered to my feet, dodging his touch. "I have to leave.

I'm not safe here. I shouldn't have come back to you."

The scratches on my legs had begun to itch and sting. I grabbed a pair of loose black sweatpants from the hamper to hide the seeping wounds. The pain kept me tethered to my body, barely, as I watched myself yank open my clothing drawer, stuff an armful of random items into my gym bag, then grope along the bookshelves for what I needed most. Julian hadn't moved, but sobs escaped his throat. "Peter...please don't end it like this," he begged. "You asked me to do it. I only wanted to be gentle with you. I told you I wasn't good enough to have that kind of power—please, be fair!"

If I didn't leave now, I never could. When I headed for the door, he fell to the ground and flung his arms round my ankles. Unstoppable instinct made me grab one of the geode bookends and hurl it in his direction. It missed him, smacking a softball-sized dent into the bedroom wall. The childlike terror on his face gave way to a stony determination that chilled me. I had killed our love, at last.

Jule brought himself upright. His eyes steadied on mine. "That does not happen in my home. Never again. I don't care what I've done or what's making you act like this. If you can't understand that, you *should* leave."

"I will!" Breaking eye contact with him, I threw more things into the bag: *The Poison Cure* script notebook, the tin where I stored my Tarot deck and emergency stash of ganja.

He followed me into the living room, keeping a safe distance. "Listen, I need to know where you're going to be. You shouldn't be alone. I'm afraid you'll hurt yourself."

"I didn't do this to myself. I'm not like this because I *want* to be. I didn't just *wake up* one day and say, hey, I want to have perverted feelings that'll wreck my life!" I yelled. Julian didn't react. He had no right to turn that face to me, that clinical judgment, that barely polite disbelief. "And don't go asking around to find me, or I'll tell everyone what you *really* did to me!"

I slammed the apartment door. Nearly blacking out, I leaned against the wall. The light behind my eyelids burst fiery orange. If he'd come out in that moment, I would've squeezed my hands around his neck. That realization was an electric shock that woke me from my mad trance, leaving me drained and feeling sick. I was halfway down in the elevator before I noticed I wasn't wearing a shirt. I dug around in my gym bag, but the door opened on another floor before I found anything useful, letting in a neighbor I knew in passing from the laundry room. He glanced at my bare chest and gave me a small knowing smile, assuming I was doing the Chelsea walk of shame. The fear came first, then the recurring memory of Nathan, of making my face as blank as his, without understanding why.

He knew about Ben. An ice pick engraved the sentence on my brain. He knew and said nothing because he loved him better than me. Now it was Nathan I could've crushed like a soda can in my numb hands. But when I pictured my cousin, strangely, I felt only the clean sharpness of loss, and longed to reach him across death's dimensions to talk honestly about what was killing us both.

Meanwhile it was the middle of the night and I was homeless—*again*. I would have to sneak back in when Julian went to work, to retrieve my laptop and more of my meager wardrobe. And take them where? Back to Dee and Kevin's place, to burden them with brokering a truce I didn't want? Or crowd in with Prue, Aisha and the cats (now five—my sister's bandmate had traded her girlfriend for a one-eyed Siamese), and twitch discreetly on the fold-out sofa, a living example of the uselessness of men? I would rather sleep on a public bench than suffocate on memories in Dad's basement, which he was renting anyway to a suspiciously beautiful NYU Law student from Nigeria.

Gateway, then. Just for the time being. My last patch of the Holy Land. I knew there was a room free on the residential floor, where the kids and live-in staff slept, because Monique had found a placement last week.

The halls of the sturdy old brick building were quiet as a sleeper's breathing. The overnight front desk guard, nodding to his headphones, hardly registered my familiar presence. No one built places like this anymore, I lamented, mounting the marble stairs worn slick and uneven by so many footsteps. No one squandered turrets and wrought iron on transients like us. Out there in its cradle of trash lumber, my mother's rogue garden was pushing out spindly tomato plants and black-eyed Susans (and probably some marijuana, if I knew my students).

Monique's old room was plain and clean, with a faint scent of the strawberry body mist she used to take from the Korean beauty supply store where she worked after school. None of the doors locked on the kids' rooms, which didn't thrill me, but it wasn't like I was planning to have overnight guests during my hopefully brief stay here. I flung myself down on the narrow bed and it promptly collapsed, the bottom right corner thumping on the floor. With a groan I rolled off to investigate. The metal bed frame leg had punched through a loose floorboard that concealed a hidey-hole with a typical teenage stash: a half-smoked joint, a switchblade with a Hello Kitty pattern in glitter on the handle, what looked like a funeral mass card with an elderly Filipino lady's picture, and a nearly-full bottle of Ritalin prescribed to someone whose name I didn't recognize. I put everything but the prayer card into my bag—no sense getting Monique in trouble retroactively—and dragged the bed onto a more secure section of the parquet.

Stripped to my shorts, as the room was stifling even with the ceiling fan, I had fallen into an uneasy doze when something pale and soft brushed against me and I shuddered.

"Peepers, is that you? What's happened? I heard a noise and I was worried someone broke in."

A weak flashlight beam clicked to life. In its fuzzy penumbra I saw Mom in her quilted satin bathrobe and the bobby-pinned headscarf she wore to keep her hair set at night, an ensemble she hadn't altered since I was a child. Could it be that the intervening years had never happened? I was absurdly glad of this one thing I could rely on to stay the same.

Coming back to now, I pulled up the blanket to hide my bare chest. "Long story, Mom. Sorry. Can I just crash here tonight? I'll be gone in the morning."

"Gone where?"

"I don't know." The tears I hadn't shed for Julian spilled over now.

She sat down on the bed. "You don't have to tell me. I saw this coming. He wasn't good enough for you, boychick."

I squeezed my eyes shut and prayed, *please don't let her touch me.* Tenderness killed. Touch let the dirt in—or out, since I was a walking disaster, spoiling every good thing offered to me. "How did you know? I didn't..."

"Ah...don't blame yourself. He was charming, and he tried very hard. But he's just one of those men who can't control themselves. I know the type."

Now she did stroke my hair. I felt Julian's fingers on my scalp, firm and soothing, holding me down while he filled me; how very badly I'd wanted it, till I didn't. Horribly, I was hard. I squirmed away.

"I—I think I should go on retreat for awhile, but I'm afraid of losing my job. What should I do?" I bunched the blanket around my disobedient lower parts, pretending to feel a chill.

Taking my performance too seriously, Mom tucked a fold of the quilt round my shoulders. I held still. She meant well. If I was going to come crying to her in the middle of the night, I could hardly blame her for handling me like a feverish six-year-old.

"We'll work something out. Where are you going and how long?"

"Well, Prue invited me to join her for LGBT Week at this Buddhist center in Massachusetts—she did tech support for them in the spring and she said the grounds are beautiful. But we'll definitely be back by mid-June when her internship starts."

"Oh, so she *is* gay now?"

"She's decided she's an asexual lesbian. I don't know how that works exactly but she's happy. Low drama. Maybe I should try it."

"I've always said, you don't need a man to be fulfilled. Well, not *always*, or *you* wouldn't be here. I hope Prue doesn't miss out on having children someday." She patted down the blanket one more time. "Are you feeling better now? Should I make us some tea?"

"I'm fine now, really, thank you. I should try to sleep. Talk tomorrow?" I lay down and rolled onto my side, facing away from her, to give her the hint.

"Of course. You need a place to stay, I'll ask the board to make a live-in position for you, but you'll have to take on the office manager job as well as mentoring, all right?"

"Oh...okay, I guess. Thanks. Goodnight." I hoped I sounded grateful. The walls of my chest were closing in for another reason, crushing my lungs, grinding to a halt on my stone lump of a heart. Of course no future looked good to me. No tomorrow without Julian's warm laugh and wistful brown eyes. But he was an illusion. It wasn't safe for us to be together.

Tomorrow, I would call Sid. I would figure out where to live for a few days until the retreat. I'd bribe Prue with a pallet of Fancy Feast to retrieve my stuff from our—I mean, Julian's—apartment while he was at work. Everything, tomorrow. For tonight, I scolded my pounding heart, we were in the safest possible place. I sent my thoughts out to the new kids sleeping in the rooms adjacent to mine, Eryka and Teo and Damon, who (of course) had laughed at the mantra I'd taught them in group: *Peace is wherever you are*. Good luck, guys. We'll get through the next minute together, and then the one after that. Pizzas wherever you are.

And in my sleep I was still counting breaths, rationing air ascending a dark mountain I couldn't see, could only infer from the labor of pushing onward against gravity. Every step was a guess at how to avoid stumbling on uneven shale or crevasses. Though I hadn't fallen yet, the tension made me feel my lungs might burst. After an unknown stretch of time I sensed someone beside me. I could hear nothing, touch nothing. But I became certain it was Ben. I was terrified to turn and see the wreck his death had made of him. Or would we be reduced to children again, reliving hidden crimes?

I spun round to face him but jolted awake instead, gasping. I was sweating and thirsty, as if my exertion had been real. Magically, a mug covered with a saucer was on the nightstand. This, too, might be the logic of a dream. Or my mother had brought it in while I was sleeping. I gulped some lukewarm camomile tea and fell back into the same darkness.

Immeasurable mountain, unseen cousin. I was less afraid of him this time. Now, as the sky began to separate from the rock, dawn faintly gray above black, I dreaded the summit where I would have to—what? forgive him, push him off? His face was indistinct, as people are in dreams, an idea more than a likeness. Which of us was guiding the other, I couldn't say, but it took our combined will to keep mounting into the barely breathable air. Our peace was broken at the crest of the hill by a heavy hand in my hair, baring my neck to a giant who brandished—

—something unseen that slashed through the veil of sleep. I sat up, grabbed my throat, tested the voice that I half believed had been severed. I croaked the *Shema*, ancient prayer of defiant worship that had raged from the crematoriums. *Surely, Adonai, you're better than this.*

And, trembling, lay down again on night's altar, bound in sweaty sheets, resisting sleep as long as I could. Over me the patriarch raised his fist. It was Grandpa Saul, holding—holding—something that gleamed and shifted, never resolving itself, dazzling me like a camera flash. I knew the old story, the holy knife. But he stood as if in a trance, like a projection from another place and time, perhaps lifting a kiddush cup for his congregation or a laser pointer at a blackboard. His unseeing eyes frightened me. Better to look at the blade. A blinding light, a clean end. Unbearable beauty of the edge.

Could you die from a dream? My throat closed up, my body went rigid—not, after all, from terror or sick desire, but a sudden agony of rage, my heart straining to break free of my bound ribs. One last effort: could he see me, could I make him care? I raised my eyes to the towering figure, but he was someone new. Beaming, bearded, with chestnut hair cascading from his antlered head down his massive nude torso. Warm scents of cut grass and spring mud, sharpened with the distinctive spice of tomato plants sprouting in kibbutz soil. The memory made the world tilt. *Danger* flashed behind my eyes. The Hairy Dude's mighty bronzed arms raised the gleaming thing over my prone form and—*poured*—

—cold liquid that startled me awake. I shook myself. My face was dripping. The bed smelled like flowers. *What*—? I was haunted, insane, or still trapped in the loop of the sacrificial dream. None of these were good news. I put my hand down, to test the solidity of the bed, and touched something curved and hard. Not a blade, a saucer. I sniffed my damp pillow. Tea, just tea? I giggled, sobbed, hysterical with relief. I must have knocked the mug off the nightstand while I moved restlessly in my sleep. Yes, there it was on the floor, the handle unfortunately broken in the fall. When I gathered up the pieces, I noticed the design and felt sad. It was one I'd given Mom for Valentine's Day as a child, with a cartoon doe and fawn under the words "You're DEER to Me!" Incredible that she'd hung onto it through moving halfway around the world and back. Maybe I'd subconsciously registered the image when I woke up before, and that's why the final figure in my dream had stag's horns. I groped around on the floor till I couldn't find any more fragments. It would be unkind to leave it for her like this. I wrapped the pieces in some tissues inside the mug and stuffed the whole thing in a pocket of my gym bag. Morning light was slicing through the window blinds. Now I knew where I had to go.

[EXCERPT OF SCRIPT FOR *THE POISON CURE*, VOL. 3, ISSUE 1]

Aerial wide-angle view of unconscious Pharmakon lying on the floor behind the nurses' station. He is drawn in monochrome green and black with dotted outlines to indicate that he's invisible to the people in the hospital. Next panel, close-up of his face, alongside dream-bubble showing Phoenix wearing a look of deep distress. Next panel, the two of them are inside a dream-bubble, full color but in pastel hues to contrast with the real-life scenes. He sits up, looking bewildered, as she reaches out her hand to him.

Pharmakon: *What happened? Is Ryder safe?*

E: *You've done all you can for him. But I must tell you—*

P: *And the little girl? Please, I think I can help her, if you'd only—*

E: (gripping his hands, with tears in her eyes): *You don't understand. The situation is not what it seems.*

P: *Then tell me! Stop forcing me to choose between losing the man I love and having innocent blood on my hands.*

E: *You made that choice. When you were tempted to be "cured" of the destiny I gave you.*

P: *Is it so wrong to want love? Must I always suffer alone, to give life to others?*

E: *You don't know what true suffering is. I've shielded you, guided you. Till now, you've never had to wonder whether you acted rightly. Can you imagine what ordinary men would pay for such peace of mind?*

P: (embraces her): *Forgive me, Eva.*

Holding each other, they are posed like lovers about to kiss, but their lips do not touch. Along the bottom of the next few panels, below the dream-bubble where the two of them are talking, a multi-panel scene of hospital activity plays out, with people and equipment rushing in and out of Samantha's room.

E: (sadly pushing him away): *Stop...I can't bring you with me. It's no longer possible.*

P: *Then what is my fate?*

E: (pulling back as he reaches for her): *Go back to Ryder, if you wish. It will be some weeks before his "cure" destroys your mortal body...enough time to say goodbye.*

P: (stricken): *There's never enough time for that.*

Bowing her head in sorrow, Phoenix begins to fade away. Pharmakon calls out: But—can't anyone help Samantha? What if I saved her instead?

Phoenix's spectral face turns the color of white-hot ash. She has suddenly aged, become haggard. Her speech bubble is shaped like an ascending wisp of smoke.

E: *Forget her, Tod! You can't endure her kind of pain. It'll never leave you. Not like the others you rescued.*

P: (falls to his knees, trying to fan her sinking flame back to life): *Why? What could be so terrible inside one little girl's mind, after all the horrors I've seen?*

E: (a crone now, hunched above a pyre of burnt sticks): *You threw away your only protection for that man... Now the child's madness will become yours...and never end.*

The fire hisses out, leaving an agonized Pharmakon in
the encroaching darkness of the dream-bubble, while
below it, we see Samantha in a coma while her mother
sobs face-down on her hospital bed. Last panel,
complete darkness except for a tiny pop of green
light to indicate his disappearance.

NAKED ON MY BACK on the dusty floor, I watched smoke clouds bump up against the ceiling, hanging like hours in a room with no clocks, like my thoughts stalled before the door that memory couldn't open. The tidal rumble of traffic from the hot streets below floated through the open windows, distant as gulls' cries over the ocean. Some time passed. My sweat cooled and dried. Orange light painted the walls of the empty room. Afternoon, then. The second day? I could measure, if need be, by counting the used underwear piled in the corner. When it ran out, I'd promised myself, everything would be over. One way or another. Was nakedness stalling? Weed supply was another hard limit on the vision quest. If I rationed it out, I wouldn't have to stand up to eat so often. Food made me sad, and not only because my one supply run, my first day here, had been limited to items I could store in an apartment with no fridge—peanut butter crackers, beef jerky, mandarin orange cups (stories about pirates dying of scurvy had made an outsized impression on me as a child).

Aside from that, my possessions consisted of a straight razor, a sleeping bag and a three-pack of boxer briefs from KMart, three shirts that were too warm for the season, two pairs of pants (both bloodstained from my scratched legs), a Universal Waite pocket-sized Tarot deck, five CDs and a portable player from my gym bag, and the notebook where I was going to finish *The Poison Cure* if it was my last act on earth. I felt like a mummified pharaoh, entombed in a haze of incense, fodder for archaeologists who would speculate why I'd chosen a Jimmy Cliff reggae mix and Liz Phair's "Exile in Guyville" to accompany me to the afterlife—birthday gifts from DeWayne and Prue, respectively. In lieu of King Tut's curse, intruders were deterred by a taped-up sign I'd stolen from a neighboring apartment, warning that it was being fumigated for termites. I hoped this would forestall any surprise visits from the realtor Mom had engaged to sell Grandpa Saul's place.

No one knew where I was. Or *when*. In my suspended state, could I *think* myself back into the past that physicists said still existed in some dimension of this room, to find the place where I'd been broken? Dizzy, I crawled over to the wall, leaned against it to remember how to stand, and found my way to the kitchen to drink a can of oranges.

THE WORLD REVERSED

Pharmakon in bed in Challis' apartment. He has
normal human coloration but is very pale and gaunt
with terminal illness. Challis, dressed up for a
performance, leans over to kiss his mouth. Next
panel, they look at each other with longing, sad
but peaceful.

C: *I thought we'd have more time.*

P: *I'd never dared hope for this much.*

C: *I never should have—*

P: (voice weakening, shown by irregular shape of
speech bubble and lettering): *Stop. You saved me...
from being a killer...*

View pulls back to show a TV next to them playing a
scene of violence on the news.

C: (anguished face): *And from being a hero.*

P: (a tear escaping his closed eyes): *No one's good
enough to be sure what that means.*

Next panel, Challis is dismayed to see Pharmakon
forcing himself out of bed.

P: *Let me come to your show tonight. What do I have
left to lose? Except every moment with you...*

Next panel, Dorothy's Cafe is packed with a festive
crowd. Jars with sprigs of Christmas holly adorn
the tables and an angel decoration hangs over
the stage where Challis sings with his guitar.
Pharmakon, bundled in coat and scarves, reclines
in a chair in the shadows at the back of the room.
His eyes are closed and he smiles faintly.

C: (singing): *By the waters, the waters of Babylon—*

As Pharmakon looks on, Challis' image dims and the
angel decoration brightens. She now has the face of

> *we lay down and wept*
> *and wept*
> *and wept*

My elbows were killing me from writing propped-up on the floor. I crawled back to the sleeping bag, with its cheap squishy-slippery material I hated, that molded itself to my bare skin when I slept. This script was turning out shit anyway. It seemed I was at the sentimental phase of baking my head, which came between "whoa, look at the wallpaper" and "binge-and-purge Slim Jims". I couldn't help it, I pictured myself in Julian's bed, dying in his arms before we could hurt each other any more, and that was it, I was soaked.

I'd only wanted to give Pharmakon an honest ending, where he returned to this world, no more grandiose destiny, but no easy erasure of his crimes. He had to pay.

And I had to avoid sleep until I was so exhausted that I'd sink right under and stay there. Despite weed, hundreds of push-ups, and the Beatles' "Golden Slumbers" on repeat, I could manage just two or three hours before I woke in a panic of disgust like a detoxing junkie, sure that horribly slow soft fingers were creeping between my legs, or seawater lapping my face, covering my nostrils. *Why?* Why did I have to relive what I already knew? I'd heard your twenties were the age for the onset of schizophrenia. Though so far I hadn't felt the slightest temptation to craft headgear in the tinfoil aisle at KMart.

> *we remember*
> *we remember*
> *we*

    the face of Eva, bending down to kiss him. A
    sparkling wisp of green spirals out of his mouth
    with his final breath. The spark is drawn up into
    the space between Eva's parted lips, which becomes a
    vast darkness and

What the fuck. Definitely half past too stoned o'clock.

> *remember thee Zion*

Sometime around dawn. Light insistent as a trumpet. Was it my thirst-sick mouth that made me imagine a tapping like water leaking in another room? This brand of hallucination hadn't been covered in *I Never Promised You a Rose Garden*. I could wait for it to morph into whispering voices while I ate my juvenile breakfast of peanut butter crackers and a juice box, or I could put on yesterday's underpants and investigate.

The source of the noise in my grandparents' old bedroom turned out to be the old guy upstairs letting his bathtub overflow, a very New York problem I remembered from my time living here. Based on past experience, the dripping would stop by 7:30 when his home health aide showed up. Meanwhile, I should put down paper towels and make sure there was nothing left in the closet that could get damaged.

Alongside a stack of shoe polish tins and a box of nearly evaporated cologne samples, the closet contained the last three boxes of photos that I'd forgotten to finish sorting for Mom. I lugged them into my base camp in the living room. So, try to kill Pharmakon again, or distract myself with these? The cards said:

8 OF WANDS

Keep it moving, Peter.

```
    the face of Samantha beaming with joy

    in a photo above the small coffin where her mother
    weeps as mourners file past
```

NO

```
    the face of Samantha smiling as she beckons
    Pharmakon toward the glowing portal that opens into
    the starry night background. Children's silhouettes
    cluster behind her. Next panel, ghost-Pharmakon's
    hand clasps hers, causing green-gold energy to flare
    along their joined arms. The other children's spirits
    are semi-transparent beings of light, pale yellow
    with dotted outlines, faces blurred. Pharmakon looks
    toward them with joy.

    Next panel, back at Dorothy's, Challis leads the
    audience in singing: —in thy tender care, and take
    me— He breaks off when he sees Pharmakon's lifeless
    body in the chair, slumped sideways, lips slightly
    parted, as though sleeping peacefully. The elder from
    the Botánica stands in back, head bent reverently,
    one hand touching the amulet at his neck. Last
    panel, close-up on Challis making the same gesture,
    grieving but accepting, as the audience, not noticing
    what has happened, continues to sing: —to live with
    thee there.
```

Ah, that was the kind of crap Julian would love. Jesus, Obi-Wan Kenobi and the Little Match Girl. Ty would barf if I asked him to draw this. Wouldn't it sell, though? Comfort, comfort ye, my people, whose sick lovers' last breaths were attended not by monochrome cherubs but by parents with a Bible in one hand and an eviction notice in the other.

Maybe it only seemed cliché to me because I didn't believe God was that obvious. Abomination was like weather. Some people were born lightning rods, regardless of how they ate or fucked or prayed. Since Pharmakon was a dead man either way, couldn't I use his ending to ease others' hellfire fears, even if it did nothing for mine? Scratch the caroling scene, though. Christmas-y shit drowned out every other flavor, same as the peppermint that food manufacturers felt compelled to add to coffees and candies at holiday time. I mean, minty popcorn Cracker Jacks, *why?*

5 OF WANDS

```
Pharmakon looks toward the children's spirits with
sudden horror as, in the next panel, their images
come into focus: naked, some bruised or bleeding,
all wailing in anger and fear. He thinks: Not the
children I saved—but the ones I couldn't! He tries
to pull away from Samantha but she grips his hand
too hard, screaming How could you abandon me?

Next panel, the children's light glows fiery orange.
They close in on him. Only his face is visible, a
sickly yellow-green, agonized but unresisting. Last
panel, an empty hospital bed with
```

singing
singing

Fuck. *No.* Where was this "Suddenly Last Summer" shit coming from? I hurled the notebook across the room. A vertigo headache nauseated me. Kneeling, bent double, I groaned, swallowing down a bitter metallic taste. I'd passed the point of diminishing returns from the weed, but couldn't tolerate the thought of food. Maybe I was already dead and condemned to fail at finishing this comic book again and again for eternity, a hundred thousand endings that never set us free. Was that blue ink on my fingertips or the beginning of decay? The possibility, however foolish, seized me with compulsive shivers. I did *smell* like a zombie, but that could be because I'd developed some kind of phobia about the bathtub. Give it another day and I'd be avoiding the room altogether and peeing in bottles like Howard Hughes. That was not the legacy I wanted to leave.

I compromised by not running the shower or filling up the bath, but washing myself from the bathtub faucet with the bottled soap from my gym bag. Luckily there was a semi-clean towel in there as well. In the scratched mirror on the medicine cabinet

this'll be the day

I was tall enough (why did I think that I wouldn't be) to see I was alive— bloodshot eyes, dark beard stubble, and

the day
the day

the wrecked face of a man who only had the courage to kill himself slowly. But no. I had stepped into Hades the moment I unlocked the front door, and I would dig to the center of the earth with my bare hands if that's what it took to understand why I ruined everything I loved. I stuffed the damp towel in my mouth so I could scream without blowing my cover. Rage tore through my lungs, a scorching wind. I bit down on the towel. *Ah, ah, aaah...* It went on till my throat was scraped raw but there was more. I pounded my forehead against the rim of the tub. Gasping, at last I fell back on my heels, with black starbursts popping and fading before my eyes. Then I passed out or fell alseep, because

that I die

I found myself lying sideways with my legs in the bathroom and my head in the hallway. I stretched, swore, massaged the worst cramps, and actually felt better once I was upright. Score one point for primal scream therapy. The '70s weren't a total write-off. Nonetheless, it was time to swap out Don McLean's flower-child elegies for peanut butter and reggae. With Jimmy Cliff promising me "You Can Get It If You Really Want", I settled down again with my snack crackers and pulled another card

THE HIEROPHANT

which I interpreted as my grandfather advising me to put my space in order. Sorting the family photos might be the mundane break I needed to recharge my writing battery—along with literally recharging the Motorola phone Julian had made me buy. *Think of it as a bat-signal for the new millennium,* he'd said. I hadn't meant to bring it, but it was in my jacket pocket, battery dead as usual.

The photos were in no particular chronological order. They mainly dated from my childhood, interspersed with some scalloped-edged black-and-white portraits of my grandparents as a young married couple with children. There was little Barbara in a puff-sleeved dress and saddle shoes, playing with a pretty toddler, my mysterious Aunt Elaine, on the stoop of this very building. While my mother and I had inherited Saul's broad Teutonic features, Elaine's fringed eyes and china-doll mouth hinted at the beauty Grandma Reyna had boasted of in her prime, which she played up by copying the hairstyles of World War II pin-up girls long after they were out of fashion. So pensive for a tiny child, was she attuned this early to the demanding gods who'd lured her right out of our family story? Or merely miswired, like me, to perceive what wasn't there?

When the crick in my neck made me pause to stretch, I was surprised to see the empty room instead of the furnished past that I'd re-imagined into being. My body thought I was still the little boy stapling his hand-drawn books on Grandpa's living-room floor, in imitation of the big man who sat above me at his great wooden desk, studying a leather-bound book that smelled like magical secrets. If I looked up quickly I could catch Grandma doing her crossword puzzle on the couch, Lawrence Welk playing at almost inaudible volume on her radio so as not to disturb her husband. I never wanted to leave them, and I wasn't going to, because Mom and I were sleeping over tonight. (I had the sense this happened often, normal at the time, but in retrospect, possibly a symptom or a cause of my parents' marital problems?) Still I was anxious to stall the moment of bathtime and bed, the same way I would check the clock while my favorite TV cartoons were playing, hating to see how little time was left to enjoy—22 minutes, 14, six...

Setting aside the earth-toned candids of my past, I hunted for more of the older generation's crisp poses. My mother, kindergarten age, sat solemnly on her father's lap in front of a dark studio backdrop. Facing the camera head-on, he was a dark-suited King Solomon on his throne. Barbara, too young to master such tranquility, betrayed her discomfort with the dull photo shoot in the odd angle of her legs, one tucked round the chair seat and the other dangling toward the floor, with Saul's knee between them like a precarious rocking-horse. I felt sure Reyna had scolded her in vain to keep her knees together like a lady, as she'd done with Prue before my sister definitively rebelled against wearing skirts.

Barbara's glum eyes and fair hair reminded me that fictional Samantha still awaited closure. I tried seeing my mother's younger self as Pharmakon would. A man who lived to save children must have so much love in his heart, love that could do good despite being tainted with poison, sacrifice that made him more than a vector of deadly desires. If that was falsely sentimental, well then, the whole project was shit. For Ty's sake, I couldn't give up on it.

Time to get this over with before I developed a hunchback from writing on the floor. I should've bought a beach chair instead of the sleeping bag. I got up to change the CD to "Abbey Road" and use the

bang bang

toilet but a wave of vertigo brought me to my knees in the bathroom. Something wet, soft, and hairy wrapped around my nose and mouth. I held my breath. I couldn't claw it away. Until it stopped (it *would* stop) I would look at the smiling orange seahorse, pink clam, friends on the shower curtain— gentle wet *something* pushing into my dirty part—seahorse again, blue bubble, purple

bang bang

octopus's garden but there *was* no shower curtain, bare tub in a dead man's house with only me and my vomit. Oh Tarot tell me, did I give myself a concussion?

Queen of Wands Reversed

Rip out everything. Start over.

```
Pharmakon regains consciousness behind the nurses'
station desk. He is able to duck round the corner of
the hallway before the returning staff members see
him. In his usual workday scrubs, he blends into the
flow of activity in the hospital, now that his skin has
lost its green hue.
```

```
He looks down at his hands, realizing he still has a
choice: go back to Challis, or become the Poison Cure
one last time. He thinks: I'm so afraid...but I have
to see her again...to see if I can bear it!
```

```
In Samantha's hospital room, Dr. Morgan tries to calm
her tear-stricken mother. A younger doctor studies the
flashing lights and spiking lines on her monitoring
machines while a nurse adjusts the IV. Pharmakon
slips past them to stand at the girl's bedside. No one
reacts to his presence.
```

```
Next panel, the other characters and surroundings are
drawn in half-tones, only Samantha and Pharmakon in
full color. He looks down tenderly at her small face
and whispers: What happened to you?
```

```
Next panel, close-up on their faces. He bends down to
rest his forehead on hers, eyes closed. At the point
of contact
```

here comes the sun

Okay, where the hell is *that* going? Black bombs exploded around my temples. Dehydrated, hungry?

After taking care of survival needs—barely tasting anything—I paced round the living room. Walking meditation. Slow the heart. The music was off. "Here Comes the Sun" was my favorite track, so I didn't want to spoil it with the way I felt now. Around first grade, I think, I'd insisted on this song as part of my going-to-sleep ritual. At home we had the record, but my grandparents didn't approve of the Beatles—considering them part of the pseudo-Indian countercultural decadence that had brainwashed my aunt—so Mom would sing it to me when we slept over here. I'd bet she would still do it now, if I asked. I missed her, and Gateway, and everything I'd left behind.

Gross but I guess that happens. Look what I suspected for awhile about Ada. That'd show them, the smug feminists in Prue's books who sorted predators and victims by what was in their pants, and Dr. Marla who wouldn't let my friends be Ty's two dads. Was the Eva look-alike a wicked stepmother, too? We hadn't laid the groundwork for that, but then again, nothing we'd written thus far ruled it out either. Trust the cards.

Droplets made impact craters in the blue ink. I checked the ceiling. No stains. I flipped over a fresh page. The lines blurred. My eyes were the problem. Tears streamed down my cheeks, mingling with the sweat that itched at my collarbones. I flinched when it trickled down my bare chest. I was melting. "'Who would have thought a good little girl like you could destroy my beautiful wickedness?'" I quoted in a cracked falsetto.

Cleanup at the kitchen sink, paper towels (I had to start being more frugal with these), then a photo-sorting break. Maybe I should ask Ty's permission before I went further with this storyline. He might be offended. His mom who died of cancer had been the best person in his life. Plus, Eva's appearance was based on Cheryl Kingston, and we all loved her. Well, we could always go the "Days of Our Lives" route and have *two* of them, one good and one evil. Surprise twins were the last refuge of a hack writer.

I lay face-up on the sleeping bag with as many photos as I could hold. By now I'd given up the pretense that I was going to walk out of here with a sheaf of memories for Barbara, or any hope of creating an accurate timeline. I was just dropping them into left-hand and right-hand piles of "interesting" and "not interesting", based on composition, my feelings about the people depicted, and how dorky I looked if I was in the shot. Ideally this exercise would wake up the discernment centers in my brain so I could discard any crazy desperate story ideas.

What a wild plot twist that would be, though! Like an Agatha Christie mystery, the person you least suspect. Yet inevitable, in retrospect, given how Phoenix operated as both mentor and antagonist for Pharmakon. Everything in his world was double-edged. My selfish zeal for an elegant creative solution swept aside my fears about how the people who'd loved me would interpret it. These characters *weren't real*. Siegel and Shuster hadn't leapt tall buildings in a single bound.

Lavender dusk crept over the sky, stealing contrast from the fuzzy colors of the aged snapshots. Closing my eyes, I could swear the sleeping bag was really the plush carpet of my parents' den, as I'd just seen it caught on film, littered with tiddlywink counters for a dreidel game that four-year-old Peter had abandoned to mash a jelly donut into his face. I felt its sugary ooze clinging there still—sticky, sated, ashamed. My heart pounded from the tension of holding completely motionless so Dad would think me asleep and carry me to bed.

No one came. They'd forgotten me. Sobs rose in my throat, were suppressed (*be a big man*), came out as short loud breaths. It was all right. I'd kept our secret. The donut. Or the comfort she gave me for being a fat little baby boy, always wrong somehow, thick and sad. No use now, trying to pretend I didn't need it. Let them all cry through me, the two whose gametes unhappily married in my cells, the photographed dead, their burned unrecorded ancestors. Poor Peter. Poor Samantha. I had to get her out of here.

come together

    she reaches between Samantha's legs and pulls the
    little girl's hand onto her own ~~thing~~ ~~vag~~ breast but
    the crying child jerks away, slips and falls and
    in another burst of light the scene Pharmakon sees

changes to Samantha drawing two figures in crayon:
a stick-figure girl (triangle dress, yellow curls)
holding hands with a tall green man. Yellow lines
radiate from his smiley face.

Samantha-in-the-vision turns around to look directly
into Pharmakon's eyes. Hers are green. He'd never
noticed before. She says to him: *You know who you
are.*

And he does.

Knight of Pentacles Reversed

I was shaking, my pen dragging holes into the paper. My crotch was sickly wet. I might literally have pissed myself, as Dad liked to say when he hit on a killer legal argument. Please God let me not have been *aroused* by the abusive stepmother. I didn't even like vaginas, they were so—so smothering and pulpy and—how the hell did I know? I thought I was a Gold Star gay. Wow, things must have really gotten out of hand at Camp Ramaz truth-or-dare night. As God is my witness, I'll never drink wine coolers again.

Next panel, the hospital room. The other characters,
still in half-tones, are bustling around her prone
form. Pharmakon, completely green, places a gentle
kiss on Samantha's closed mouth. Next panel, a wisp
of green smoke, all that remains of Pharmakon,
enters her parted lips, as her eyes open halfway.

Next panel, everyone in the room is in full color.
They are shocked to see the girl wake from her
coma. Eva brings her hands up to her face and cries
out. Next panel, close-up on their reunion. Eva's
hands are clenched on the girl's blanket. She leans
over with an eager, anxious smile. Samantha weakly
lifts her head.

Stop there tonight, before maudlin bullshit took over. I'd written myself into a fucking corner again. Who would protect the kid, now that Pharmakon had evaporated into her imagination?

I set the notebook aside and started tidying the piles of photos so I wouldn't trip over them at night. Wash up, smoke up, pass out. That was the plan.

As I straightened the stack that I hadn't yet reviewed, a purple *tentacle* poked out of one corner. My heart slammed into my ribs. No

no no no

mystery, it had to be a toy or

not that not

what it actually was, a shower curtain decorated with cartoon sea creatures that used to hang in this apartment. I could hear Mom saying *Papa how cute won't you take a picture* because, God help the children of the '70s, she and I had had shower caps to match. Doughy, blank-eyed little Peter, probably overtired past a five-year-old's bedtime, wore only a pair of Batman underwear, while Mom

can't remember

held closed the neck of a quilted lime-green bathrobe, nearly identical to the one she'd worn at Gateway, my last time

seeing her

orange seahorses, pink clams, purple octopus, round and round my head. Her head. My small damp face. Her

NO

embarrassing taste in photo ops was distracting me from my real problem, the ending. Samantha. Pharmakon. Everything he was, was in her too. Poisoned pleasure and avenging guilt. Because she'd opened

the kissing game
open up your legs
now clean mine

No— I beat my head with my hands till both were sore. I was sick, and confusing this twisted story with my life. Write it out, get it out and then destroy it. I could barely see the page because sights were flashing past me like a slide carousel stuck on triple speed. I was writing by feel, missing the lines.

> Next panel, Samantha, with surprising strength, grabs Eva's hand, pulling the woman closer. The hospital staff are moved to tears by this apparently tender scene. But the reader can see, as they do not, the fear on Eva's face as the girl speaks her first words in a year:
>
> Mother. It's you.
>
> Next panel, Samantha throws her arms round the woman's neck and kisses her hard on

her mouth
on my little little thing
(that's what people do)
now my turn
i don't like it
(when they love each other)

her mouth. Green color spreads over the woman's face
and neck from the point of contact. Next panel,
Samantha falls back onto her pillow. The woman faints
into Dr. Morgan's arms, clutching her chest with one
hand, her face distorted in pain.

Next panel, an exhausted and despondent Challis
watches TV news in his apartment.

Newscaster: *In local news, a bittersweet story from
Greenville's Mercy Hospital. Samantha Stone, winner of
the Little Miss Queens County pageant two years ago—*

Samantha's pageant photo appears on screen. Challis
is startled to recognize her.

Newscaster: *—woke up from her coma yesterday, to the
delight of her fans and caregivers—and a shocking
loss. Her mother—*

little darling

sleep so safe
with your legs between mine
(that's what)
wet
(when we love)

Oh I couldn't I couldn't I couldn't
(write)

*—Eva had a heart attack and tragically passed away,
just minutes after her only child's miraculous
recovery. Doctors said the 35-year-old single mother,
a school counselor at P.S. 12, had a congenital heart
defect that was exacerbated by the strain of—*

Challis' hand switches off the TV. Eva's image
disappears from the screen...with a tiny flash of
green.

I did it. I killed her.

I had to hide it, I couldn't—I clawed through the stack of pictures. My stomach lurched when I revisited the shower curtain photo. Because I *saw* what was next. Pale damp belly I'd somehow fit inside, C-section scarred, folded above the mound of tight light-brown curls I

her hand in my hair
rubbing my face into
wet

shouldn't have seen, shouldn't know. *Didn't believe.* I meant to rip the photo in half, but my fingers wouldn't cooperate. Had to save it. To

remember

prove I could stop destroying everyone who loved me. These other pictures would show how normal my childhood had been.

A crowd woke up in my head. *Look, here we are, we've always been here.* Like knowing someone is standing behind you, knowing so long that you almost stop noticing, except for the prickling on the back of your neck, the constant low-level fear of the mysterious watcher. And then you turn around and see yourself.

Picture of Dad and me playing checkers

opening closing bathroom door

picture of me blowing out candles on a blue spaceship cake *wrong-tasting mouth* picture of me tucked into bed with a stuffed Peter Rabbit

soft fingers pushed under my waistband in the dark

They—the new ones, the other ones who wouldn't shut up—forced my inner eye to follow that hand up the wrist to the quilted sleeve

not her face
don't make me
(love each other)

I loved my mom so much. I needed her right now, more than anyone. I swore, I wouldn't cringe when she called me "Peepers" and "boychick" and made me throw my weed in the trash. She wouldn't judge me for being a helpless mess with no steady income and my underwear on backwards. With one phone call I could have clean clothes and chicken soup. And we would go on like that, from crisis to crisis, just the two of us, for the rest of my life.

Was that all this was? An overly dramatic attempt at individuation? Internalized homophobia of the Jewish mama's boy, a case study.

The Sun

My lullaby. With my eyes closed, her face came into view. Her alto voice superimposed itself on George Harrison's gentle tenor. The CD player, low on batteries, cut out in the middle of the second chorus, but the memory-voice went on. Her tender, abstracted expression, her eyes searching a point in the distance where her own frustrated dreams or childhood memories replayed, with that underlying sadness that had made me both scared and protective of her...even while she was the one singing me to sleep, even when, with the same look on her face, she touched

no no no

I howled. This, too, I'd always known. My body seized up, spasming with the release of muscles that had hardened against the memory of feeling. Oh, if my first sensations were broken...if *she* wasn't good...nothing was. I had to end this now or I would tell someone and then it would be *real*.

The boy on the Tarot card shone up at me. Naked, sunflower-crowned, parading on a milk-white horse. I'd never been that pure and never would be.

I was done here. I returned all the pictures to their boxes and stacked them against the back wall in plain view of the front door. My closed notebook and pens went on top. Everything else I'd brought, except the unopened food and the razors, went into my gym bag, next to the boxes. My mobile phone, blinking green to show it was finally charged, was still plugged into the wall. I left it there. Lastly, I unlocked the door and took down the fake fumigation notice. I wished I could play my music, but I hadn't thought to buy spare batteries. Then again, it would be ghoulish for whoever found it, playing over and over, with me gone.

Quickly now. Wipe this out. Release myself, every conflicted surrender a training for this. Because I'd always known the truth would end it all.

Water thundered from the bathtub faucet, steaming up my vision. I pleaded with myself: be confused, be wrong. But more sights cut through the fog, bits of mirror shattering. Flashes of skin, half a face, a kiss, the part in my mother's honey-brown hair as she bent her head down to lick my

NO

That image broke me, because I saw every strand, the line of coppery pins that held it in place for bedtime, the rosebud-shaped earring, her hand where it was

Natural

I heard her voice sing in the echoing stream. A word that meant disappointment even then, sensation cheated: chalky carob bars that only looked like Hershey's, rough soap studded with kelp bits. *Natural* a suffering to accept. A name for innocent love between mother and child, that never had to change. *I carried you in my body*, she'd say, pained and proud, guiding my small fingers to her stretch-marked belly and

do you want to see where you came out of me

blackness opened and I sank beneath. Relief in the hot waters that sealed over my head. Maybe I could do this neatly. Hold my breath. And then not.

Fighting my body's instincts, I opened my eyes to the water that pressed in and stung. A round glare wavered overhead, lightbulb swollen by refraction till it seemed to shoot out curling rays like the Tarot Sun. My heart lurched with sorrow for the pictured boy. He had no idea what crouched in wait on the other side of that wall. My stifled sob bubbled out the last of my air. A choking green-black cloud descended on me.

Involuntarily my body spasmed upright. I gulped in painful, noisy breaths. Foolish. I had a backup plan for this.

Trembling, I tested the razor blade's merciless edge on my forearm, to see if I had the courage. Do it fast and hard, that was the secret. Like tearing off a bandage, only the opposite. And vertical, along the vein—that much I knew from one of my stepmother's more sincere attempts. Thanks, Ada. I hope you get a good poem out of me so Prue will think you care.

I was able to blank out my mind for the first slash but the second, with my weakened hand, was ragged and hurt like fuck. I dropped back into the tub. That's how they did it in "I, Claudius," a dignified sleep, noble crimson life ribboning away. The Sun child's billowing red cape was blood, covering his face, drowning him. Child killer. This wasn't peaceful at all. It was me. I'd cut his throat, ripped out his vision. Thrashing in murky water. A stone for a head. Trying to rise but every direction was down. A shining circle. The light—the drain—

Water roared out through the opened plughole. Air hit my clammy face as the level in the tub dropped. My body was a thousand pounds of wet sand. Red branches twined round my forearms. I craved sleep more than anything but I couldn't. Had to find him.

I dragged myself over the porcelain edge. Watery red streaks on the tiles marked my path to the rack where I grabbed the towel and wrapped it round my wrists. Now my arms were bound together and I couldn't steady myself to stand up. Crawled down the hallway that expanded like a recurring nightmare, the half-familiar but never comprehensible maze where my sleeping self would chase a missed connection through shadowy subway stations. Turn around, Adonai. Show me your face and incinerate me. But let the boy shine on.

I couldn't see him anymore. The card was gone. I groped along the floor with rapidly fading strength. Night blurred the room, except for the faint green circle of light around my plugged-in phone on the floor. I wept with gratitude. We had a way out of here. The first *NO* the second speed-dial— oh, the sweet *hello*—

"Jule, I'm sorry...please help...Grandpa's apartment...I've hurt myself really badly..."

Then I knew nothing

bang bang

the phone hitting the floor my head cracking the bed banging the wheels the bed up and down
rocking in a bed in a metal room that sped over a bumpy road wailing flashing lights and everything white clean around me his arms
keeping me safe

PART IV

VAYEISHEV

JUNE, 1997 AND SEPTEMBER-OCTOBER 1997

And here you will ascend into the black mouth of God
I don't know how to do it but I am fuck well doing it
I am doing it
That's life I guess

—Ariana Reines, *A Sand Book*

I HAD SHOES WITHOUT LACES and three meals a day with a spoon. I had exactly two pills twice daily in a paper cup and a sealed window that overlooked the gray perpetual-motion loop of the FDR Drive. I had no desire to sing "Folsom Prison Blues". Pencils were too sharp for me but I had a blunt fat ballpoint pen that would click like a morphine-injection button when I wrote down my nightmares on the free notepads promoting Prozac. I didn't have the pages I finished because I threw them away. At least they let me do that. Or pretended. I was happy as a wall. And the evening and the morning were whatever day it was.

"Five," said Prue. She was family so they let her sit with me in the day room where two people whose names I hadn't learned played Gin Rummy. Julian was nothing to me legally. I could have put him on the list that Dr. Mirsky offered me but somehow the time seemed to go by and I couldn't decide anything. She also said I could make a list of banned people, which I thought was a nice gesture. Everything hurt when I tried to write their names. Even in my shredded dream-notes I could only say *SHE*. As memories came back to me, bright lights would burst like gunshots inside my skull and the sickness would rise up. I told myself the story had happened to someone else, who died. So my forbidden list simply said "EVERYONE". Dr. Mirsky looked like she approved.

"Where do they think I am?" I ventured to ask my sister. If this was the fifth day since Julian and the paramedics had found me bleeding on the floor of the rabbi's apartment, I had only five more days to enjoy the hospitality of NYU's locked psych ward, unless I convinced them I was a danger to myself and others.

"The meditation retreat story was good cover. I can extend it for you as long as you want. Tell them you're observing three months of silence in the forest."

"Not a bad idea."

"Don't you dare. Not yet anyway. You need people around you to keep you nailed down." She followed my glance around the dingy room, at my fellow patients who shared space but not awareness, each one dully focused on their inner monologue or time-killing hobby.

"Prue, I'm sorry to bring you back to a place like this."

"It's okay. I know my way around."

"That makes one of us."

"Is it helping?"

"No. Nothing helps. Limbo is just a break from hell." Here came the palpitations again. I fought for control of my breath. I didn't want to scare her.

"What are we going to do?"

That little word, *we*, spread warmth in my chest like a calming inhale of ganja smoke. "I don't fucking know. It's like walking on a glass bridge. There's nothing underneath me anymore." Be present, damn it. Feet on the floor, linoleum the color of old turkey slices. Smell of soap and cigarettes. White light. Infinite sensations of the moment, more vivid than ever, but sliced unpredictably by flashes of my long-buried life. "How can I go on living without trusting anyone?"

"Do you want to? Live, I mean," my sister asked, as if these were options we could debate rationally. That was her way. She was willing to consider the unthinkable, but unlike her mother, she wasn't excited by it.

"Please, Prue, I mean it, this isn't your responsibility."

"It kind of is. I'm sorry I didn't want to believe you before. Defending Ada was my job for so long—to make people see what I saw, that she really did love me, so they wouldn't take me away."

I forced myself to press her hand lightly. Touch set it off the worst. The cautious etiquette of this place pleased me. The other hospital guests might bend your ear about possible spy cameras in the air shaft, but no one forced you to hug out your feelings.

"It's not Ada," I said.

She couldn't hide her relief. "Are you sure?"

"Fuck no—aren't you listening? I could remember tomorrow that all of Dad's girlfriends passed me around at a Dionysian ritual. Nothing is sure. But for now, the Porter family honor is safe. You can stand down."

"I wish you could tell me what you remembered. So you're not going through this alone."

"A man with a split personality is never alone."

She laughed despite herself. "That sounds like one of Julian's jokes. Which reminds me, he sent you another note."

I accepted, but didn't open, the folded paper she retrieved from a pocket of her cargo pants. "H-how is he?"

"Sad."

"Tell him it'll be all right."

The day nurse came in to give a ten-minute warning about the end of visiting hours. Prue glowered at him behind his back.

"It's okay. This place isn't bad. It's like a monastery with really ugly furniture," I assured her.

"When they spring you, you're staying with me and Aisha for the summer, or until you and Julian patch things up. I promise I won't ask any questions."

"Like how I'm going to pay rent?" I'd have to quit Gateway. Any job at all seemed like a stretch until I learned how to lower the volume on the horror-movie highlights reel looping in my brain.

"I'll cover your share for now. I'm embarrassed to tell you how much my summer internship pays. Honestly my only big expense is Quan-Yin's specialty cat food. She has irritable bowel syndrome."

"Thanks for being there for me. I'm not trying to push you away, it's just—the less you know, the less the family can pump out of you. Don't get caught in the middle."

"That's where I was born."

"You and me both, kiddo—you should only know."

"Hey, fuck you with the dramatic foreshadowing. 'Do or do not—there is no try.'"

I hugged her goodbye without hesitation. "Ah, I'm glad you're my family. I do feel thirty percent less like death now. Seriously, you would make a good therapist."

"Ugh, no. I don't empathize for *money*. I'm not a sex worker." And my sister clearly didn't care how many staff members heard that, as they shuffled us off to our solitary rooms.

Sitting cross-legged on my thin mattress, I wished for the hundredth time that I had some weed, as much for the fidgeting potential as for the calming high. Rolling a joint was superior to basket-weaving; who the fuck needed more baskets? Also healthier than the cigarettes my neighbors chain-smoked in the break room. I didn't want to acquire that smell of second-rate addiction substituted for true desire.

Instead, I opened Julian's note.

> *Peter—your life is the most precious thing in the world. Remember that, whether or not you want to see me again. I'll do whatever you ask. Love, Julian*
> *PS—Someone named Felix Taylor from DC Comics wants you to call him. What should I do?*

This was followed by an unfamiliar Manhattan phone number. For a moment I forgot where I was and what I'd done to myself. Could it be that a real comics publisher had noticed *me*? Then the trapdoor opened under me, weightless elation turned to choking shame. I could never show anyone that notebook (where was it?) with *The Poison Cure*'s only possible conclusion. What a sick person I was for dreaming up such a story. Forget about convincing my family of its truth. Even as fiction it was a waste. I was not the boy they'd groomed to improve the world.

I dug up Julian's other two unread notes to me, which said pretty much the same thing: he loved me, he was sorry, he was mine to command. The earliest note contained other useful information. He would be coming to the hospital every day at 2:00 in case I felt like seeing him. (I couldn't help thinking that was kind of romantic, like a dog in a movie visiting his master's grave.) And he had salvaged my script notebook from the carnage at the apartment, but he wouldn't read it without my permission.

I could put him on the visitors' list right now and see him tomorrow. I mistrusted my joy. After all, I still missed Mom terribly, though I woke up trying to scratch my skin off after cloying wet nightmares of her. In my mind, my family waited behind a door, that if I never opened, I could see them as they ought to be—generous, normal, creative, affectionately bickering but united by a history I couldn't spoil. Aunt Nora's seder seemed like it had happened a century ago.

D R. MIRSKY HAD LEANED on me to let Sid visit, so that was my next ordeal. I preferred strangers around me, people I'd never see again, who wouldn't remind me of the life I would have to shatter and rebuild. But my insurance didn't cover that. Only five more days to pretend I was dead.

To my surprise, I melted inside when I saw Sid. Short and stocky, he reminded me of a bristly gray-bearded teddy bear. (Everyone looked smaller to me now, it was weird. I'd thought it was just Dr. Mirsky, who resembled a midget Ruth Bader Ginsburg.) I gave him a quick hug, which he returned. It didn't feel terrible.

The private meeting room's old vinyl couch wheezed when we sat down. "Private" was something of a misnomer because an orderly watched us through the thick plexiglass window to ensure that no pills, sharp objects, or body fluids were exchanged. The day-room crowd might disagree, but I found his surveillance reassuring. My bed, my dreams, my mother's womb—if only someone could have put a camera there, to record what only my skin knew for sure.

The first thing I could think to say to Sid was, "You must be so disappointed in me."

"What? No. Never. You're doing the best you can, Peter. You always have been."

I hung my head. "Yeah, but I promised you, if I felt like—you know—" I mimed cutting my throat because it felt too melodramatic to say the word. "I was suppposed to tell you first, but I got caught up in writing, and..." How to describe the call that had compelled me? "It was like, I had to get down to the bottom of this or it would never end, and if I stopped for anyone, I would lose my nerve."

Sid nodded like he understood. "Did you get there?"

I shuddered. "Yes."

We were silent for awhile, him obviously waiting for me to hand over the key to my psyche, me praying I could leave it at that. "Did you bring your cards?" I asked at last.

A wry smile. "No, when they checked inside my bag at the front desk, they said I'd have to fill out a form for permission to conduct religious services."

"Gotta love this place."

Sid waited to see if I'd share more. I didn't. "Telling me makes it too real, doesn't it."

"Fuck. How do you know."

"This isn't my first rodeo in Flashback City."

As usual, his humor made my problems seem less monstrous. "Okay cowboy, then tell me how does someone move on from this? How do I *live* in this world?"

"People do lots of things. Some of them try to forget again. Some bracket it and go back to their families and keep things normal at arms' length. Others decide those relationships are bullshit and go into exile with other folks they trust. It's fine to go back and forth among all of those modes till you find your balance."

"Those choices suck."

"Yep, they do. Some lead to better places than others, but they're all going to hurt." His voice was warm and gentle. "You can't think yourself out of a bad thing someone else did to you. Your brain did an excellent job protecting you that way when you were a kid, but now it's saying you're strong enough for the truth. Which I know you are."

"Even if I am...no one else is." My father, crushed by Ben's death. Prue, so clever, so defensive of her isolation. And Mom? Surely she couldn't remember, either. She'd only wanted to love me and hadn't understood how.

"I am," Sid said. "Whenever you're ready."

"I'll come see you when they release me. Promise."

"Yes you will. We're making an appointment today. And we have to discuss how you'll stay safe when you're on your own again."

We went over the details of where I'd live, who I'd call if I felt like hurting myself (not my dungeon master!), meditation, breathing exercises, et cetera. The absurdity of planning a life with this black hole at the center—I didn't know whether to laugh hysterically or punch a wall. So I did neither. I was a *good* patient.

The next morning I resolved to enjoy my banal institutional existence until Julian's visit, because I could only feel so many emotions in one day before total systems failure. It's a funny thing to be on the other side of the bulletproof glass after working in social services. A group of strangers in crisis will fumble around for familiar roles to play. In this week's random scoop of nuts, would I be the sullen superior loner, anonymous middle child, tragic burnout, or kiss-ass who did the art therapy assignment exactly as described? (Draw your dream vacation.)

Stick-figure man in the woods. Sheltering green crayon pines. Thick brown crayon earth. Silver circles of boulders for some mature artistic detail. I knew how the game was played. The content didn't matter. A hook for interrogation was the point. Leave the figure alone and they'd ask me why. Draw him a companion, they'd ask who. Valuing anything enough to keep it secret would only betray me as a liar. The joke on me was that no one cared about my strange gods or grossest arousals. They wanted to pry open the clam, not find the pearl.

I drew Julian, an orange-haired stick figure, off to the side of the page, standing on a rock. He held a rectangle with a circle inside to represent a camera. On my avatar's other side, I found myself drawing a large brown humanoid figure that loomed as tall as a tree. What would the head look like? The body resembled a bear, but I didn't want it to be something that dangerous. I closed my eyes, took a deep breath, reliving my mother's night-time cold-cream scent, my wet face, a shattered cup. The huge smiling head I drew looked vaguely canine—I was no artist—till I added the spreading rack of antlers. I imagined Dr. Mirsky's case notes: *Diagnostic code 301.2, phallic symbols (multiple)*.

What I'd told them when I woke up strapped to a hospital bed: *I remembered some bad things from my childhood and became depressed.* What I meant was: *I'm a disgusting person and I can't live in this body.* Happy couples would refuse to buy a house where a murder had occurred, though the blood had been sanded off the floors and the echo of gunshots dampened by new carpeting. How then could I eat, talk, breathe with this mouth that had *touched*—I couldn't even finish the sentence in my own head.

This was not how I expressed myself to the good people of NYU Hospital. They weren't ready for metaphors to come true. I was afraid they'd tell me my new language was meaningless before I myself learned to speak it.

Don't get me wrong, I was glad to be here. It beat the alternative—a bloated corpse depressing the value of my mother's real estate. I was soothed by the mundanity of filling out psychological questionnaires that asked whether I was afraid of lightning and how many times a week I took a shit. Was my father a good man? Did I prefer engine repair to needlepoint? Did I sometimes see patterns that weren't there?

In my room, after picking at a starchy lunch, I did some low-impact yoga and then flipped back and forth between two paperbacks I'd scavenged from the day room, a Tom Clancy thriller and an illustrated book of positive affirmations. *You are more than your worst thoughts.* Okay, cartoon frog sitting under a raincloud, I fucking hope you're right.

I almost forgot why I was being summoned to the private visiting room again. I panicked that Dr. Mirsky was about to break it to me that I had schizophrenia, which would probably make me unemployable at DC Comics for liability reasons. Uh oh, was that paranoid? I dunno, kids, is it *normal* to be a wee bit suspicious of the world when the person who gave you life is literally sticking her finger up your—

Then Julian was there. The most beautiful sight in the world. His radiance, his worn-out gentleness. The soft, safe pressure of his body in my arms. I didn't hesitate to wrap myself around him. He held me lightly, waiting to see what I could handle. Poor Julian. I was all extremes. I sniffled into his sweet-smelling hair. My death hadn't worked; I'd have to find a way for us to have peace while I was still alive.

I pulled back and looked at him again. Everything was new. Uncontainable warmth spread from my chest. I cupped his tear-stained cheek in my hand. "Please forgive me for—"

"I'm so sorry I—"

Speaking over each other, we broke off and laughed through our tears. With a sigh, he stepped back, giving me space that I no longer needed. "As long as you're alive, nothing else matters. Just tell me what to do. Or what not to do, if that's an easier place to start."

"Could I...hold you again?"

"Oh, God, always." This time his embrace was firm.

I made myself look into his eyes. That was still painful, because I felt guilty, unworthy to make promises. "None of this was ever your fault. I love you so much."

"I know you do." He bowed his head.

"How do you know?"

"Because you called me, when..." He swallowed hard, unable to put words to the bloody scene I'd forced him to witness.

Closing my eyes, I was underwater, watching the light fade, fighting my way toward the sun. "Because of you, I know what being alive should feel like."

He gripped me tighter and buried his face in my neck. I let him weep quietly. A brief peace descended on me. I had said something true.

"Okay, that's it, you have destroyed me." Jule found the nearest of the tissue boxes they stocked the rooms with and blew his nose.

"Sit down, it'll be okay."

"You're right, it's hard to swoon in a plastic chair." He reached for my hand across the formica table. "Listen, you can take your time telling me what you remembered, but it would put my mind at ease if I had some idea what we're dealing with."

"You still want to...be part of this?"

He rolled his eyes. "Can we *please* have a moratorium on breaking up? It's such a waste of time."

Julian could make me smile under the worst circumstances. "So, do you want a year's lease on my soul, or month-to-month?"

"Jesus, I can't go through this every month."

"We won't." I caressed his arm. We both knew I was stalling.

"What sets it off, then? How do we keep it from happening again?"

"If by 'it' you mean me trying to check out permanently, I don't think I'm going to do that again. If you mean me being triggered and mistaking you for...the person who fucked me up...well, I hope not, but my reality is still kind of smashed up. Pieces of *then* get stuck in the *now*."

He stroked my hand, grimacing when he touched the bandage on my wrist. "Why did you do it?"

"I found out something I wasn't supposed to know." The old me would have stopped there, but he was dead. Everything he'd lied to preserve was gone down the drain with his blood. I couldn't spare Julian either. "I wouldn't have gone through this ordeal unless I wanted to live, actually—really live, for the first time—but the truth is..." My breath felt like knives in my chest. "When I think of the rest of my life, sometimes all I see is pain that I can't tolerate for another second. How to live with losing...*someone*... not only in the future, but the past too, all my good memories made filthy."

Jule brought my hand to his lips, softly kissing first the back, then the palm, near the covered scars that remained sore. I leaned into him. My skin thirsted for this touch that didn't feel wrong. The old terror lapped at the edges of my awareness, the dark waters I'd shied away from whenever he got too close, but for the first time I recognized them as separate from us.

"I don't think Abraham got Isaac back in the end," I said. "I think once he saw the knife, Isaac lost his family and his God, and everything in the Torah after that is a lie. Do I sound crazy, Jule? I'm sorry."

"No, I follow you." He lowered his voice. "Was it, uh, your grandfather?"

I hesitated, chasing a glimpse of hope that it *had* been his fault, some way to spin my memories that made Barbara into another person's unwilling puppet. "You have my notebook from his apartment, with my *Poison Cure* script? You can...you should read it, but don't show it to anyone. Especially not Ty or Prue. It's not their burden to bear...yet."

The practical problem of our unfinished comic-book series, now apparently in demand at the Daily Planet, was a matter to work out with Sid. I could count on Ty to be blunt about whether he hated my plot twist. I was mainly afraid he'd guess my real-life inspiration and it would stir up his old defiance of his Gateway caseworkers, just when he seemed to have accepted his placement.

"You're staying with her when you get out?"

"Just for a couple weeks, while I figure out where I go from here. I need to lie under a pile of cats and listen to folk music. Are you okay with that?"

"I trust you to do what feels right. As long as you don't disappear again."

"I won't."

"When—*if*—you come home, we don't have to sleep together. I can stay on the couch."

My eyes welled up. "You deserve better."

"All right, *you* sleep on the couch. I can afford to buy a new mattress for it, I had them cash me out of Shooz.com this week."

"Way to bury the lede! Why?"

"You were right, I don't care enough about that masters-of-the-universe Wall Street bullshit to let it take over my life. I have more important things to focus on."

"You didn't give it up because of me, did you?"

"Fuck, are you really going to be like this again? They're not the kind of people I want to spend all my time with. You are. Deal with it."

Under his irritation I heard the fear and exhaustion he'd been covering up for my sake. "It's okay to be mad at me. I know I put you through hell."

"You *don't* know." His eyes blazed. "I watched my first boyfriend die. I saw my father break my mother's wrist with a Waterford crystal decanter. But finding you nearly dead—that's the one that almost killed me too."

I pulled him into my arms. "Never again. I swear."

Time's-up knock on the door. Julian wiped his face. "Can I come back tomorrow, or do you need a break?"

"That's kind of you...maybe, the day after?"

He nodded, resigned. We agreed he'd call DC Comics and tell Felix I was on a meditation retreat, then later this month I'd go for an interview (if I was lucky) and explain the bandages on my wrists as carpal tunnel syndrome—a trick I learned from a girl in our coping skills group.

I was restless when he left, finally eager to get out of here, not waste another day of my resurrected existence doing jigsaw puzzles under supervision. I read some more of the inspirational quotes book and doodled pictures of vampires and werewolves saying things like "Happiness is not by chance, but by choice."

Like every evening, I fought the impulse to call Mom and tell her I was all right—even though, number one, I wasn't, and number two, she had no idea that I wasn't sitting quietly in the woods around the Quabbin Reservoir with the other homosexual dharma bums. In my mind I had two mothers, the dreadful new one who touched me in the shadows, and the normal one, whose solid familiarity argued for more credence than that fragmentary intruder. I couldn't have expected the one to recognize the other.

you can't tell

Whispering woke me from a restless doze. I cried a little, homesick, crushed by the dull weight of each minute. I hadn't heard anything, of course. Only sputtering disconnected wires in my brain that

he couldn't understand

I broke out in a cold sweat, regretting that I'd asked Julian to read my perverted script. If he read between the lines, he'd see

our love

my filth, my betrayal of the purest bond. I'd had a *good* home. I wanted to go back there, to find the kernel of love untouched by this aberration. Eyes closed, I caught a whiff of her lotion scent on my childhood pillow, a storybook whisper

they'll take you away from me
crazy people get put away
don't say crazy things

Her lips...soft whisper...her fearful eyes. Helplessly I was compelled to look, to recognize who

no please no

and what she knew.

"Mom, no, please NO—" Tearing sounds came from my throat. I pounded the thin mattress till my fists ached. My sobs rasped like a death rattle.

Footsteps in the corridor. Instantly I stifled my cries in my pillow. As a child, I'd been afraid I would suffocate to death in my sleep, but simultaneously fascinated that I might have the power to end the world I knew. A glimmer of that temptation danced before me, to scream and scream till an impersonal hand injected me with oblivion. But I lay frozen, half in and half out of the past, till the ward fell silent. I'd promised Julian. I'd promised *her*. If speaking and silence were both unthinkable—well—

I scrambled out of bed to write on the first unripped page of my new black-and-white composition notebook:

It happened.
Don't destroy this.

[EXCERPT FROM RADIO PROGRAM ON FAITH TALK ATLANTA WNIV-970, DEC. 13, 1997]

...I've been a star athlete, a nationally acclaimed bodybuilder, a political strategist. And I've been lonely and suicidal. I've misused my God-given gift of sexuality. Through it all, Jesus has loved me. He's all I've ever had. And that's enough.

Not that I haven't been led astray sometimes. There was once a guy I cared about a little too much. He struggled with same-sex attraction because he'd been beaten by his father, and he sought out other victims of child abuse, to try to fill that void together. But relationships that are against God's will can't last. They just can't. He even told me that himself.

I've found the one love that the world can never take away. That's always there to pick me up when I fall. And you can too.

Radio Host: That was Brent Harrison, the new Communications Director at Love In Action Ministries. If you, or someone close to you, would like help moving from homosexuality to holiness, call this number today...

Down on hands and knees…back bent…sweat dripping eyes blurred… she's watching…she's touching.

"C-cat pose," I rasped, fixating on the electric blue fibers of the yoga mat under me to bring my awareness back to the 7 AM class I was leading at the Ironman Gym. The thick air parted briefly as Suzanne, the new instructor I was coaching, made her brisk transit around the hot studio to manipulate students' limbs into correct positions. Out of the corner of my eye I saw her straighten the elbow of a woman whose arms were trembling with the effort to hold still. The student, a longtime but sporadic visitor to my classes, was sweating in the baggy long-sleeved tunic she wore to disguise her top-heavy frame. Suzanne had the type of body you see on the cover of runners' magazines, her slight curves as disciplined as the straight black hair she wore in a high ponytail.

"Half hero pose," I said, more decisively, and the students gratefully fell back onto their haunches and slumped forward. They were supposed to hold each position for three minutes but my instincts told me to release them early. I certainly felt less vulnerable with my ass securely tucked against my feet instead of presenting in mid-air. We shifted to butterfly pose, spreading our legs in a diamond shape, some of us more adept than others at making them lie flat against the floor. Suzanne rose from her perfect posture to place her hand on a squirming man's knee till he sat still. I counted my breaths like they were soldiers marching past a parade stand. First day back at work after my "meditation retreat" in the rubber room, and this was supposed to be the easy part. No such luck.

"Only hold the position as long as you feel safe and comfortable," I told them. "If something hurts, feel free to adjust it." This was a new direction for me. I'd always assumed that, being New Yorkers *and* motivated enough to wake up at 5 AM, my clients would do whatever they damn well pleased. But I myself needed an excuse to stand up that very second. In tree pose I felt tall and weightless, a hairy 200 pounds of improbable gracefulness.

Suzanne and I lingered after class for post-game analysis. She normally taught Tae Bo, but management wanted me to train her to pick up a yoga shift, because another instructor had been poached by David Barton Gym. I was going to lead with a positive comment about her form, but she jumped in: "Why did you let them end the poses early?"

Because you don't want to watch me decompensate was not a professional answer. "Just instinct. We want them to come back. Yoga is about learning to appreciate being present in your body. You can't rush that." In fact, it could take 27 years...and counting.

"I felt you undermined me out there."

"How's that?" I tried for a neutral, controlled tone.

"I'm working hard to make them do the poses right, then you act like it doesn't matter."

"That wasn't my intention. It's just that...'right' could be different for everyone. We don't know what injuries or, uh, negative feelings in certain body parts our students come in with."

"Then they shouldn't be here. They should go to a doctor and come back when they're ready to push themselves outside their comfort zone."

"Some people have never been *in* a comfort zone to begin with." I was raising my voice, so I took a beat. "In any class that I'm teaching, we're going to ask students' permission before we touch them."

She rolled her eyes. "Oh, is this a liability thing? Got it."

"Best to get out in front of it now, before management has to issue a statement." Though I was annoyed she didn't value consent for its own sake, Suzanne had given me a good idea for how to sell this as a gym-wide policy change.

Standing my ground with her had left me in a cold sweat. My hands twitched, craving the soothing routine of rolling a joint, but I was strictly limiting myself to one per day and I needed it before bedtime to take the edge off the nightmares. I substituted a quick, punishing session with the punching bag in the weight room. My surroundings blurred, the impacts vibrating through my overheated body till I was both weapon and target, raging fists and pummeled sack of sand. Shaking myself alert, I stepped back, slow to process the silky-voiced question, "Work in with you?" from a guy with G.I. Joe neck muscles and a buzz cut to match. He leaned in toward me, spreading his hand against the swaying leather bag as if cupping its nonexistent ass cheek.

"Sure, I'm done." I lay down to stretch while he danced around the bag, landing percussive little jabs. He stopped as soon as he saw me head for the door.

"Whew, time to hit the shower, huh? Or maybe the sauna?" He was following close behind me.

"Sauna in June? Nah, I'm hot enough already."

"You sure are."

I forced a smile. "Guess I walked right into that one."

"What else do you like to get into?"

I looked him over. Healthier than weed for a distraction. Nice bulge in the sweatpants. I'd forgive him the reactionary politics implied by their "Princeton Tigers" logo. Julian would be on his ass in a second. He wouldn't blame me for doing the same. But the desire was all in my mind, while my body cringed. I wanted power, not touch.

"Ah, well, right now I'm late for work, but..." I casually brushed my hip against his pelvis on my way out, to preserve the opportunity for a time when I wasn't insane. "Before you ask, yes, I do come here often."

"I'll make sure that you do." No subtlety for this one. Probably majored in economics with a minor in Coors Lite.

In the locker room shower stall, the water's forceful pulse on my thighs reawakened the momentary arousal I'd felt when the stranger's hard-on pressed against my leg. I looked down at my dick in its nest of black hair—a man's body, nothing to do with that horrified child—and gave it a tentative stroke with soaped-up fingers. My breathing quickened. White noise fizzed in my brain, curtaining out all sensations but one. I watched my hand to make sure it was mine. Thrusting feverishly into my clenched fist, I staggered and bumped my head on the faucet. The pleasure I'd been chasing slipped away, as quickly as it had overtaken me. I'd been trying too hard not to fantasize about anything while I beat off, purely a body meeting its needs, a stupid animal. I shoved open the fogged glass door, barely stopping to wrap the skimpy towel around my limp bruised dick before I rushed to a toilet to throw up my breakfast smoothie.

Ginger ale and Tums tablets from a subway newsstand would have to satisfy me till lunchtime, since I had a long ride uptown to Gateway. I re-read a back issue of *Aquaman* and daydreamed about where the character might be headed. Bastian from GalaxyCon had kept his promise to put in a good word for me with his Uncle Felix, who now wanted to try me out on the writing team for a reboot of the undersea hero—contingent on whether I nailed the ending of *The Poison Cure*. Four-color ink came off on my sweaty fingertips. So far Julian was the only person who'd seen my script with Eva's downfall and Pharmakon's transmutation. "Wow, that's pretty dark. Incredible twist, but...do you want to talk about it?" Jule had ventured. But I merely shook my head and urged him to hide the notebook somewhere safe in case I was tempted to rip it up.

Warm cooking smells of vegetables and herbs greeted me inside the Gateway building. I met Teo in the hallway, bearing a dirt-speckled bouquet of chives from the community garden. In the kitchen, a new girl with braces on her teeth and a large baby bump stirred a tall silver stewpot. As I'd seen her do on so many Friday nights, Barbara expertly quartered a raw chicken and added the fatty yellow-skinned pieces to the bubbling mixture.

My stomach turned over. My hope, only recognized as it seeped away, had been that her sturdy physical presence would expose the unreality of my sickening visions. It hadn't worked. *She didn't know*, I pleaded inside. If not my delusion, hers. Something had overtaken her. How else could she smile at me now?

"Boychick! Welcome home. Come peel some potatoes and tell me everything." She scrubbed her hands and hustled over to the doorway where I stood paralyzed. "You don't look so hot. Was it hard work, sitting in the woods and eating beans for a month?"

She reached up to touch my face but I flinched away. My tongue felt coated, thick with words no one would hear, words that I couldn't have known for her

holding down my head

expression of tenderness chilled to blank disappointment
in me
between her legs
in her wet
in her

A knife. My hand on the knife, on the slick sweet-rotten earth smell of the cutting board. Potatoes. A table to lean against.

"Just tired today," I forced out. "Taught an early yoga class."

"Hmph. Well, we're all ready for you to start as office manager. These part-time jobs are spreading you too thin."

"About that—" My planned speech, such as it was, went out of my head. The comics gig wouldn't replace a full-time salary, and forget about benefits. Without running the numbers, I'd been relying on wishful thinking that extra gym shifts and freelance jobs would make up the difference. For shelter, I always had the option to move back in with my suddenly rich boyfriend. But how plausible was it to organize all that, when I could barely rouse myself to eat one meal a day and change the litter boxes for Lena, Reilly, Murphy, Quan-Yin, and Boadicea? For the past two weeks, as soon as Aisha and Prue left for work, I would get back under the covers, turn on the Cartoon Network for company, and cry.

Barbara filled the pause in my unfinished objection. "Taste this lettuce. Teo and Eryka have done wonders with that garden." She popped a curly pale-green leaf in my mouth. It was tender and soft like skin.

"Can I stop now?" the new girl whined, shifting from foot to foot.

"I'll bring you a stool," Barbara replied. Then, to me: "This is Callie. She's fourteen. Callie, my son, Peter. He'll be your mentor. He's so good with babies. Peter, have you seen Amy and little Mae lately?"

I shook my head. The smell of the stew made me hungry and sick at the same time. The kitchen dimmed, morphed into Aunt Nora's dining room with the aromatic steam of the Passover feast and the unending replay of Ben and my mother spreading the baby's legs to clean her

special place
soft
how you like it
before we sleep

"—fucked my stepbrother."

"Wait, *what*?" I yelped.

"Callie, we don't say that word here," scolded Barbara.

"*Excuuuse* me. I *said*, my father threw me out because Ricky and I made *this*." She patted her belly. "I promised Ricky I wouldn't get rid of it because he's, like, super Christian. I am *so* done with this stew." She slid off the stool my mother had just dragged over to her.

Barbara sighed. "All right, maybe it is too hot in here for a girl who's expecting. Go upstairs and work on your book report."

When the girl had escaped, Barbara filled me in. "Summer school—so she won't fall behind when the baby comes. She's smart, but she's stupid, you understand? This 'Ricky' is 22, shouldn't even be living at home anymore. Statutory rape is what it is, but of course their father won't hear of pressing charges. And she thinks this is something she *chose* to do."

Like I did. She'd have stopped. If I stopped. Liking it. Soft—

I flung myself onto the seat Callie had vacated. "Mom, I don't want to do this anymore."

"What are you talking about?"

I made myself meet her eyes, the same hazel shade as mine. What if I was wrong about everything? If only she would protect me, like Callie and the baby...the baby...what would she do to him? No, it was only me (*little darling*) she loved that special way—

"I've figured some things out." I waited for my direct gaze to make her squirm with guilt, but she merely seemed perplexed. "Nothing's been the same since Ben died. I've had to face the fact that I run around doing 'good works' to avoid seeing the emergency right in front of me. This job—it's not right—I can't be here."

"Peter—as your mother, of course I want you to take care of yourself. But I'm responsible for other kids besides you. Look at Callie. No way her father and stepmother will take her back, not that it would be safe anyway with that Ricky around. A real Cinderella, without the prince. As usual."

"What are you going to do with the baby?"

"Oh, we'll get her to adopt it out. You saw her, she doesn't have the attention span to make soup. We need you to honor your commitment, Peter, I can't be the only adult around here." She passed me the paring knife, a brisk gesture indicating that the case was closed.

Couldn't I bear it for a little while, knowing what I knew but putting it aside (as she must have done), for the kids who were more helpless than I was—a bodhisattva re-entering the cycle of ignorant suffering? In silence, I worked beside her, unfurling a long spiral of potato peelings from the small blade, then another, and another, falling back into the automatic motions learned in the kibbutz's steamy cafeteria kitchen.

Her arm brushed mine as she scooped the raw chunks into the stewpot. A feather-light touch, but my knife hand skipped. I gazed at the deep red bead of blood welling from my thumb. I hadn't felt anything. Red clouds, red ribbons in water... My vision doubled, then refocused, clearer than before.

"You're right. I have to grow up. That's why I'm quitting—to take some time apart from the family."

"I'm not 'the family'. I'm your mother. All I've ever done is be supportive of you. You've been the most important person in my life since the day you came out of me. I pulled a lot of strings to get you a better job here, don't leave us all hanging because you want to go find yourself in the woods. You're not like your father, you can do better."

An old weight settled on my shoulders. She was right, I'd been unreliable to everyone who cared about me the most. For instance, I was dripping blood on these innocent vegetables. That couldn't possibly be kosher. Smothering wildly inappropriate laughter, I blotted my stinging hand on a dishtowel.

"Maybe you expected too much from me."

"I shouldn't want the best for my only son?"

"No, I mean... Mom, is it possible you might have been, like, *too* involved with me? Like, sort of, love me the way you should've...loved Dad instead?"

"Ridiculous! A mother can't love her child too much." She narrowed her eyes. "Is your therapist a Freudian? You can tell him, I didn't make you homosexual. They think now it's brain chemistry, I saw it on PBS. Besides, there's nothing wrong with you, as long as you stay faithful and don't catch any diseases—oh my God, is that why—"

"No, Mom, calm down, I'm clean!"

"You look sick. Did Julian hit you again? Is that why you're wearing long sleeves in the summer?"

I yanked away my arm before she could roll up my sleeve and see the razor scars. "Mom. *Chill.*" She recoiled from my angry voice. I dropped the volume. "I'm really, really sorry this is inconvenient for you, but I wouldn't be able to do a good job here anymore. I thought I could handle it till I walked in the door and realized it was too much."

"How is working in an office 'too much'? I'm trying to help you build a steady life for yourself, where you aren't depending on a man who blows hot and cold. What aren't you telling me, Peepers? Are you in some kind of trouble?"

Fatigue wrapped its lead blanket around me. None of my disguises had worked as well as I'd always believed. Who knew me better than my mother? She saw the real me. The boy who'd never refused her soothing touch, who hadn't hidden his dirty places from her.

"I told you before...I'm trying to understand some new memories... about the way I was touched, that confused me, when I was little..." I could scarcely hear my own voice.

She withdrew the hand she'd laid on my arm. "Who put that idea in your head?"

"I just think I shouldn't work around other kids with trauma till I get clear on what's real, you know?"

"Believe me, if something like that happens to a person, they never forget it." She stood up and turned away from me so I couldn't see her expression.

"Were *you*—"

"Of course not, and neither were you. I'm not naïve like some parents. I always made sure I knew where you were going and who you were with, even though your father said I was turning you into a *feigele* by overprotecting you. He's another one who wants to convince people that a cigar isn't a cigar." She banged the stirring spoon around in the stew pot, sniffed the mixture, and clapped the lid back on without tasting it. "Peter, if you want to leave that badly, then leave. Don't play the victim."

"Not like you, huh, Mom? Everyone's done *you* wrong. *Your* intentions are always good."

"Ugh, don't take my kishkes out about Tyler again. And go wash your hands, you're contaminating the food."

I licked the wound on my thumb, instead. "They say saliva has healing properties." Her look of disgust goaded me. "Is that what you told yourself when you were sucking my dick?"

Her face frozen white with sudden fury, she slapped me across the mouth. I swallowed down bubbles of mad laughter. Did she think that *hurt?* Was I, like, some kind of punch-in-the-face *virgin?* What a fucked-up thing to be proud of. No more. No more of this life.

I seized the handles of the huge boiling pot and swept it off the stove onto the floor. Barbara shrieked as the hot stew splashed at our feet. Then she sank down at the table, weeping into the apron she held over her face. "I tried so hard... I don't know where I went wrong with you... I gave you everything."

I fought the instinct to console her as I always had. Unable to hold still, I began to wipe up the mess I'd made. But the half-cooked chicken parts, their flabby skin peeled back like a nightgown baring pale pink flesh, looked like something I never wanted to touch again.

"Are you telling me it didn't happen?" I demanded—pleaded, really. Which answer did I fear more? I gripped the edge of the table, to stay anchored in this body that I'd almost abandoned.

Barbara raised sorrowful eyes upward. "I knew you were unwell when you disappeared like that for a month. Meditation retreat, my foot. It's drugs, isn't it! Filling you with these paranoid hallucinations. My poor boy."

"No, Mom. The weed was to help me forget, but I don't want to do that anymore."

"I hate to say this, but your father was right about something. These quack therapists out there, they can't fix what's wrong with you, so they send you on a wild-goose chase for someone else to blame."

"Why were you and Dad talking about *that?*"

"Who remembers, now? Nathan has an opinion about everything, and two on Fridays." Recovering her composure, Barbara started cleaning up the remains of the stew.

"I thought I heard a crash—is everything all right?" Dr. Marla, entering the kitchen, directed a concerned look at my mother. A brief, flat glance acknowledged my existence. Relations had been chilly since DeWayne's lawsuit.

"Too much schmaltz on my hands," Barbara covered with a self-deprecating shrug. "Peter was just running down to Gristede's to buy fresh ingredients. Oh, and he was wondering if you still had the number of that residential detox program in Riverdale?"

"There's been a misunderstanding," I said. "I don't work here anymore."

The two women drew together in quiet conversation, treating me as gone even before I walked out.

Dizziness struck me when I emerged into the white-bright sunshine. I detoured into the garden to sit for a moment in the privacy of the board fence. The raised beds baked in the June heat. I inhaled the scents of mulch and vegetation competing with the burnt-rubber odor of the city in summer. Breathe in, one two three four, breathe out. My vertigo eased. Enthusiastic but not thorough, the Gateway teens had weeded half the plots and left their tools scattered among the crabgrass and chickweed in the unfinished patch. Kibbutznik discipline had not yet taken hold. On a real farm, that would be a fine way to slice your foot open on a hidden blade.

I picked up a slim-handled digging tool with a sharp half-moon blade for tearing out roots. The metal edge was bright and tempting against the soft skin of my wrist. I held it there, imagining the decisive blow, the opening through which my pain and fury could drain away.

The sun beat down on my bare neck. My stomach rumbled. Laying down the tool, I sifted a clump of chocolate-brown soil through my fingers. A row of little strawberry plants grew nearby, the season's first red fruits nestled under their frilly leaves. I plucked one and rolled it slowly around in my mouth, absorbing its nubbly texture and earthy, tangy flavor. After I'd eaten a few, I took up the weeder and chopped away at the tangled greenery that was choking them. I ripped out dandelion roots, pale and bristly as rat tails, till the garden beds were as manicured as a Long Island cemetery.

My work done, I walked downtown for uncounted blocks till I found a diner. I sat on a vinyl stool in the stale air conditioning and finished every bit of my pancakes and iced coffee, not caring how filthy I was.

[EXCERPT FROM *THE AKEDAH, SACRIFICE AND SANITY* BY RABBI SAUL HAUSER (HEBREW STUDIES PRESS, 1981]

...The ethics of Abraham killing Isaac are ultimately irrelevant. To accept the challenge of the Akedah, we must stop debating it as *a story that happened to someone else.* Nor should we expect its crisis to take the same form in our own lives. That, also, would be to misunderstand it as something that could be prepared for in advance. We will recognize it (if we dare) solely by its refusal to be worked out within our old systems of beliefs and relationships.

An example from real life shows the protean forms this crisis may take. A youth in my congregation was hospitalized for a near-fatal overdose of sleeping pills and liquor when he was eleven. His mother refused to consider any explanation other than accident—an ignorant experiment by a naïve child succumbing to peer pressure. Was she a neglectful woman? No! So devoted was she, like the grieving Abraham before he ascended Mount Moriah, that she could not "kill" her idealized image of their happy family in order to see her son's painful struggle with unnatural feelings.

Thus does the eternally occurring Akedah—not a moment in history, but an attribute of the timeless G-d—demand to shock us out of complacency and re-evaluate the unconscious bargains on which our current life rests. What price, that we assumed was too high, could we actually bear to pay, in order to live an awakened life? We will not see the ram in the thicket until we are willing to act *despite* the chance that it is not there...

[Excerpt from Elaine Raindaughter, "Supermodel to Sage: An Interview with Cheryl Kingston," WomynWise Magazine, June 1997]

ER: When I founded this magazine, I wanted to explore how the myths we tell ourselves affect the memories we're able to have. Maybe I caught that obsession from my father, the rabbi. His Bible says we can remain in paradise only if we keep our eyes shut. But in this world, we stay alive by asking questions—especially the forbidden ones.

So I'm wondering how you've resisted being silenced, as a new Christian, bringing your radical message that it's holy for women to seek pleasure and beauty. What makes it worthwhile to keep fighting from within, against the tradition that sees our bodies as sinful?

CK: Nothing's pure, right? Not even Ivory Soap! I guess there will be people in any faith who are still stuck at a lower vibration of negativity, but that doesn't change who Jesus is for me. He was all about seeing God in people who felt too dirty to see it in the mirror. Like me at my lowest, when I was doing those gross centerfolds to feed my drug habit.

I'm grateful for it, though. There's a lesson in even the worst experiences. Just like every religion has a piece of the truth in it. Do you feel that way about your years with the Hare Krishnas?

ER: It's been a long journey, but I do, finally. Don't get me wrong, it's a cult, and I stayed much longer than I should have, because they make you too exhausted and isolated to imagine an exit strategy. But it cleared away the weeds, so I could see what was underneath. Chanting, meditating, being cut off from my family—my father's stories were silenced for the first time in my life. The wounded goddess in my body woke up. That's when I got my first incest memories...

A HOT, GLASSY-BRIGHT morning, the last Sunday in June. The ancient clanging of tower bells echoed down Fifth Avenue, over the din of police sirens and honking traffic diverted from the cleared street. My destination, a couple blocks north of the Washington Square marble arch, was a cream-colored stone church with a small garden behind an iron railing. The first marchers wouldn't reach this end of the parade route for another two hours, but some dedicated spectators had begun claiming their spots behind the blue wooden police barriers. Girls with buzzed haircuts and fishnet stockings, and guys in booty shorts and not much else, lounged on the stoops of businesses that had given up shooing them away. You could tell the first-timers by their obvious rainbow attire—pins, knee socks, plastic necklaces, and in one case, a beer can hat with two curly multicolored straws for the guy to suck on. Longtime New York gays pretended they were "over" Pride, but you'd invariably see them out here, flashing their freshly waxed pecs to lure the new boys whose rainbow merch they disdained. Eyeing them with salacious disapproval, a huddle of counter-protestors held signs with the usual phrases about sodomites and hellfire in unattractive black capital letters.

Positioning myself to block Julian's view of the Christian hecklers, I wiped my forehead with the sleeve of my olive-green dress shirt. No outfit I owned could meet the conflicting demands of Sunday best and summertime parade wear. "How can you look so fresh? I'm dying already."

"A Southern belle never sweats." His tight gray slacks were crisply pleated. The open collar buttons on his short-sleeved maroon shirt were his one concession to the weather.

"Those folks have the right idea." Three people who'd come out of the church were setting up a long folding table to hold coolers full of water bottles. They wore white T-shirts reading "Proud Episcopalian" on the front and "Church of the Ascension" on the back, with a cross-in-shield symbol trailing rainbows.

"Cassidy!" Julian ran over to one of the water table volunteers, a rangy middle-aged woman in jeans and sandals, with wavy salt-and-pepper hair and large round tinted glasses like a high school girl in the '80s. She gave him a big hug. He introduced us: "Cassidy Gilman, my Al-Anon sponsor—Peter Edelman, my boyfriend."

I was glad he still wanted to call me that. "Happy Pride," I greeted her.

"And also with you! Don't tell me you've heard a lot about me, I don't want to know," she joked.

"Hey, you stole my line."

Everything Julian had told me about his new local sponsor seemed promising: The ex-wife of an alcoholic Lutheran minister, Cassidy was now a hospital chaplain at St. Vincent's and an active member of the 12-Step group that met in the basement of this very church.

The bell changed its tune, shifting from melody to insistent banging that signaled us to fill the pews. Sensing Julian's anxiety, Cassidy kept hold of his hand so the ushers would seat us together. Rich music swept over us—a Bach organ composition, I thought. It brought back memories of listening to WQXR with Dad on the weekends. We were in a living museum ornamented with gold brocade altar cloths, stained glass, and gleaming candle holders borne in procession by lace-gowned men. I felt under-dressed. Even the lesbian couple across the aisle were wearing bowties. Their little son, though, had on an oversized Power Rangers T-shirt and only one muddy shoe that he propped on the seat in front of him. We made silly faces at each other. Two young guys in tank tops sneaked in behind the procession, smiling nervously as they settled into a rear pew. I turned to point them out to Julian, to show him we weren't alone. His wet eyes were fixed on the crucifix carved in dark wood that hung directly in front of us, its suffering figure unaltered by the festivities below. "How are you holding up?" I whispered.

"Awesome. This place is like the Met Gala, but for Jesus." He smiled faintly.

"Because we can leave anytime, just say the word."

He nodded. Cassidy and I held his hands on either side. Then there was a lot of singing, standing up, sitting down, Bible reading, kneeling, chanting, and so on. The regulars discreetly oriented us in the 800-page prayerbook. I pretended to move my mouth to the words and just enjoyed the music. Julian sniffled. An elderly lady with peach-colored hair gave him a perfumed tissue.

"When you have a choice of two beliefs," the priest said, "pick the one that doesn't kill you."

My heart stuttered. Every day, facing memories too tangible to dismiss as a fever dream, I felt oblivion's tempting undertow, a dark sea into which I would throw myself to escape panic's agonizing flames. I tightened my grip on Julian's hand. He leaned against my shoulder.

The priest, a boyish-looking woman with short black hair, spoke without notes, throwing her whole body into the rhythm. When the sleeve of her robe fell back from her bare tanned arm, I glimpsed a complicated tattoo involving wings and a crescent moon.

"How can we trust Jesus to meet us here, loving us as we are, when some people right outside these walls are invoking his name to wipe us out? Because he said, 'I came that they might have *life*, and have it abundantly.'" She spread her hands wide. "Do any of you know the Broadway musical 'Falsettos'?" (A murmur of recognition.) "The family finally accepts the dad's boyfriend because he *dies*, right? An AIDS martyr, like Harvey Milk was a hate-crime martyr. We parade such tragedies before straight society to move their conscience. And we should keep mourning and being outraged by these unjust losses. But today's parade is about something else. It's about abundant life. Just as the Christian story is different from other martyrdoms, because it ends with triumph, not pity. Death is not our end, Jesus says. We have a better language than pain. Pride is a Resurrection!"

Through the side windows, propped open to dispel the mounting heat, the sounds of the gathering crowd entered: laughter, motorcycle engines, snippets of music from portable radios. The organ played while the congregation filed up to the altar for communion. I welcomed a moment alone to let the priest's words sink in. It was a very artistic service but there wasn't enough quiet in it. Choosing life was also choosing death, I thought. If I believed—if I *said* what I believed—I'd be dead to my family. But I'd still be here.

After the service, a lot of us hung around by the church steps to wait for the Dykes on Bikes, the traditional vanguard of the parade. We could hear their engines growling in the distance. Julian joined Cassidy to hand out water bottles. I staked out a ledge on the side of the church wall, from which I could see above the crowd a little. We'd told our friends where we'd be, but making plans to meet someone during a New York parade is an exercise in wishful thinking.

The street was soon littered with candy, decoratively wrapped condoms, Mardi Gras beads, and promotional postcards for nightclubs and health hotlines. Floats loaded with buff shirtless men crawled along ahead of stop-and-start marchers whose banners sagged in the heat. The Lavender Choir tried gamely to perform a song as they walked in loose formation, but I could only see their mouths moving, the sound swallowed by the blasts of salsa and house music from the floats' speakers. Drag queens' feathered headdresses glided above the crowd. There were contingents from the NYU and Columbia gay student groups, a women's domestic violence shelter, several AIDS organizations including my old employer Housing Works, and (so far) one brave synagogue. Kevin had said he'd be pushing DeWayne in a wheelchair with the Gay and Lesbian Teachers' Association, but they were a long way off and I wasn't sure I could tolerate the scorching sun for that long. Julian had gone bare-chested already, shirt tied round his waist as he distributed sweating-cold bottles to a fire truck crew. That torso was the church's best strategy for new-member recruitment.

Just then Mrs. Becker and Ty found us. They made an unlikely pair: Aletha in a fancy sun hat and white dress printed with orange trees, the teenager in a tank top and cut-off denim shorts, with bronze eyeshadow, mascara, and glossy burgundy lipstick to complete the look. "Whew! Sorry we're late. I got out of church an hour ago but the trains were so slow," Aletha said to me.

"It's wonderful that you came."

She looked fondly at Ty, who was pretending not to know us old folks. He stuck two fingers deep in his mouth and whistled at a float of dancers in thongs. One of the performing men imitated the gesture, licking his fingers as he pulled them out, and the kid screamed in delight. Aletha made the effort to keep smiling. "Harold said he had to work today…"

"One step at a time, right? And this scene is, maybe, step 20." As if to prove my point, a young woman wearing glitter on her nipples walked by.

"We're seeing a counselor about transsexual issues. She's invited Tyler to a party today at the Gay Center in Greenwich Village. Young people, no alcohol. What do you think?"

"Fantastic. You should definitely go."

Mrs. Becker had come a long way in the past month. Compounding Ty's disappointment at not getting into Cooper Union this year, she'd balked at letting him go away to a Hampshire College summer program that my professor friend from TropiCon had suggested. Harold and Aletha felt Ty wasn't responsible enough yet to live away from home. To compensate, they were trying to understand Ty's two gender personalities.

Now, seeing Aletha hover lovingly behind her reckless, flamboyant teen, I had to pretend it was only sweat I was wiping from my face, not tears—of gratitude, envy, mourning.

Julian pressed a cold water bottle into my hands. "Oh thank God," I said. "Is there room in that cooler for me to jump in?"

"I've got a better idea." He teased open my top shirt button. His hands were refreshingly cool against my chest. I kissed his forehead. "I'm so happy we're here," he sighed.

"So am I. You deserve this." I put my arms around him.

"Not necessarily, darling, but Jesus doesn't care." He undid another one of my buttons. The air on my bare skin brought relief, but I pulled away. "I'm sorry—too soon?" Jule asked.

"It's not you, babe. I'm dying to take this off, but I'm kind of embarrassed by my scars."

He rubbed my wrist through the stiff shirt cuff, a gesture that had become habitual with him since my hospitalization. "Why?"

"I don't need to air my dirty laundry in public." A phrase I'd picked up from my mother, repeated out of habit. Would I have to hate my own voice now, too?

"Darling, the boys from Gay Men's Health Crisis are right in front of you, dancing in thongs, with big red plus-signs painted on their chests— not as nice as yours, I might add—and a banner that says 'Poz and Proud'".

"I suppose that *would* distract the crowd from my insanity."

"You know that's not what I'm saying."

I took a deep breath and looked again at the slow carnival procession. The sun glinted off windshields, tinsel, boom boxes, cop helmets, multicolored sunglasses on a thousand faces, making a complex glittering mosaic. Slowly I unbuttoned and peeled off my sweaty shirt. Ty whistled. "Don't creep on me, kiddo, or I'll tell DeWayne to assign you a hundred extra math problems," I teased. Mrs. Becker pinched Ty's earlobe playfully. Julian put his arm around my waist and we held each other for a long time while the whole queer world went by.

INNUMERABLE FIRE TRUCKS and lesbian softball teams later, I begged off to go wash up and rest at Prue's place, which was my place for another week. Some friends were coming to stay with them for July 4th weekend, a logical transition point for me to try moving back in with Julian. It would be a nice early birthday present for him, and if nothing terrible happened, I'd stick around.

On impulse, I asked him, "Come home with me? Not for...you know...I'm sorry I'm not ready for..."

He kissed my lips. "Don't ever apologize for that. I can scratch that itch anywhere, but there's only one you."

"Actually, I'm kind of a hive mind at the moment, but unity is the goal."

Our destination was downtown on the east side near Astor Place. We had to head west first and skirt around because Fifth Avenue would be impassible for hours. We were both wrung out and starving by the time we opened the door, stumbling into an oasis of coolness because the girls had left air conditioning on for the cats. With no need to discuss it, we showered separately. I loaned Julian my one bathrobe and changed into boxers and a GalaxyCon tee. While he primped, I set up snack bowls of chips, hummus, fruit, and a bag of dried shrimp treats for Lena, the other regular occupant of my small bedroom. She was loafing in her usual spot beside my pillow, her striped tail curled over her half-closed eyes. "Be charming," I directed her. "Act like you're Little Orphan Annie and Daddy Warbucks is coming to give you a look-see." Lena opened her mouth, baring her little lioness fangs, but nothing more melodic than a yawn came out.

Julian collapsed dramatically onto the bed. "Ahh...I never want to go anywhere again."

I stretched out next to him. "That's my kind of homosexual lifestyle."

"Hey, is it okay that I'm in here? I just lay down without thinking."

"I love you." It felt natural to say it now. Life was too short for anything less.

He rolled over to nestle against me. "I'll never get tired of hearing you say that. Not for a hundred years...and yes, I know you can't plan that far ahead."

"Who the hell can?"

Eventually we made ourselves sit up so we could have snacks and cold sodas. The girls stocked this knock-off health food brand of Hawaiian punch that tasted almost like the real thing. We debated our options for the evening: Frank's drag cabaret, Aisha and Prue's set at Meow Mix in Alphabet City, a dance party in the Meatpacking District sponsored by *FHM* magazine. None of them sounded as appealing as Chinese takeout, a video, and a walk in the long evening light when Julian's hand-washed underwear was dry.

Holding a treat in his palm for the cat to lick up, Julian examined the package. "Wow, this little bag cost five dollars? I wonder how they taste."

"Only the best for my therapist."

"Does she tell your future with Tarot cards too?" He popped a dried shrimp in his mouth. "Not bad—needs more garlic butter."

"Lena's the only one I've told about...what really happened. Or what I remember, anyhow."

"Why not Sid?"

I chewed my lower lip. "It feels like something that shouldn't be said. Or thought about. Or happen."

"But it did."

"You believe me? When you don't even know who..."

"I don't have to. If I know one thing about you, it's that you don't turn against your loved ones to feel better about yourself. Which puts you in the top percentile of humans, by the way."

He reached for me, but I curled into myself, hunched over, unable to face him. "It's the worst thing, Jule. The thing you kill yourself for doing." I heard his choked cry, but I couldn't reassure him. The closer I came to spilling my secret, the more I was terrified that I didn't deserve the joy and cleanness this day had brought.

"No! You were just a kid."

"I'm still me, though. Still in the same body that did it."

From the corner of my eye, I saw his hand kneading the blanket with agitation. He must have been dying to touch me, to claw me back from the tempting abyss. Because he held back, I suddenly knew, with calm clarity, one person I could trust. Still facing away, I laid my hand over his.

"You have to talk to someone soon. You know that, right? If not me, then Sid, or even your mother." At the shock of hearing him mention Barbara, I began to cry. Misunderstanding (of course), Jule went on, "Come on—it's sweet that you try to protect her, but she would want to help. Maybe if you didn't shut her out, she wouldn't fuss and worry so much. And she must have experience with childhood trauma."

I laughed wildly through my sobs. "Oh, she does. She does."

Julian hesitated. "I don't get it."

"Did you read my last script for *The Poison Cure*? What did you think it meant?"

"I...don't want to put words in your mouth."

"*Tell me.*"

"No."

We locked eyes. For a split second I wanted to hurt him, choke the confession out of him so the stain of saying the unspeakable would be his and not mine. Exactly the opposite of the man he believed in.

"My mother..." I stumbled over the words. "She touched me...made me touch her...not just with my hands but...everything, everything we shouldn't." I broke down. Nausea and vertigo overtook me. I was speeding backwards through a dark tunnel.

"No, oh no..." Julian caught me. I collapsed against him. He held me while I let out sounds halfway between crying and screaming. Prickles of pain on my thigh turned out to be Lena burrowing into my lap, making a nest with her claws. I scooped her up and cradled her against my chest.

When the worst of it was spent, I dared to look up at him. His eyes were watery too. "You don't believe me anymore, do you," I said.

He looked surprised. "No, of course I do. More than ever. My poor darling. You wouldn't break your own heart for nothing."

This made me cry all over again. "Everyone says this kind of thing doesn't happen...mothers and sons...women aren't supposed to be like that. I've looked in all the books, there's no one like me."

"Let me tell you something—I don't care about any experts, shrinks, feminists, whatever, it could be in the *Bible* and if it's a choice between that and keeping you alive, I'd burn it all the fuck down."

"*Thank you.*" I gripped him tighter. "We might have to."

"Let 'em come at me."

Finally I untangled myself from his fierce embrace and lay back on the bed, sweaty and wrung-out like I'd run a marathon. "I'm out of a job, obviously."

"Did you confront her? What did she say?"

My face heated up with irrational shame. "Same thing that my family has always said about me—I'm either crazy or on drugs."

"I'm sorry. But now you can tell them the truth, right?"

I shook my head. "I'm just avoiding them for the time being. I have to get clearer in my own mind what happened, or Dad will cross-examine me right back into the rubber room. Why be a shit-stirrer when I can't change the past? Better to let them go on thinking I'm an unreliable slacker who's good for nothing but pumping iron."

"Frivolity can be very liberating. Look at me, I made a killing by *not* selling shoes on the Internet."

"Oh Jule, I'm so scared." I rubbed my wet eyes with my fists till I saw stars. "I've trashed every career I've started. I hate depending on people but I'm basically homeless. I have barely enough to live on, unless this DC Comics gig comes through. So, great, now I understand *why* I ruin everything, but because of that, I've lost what little I did have."

"Don't second-guess yourself. You've have died otherwise. Fuck the rest of it—it's just money."

"Easy for you to say." It was hard to look him in the eye after what I'd told him, so I put my head on his chest. "I'm sorry. You're the last good thing left in my life."

He ran his fingers through my hair. "No, I'm not. You have God, and this little beast who is waving her anus in my face. And yourself, all the people in your head, the amazing comics you're going to write."

"How do you understand me so well, when no one else does?" I kissed him.

He shrugged. "Why did any of this happen to us? Are Christy Turlington's cheekbones proof of a benevolent creator? I don't try to figure that shit out. It just is."

We lay together for a long while in the cool, shadowy bedroom. I cried some more. Jule held me, not needing to say anything.

"I want to get out of here, but I don't know where to go," I said at last.

"Tonight, or in general?"

"Well, my immediate destination is Sammy's Noodle Shop, but after that...I feel bad that I'm not ready to go back to your place. Could you stay the night here, instead?"

"Absolutely, darling. And about *our* place—I agree, it has too much bad history. I've decided to pretend I'm a responsible adult and buy real estate. What would you say about looking at condos with me, very soon? We could find a two-bedroom where you could have your own writing space and...a bed you don't have to share with me, for as long as you feel that way."

"Jule, I can't." I wanted to, God knows, but it was humiliating, frightening, to trust that my fairy godfather could solve all my problems. "It sounds like a great investment, but what could I contribute?"

"Consider it my dowry to you from Selkirk Builders. A wealth transfer from The Man to the homo revolution. Or, if you prefer, an advance on the superhero movie royalties with which you will support me in my old age."

"What if we—I hate to say it, but—if we break up, for real? I love you more than anyone, but I don't know who I am from one day to the next."

"Then we'll sell it and split the proceeds, or draw a line down the middle like that awful couple in 'The War of the Roses'." He tugged my hair lightly. "Come on, you're supposed to be a submissive."

"I told you, it doesn't work that way."

"Pushy bottom."

"Yes, Daddy."

"*That*...is kind of disturbing."

"That's my brand. Take it or leave it."

"I'll take it, of course. What about you?"

"All right, I surrender. I'll think about it. Thank you." I slid off the bed in a hurry. Our banter was waking up desires that I was afraid to express. My skin felt more sensitive, prickling with the electricity of his imagined touch. Maybe we'd try something tonight and maybe not; either way, we would pick up the pieces and go forward, as we always did. One more truth that was finally clear. "Let's get dressed, sugar daddy. I have just enough cash to buy us half a Peking duck, and I won't even expect you to put out afterwards."

[EXCERPT OF SCRIPT FOR *THE POISON CURE*, VOL. 3, ISSUE 2]

Caption: *Six months later...*

Afternoon at Dorothy's Cafe. Challis on stage, pensively singing with guitar, eyes downcast. Mood in room is festive. Pride flags in window, mixed-age crowd at tables with rainbow flags in the bud vases. Several children are there, including a little boy with two mothers and a pair of tween girls in butch clothing.

Next panel, Challis on break between sets, observing the scene with Mal, who wears full makeup, a sparkly bow tie, and a sleeveless button-down shirt that shows off his muscles. Mal inclines his head toward the gay male couples flirting in the restaurant, saying to Challis: *Now's the time to find someone new.*

Challis (shaking his head): *Still so hard to let go... If I only knew what happened to Tod...*

M: *What would it change? Way I see it, we have to live extra hard for the ones that are gone.*

C: *But if it was my fault—because I tried to change him—maybe I don't deserve to try again.*

M: *Honey, love isn't for deserving, it's for staying alive.*

Next panel, Challis at the bar with an empty glass. The bartender raises an eyebrow but slides another drink over to him. A man and a young girl approach, but their faces are not yet visible.

Girl: *I liked your songs. They're happy and sad together, like me.*

Next panel, Challis leans forward on his stool, face to face with Samantha, whom we can now see in profile. Her adult companion is behind her, but his head is not pictured because of the close-up view at the child's eye level. Samantha is smiling and healthy-looking, while Challis is in shock.

C: *You're the girl in the photo—I mean, from the*

news, in the hospital! What are you doing here?

S: (beaming, holding the unseen man's hand): *I marched in Pride today with my uncle!*

Next panel, Challis stands, faces the man for the first time. He is tall, slim, well-built, with fair hair.

C: *I'm sorry. Didn't mean to embarrass you. You must get that a lot.*

Next panel, the men shake hands. The angle of view shows more of Challis' face, now smiling in a star-struck kind of way, as one does when meeting someone attractive. The other man is in three-quarter rear view so his full face is still concealed.

C: *I'm Ryder Challis. Welcome to Dorothy's.*

Man: *Pleased to meet you! I'm Theodore Stone, but...*

Last panel, close-up full frontal view of the man's handsome face and warm smile. His eyes flash a dazzling emerald-green light.

Man: *...everybody calls me Tod.*

THE DRUM'S SOFT HEARTBEAT filled the forest clearing. The crisp breeze carried the scent of drying pine needles and the whispers of sun-dappled leaves just beginning to be edged in red and gold. Shifting position to follow a patch of sunshine, as the day was cooling toward afternoon, I pressed my bare back against the earth, cradled in a dip between tree roots.

I was on a two-day men's retreat in the Palisades—for real this time—led by Sid's colleague Mercer Hart, Jungian analyst and weekend shaman. The weather had mostly been warm enough to go clothing-optional, but this was no 1970s encounter group. The first morning, in the campground's main lodge, Merce put the fourteen participants through a long workshop about consensual touching, privacy, and triggers that arise in spiritual work. The main purpose of our semi-nudity was to release shame and lower the barriers between ourselves and the natural world. It was understood that some people might become intimate, but they had to do it in private or ask consent from whoever might be watching, "and don't leave your damn condoms in the woods for the squirrels to choke on."

Merce was leading us in a guided meditation journey to discover our loving creator. Seated cross-legged before a large drum decorated with a snake biting its tail, he was nude except for a sort of leather loincloth/shorts garment. Twin ivy vines were tattooed over his top surgery scars. I wondered what Julian's style verdict would be if I had my wrists inked. Perhaps a detail from the Sun card, the radiant child a daily reminder to keep my blood inside my body.

I almost hadn't come to this event, struck with last-minute anxiety even though I'd looked forward to it for weeks. Meditation in a group was no longer possible for me. I feared falling too far into my own mind and setting off a rockslide of memories that would turn me into a twitching, moaning mess. Concealing my secret from other people was nearly as exhausting as hiding it from myself had been.

But out here, the trees didn't judge. So different from the blankness of a silent meditation room, the forest breathed with a hundred thousand lives, none of them concerned with human shame—pines drawing up their slow sap, bugs zigzagging in a shaft of light, unseen birds that whistled and clucked. Merce's drum thudded faintly, accompanied by a tape recording of a meandering bamboo flute melody. I tried slowing my heartbeat to match. Did I even believe in a creator? And did I want to be "loved" by an inscrutable, all-powerful being? Was there a safeword for the Almighty?

Stick to the known real. I was part of the earth. Someday I would die, like the brown leaves I was lying on, breaking down into the soil. I let my cells surrender to that future, and the dead caught me, showing me their dance underground, joyfully busy feeding the earth. They were creators too. It would be okay, somehow, to release every image of my loved ones in my mind, every story that pretended to shield me from loss.

I was a baby, a new-laid egg, all soft and fragile surfaces, dying to be enfolded in a safe warm embrace. Hypnotic heartbeat drum. Water crashed over me—ocean pressure, the shower, the tank where soul-cleansing and *that touch* slickly intertwined—but my dissolving body also recalled muscular arms and soft fur, a giant's mighty chest that could absorb my screams.

Flung back to the everyday world, I found myself curled up on the forest floor, hyperventilating and shaking. Merce's hand on my head was warm and steadying. A couple of other men from the group squatted beside me, their body language offering touch without forcing it. I crawled into their arms. I breathed in the varied musk of their sweat, soil and leaves, fading deodorant, shampoo, the indefinable pheromones of arousal. I pressed against them, skin to skin. Quietly, more joined the huddle, till we were all connected in a gently rocking mass under the pines' lengthening shadows.

After a light vegetarian supper, we went outside again to a grassy clearing behind the big lodge for some low-impact yoga. A couple of the men, myself included, had taken the option of presenting workshops in exchange for a tuition discount. Today we'd had a dream journaling session and tomorrow morning would be Tai Chi. Most of us were now partially clothed since the approaching evening brought an autumnal chill. Yellowish outdoor lanterns cast a campfire glow as the rose-tinted sky dimmed behind the treeline.

Merce drew me aside. "Are you up to teaching tonight, or should we ask Cliff to swap tomorrow morning with you?"

"Thanks, I'm good now. Yoga helps me find my way back to Planet Earth."

"Don't be afraid of the journey. You can't get lost forever. There are allies around us everywhere—the elements, the ancestors, plants and animals. When you're out on the edge and need to come back, ask one of them to guide you home."

I wanted to ask him more about this, but it was time for my class to start.

Besides, he'd said earlier that we each had to find our own "right way" (with an ironic eyebrow-raise at the very concept of shamanic orthodoxy). Leading the men through animal-named poses, I imagined the creatures themselves beside us, instructing us in their ways: the graceful wariness of the cat, the cobra's proud stretch. I felt like Mowgli in *The Jungle Book*.

At day's end I fell asleep in my tent at once, but my dreams were confused and violent. The sleeping bag's clingy fabric trapped me in memories of Grandpa Saul's apartment. Frustrated, I crawled out and peeled back the tent flap. The stars were so much brighter outside the city. The fine branches overhead were outlined in silver. I gave in to my craving for a walk in the woods, armed with my pocket-sized flashlight and a pair of sandals so I wouldn't step on anything sharp in the dark. Call me a cautious city boy, but I could do without a shamanic journey to the ER. Besides that, I wore only the shorts I slept in. I was still overheated from my restless night.

Without any direction in mind, I found myself following a gently downward-sloping path to a stream we'd visited earlier in the day. A massive willow stood guard over it, tall as a three-story house, its feathery trailing branches oddly delicate compared to the thick trunk that bulged with rough boles like the Elephant Man's tumors. The scrape of the bark on my palms was pleasurably sharp, but I didn't succumb to the frenzy of seeking more pain than that, though sudden anger overtook me. Whatever gods there were, fuck them for punishing me with nightmares! Wasn't it enough that my childhood sleep had been violated? Why did that touch have to slither into my exhausted body a second time, even pursuing me here, where I'd broken through to a dimension that was sacred and pure?

I flung a stone into the stream, then another. Flying water droplets danced in the starlight, a firework splash. I threw myself face-down on the mossy bank. The ground was a giant's body under me, quiet and strong, furred with grass. Damp loam, yielding. As I calmed, breathing in sync with the earth's imagined breath, I became conscious of my ass in the air, positioned just like I was waiting to bottom for a lover. I laughed a little, letting the idea play out. Allies everywhere? Why not the Hairy Dude, tree-trunk cock jutting out of his mud-slick hand, coming to spread me open right...*now*. I moaned and pushed my hardening bulge against the ground. With my eyes closed, the fantasy took over. I was fucking him, rubbing and thrusting. When I was crazy for release, I stood up, pulled off my shorts, and stroked myself greedily. My cum arced into the stream. I pictured his great mouth drinking it up, and shuddered with a second wave of pleasure.

Dizzy with happiness and spent tension, I carefully lowered myself onto the rocks in the shallow water and cleaned off. My shorts were ruined in a way that clearly showed what I'd been up to, so I just folded them under my arm and walked naked back to my tent, where I spent the rest of the night in peace.

I woke up missing Julian. He had planned to come too, but between photo shoots and closing on our new apartment, his schedule was packed. Right now he was shooting his second ad campaign for Juicy Couture, a new brand that sold velvet sweatpants to white girls pretending to be rap stars.

Naked Tai Chi was a new frontier for me. Cliff gave us the option to wear clothes but nobody did. Merce wore his packer in a strap-on pouch. Afterwards we were sent on a "wisdom wander" to find items in nature that spoke to us for the arts and crafts session. I discovered a smooth white rock from the stream I'd visited at night, and glued a pattern of fallen willow leaves onto it. We made self-conscious jokes about summer camp and macaroni collages. Merce gravely told us to embrace the childishness of playing with materials for its own sake, before we were burdened with ideas of being "good at" something or making ourselves understood. Was there ever such a time? Not in my family. Thinking back to my crayon drawings in the hospital, I reflected that recovery seemed to involve making a lot of bad art. Still, the rock felt good in my hand, fitting comfortably into my cupped palm. When the glue dried, I flipped it over and painted a Hebrew *chai*, for "life", on the other side.

We closed the retreat by writing wishes on paper scraps that we tossed into the sacred bonfire to send them up to the spirits. There's no assignment so small that you can't get writer's block. My wishes, or maybe worries, would fill a jumbo-sized roll of hotel toilet paper. Let me not lose my mind; not break up with Julian again; hurt no one; tell the truth; write good comics; not alienate my entire family. Incompatible demands on the gods. If I threw them all into the fire, it might explode, like Coke and Pop Rocks. Following King Solomon, I settled on writing "wisdom", and hoped I wouldn't be the baby that got cut in half.

A COUPLE OF DAYS after my return to civilization, Julian and I were hosting a housewarming dinner in our brand-new two-bedroom condo on 9th Avenue. We didn't own anything as bourgeois as a dining-room set, but we had a handsome gas stove with sealed burners, a discontinued-pattern

Mikasa chinaware set from Fishs Eddy (only two salad plates and a teacup missing), and plenty of unopened boxes to throw a tablecloth over. A premature celebration, maybe, but Julian really wanted to include his Fashion Institute of Technology classmate Ariana, a TV costume designer in L.A., who was only in town for three days to see her parents for the High Holidays. And I had my own family obligations to avoid. So we borrowed a stack of folding chairs from the community room and filled the oven with roast chicken.

"I've never lived in a building with a community room before. I feel so fancy," I joked to Julian.

"Wait'll you see the silver napkin rings I picked up at ABC Carpet.""We have cloth napkins?" Another load of laundry for tomorrow.

"Well, no, I was waiting for us to decide on a color scheme for the living/dining room. But I got the good paper towels, Bounty, not the cheap kind."

I hugged him. "It'll be perfect."

And it almost was, except that Prue wasn't there. Of course, she had to go to Aunt Nora's with Nathan and Ada. My sister and I still had a "don't ask, don't tell" arrangement about my memories. Other than reassuring her that her parents were (so far) in the clear, I kept the details to myself. I was trying to be a good big brother and not put her in the middle of family conflict. But the more cagey I was, the more my secret grew to fearful proportions in her mind, making her hesitate to break down my walls.

So be it—this was a new year, by my people's calendar, and I was alive and not alone. We had enough plates for eight people if we served the arugula salad in soup bowls: Kevin and DeWayne, Stan and Frank, Ariana, Tai (looking fresh in a black lace crop-top, jeans, and sparkly platform sneakers), and your hosts. I lit a candle and said the Hebrew blessing.

I admit I hadn't liked Ari much when she was Julian's brief experiment with heterosexuality, but she won me over with her enthusiasm for *The Poison Cure*. She'd made a niche for herself designing costumes for paranormal TV shows and the occasional surreal music video, while trying to make a go of her own couture label. Tai was smitten. They talked about the importance of including non-traditional body types in high fashion (Ari was a grapefruit in an industry of string beans). It was good to see Tai smile again. She had started two classes at City College this term, laying the groundwork to apply to Hampshire next year, but she was easily discouraged and pissed-off by the bullying about her gender-switching appearance. "Those people are so banal. Clothes shouldn't have a gender," Ari scoffed. "I mean, David Bowie? Prince? *Elvis?* All the sexiest men are androgynous, according to Camille Paglia."

Julian gave me his "footnote, please" look. "Right-wing lesbian," I whispered. "Dresses like k.d. lang, writes like William F. Buckley."

"Try to wear something that makes both sides of you happy every day, instead of flipping between b-boy and beauty queen." Ariana sketched an outfit for Tai on the pastry box of cannolis she'd brought from Veniero's. The teen's mood brightened.

Since it was the first night of Rosh Hashanah, Ari and I led the group in singing "Shana Tovah", a children's song we'd both learned in Hebrew school. We threw in an improvised chorus of "lai lai lai's" so the goyim could keep up. *Shanah halchah, shanah ba'ah; Ani kapai arimah—A year went, a year is coming. I raise my hands.* My throat caught on the next words: *Shanah tovah lecha, Aba; Shana tovah lach, Ima.* Daddy, Mommy...

Suddenly this patchwork family, attempting to harmonize on a song they didn't know, seemed as makeshift as the linen-draped stack of boxes on which our holiday meal was spread. I flashed on my mother's younger face in the glow of other candles, and read only devotion there, as my father wiped honey from my sticky cheeks. *(The wicked child asks, what does this mean to you?)* What good was the new year now?

I shook myself back to the present. The song had ended without me. Julian and Ariana were cackling over some bit of fashion gossip that I wouldn't understand. He leaned close to her to deliver the punchline, draping his arm around her shoulders. The other guys were listening to Stan's rumors about new AIDS drugs in the pipeline. He was part of a group of pharmacists lobbying the FDA to fast-track some experimental treatments.

Would it hurt to call my mother and wish her a happy new year? Would it hurt worse than *not* doing it? I'd dodged any meaningful conversation with her since quitting Gateway three months ago. She'd chosen to pretend that my unspeakable accusations had never been made. In her mind, my sudden exit was merely another irresponsible decision from which she would eventually rescue me. Email flustered her, so she left messages on our phone, encouraging me to look at the current issue of *Newsweek* or *Prevention Magazine* for an article about mindfulness-based treatments for substance abuse. If he got home before me, Julian would delete her voicemails. He was ready to change our number whenever I gave permission. Sometimes when I was alone I'd replay the most innocuous message I'd saved, about a new health food store on University

Place that carried my favorite cereal from childhood. *Cinnamon Wheat-O's cost $3.49 now!* I had it memorized. I even went and bought a box, but they tasted like stale oatmeal cookies.

None of my friends at our Rosh Hashanah dinner noticed that I wasn't paying attention to their animated cross-talk. They wouldn't miss me. Pretending things were normal was the best way to keep her off my back, I told myself.

I made it as far as the kitchen but couldn't lift the cordless phone out of its cradle on the countertop. Not yet. The old dullness came over me, the grey weight of its fog. I was ashamed of the dishes in the sink, the crumbs of our attempt to celebrate, the dirty knives.

Perfume, but not hers. A hand on my shoulder, soft, brief. "You're not sick, too, Pedro...?"

"Tai! Oh...no, I'm not, that's not it..." I fumbled, too grateful to see her. "I was trying to decide...whether to call someone."

"Crisis hotline or shitty ex-boyfriend?"

I gave her a long look. "You're not a kid anymore, are you."

"Haven't been for awhile."

"Yeah..." I exhaled heavily. "Look, you deserve the truth, but I don't want you to feel that you have to take care of me, or solve my problems. If you're out there focusing on your future, making your artwork, I can be happy that I did right by you."

"I'm trying." Self-conscious now, she studied her sparkly manicure.

"You're *succeeding*. You're very strong. So...you've probably noticed that despite my amazing skills as a youth mentor, mental-health-wise I'm a few fries short of a Happy Meal?"

Tai snickered. "I've met worse." A hint of fear showed through her cool pose. "Are you, like, depressed? Did you hurt yourself?"

"How did you know?"

I could see in her eyes that whatever she recognized in me came from a memory too difficult to discuss tonight.

"Never mind, the important thing is, I understand what happened now, I'm getting help, and I'm not going anywhere." I reached for her hand, and she gladly gripped mine. "Someone hurt me when I was a kid—you know what I'm talking about—and now I'm strong enough to deal with it."

"What are you going to do?"

I laced my fingers through hers and smiled. "*We're* going to have dessert with our friends."

The party broke up early, around nine; it was a school night for Tai, Ari still had to drive to her parents' house in Teaneck, and DeWayne tired easily these days. "We're getting old, darlings," Frank lamented.

"'I'm a quarter of a century—it makes a girl think,'" Julian quoted, fluttering his eyelashes.

"Marilyn Monroe, 'Some Like It Hot'!" Stan called out.

Ariana got into the act. "'Osgood, I'm a man!'"

All of us except Tai—whose queer education we'd really have to take in hand—shouted the movie's last line: "'Nobody's perfect!'"

Our bubbly mood lingered after our guests left. Julian cleaned up the kitchen while I broke down the makeshift furniture. "Praise Jesus, this place has a dishwasher!" he sang out.

I rushed to his side. "Wait, is that china dishwasher-safe?"

"Isn't everything?"

"You're such a savage. Didn't Bitsy teach you anything?"

"Alas, we never reached the chapter in Leviticus about abominations involving flatware."

Unable to find instructions on the back of the plates, we played it safe and washed them by hand. Our fingers touched often in the warm soapy water.

I had my own bedroom, where I'd stayed since we moved in two weeks prior. Before that, in Julian's old place, I'd slept on the sofa bed with Lena the tabby on my chest, just like in Prue's apartment. The shy little cat was officially mine now.

As for sex, we had tried twice, once in the old apartment and another time in the backroom at New Eden on Madonna karaoke night. The first time, I was able to suck him off but couldn't get hard. He felt guilty, struggling to accept that I still enjoyed being close to him and pleasing him. Something about the combination of love and desire—the most natural thing, for a normal person—was too much like *the other* for my twisted circuits. In the nightclub, thanks to the sultry beat of "I'm Burning Up", I'd managed to suspend these thoughts for the minute and a half I took to rub one out. But I had skin-crawling flashbacks and no sleep that night. We talked through the issues in a joint session with Sid, but hadn't dared a third attempt yet.

My half-furnished room reminded me too much of other temporary homes where I'd lived and almost died. I would really, truly set aside a day next week to install brackets for my hanging plants and unpack the book boxes that doubled as my laptop desk. The walls sported two posters so far: a Jewish Museum gift shop print of the Tree of Life with the *sefirot*, and a mist-wreathed New England shoreline at night, a fan-art rendition of "The Shadow Over Innsmouth" from NecronomiCon 1997. We'd finished *The Poison Cure* too late to book a vendor table, but no one refused a free copy from the messenger bag I shlepped to every panel discussion and tabletop gaming night. I made another mental note to get my posters framed like a real adult.

Before my evening meditation, I toyed with the tin where I kept my weed, but decided to abstain. I placed the decorated rock from my retreat on my bedside table.

In the dark, I waited to be swept away. For now, my dreams didn't scare me. They were only shadows of what I'd already survived. I gathered my selves around me, little unwanted messengers, dirty and torn. They slept, but I didn't want to. I opened my door. Faint sounds of a running faucet, the squeaky cabinet door in the master bathroom. I smiled. Julian had more creams for his face, hair, and body than Michelangelo had tubes of paint. Might as well watch the artist at work.

"Pardon me, do you have any eyebrow lotion?"

"You jest, but you ought to moisturize more if you're going to spend your weekends climbing trees in the nude." He dabbed some soft, cool paste under my eyes. It smelled like fresh-cut lemons. The door squealed again as he shelved his supplies. "Sorry, am I keeping you up?"

"Not in a bad way..." I embraced his warm, clean body. His groin twitched beneath his white bathrobe. In such a short time, he'd trained himself to lean away from me when he got hard, sparing me any touch that might make me feel pressured. I drew him back onto me, with my hands cupping his ass.

"Mmm?" I felt him tremble with the effort of not rubbing against me, until he was sure what I wanted.

"Stay with me tonight, Jule? I don't know what'll happen, but whatever it is, if I'm with you, it's good."

"Always. Always, my love."

We lay down, dressed only in our undershorts. My new mattress, not yet shaped by our particular curves, was smooth and fresh as a hotel bed. The cat leaped to the windowsill, sharpening her claws on the carpet strip I'd tacked to the ledge to make her perch more comfortable. I explored the sensations of pressing my bare skin against his, thigh to thigh, chest to chest. We breathed together, our bellies touching, rising and falling as one. Just a brief kiss, or I'd drown. I didn't have to explain; he knew. He moved his mouth to the hollow of my throat. I tilted my head back, eyes closed, imagining stars above me, a brimming well of darkness ringed by treetops. I wanted him to go lower. Not all the way—my insides clenched, like machine gears seizing up, at the thought of my cock in anyone's mouth, even his. But close.

I folded the cover back and inched upward. Understanding, he trailed his tongue down my breastbone, all the way to my waistband. My aching bulge thrust upward to graze his chin—my body's decision, not mine. He slipped his fingers into the opening of my fly, but withdrew them when I twisted away. That slight touch on my bare shaft had been so intense I didn't have a word for it. Jule sat up and kissed my forehead. "What next, darling?"

I sighed, my thoughts muddled by a mix of desire, fear, and embarrassment. To think that last year I paid good money to be pissed on in a basement, and now I was afraid of a hand job? "I don't know...maybe, let's be naked but keep the blanket off? I need to see what's happening."

"Of course. And you don't need a safeword—if you forget what to do, you can just say stop, or...punch me in the balls, or whatever."

I laughed. "I hope I'm not that much of a caveman. But it's good to have options...in case my mouth is full."

Taking the hint, Jule rolled onto his back, pulled off his briefs and spread his legs. His dick arched gracefully upward, the tip gleaming with wetness. I teased the slit with my fingertip, enjoying his groans, then licked it, savoring the salty taste, a return to the waters of a welcoming shore. I took all of him into my mouth. His total absorption in his pleasure satisfied me. I would never be too much for him. I sucked greedily, rubbing my erection on his leg. The world faded away. When I thought he was close to coming, I released him. "Lube?" I asked.

"Yeah! You want to..." He drew his knees up slightly.

I felt bad turning him down. "Maybe next time—we shouldn't bareback, and—I don't want anything separating us."

That gave him the greatest pleasure of all. We lay face to face again. He kissed me, tonguing my mouth, tasting himself on my lips. I pushed against his fingers inside my ass, clenching and releasing around his deliberate thrusts that were firm but not rough. Our breath deepening to low groans, we pumped each other's shafts at the same time, till I could hardly tell whose hand was whose, the climax his or mine, pounding into each other's palms in a sticky flood.

We lay quietly, his forehead against my cheek, our hands resting between each other's legs, a sweet and fragile stasis. The tide of fear lapped at the edges of my cooling body. Inevitably, I thought, bracing myself, this perfect merging of skin on skin would creep over the line into sickening excess, sucking me in to the dissolving rot. Soon I would be driven to outrun it.

But where? This was *my* room, my final turf. I was done moving. Carefully, so as not to disturb my dozing lover (whose ability to fall instantly into unconsciousness was truly enviable), I reached for the forest stone on my nightstand. I cupped its smooth cool weight in the hand I tucked under my pillow, laying my other arm on Julian's warm body once more. Time and space wobbled nonetheless, but not as much. I couldn't remain suspended between restless fear and frustrated longing. So what if he consumed me; was there any better place to be than in his arms? Inwardly I fell forward, deeper into the dark waters. Everything in me that strained to pull away, I reveersed, pressing him closer, sinking into the smell and touch. Such a thirst awakened, a pure infant loneliness, seeking comfort and softness. There was nothing on the other side of the barrier after all, nothing but me and my tears, which finally woke him up by dripping on his forehead.

"Oh no, was this a bad idea?" Julian pulled up the blanket to wipe my eyes.

I shook my head, hoping he'd give me time to become capable of speech, before tormenting himself with apologies. "I can feel...*everything* now."

He moved his hand off my soft dick, touching my shoulders but making space between us. I closed that space back up, and he snuggled gratefully against my chest. "You can talk to me. Sorry I fell alseep. You made me so happy, I couldn't think anymore."

"I'm happy too." I caressed the delicate line of his jaw. "Unless you have to pee, all I want is to stay exactly like this till my alarm goes off tomorrow morning."

"Consider me glued to your side."

T HE WEIGHT ON MY CHEST in the morning was only Lena, hooking her claws into the blanket to stretch. She bared her minature fangs in a contented yawn. I rubbed under her chin. Julian slept, his legs intertwined with mine, one arm flung over his eyes to block the morning sun. I even loved the smell of his sweat. Both of my bedmates would be unhappy that I had to get up for my yoga class. I wouldn't be cruel and tickle his armpit, though. Well, maybe a little.

I cooked as nice a breakfast as our schedules would allow—thank goodness for pancake mix. Julian would be out until late evening, auditioning models and setting up a shoot that called for a nighttime street scene. After my morning classes at the Ironman, I planned to come back here and knock out some pages for DC Comics. Then I had to call some potential weight-training clients who'd seen the flyers I tacked up in the neighborhood gay bars. Our apartment's monthly maintenance was steep, and we'd barely bought any furniture yet. "Buddha was right, possessions are an encumbrance," I said.

"Yeah, but you have a hard-on for that new stove."

"Oh no, I've become a 1950s housewife! Where's my Valium? But seriously, I was raised to fear credit card debt, so I think I'd better pick up that Tuesday night shift at the Ironman. Powerlifting—buns of steel, baby!"

"Weren't you going to try out the group that night, the one that Sid recommended—"

"I don't need that," I cut him off. "I'm doing so much better now, really. Look at last night—no flashbacks. And Merce's retreat was transformative. *Nature* is my support."

"Should I buy you another houseplant?"

"Don't be a dick."

"I don't care if you hate me, I'm not letting you end up in the hospital again."

"I'm sorry. I promise I'll be okay. It's not what I need right now—I just think I'll feel worse having strangers know my business." We hugged to clear the air. I hated to worry him, but I had to recover in my own way. Nobody knew what it was like in my head—sometimes, not even me.

Later that afternoon, I was outlining Aquaman's next adventure on my new computer when our apartment door buzzer sounded. I wasn't expecting anyone, but maybe Julian had ordered a package, so I saved my work and pressed the intercom. It was Prue, bringing me a care package of food from last night's Rosh Hashanah family dinner. That was a welcome surprise since I hadn't made time for a decent lunch.

When I opened the door, though, I got a second surprise. Dad was with her. He walked right in, carrying two shopping bags of food containers. Lena wreathed around my sister's legs, happy to see her former foster mom. Dad wrinkled his nose at the cat, though his allergies couldn't possibly be acting up this soon. "So this is where you've been hiding. Nice place. Very good investment. I hear this neighborhood is coming up."

"Dad...hey. Uh, thanks for the food." I relieved him of the bags. "Sorry Julian's at work. I didn't know you guys were coming by."

"You didn't?" Prue shot an annoyed, perplexed look at Dad, who shrugged it off.

"Peter, forgive me for just showing up. I thought we needed some family time, but it's been impossible to get ahold of you."

"Sorry, I've been working really hard. My schedule's in flux." I bought myself some time by unpacking the food. My hands shook untying the handles of the plastic bag. The cat heard the sounds of meal preparation and trotted over to see what was in it for her. I petted her stripey head and told myself I had nothing to fear. I hadn't done anything wrong.

"I'm having some soup. You guys want anything?" I called out.

Dad patted his belly. "If there's enough to go around, I never can resist Michelle's pecan coffee cake. Made with margarine, Prue—vegan."

"Yeah I know," my sister muttered, pulling up a chair with a loud, slow scrape. This was hardly the first time I'd seen my articulate feminist sister revert to a pouty teenager around our father. While I feared his compulsion to pry silent people open like a mussel in linguini, Prue incited it, either to make him prove he cared or to win his respect in a battle of wills.

I tried to be happy to see them. Damn my memories, anyway. It wasn't fair to punish the rest of my family for what Barbara and I had done. Before we ate, I gave Nathan the tour. (Prue had been there several times already, which we both tactfully avoided mentioning.) He enthused over the closet space and the vintage ceiling light with painted-glass globes that the previous owner had left in the hallway. Work news and family updates kept mealtime light. Cousin Noah read a board book all by himself, "and he only just started kindergarten!" Grandpa Abe had had a minor scuffle with a fellow resident of Shady Gables in Boca Raton when the other guy tried to cross the janitors' picket line. How I missed them. Pretending to wipe chicken soup from my mouth, I swiped at my tears with a napkin.

As soon as she was done eating, my sister invented an errand to the one health food store across town that sold the correct brand of kombucha, so that Dad and I would be forced to talk one-on-one. I could only stall so long by washing dishes. My father made coffee without being asked, and brought the mugs to the table.

"It felt too empty last night at Nora and Leo's place, with you missing in action, and Mae and Amy at her mother's. I guess it'll never be like it was," he said.

"I'm sorry."

"No, I am." Dad compounded my surprise by putting his hand over mine and squeezing it awkwardly for a moment. "Are you trying to send me a message? Did I make you feel unwanted by taking Ben's death so hard?"

The habitual evasions rose to my tongue, but I'd vowed to be straightforward from now on—or at least, to be honest that I was hiding something. "I just wanted you to support me in looking for the truth. You always taught me how important that was." Saying this, I realized I did have a reason to be grateful to my father—a role model for the willpower that had driven me to dive into the wreck and (barely) resurface.

His face softened at this unexpected praise from me. "Yes...you were honoring your cousin in your own way, I know. But I wish you'd been able to put it aside for one night. The family's not ready to deal with anything else upsetting."

"Are you?"

"What have you found out?"

"Not about Ben..." I squeezed my eyes shut (*breathe one two three four*), gathering strength. "I didn't come last night because...I'm going through something serious, that I need privacy for, and it doesn't work anymore to keep pretending I'm okay."

My father wrinkled his brow. "You're not becoming a woman, are you?"

I was startled into laughter. "What? No! Why would you get that idea?"

"Well, this sounded like your coming-out speech, and you're already gay, so...eh, never mind." He scrutinized me more closely. "It would be odd, but better than your mother being right about the drugs."

"Wait, you talked to Barbara about me?" My voice cracked with fear.

"She sought *me* out, actually, so I already knew something must be wrong, for her to talk to me voluntarily. That woman nurses a grudge like it was her second baby."

"You *did* cheat on her," I automatically fired back.

"Because your mother and I had a dead marriage! She got pregnant, we tried to make it work, but there was nothing there."

"She gave it all to me," I said, flatly.

Dad picked up on my unusual tone. He didn't quite know what to ask, and I wasn't ready to elaborate, but it gave him an opening to present his case. "I shouldn't be so critical of you. It just made her baby you more. Only, sometimes I feel that you hurt yourself to punish me. That you'll never let me get over divorcing Barbara, even though I would support *you* in having any kind of partner who made you happy."

"Yeah, you're right."

"What, really?" Like a judo fighter, Dad lost his footing when his attack met empty air.

"I'm sorry. I didn't understand what I was doing. I was in pain, and part of me had to wreck things over and over again until the other part got serious about tracking down the source."

"It's okay. It's okay." He gave me a clumsy but long-lasting hug. When he pulled away, his eyes were watery. Spitefully, even at this moment of greater tenderness than we'd shared in years, I felt a little satisfaction that not all his tears were saved for my poor cousin.

"So, should we talk about getting you into rehab? Don't let money be an issue."

"I'm *not* on drugs." Fed up, wanting to shock him, I rolled up my sleeves. The sight of my scars reassured me. Here was a fact. A record of history. "I tried to kill myself in May. I spent two weeks in the psych ward at NYU."

"No—Peter, no! Why didn't you come to me? How long has this been happening? Is that why you thought Ben—"

"Fuck Ben. Sorry, may his memory be a blessing, but not right now. This is about *me*. I remembered...something bad."

Nathan opened his mouth, pressed it shut again in a tight line, fixed me with a skeptical eye. Here it comes, the playing out of the rope for the dumb witness to hang himself. The death by a thousand objections. I groaned impatiently and stood up. "Maybe you can't handle this, Dad."

"Ssh, calm down. There's nothing to worry about." He took a cautious step toward me, like I was a large unfamiliar dog. "Your mother said you were acting...afraid of things that weren't real."

"My *mother* stuck her fingers up my ass at night when you were too busy with your other family to notice. What's real? How would you know?"

I braced myself for a companion to the slap she had delivered, but Nathan simply paled and backed away. "T-that's impossible. *Barbara?* She's the most normal—I mean, she doesn't even *like* sex! Why would she... Ugh." He shuddered.

"If *you're* disgusted, imagine how I feel," I snarled. Indeed, his expression of repugnance—this lifelong aversion to me, which neither of us had understood, now out in the open—made my stomach lurch with shame. I wanted to turn inside out.

"Confused. You must be feeling so confused." His soothing tone returned. I didn't trust it. "Who else have you told?"

I leaned heavily against the wall. Gravity was doing strange things. "Just Julian and my therapist. Prue knows about the flashbacks and—and this —" I held out my wrist, unable to say the words again—"but not who did it. I was trying to protect her. To protect all of you. Always. I wanted to die so I wouldn't remember and ruin everything."

I didn't know if he understood my last words because I'd broken down in tears as I spoke. He came closer, palms out in a don't-shoot pose. "Stop, stop. Don't get hysterical. We'll straighten it all out."

376

"Do you believe me?"

Nathan exhaled heavily. "I don't need to have an opinion."

"No? Either you want me to live or you don't."

He reached up to put his hands on my shoulders, in what was supposed to be a steadying gesture. I regarded the top of his head. More gray hairs had wormed through the thinning reddish ones since my cousin's rendezvous with a concrete wall.

"This is the best thing I can do for you. Give you breathing room to sort out fact from…well, emotional truth. No question, Barbara was too much. Maybe the rest is just a metaphor…?"

"I need some time to myself now, Dad. I'm on deadline." DC Comics was expecting four pages on Aquaman's battle with the Hypno-Kraken by tomorrow morning.

"All right, but don't be a stranger. The whole family misses you."

I sidestepped his attempt at another hug. "What are you going to tell them?"

"They have enough on their plate." Forestalling my objection, he argued, "Look, I'm protecting your privacy. This repressed memory business, it's always seemed far-fetched to me. People do change their minds. You don't want to be embarrassed if you go back on it later."

That sounded so reasonable. But then, so had slitting my wrists.

"I have flashbacks. Panic attacks. I have to leave places without warning. Sometimes I forget where I am. How are you going to explain that at the next family dinner?"

"Peter, everyone already knows you have troubles. We love you. You don't have to fake being okay. Just show up."

On his way out, he extracted a promise from me to call him or my sister tonight, to confirm that I was still alive. After all these years of bemoaning my dad's emotional negligence, I wasn't sure I liked this version much better.

Lena crept out from under my bed when the apartment was quiet. She didn't like arguments. I picked her up and rocked her in my arms, huddled on the couch. Her tiny claws needled my shoulder as she adjusted position. I didn't mind. We were here, on this earth, this moment, and pain wasn't the worst thing in the world. Her soft breaths snuffled in my ear.

When I sat down at my computer, the cat sprang up to her favorite warm spot atop the laser printer. I lit a soy candle from the set that Prue had given us as a housewarming gift. The pine scent allowed me to pretend I was in the woods if I closed my eyes and recast the honks of New York traffic as some very loud migrating geese. A realist at heart, I didn't waste much time struggling with temptation. I lit a joint from the candle wick and began:

Aquaman speeds upward through churning waters. Below him, a shipwreck lies tilted on the rocky sea bed. Shadows of two boat bottoms overhead. He thinks: *Quick—before the Hypno-Kraken claims another victim!*

Surface scene. Moonlight on water. Deck of the lead naval ship. Sailor with telescope says to captain: *Those must be the cliffs where the Intrepid went down! Steady now—I see a gap we can sail through!*

Aquaman breaches the surface in front of them. He raises his shining trident. *Follow me!* He swims fast as a torpedo—*toward* the sharpest rock wall!

Sailor with telescope: *Hard a' starboard!*

Captain: *Are you mad? We'll crash. He must be under the spell of the Hypno-Kraken!*

Their ship continues on its course toward the narrow channel. The sailor looks behind him anxiously, seeing that the rising gale makes retreat impossible. The other ship, however, turns to the right, following Aquaman. The hero's teeth are gritted and his eyes bulge, as if struggling with all his might against an irresistible compulsion.

The gale pushes the boats forward on higher and higher waves. A mighty surge flings Aquaman against the deadly rock face—which disappears! The ship that followed him speeds away into calmer waters. Aquaman bows his head and closes his eyes in relief: *My hunch was correct! A near thing—*

But turning around, he sees the waters boiling under the unfortunate other ship, which the Kraken has lured directly over its lair! Giant snaking metal arms start to drag it beneath the waves.

Undersea shot of the villain Black Manta in the cockpit of the Hypno-Kraken, controlling its arms with levers. *This will fetch a fine price on the black market!* he gloats.

Aquaman's trident smashes through the cockpit window. Black Manta presses a button and drops into an escape pod that darts away. Aquaman says to himself: *No time to pursue him! I can rescue the crew—or retrieve the*

I NEEDED GUIDANCE, and there was only one man who could give it to me.
"What should I wear to this meeting?"

Out of all the gut-wrenching challenges of my current life, this was the
one I could control. I couldn't stave off the flashbacks that made daily life
into a bad LSD trip. I gutted my way through teaching my classes at the
Ironman, slept in one-hour increments and had a resting heart rate so high
that I was losing weight despite my muscle-building regimen. I noticed
this again as I adjusted the belt on the black jeans that Julian selected for
me.

"Wear layers. Your body temperature goes haywire when you're stressed."
Julian laid out two combinations on the bed, an olive-green tee with a blue
and green striped shirt, and a dark-gray tee with a brick-red plaid. I closed
my eyes and pointed to one. All right, dealer, put my money on red. I
immediately regretted it. It felt so...*conspicuous.* As if that was avoidable,
at this point.

"What if I'm making the worst mistake of my life?"

"The worst mistake was when you tried to—" He forced himself to
avoid his usual euphemisms—setting an example for me, no doubt. "To
end your life. It's all uphill from here. Or downhill? Actually neither of
those sound good, but you know what I mean." He put his arms around
me, and I was able to breathe again.

I pulled on my windbreaker and slipped the painted stone into the
pocket. "Okay, I'm as ready as I'll ever be."

"Nope, ugly jacket. Wear a blazer." Julian hauled out my basic black,
swatting cat hair off the lapels.

"It could rain."

"Then take an umbrella. You're stalling, babe."

I obeyed my master, but pretended not to see his disapproving look when
the stone made my pocket sag.

"Sure you can't eat something?" he fussed instead. He was training to replace a whole Jewish family.

"Too nervous."

"Okay. I'll wait for you in the coffee shop and read my book, and when you're done, I'll take you to dinner. You can do this, darling." Julian was unexpectedly hooked on Robert Jordan's *Wheel of Time* series from my sci-fi collection.

We parted ways in front of the New School for Social Research on downtown Fifth Avenue. The meeting facilitator, whom I hadn't met yet, taught psychology classes there and so was able to secure a seminar room for us. I wandered identical brown-tiled hallways till I found the room number that Sid's contact had given me, but there was no sign on the door. "I hope this is the place," I thought aloud.

"Yeah, I hope it *ain't*," a deep voice drawled. "This is one club I wish I *wasn't* in, know what I mean?"

The big man beside me had close-cropped gray hair and a rugged, sun-wrinkled face. He held a portly brown Labrador on a leash attached to a service harness with the "Semper Fi" Marines logo. "Dr. Barnett's group?" I asked.

"The very same. I was in the last cycle but I re-upped. Name's Sonny. This here's Rosie. She catches me if I have a seizure. Took a projectile to the head in 'Nam."

"Damn. Glad you made it out alive." We shook hands.

Soon after, Dr. Barnett came along to unlock the door. I recognized his British accent from the phone. He told us to call him Ian. He was a skinny, rumpled, middle-aged professor type with sparkling blue eyes behind wire-rimmed glasses. "Sorry I'm a minute late. Jim was putting our daughter to bed but she insisted that I read her a story." Good, so I wasn't the only gay one here.

We numbered eight in all, plus Ian (and the dog). One withdrawn-looking Hispanic guy barely out of this teens, a handsome black man my age with a beard and turtleneck (not appropriate, Peter! don't cruise!), and assorted white guys from their thirties on up. In short, a cross-section of the people you'd bump up against in a subway ride to the West Village.

"Welcome to Hero's Journey. We are a group for male survivors of childhood sexual abuse," Ian began the meeting. Instantly, as Julian had predicted, I broke out in a cold sweat. Did he have to be so...explicit? I mean, what if we weren't ready to call it that? *Abuse* is a big word. Like, maybe, some of these other guys, somebody pulled them into an alley and raped them or something, but not me. Okay, *Jonas*, but thirteen isn't a child. My mother would *die* if she knew I was here. She didn't even want anyone to know she wore a girdle, let alone...*never mind.* I gripped the sides of my chair, ready to bolt.

The dog thumped her tail on the floor. I glanced at Sonny, sitting up military-straight, clenching his jaw as a tear rolled down his leathery cheek. Rosie laid her head on his knee with an adoring look. Warmth flooded my heart, for everyone here—their precious trust in me, a stranger, to behold their lives cracked open.

"My name is Peter," I said when it was my turn. "And I'm an incest survivor."

now may the words of my mouth
and the meditation of my heart
be acceptable in thy sight

Acknowledgments

The Tarot Write-A-Torium writing group at Soul Path Sanctuary provided spiritual support, craft guidance, and deadlines to keep me working on this novel. Director Carolyn Cushing and fellow authors Grace LeClair, Mistinguette Smith, and Sharon Vardatira have been faithful friends of Julian and Peter since 2015.

Trauma therapist Rythea Lee helped Peter and me keep the faith in our healing journey. Rythea also consulted on incest family dynamics and how to describe flashbacks. Check out her YouTube series "Advice from a Loving Bitch".

Denne Michele Norris was a stellar developmental editor who always asked the right questions. She helped make Tai's character more true to the Black transfeminine experience and the perspective of a younger generation. Follow her work at Electric Literature, where she is now Editor-in-Chief.

Beta readers Ellen LaFleche and John Ollom helped refine the novel's themes and pacing. Ellen's prizewinning poetry includes the collection *Walking into Lightning* from Saddle Road Press. John is the artistic director of Ollom Movement Art in New York City. His books include *Rocks in the River*, a guide to healing through creativity.

Survivor advocate and former social worker Sovey Seabright figured out Peter's trauma history when I was still writing *Two Natures* and fretting that he wouldn't talk to me. She consulted on the process of memory recovery and suggested resources that would make the story more realistic. Some of those books are listed below.

Flame Con, the queer comic-book creators' convention hosted by Geeks Out, showed me who my people were. This fun annual event takes place in midtown Manhattan in August. Writers, when you're planning your next book, pick a topic that allows you to buy gay erotica for "novel research".

The Black Walnut Inn in Amherst, MA was the perfect place to sequester myself in March 2020—the weekend before COVID lockdown, as it would later turn out—to write Peter's climactic flashbacks scene. Thanks to journalist and comic-book critic Noah Berlatsky for introducing me to the music of Liz Phair and Jimmy Cliff on his eclectic "105 Greatest Albums Ever" list, now collected in his Kindle e-book *The Best Greatest Albums of All Time Ever*.

The Poison Cure's "origin story" can be traced back to 1992, when I was introduced to the concept of the *pharmakon* in Plato and Derrida during Prof. Steven Hopkins' "Love and Religion" undergraduate seminar for the Comparative Religion Department at Harvard. I knew I'd write fiction about it someday, but I wasn't ready yet in terms of craft or life experience. Thank you, Steve.

My steadfast family—husband Adam R. Cohen, son Shane, and mom-of-choice Roberta Pato—are the future that I survived for. Theodore "Big Pussy" Cavalieri DiMeow improves my manuscripts by sitting on them.

Resources

Brown, Joanne Carlson, and Carole R. Bohn, eds. *Christianity, Patriarchy, and Abuse: A Feminist Critique.* New York: The Pilgrim Press, 1989.

Fredrickson, Renee. *Repressed Memories: A Journey to Recovery from Sexual Abuse.* New York: Fireside Books, 1992.

Miller, Alice. *Banished Knowledge.* Translated by Leila Vennewitz. New York: Anchor Books/Doubleday, 1990.

_______*Thou Shalt Not Be Aware.* Translated by Hildegarde and Hunter Hannum. New York: Meridian, 1986.

Napier, Nancy J. *Getting Through the Day: Strategies for Adults Hurt as Children.* New York & London: W.W. Norton & Co., 1993.

Patterson, Jennifer, ed. *Queering Sexual Violence.* Riverdale, NY: Riverdale Avenue Books, 2016.

Real, Terrence. *I Don't Want to Talk About It: Overcoming the Secret Legacy of Male Depression.* New York: Scribner, 1997.

About Jendi Reiter

Jendi Reiter is the author of the novel *Two Natures* (Saddle Road Press), the short story collection *An Incomplete List of My Wishes* (Sunshot Press/ New Millennium Writings), and five poetry books and chapbooks, most recently *Made Man* (Little Red Tree). Their work has appeared in numerous journals including *Action, Spectacle, The Iowa Review, The New Guard, New Letters, Quarter After Eight, Solstice Lit Mag,* and *Wicked Gay Ways.*

Two Natures won the Rainbow Award for Best Gay Contemporary Fiction and was a finalist for the Book Excellence Awards and the Lascaux Prize for Fiction. They are the editor

of WinningWriters.com, an online resource site with contests and markets for creative writers.